continued ...

**Other Crime of Fashion Mysteries
by Ellen Byerrum**

Shot Through Velvet

A CRIME OF FASHION MYSTERY

Ellen Byerrum

AN OBSIDIAN MYSTERY

OBSIDIAN
Published by New American Library, a division of
Penguin Group (USA) Inc., 375 Hudson Street,
New York, New York 10014, USA
Penguin Group (Canada), 90 Eglinton Avenue East, Suite 700, Toronto,
Ontario M4P 2Y3, Canada (a division of Pearson Penguin Canada Inc.)
Penguin Books Ltd., 80 Strand, London WC2R 0RL, England
Penguin Ireland, 25 St. Stephen's Green, Dublin 2,
Ireland (a division of Penguin Books Ltd.)
Penguin Group (Australia), 250 Camberwell Road, Camberwell, Victoria 3124,
Australia (a division of Pearson Australia Group Pty. Ltd.)
Penguin Books India Pvt. Ltd., 11 Community Centre, Panchsheel Park,
New Delhi - 110 017, India
Penguin Group (NZ), 67 Apollo Drive, Rosedale, North Shore 0632,
New Zealand (a division of Pearson New Zealand Ltd.)
Penguin Books (South Africa) (Pty.) Ltd., 24 Sturdee Avenue,
Rosebank, Johannesburg 2196, South Africa

Penguin Books Ltd., Registered Offices:
80 Strand, London WC2R 0RL, England

First published by Obsidian, an imprint of New American Library,
a division of Penguin Group (USA) Inc.

First Printing, February 2011
10 9 8 7 6 5 4 3 2 1

ACKNOWLEDGMENTS

When writing a book, you can't get far without inspiration and information and a host of people who are willing to help—whether it's with the writing or just keeping up your spirits. A lot of people kept me going during the road to publication of *Shot Through Velvet*, and I offer them my wholehearted appreciation.

I'd also like to explain that while there is no little town of Black Martin, Virginia—nor is there any velvet factory called (or exactly like) Dominion Velvet—there are several parts of that state that have been deeply affected by the demise of the textile industries. My friend Regina Cline alerted me to the last velvet factory in Virginia, and also inspired my interest in visiting beautiful Lake Anna, for which I am deeply grateful. Paul S. Majeika of A. Wimpfheimer & Bro., Inc. opened my eyes to the plight of the velvet industry in Virginia and across the country. He was generous with his time and experience, and he gave me a fascinating tour of a well-managed velvet factory, for which I am very grateful. Any errors and omissions in the history and practice of making velvet are, of course, my own, as are the imagined details, characters, and situations in my fictional Dominion Velvet. Corrine Geller, public relations manager with the Virginia State Police, also answered my questions in the midst of her busy schedule.

Many thanks to my fabulous agent, Paige Wheeler, who has gone above and beyond the call of duty on my behalf.

And I would also like to acknowledge the efforts of my terrific editor at NAL, Sandy Harding.

As always, I wouldn't be here without the support of my husband, Bob Williams, as well as his keen eye, critical insights, and back rubs. Honey, there just aren't enough words.

chapter 1

The body was blue.

Not merely wearing blue, he *was* blue—and not the blue pallor of death. He was sapphire from head to toe, a deep shade of mood indigo.

Oh, that's taking the matchy-match thing way *too far,* thought Lacey Smithsonian, fashion reporter for *The Eye Street Observer. No, Lacey,* she told herself. *This is not* What Not to Wear. *This is how not to be caught* dead.

The corpse was lashed to the bottom of a giant spool of velvet, fastened with strips of the same velvet, as blue as his skin. He rose dripping from a vat of blue dye, splashing inky blue liquid on the factory's cement floor. Everywhere Lacey looked there was a serene shade of blue made obscene by death.

The dead man's head was swollen, his hair matted blue-black, his lips and tongue a royal blue, his protruding eyeballs a lighter shade, perhaps cerulean. A human gargoyle in death, he was a sight both horrible and fascinating.

A song played unbidden in Lacey's mind. *He wore bluuuue VELLLL-vet . . . Lacey, stop! NOW!*

How long would his blue skin last? Lacey wondered. Through all eternity? Or just through decomposition? *With Valentine's Day less than two weeks away, maybe he should have been dyed red instead of blue. Then again, maybe not.*

Although the man had been completely submerged in the tint, the spool of velvet was only half dyed, the unsubmerged part still cream-colored. It was a sodden mess hanging from a long heavy chain attached to the overhead machinery of the dye house.

Lacey had been touring Dominion Velvet, the last velvet factory in Virginia, on its final full day of operations, for a special report for her newspaper on the vanishing U.S. textile industry. She was planning to write a fashion-related feature article, one with more substance than style. Her agenda for the day was not supposed to include murder. Murder was never on Lacey's game plan, and yet here it was. Again.

This time death wore blue velvet.

Lacey spared a sigh for the velvet, the deceased, and the factory workers. And herself. She wondered how the man's demise would affect her feature story. There were days Lacey detested being a fashion scribe. Today might be one of them. *I can't believe this is happening.*

Standing next to Lacey and also witnessing the royal blue debacle was Dominion Velvet's newly hired security consultant, Vic Donovan, her boyfriend. He was supposed to start working up a security plan the next day and have new guards and a new security system on-site within a week. He was there to get a look around, but he was getting far more than he'd anticipated.

Vic was dressed in his professional attire, a close-fitting black turtleneck that showed off his muscles, a black leather jacket, black boots, and gray slacks instead of his usual jeans. One pesky dark curl fell over his forehead. Lacey restrained the urge to push it back and gaze into his green eyes.

Vic Donovan, the man in her life, had tipped her off to the factory closing story. He invited her along to the little town of Black Martin, Virginia, to see the factory firsthand while he initiated the security contract for Dominion Velvet in its waning days.

After angry graffiti had been scrawled on a factory wall one night, the company had instituted some stopgap security measures, but its original plan was not much more sophisticated than locking the doors and turning out the lights. The workers were unhappy about losing their jobs. The local economy was devastated; there were no other jobs in town. Dominion Velvet was afraid an empty plant would just encourage more vandalism. The company had hired some local good old boy to watch the plant at night, but he wasn't a real security guard. Donovan's company was hired to install a serious security system to ensure there would be no more incidents on-site. When and if the building and the machinery were eventually sold, security would be the new owners' problem.

For Lacey and Vic, this foray to Black Martin was supposed to be a quick road trip away from Washington, D.C. Lacey could work on her serious fashion story, Vic would meet his new client, and she and Vic could have a romantic dinner somewhere. But their plans for a little romance were spiraling down the drain, along with the blue dye dripping from the corpse.

Things had gone wrong from the start that morning. Vic and Lacey were supposed to meet with Vic's contact, a company official named Rod Gibbs. But Gibbs hadn't shown up, so general manager Tom Nicholson had filled in. He was giving them what he called the five-cent tour.

Rod Gibbs was also the company official Lacey had intended to interview. He had promised her on the phone that the shutdown would be temporary and he would give her details of "an exciting new plan" for the factory's future.

At the moment, Vic was taking a deep breath, no doubt trying to control his emotions. "This is a disaster," he whispered and shook his head.

"This is not my fault, Vic Donovan," Lacey whispered back.

"I know that, Lacey."

"That's not what your tone says."

"My tone? Are you telling me this is one of your infamous crimes of fashion?"

"Just what would you call it? He *is* tied to a spool of velvet. He *is* blue. Do the math."

"It's a workplace homicide," he said. "Just so happens the workplace is a velvet factory. Besides, I didn't mean this was your fault. I meant mine."

Lacey raised an eyebrow in response. "Your fault? How do you figure that?"

"I should have started this job yesterday. Then this wouldn't have happened."

"The company set the timetable, not you. The client is always right. Right?"

"Yeah. That was my first mistake. The client is usually wrong."

A handful of other witnesses were sharing this spectacle. Vic and Lacey's tour had picked up a few hangers-on, employees who trailed along in a kind of melancholy parade, not knowing what to do to fill their time on their last day on the job. They collected their personal mementos and cleaned out their lockers, but they had nowhere else to go. It didn't feel like a brand-new day waiting around the corner for the factory, as Rod Gibbs had promised. It felt like a heartbroken good-bye. *A deep blue good-bye.*

This is what happens when people lose their jobs. The irony didn't escape Lacey. She was writing about job loss at a time when newspapers were closing all over the country and her own newspaper was in trouble. She could lose her own position just when the job horizon for reporters was rapidly dimming. Lacey had expected her journalism career to move from paper to paper, onward and upward, with better positions at every step along the way. But what if *The Eye Street Observer* was the end of the road for her? Newspapers were threatened daily by the Internet and twenty-four-hour broadcast news. Lacey shook her head to clear her thoughts. This wasn't about her. This story was about Black Martin, Virginia.

The group had turned a corner, from the velvet-shearing operations on the main floor to the white-tiled room that was called the dye house. Six large gray steel vats sat in a row, partly sunken in the floor. Five of them were empty. Each vat was seven feet deep to accommodate the heavy steel spools of fabric six-and-a-half feet wide. Nicholson, their tour guide, had been surprised to see there was a problem with the sixth. The spool of velvet seemed to be stuck half in and half out of the vat. When the spool was slowly lifted by the heavy machinery, the blue corpse came up with it.

In the ensuing confusion and gasps of disbelief, Lacey

felt Vic's hand on her shoulder. His face was stern and his jaw was set. She'd seen that look before. She whispered, "I do not have a murder mojo."

Donovan snorted. "I didn't say that. Today."

"You're the one who gave me the tip the factory was closing."

"I should have my head examined."

"It's a good story, Vic. Factory closing, workers out of jobs, American industries killed by cheap foreign imports."

He nodded toward the body. "But it's a better story now, right? With Blue Boy hanging there?"

"It's a more complicated story now." Lacey was beginning to regret not bringing a photographer, but she didn't mention that to Vic. He had his own problems. She would have to make do with her small digital camera. She took a few quick photos, but she put it away after being glared at by Vic.

Lacey whispered as they moved a few yards away. "Vic, you know that old song, 'Blue Velvet'? It keeps running through my brain. *And I still can see blue velvet—*"

"—*through my screams*. Thanks, darling. Now it's running through *my* brain."

Tom Nicholson stood next to the spool, shaking his head and staring.

"Do you know who it is?" Vic asked.

"Well—" Nicholson began. "It's a little hard to say."

A latecomer to the party joined the tour. Kira Evans, the bookkeeper, screamed and clapped her hand over her mouth. She looked ashen. A nearby worker reached out to prop her up.

Another woman gasped, "Oh my God. Is he dead?"

"Is he dead?!" A workman named Dirk Sykes answered. "Inez, honey, he is dead blue."

Sykes looked fierce, even in his bright turquoise Hawaiian shirt, which revealed a scorpion tattoo crawling up his right forearm. He wore his black hair pulled back in a ponytail, but with a finely clipped Julius Caesar fringe around the nape of his neck. He was definitely dancing to the beat of a different fashion drummer. Lacey had just learned his now-defunct job was shearing the fabric. The velvet was woven with the soft nap connecting two heavier sheets of backing material. Sykes had been the one who sheared the woven material in half, producing two sheets of velvet with the nap exposed. Scars on Sykes's hands and face testified to the sharpness of the huge blades he used.

"Why, Mr. Blue looks like one of them troll dolls, only not as cute," Inez Garcia said, after catching her breath.

A pretty Hispanic woman about thirty-five, Inez barely topped five feet, but she fearlessly stepped right up to get a better look at the dead man. She held on to her long, black braid to protect it from the dye.

Like most of the other workers, Inez was dressed as if for summer: shorts and a thin cotton top. The shearing machines, the washers, dyers, and dryers pumped out heat and made the factory almost tropical inside, in sharp contrast to the bleak Virginia winter outside. It must have been almost ninety degrees in the dye house.

"That looks like a goat-sucking *chupacabra* to me," Sykes said.

"That's no *chupacabra*. It's a coyote with mange," Inez responded. "Blue mange."

"I always wondered what'd happen if you fell in the dye vat," observed Hank Richards, the maintenance chief. "Now we know. I guess he's been in there a while."

Richards appeared to be in his late forties, tall and fit with a soldier's bearing but an aging surfer dude's shaggy blond hair, mustache, and goatee. He wore a navy short-sleeve polo shirt with dark blue slacks, which were neat and tidy. He had sad brown eyes that watched everything, and he had reached out to Kira Evans when she screamed.

Everyone fell silent for a moment. They seemed to know who the dead man was, but no one was quite ready to say so. Perhaps because he was so changed from life? The velvet factory workers had never seen anything like the blue body before, and they were unlikely to again. Not just because murder was rare in that rural part of Virginia, but also because their jobs in the factory were lost and gone forever.

Lacey Smithsonian had never witnessed anything like the blue man either. She'd seen a few dead bodies—bloody ones, cold ones, and ones with terminally bad haircuts—but none like this. She held her breath, her heart beating wildly. It was a last day of work no one here would ever forget. The ruined velvet was more than the last batch of the day: It was the last batch. The final spool of Dominion Velvet ever to be dyed at this factory. And now Lacey had missed her chance to see how the dyeing process actually worked from start to finish. This was the finish.

As Dominion Velvet General Manager Tom Nicholson had put it earlier, "The world keeps on getting smaller. You see, Ms. Smithsonian, making velvet isn't just a manufacturing operation. It's more of an art, and very labor-intensive. It's expensive to produce."

When Lacey asked about the new plan for the factory that Rod Gibbs had mentioned, Nicholson said that was a fantasy. In better days, the factory had close to a hundred looms and more than a hundred workers. Now it was just a ghost of its former glory. The half-dyed spool of velvet was a reminder that dyeing the last batch of "greige goods," the cream-colored, undyed fabric, was the final task on this ultimate day of full operations.

Dominion Velvet had picked this bitter cold Monday in February to let their factory workers go, supposedly to avoid the deeper depression that comes with shutting down at the end of the week, according to Nicholson.

"I don't understand it either," he had told her and Vic in the office. "Some psychobabble mumbo jumbo. My people aren't any happier to be let go on the first day of the week than the last, far as I can tell."

Once the fabric of kings and queens, of luxury and wealth, velvet was subject to the whims of fashion and the hard economics of trade. Like Dorothy Parker's ode to a satin dress, velvet too had the ability to soothe and comfort and "ease a heart." Nothing was as deeply textured or as warm or as comforting as velvet.

Lacey was rather sorry that she hadn't worn something velvet today. *In memoriam.* Her wardrobe held some favorite velvet pieces in black, green, and burgundy, which intensified her blue-green eyes, and rich jewel-toned velvet always contrasted nicely with the highlights in her light brown hair, which she wore today in a French twist. With the economy so dreary and depressed people all around her in Washington wearing nothing but shades of gray, Lacey thought it was time to dress up in the downturn. But today she had decided to go with a simple vintage purple wool jacket and black slacks, as if wearing velvet would be giving it too much favor, as if she were taking its side against other fabrics.

Nicholson cleared his throat to break the spell. He stepped a bit closer to the corpse, taking care not to touch anything. Nicholson had a young man's face and an old man's worried air. Casually dressed in a tan shirt and khaki slacks, his shoulders seemed to take on weight, dragging him down. With exasperation, he turned and gestured to Donovan. "About this security contract. We're going to need some changes."

Vic nodded in response. "Goes without saying."

"I'm afraid this tour is over, Ms. Smithsonian," Nicholson said. "I have to call the police."

Lacey nodded, but she knew it didn't mean the story was over. Her story here was just beginning.

"Who is the blue man?" she asked.

"That man is the Blue Devil," Inez murmured, still clutching her hair and pulling tight on her braid.

"Who is the Blue Devil?" Lacey asked. "And where is Rod Gibbs?"

"I believe you're looking at Rodney Gibbs right now," Nicholson said. "He's had better days."

chapter 2

Lacey and Vic shared a look. This day had just gotten worse.

To Lacey's unasked question, Nicholson added, "Rod Gibbs, the man you were supposed to meet. He was part owner of the company, a partner. Liked to come around, keep an eye on things. Called himself the night manager." Nicholson wiped the sweat off his forehead. "When I agreed to show you around, I sure as hell didn't plan on this. I'm real sorry."

"Not your fault," Lacey said. "Ms. Garcia called him the Blue Devil?"

"Yeah." Nicholson took a moment before answering. "It was Gibbs's nickname. He thought it was funny. Had a strange sense of humor. Anyway, he keeps a boat out on Lake Anna. Calls it the *Blue Devil*." Nicholson walked around the corpse and gestured mournfully at the ruined spool of velvet. He seemed lost in thought.

"Rodney Gibbs." Lacey wrote the name down. "You're sure this is him?"

"He's not looking his best right now," said Dirk Sykes. "I imagine he's got one ferocious case of blue balls."

The little crowd laughed uncomfortably. Vic's lips were twitching, but he kept his professional cool. Lacey continued writing notes.

"It's kind of hard to tell what he looked like." Lacey took another look at the body, craning her neck for a better angle. She was sure his eyes didn't bulge like that in life, or his tongue hang out that way. But he was so transformed by the dye, he might have been an alien.

"I only talked with him on the phone," Vic said. "And e-mail."

"What did old Rod look like? That's easy," Sykes said. "I'll be right back."

Sykes trotted from the dye house toward the front entrance of the factory, where a Dominion Velvet sign announced the company was owned and operated by Symington Textiles, Inc. The sign was flanked by eight-by-ten pictures of the company's various executives and managers. Sykes returned with one and handed it to Lacey.

The picture of Rod Gibbs was typical of executives' publicity photos. Each was posed in front of the same backdrop, their heads at the same slight angle, with big pasted-on smiles. Lacey stared at the likeness for a few moments and handed the photo to Vic.

Judging from the picture, the man was in his early forties, though hard living might have made him look older. Lacey thought Rod Gibbs looked like a high school or college jock who had gone to seed after the last game. He might have started out handsome, but something had taken its toll. Perhaps drinking. His watery blue eyes were bloodshot, and his pasty white skin had taken on flab. His dark hair had thinned. His smile, however, was still toothpaste perfect. The very picture of a big fish in a small pond.

"I put that velvet on the spool myself yesterday. I tucked up the selvage on both ends so it would be perfect." Inez sounded mournful. "I always do. Especially since it's the last batch and all."

"Damn it all! That filthy pig ruined my last batch of velvet!" A woman who had just walked into the dye room offered her opinion unasked. Her name was Blythe Harrington, Lacey learned later, but she was anything but *blithe*.

She looked like any soccer matron, although with an impressive set of biceps from lifting heavy velvet and running the dye house. Blythe Harrington had short dark hair in a classic suburban-mom hairdo, red glasses, and a downturned mouth. She wore a smock over long pants and a T-shirt, and steel-toed shoes.

"Wouldn't you know it'd be the Blue Devil," Blythe

continued, much aggrieved. "Leave it to Rod Gibbs to ruin my very last spool! Just like he ruined this company."

That didn't sound like the man who had promised Lacey a story about how the company was headed for a sparkly new future.

Blythe grabbed a pair of scissors from her smock pocket and launched them at the body. They stuck in the victim's thigh, not that he would feel it. The crowd gave a collective gasp.

Lacey flinched, but Vic stepped forward and put out one arm to block Blythe. "We have a crime scene here, people. Time to calm down. We need to secure the area and get the police. Has anyone called them?" He looked at Nicholson, who seemed frozen in place. Vic handed Blythe off to Nicholson, took out his cell phone, and punched in 911.

"He ruined my velvet, my very last spool. My beautiful, beautiful velvet." Blythe was not at all sorry for her scissor toss. "If someone had to kill Rod, why did they have to spoil my velvet? I could have killed Rod myself. Asshole didn't need to ruin my velvet."

"I'm sure many of us would like to take all of the credit and none of the blame," Nicholson cautioned her. "Don't borrow trouble, Blythe."

"Too late, Tom. Trouble is here," Blythe said as he released her.

Kira gave Blythe a hug. "It's going to be okay. It's got to be."

Kira Evans had found her voice and seemed steadier on her feet. She was a pretty but frail-looking blonde who appeared about forty, though she might be younger. She looked as if she had given her best years to the job and received little in return. *It must have even taken the heat from her bones*, Lacey thought. While others were dressed in short sleeves to deal with the factory's heat, Kira wore a heavy turtleneck sweater and rubbed her arms as if she were chilled to the core.

"Don't worry, Blythe," Inez said. "Rod will never ruin anything else ever again."

"That's right," Hank Richards said. He'd been quiet through the discovery of the body, but he'd been listening to everything. His face was etched with deep worry lines, and the lines grew deeper as he stared at the body. "Rod Gibbs was a ruiner. Everything he touched turned to crap."

"Like my velvet," Blythe complained.

"This is horrible," Kira said.

Hank put his arm around Kira's shoulder. "It's not like it happened to somebody who didn't deserve it."

"I can't stop staring at him," Kira said. "He looks like something out of a monster movie."

"Careful, honey," Inez put in. "He might come back to life, like an alien. A big blue head might pop right out of his stomach." Inez seemed to find Gibbs's death funnier than the others. Lacey wondered exactly what Rod Gibbs had done to deserve this fate.

"I hope he burns in hell," Blythe spat. "Blue flames." She reached out to touch the spool of ruined velvet. Vic stopped her.

"One day to go, and y'all couldn't get through it without a major crime," the cop complained, glancing at the body. "Colorful too."

Two of Black Martin's finest, Officers Gavin Armstrong and Russell York, had arrived on the scene in a few minutes. Lacey put their ages at midthirties. Armstrong was an intimidatingly large man, but his freckled face and a mop of wavy light brown hair made him look like the cop next door. York was smaller, darker, and quieter. Armstrong took the lead. He walked around the dye vat over which Rod Gibbs's body hung, and he conceded that the death "was a little baroque for Black Martin."

He looked a little closer, and this time he sounded disgusted. "Oh, my God. Is that Rod Gibbs?"

Murder alone would be enough to merit attention in this little town, but the demise of one Rod Gibbs, and the added attraction of his new tint, seemed to be a big draw. They were soon joined by other officers. Lacey thought it must be the entire police force.

"So it's murder?" Nicholson asked, for lack of something better to say, or maybe simply to put a name to what had happened to the gargoyle hanging in their midst.

"I'm not the medical examiner. I can't make that determination," Armstrong said, all business. "But hell, Tom, you know this machinery better than me. Does this look like your typical workplace accident? And just between us, I don't think Rod climbed up there by himself, lashed himself to the spool, operated the hoist by remote control, and committed suicide. But if you've got a theory, I'm willing to listen. Especially if you think it was some kind of kinky sex thing." The two cops smirked. Their fellow officers chuckled.

"That would be like Rod," Officer York said.

"No need to be crude," Nicholson said.

"That wasn't crude, Tom," Armstrong protested. "I could show you crude, but I'm holding off because of all the ladies. I got to be honest, though. Someone really had it in for old Rod."

Vic offered his hand to the lead officer and filled him in on what he was doing there—meeting a new client for his security firm, touring the site.

Armstrong pressed his lips together. "Hell of a time to start a job like this. Client turns up dead." Vic nodded in agreement. "You're ex–law enforcement? You know the drill then. Stay out of our way, and we'll get along just fine."

"Works for me," Vic said. "I take it there haven't been a lot of murders around here."

"This ain't Richmond, or God forbid, D.C.," the cop said. "We take personal affront to murder in Black Martin. Isn't that right, Officer York?"

"That's right," York responded. "Too damn much paperwork."

"We had a nasty killing a few years back, but it was cut-and-dried," Armstrong said conversationally. "Love triangle gone wrong. Husband killed the wife's boyfriend. Three witnesses. Now, that's the way you want it. This thing looks downright complicated."

"It's a mess, no matter which way you look at it," York said. "Big, soggy blue mess."

Armstrong scanned the room and noticed Lacey for the first time. "And you are, ma'am?"

"Lacey Smithsonian. I'm a reporter for *The Eye Street*

Observer." She hoped she wouldn't get tossed out on her cute reporter's notebook.

Armstrong brought out that special look that cops reserve for the media. "Ah. Reporter, huh? What are y'all working on way down here in Black Martin?"

"I'm writing an article on the closing of Dominion Velvet."

He rubbed his chin. "*Eye Street Observer*? That wouldn't be Ms. Claudia Darnell's little paper up in Washington?"

Lacey nodded. "You know Claudia Darnell?" *Claudia Darnell, The Eye's publisher Claudia? How does this small-town cop know her?*

Armstrong smiled as if he could read Lacey's mind. He had a lot of teeth. "Everyone knows Claudia Darnell round these parts. Why, she's our little hometown gal."

Lacey thought she knew Claudia pretty well, but she didn't know that interesting factoid. She felt like a fool, and worse, professionally uninformed. "When you say *everyone* knows Claudia Darnell, you mean—"

"Everyone in *this* town," Nicholson offered. "Washington too, I guess. Claudia is the fair-haired country girl who grew up here and moved away. And made a big name for herself." He didn't add *like a traitor who forgets her roots*, but his voice conveyed that feeling.

Lacey wondered if she somehow should have known that little tidbit. Were there bad feelings toward Claudia's newspaper because of Claudia's history? Lacey hadn't run her Dominion Velvet story idea past Claudia. She didn't always even tell her editor, Mac Jones, what she was up to. Would Claudia have tried to steer her away from the story? But that was ridiculous. Reporters didn't run story ideas by the publisher. They used their own judgment.

"Not only that." Hank Richards joined the conversation. "Claudia Darnell is a silent partner in this factory. Why, she pulled the plug on us, along with the Blue Devil here. Claudia Darnell helped put us all out of work. But at least she isn't feeling blue about it."

chapter 3

Oh holy—conflict of interest! Claudia's part of this story? This day gets worse every second.

Lacey smiled brightly. "You learn something new every day."

"With Claudia Darnell, there's always been a lot to learn," Hank said. "She was maybe a decade ahead of me in school, but there were always tales about her, if you know what I mean."

Once a key figure in a spectacular Washington scandal, *Eye Street* publisher Claudia Darnell left town in her twenties in a blaze of notoriety. She had been a "secretary" to a married congressman and became famous for *not* typing. But Claudia had other skills. She turned out to be much smarter than the average scandal-scorched bimbo. After she had licked her wounds and learned to type, she wrote a bestselling roman à clef and proved adept at making money. A lot of it.

Claudia eventually returned to the scene of her previous alleged indiscretions, now as publisher of *The Eye Street Observer.* She also retained her famous looks and magnetism. She was a woman of a certain age, but she could still wrap men around her finger with a beguiling smile. Claudia had taken back her place in the Washington firmament, and then some.

Lacey's publisher apparently had several little-known chapters of her history that Lacey wasn't up on. But then, didn't everyone have secrets? Lacey wondered how Claudia's role would affect the Dominion Velvet story. At the very least it would require disclosing the newspaper's relationship to the factory. *Damn it all anyway.* Lacey had to call her editor as soon as possible. *Mac's gonna kill me,* she thought and groaned.

First a dead body, and now Claudia was involved somehow, even if only tangentially. Did she really pull the plug on this factory? Another old song began playing in Lacey's head. *Am I blue, am I blue-hoo-hoo—*

"They're not the only ones," Kira whispered. "Don't forget the others that sent us down the road to ruination."

"Looks like you got a lot more to learn, Ms. Smithsonian," Sykes noted with a grin.

Armstrong looked at York. "Having a reporter here from a bigger paper is really gonna piss off Will Adler." They both laughed. Armstrong turned back to Lacey. "This town may not be big enough for the two of you, Ms. Smithsonian."

"Will Adler? Who's he?" *Another complication?*

"Local reporter for the daily scandal sheet," Armstrong answered. "Thinks he's Woodward and Bernstein rolled into one. He'll show up here sooner or later. We like to take bets on how soon it'll take him to demand his First Amendment rights. Course, you being a reporter too, and for Darnell's paper? Hell, I don't know what to do with the two of you. Maybe you and Adler can fight it out. I'm not giving you anything more. No comment."

"Doesn't matter," Vic said. "She tends to find things out."

Don't forget I just witnessed the body, Lacey thought. She smiled and remained silent.

"Journalists are a nuisance." Armstrong stared at Lacey, hoping to make her uncomfortable. "Now, why would y'all want to go and write a story about this dead man here? Don't they have enough dead bodies in Washington, D.C.?"

"Because it's news, particularly with the factory closing. And if you hadn't noticed, he is blue." She knew the cop was just playing with her. The key was showing no fear.

"No skin off my blue suede shoes." Armstrong shrugged his large shoulders.

"In a town like this, the Blue Devil will be the topic of

conversation for quite a while," Hank pointed out. "He might as well give folks something back, after all he's taken."

"That's enough, Hank," the cop said. "All of you. Y'all will get your chance to bitch about the Blue Devil later."

"You knew his nickname?" Lacey asked.

Armstrong lifted an eyebrow. "We're not as dumb as you might think. Everyone in town knew Rod Gibbs was a devil. Hell, he drove that boat of his like a speed demon. This will only cement the legend of the Blue Devil."

"That's telling her," Sykes laughed.

"Okay, back away, people," Armstrong ordered. "Y'all will have your moment in the spotlight. And don't talk about this with each other anymore. I'm sure y'all've been jawing plenty, but it stops now."

The whispering in the background did not abate. "How are you going to go about the investigation?" Sykes asked. "You gonna grill us all?"

"*Grill* is an unattractive word, Sykes. Sounds like we're gonna barbecue you. The Black Martin PD conducts witness interviews in an orderly fashion."

"How can the department handle this one?" York asked.

"We're not. I'm calling in the state troopers," Armstrong said. "This kind of mess is right up their alley. Let them barbecue the witnesses."

Lacey looked at Vic for explanation. "Up to them," he said. "Smaller jurisdictions call in the state police for crimes that require special investigatory skills."

"We got the investigatory skills," Armstrong said, slightly affronted. "We just don't have the manpower this kind of nonsense is gonna take." Before Lacey could process that information, Armstrong turned to other matters. He jotted notes and peered at the body. He addressed Nicholson. "Will this blue dye wash off old Rod?"

"Not any time soon. Looks like he's been in the tub long enough for the color to set," Nicholson said. "These dyes are permanent. If you get it on your hands and skin, you can have a dye shadow for days." He sighed deeply. "If he's been in there a while, I'd guess he'll arrive at the pearly gates in what we like to call Midnight Blue."

"If he's been in it overnight, he'll be cooked," Inez added. "When the heat's on over two hundred degrees, it's like a crock-pot."

"No, Inez, it was just standing dye. These vats were all turned off over the weekend. Couldn't have been hot when he went in." Nicholson stroked his chin and pursed his lips. "And if the heat was on, there would be a different smell."

"Thank God for small blessings," Armstrong said.

Lacey wrinkled her nose. There was a definite acrid aroma in the dye house. It reminded her a little of a nail salon. She had assumed it was just the chemicals in the dye, but now she caught a strong whiff of death.

"Rod Gibbs will never get past the pearly gates. He'll be a blue devil in hell," Blythe claimed. "Make a nice contrast to all them red devils."

The cop crossed his arms. "He'll amuse the medical examiner, for damn sure."

"You can't keep me out! I'm the press!" someone yelled.

Lacey couldn't see the front doors through the little throng of witnesses and cops, but she could hear someone complaining. The local reporter had arrived.

She got a glimpse of a slightly built man in his late twenties with a receding hairline. He was arguing with Officer York just inside the entryway. She wondered how he'd found out about the body so fast. One of the velvet workers or one of the cops? *It's good to have sources.* She just didn't want the competition to have all the good sources.

"No one gets in to a crime scene who isn't already in. You know that, Will," York said.

"*The Black Martin Daily Ledger* has a right to know!" he shouted. "Tell me one thing, York. Is the body really blue? I heard it was Rod Gibbs. Can you verify that? And I want a picture."

"He'll get a picture when hell freezes over," Armstrong bellowed. "We take the pictures here, Adler."

York hustled the man out and locked the factory doors. The state police Bureau of Criminal Investigation was in Richmond. It would be a while before the state troopers and their crime scene van showed up at the factory. The local cops ordered everyone to different locations in the

factory so they wouldn't swap stories or agree on their re-
actions to seeing the dead man, though Lacey thought it
might be a little too late. She was irritated to be left cooling
her heels while Armstrong allowed Vic, a former chief of
police, to accompany him to look at the rudimentary security measures that had been in place. Some ancient video
cameras would be dusted for prints. It was unclear whether
they would prove helpful. It was also unclear whether the
cameras were even working.

Lacey was ensconced in one of the glass-windowed offices with a view onto the factory floor. Though she could
see flashes from the police cameras in the dye house, no
one was around to see her. She fretted that the local reporter might already be filing his own story. It might not
be accurate, but it might scoop her own, practically eyewitness, account. She thought about it. Although Armstrong
had cautioned the witnesses not to talk with each other,
he didn't tell Lacey she couldn't call her newspaper or her
editor. She pulled out her cell phone and dialed Douglas
MacArthur Jones.

"Mac, it's Lacey." There was a pause on the other end.
He wasn't expecting her to call. "You remember. Funny
name? Fashion beat?"

"Tell me now, Smithsonian," Mac said. "Do I open the
Maalox, or is this a social call?"

"Well—" She hesitated. This was always the hard part.
"Does Maalox count as a social drug?"

"You're writing a feature, Smithsonian. A simple feature, tugging at our readers' heartstrings. Workers out of
jobs, fashion down the tubes. That's all. Right? That's the
deal. No dead bodies. No problems." Mac was trying to be
funny, but his voice was questioning. He always jumped to
dire conclusions. Not that he wasn't sometimes justified.
She wasn't supposed to have any reason to call in.

That's what comes of having a history. Lacey took a deep
breath. She could imagine Mac unscrewing the cap of the
blue bottle of antacid and taking a big slug.

"I'm waiting, Smithsonian. We're on deadline here."

"All right. Just let me get this out. Yes, there's a dead
body."

"There is no dead body in this story, Smithsonian," Mac said.

"Do you want to hear this or not?"

He moaned with dramatic flair. "Go ahead."

"A man was pulled out of a tub full of blue dye here at the velvet factory, and, yes, the corpse was dyed blue. Midnight Blue is the exact shade. Looks like homicide," Lacey said in a rush. "Name of the victim is Rodney Gibbs. And yes, he was the guy I was supposed to interview. And Houston, we have another problem."

"Beyond the fact that you can't go a month without stumbling over a dead body? And not just a body, *a murdered* body? And check my hearing here, Smithsonian: Did you say the victim is blue, as in the *color* blue? Not black like me or white like you?" Mac was actually a little of both, but she didn't quibble.

"Yes, he is blue. Like a crayon is blue. And I like that rhyming thing you do."

"I do not rhyme and we're wasting time. Now talk to me, Smithsonian."

"I didn't 'stumble' over him. He's actually hanging out to dry. But listen, Mac, here's the rub: The dead guy was part owner of the last velvet factory in Virginia. But so is our publisher, Claudia Darnell."

"What the hell—"

"I didn't know about Claudia. Turns out she's from here—Black Martin, Virginia, where the factory is. Did you know that? The factory is closing, she owns a stake in it, and people down here blame her and this dead blue guy. She could be involved somehow."

"Smithsonian, when you put your foot in it, you really—"

"So I want to know, conflict-of-interestwise, what does this mean for my story? A disclaimer or what? Do you want me to forget this feature? It's visual, Mac. Very visual. I know how you like visual."

There was a pause. Lacey could envision Mac wiping sweat off his chocolate brown forehead, his eyebrows dancing a troubled tango. She heard his irritated whistle. Lacey was glad she wasn't there.

"Keep on the story. We'll do full disclosure. Claudia may

be part owner, but we won't hide that, especially with a death on the premises. A particularly lurid death, the kind that only fashion reporter Lacey Smithsonian can find."

"That sounds suspiciously like that sarcasm thing," Lacey said.

"Now send me what you can about this royal blue mess."

"A little tricky, Mac. My laptop is in the car, I'm sequestered awaiting questioning, and the cops might come back at any moment and tell me not to talk to you. And there's a local reporter who might be writing something for the neighborhood rag right now. But he wasn't lucky enough to be a witness, like me."

"Great. That's just great," he snarled. "Give me the facts. I'll write a brief. We'll have something on the Web in twenty minutes, nothing razzle-dazzle, just a brief. And remember, Smithsonian, this murder, as rainbow-hued as it is, is *not* a big story, not in D.C. You are a long way from the District. But we can't ignore it either, not while you're there working on the human-interest side of fashion. Human interest, not homicide," Mac reiterated for her benefit. "And what about your column?"

Officer York entered the corner of her vision, pacing the factory floor, followed by a newcomer. Lacey assumed he was from the state police.

"Ma'am, you better not be talking on that phone," York warned her. The newcomer scowled at her.

"I gotta go, Mom," she said into the phone. She smiled at York. "Calling my mom."

"Okay," Mac continued, "you figure out how the blue guy fits into your factory closing story. I'll write a brief and talk to Claudia. Stay out of trouble. I mean it." Mac hung up.

"I'll call you back, Mom—" Lacey said to dead air. She made a show of putting the phone away for Officer York.

"You flouting the law, Miss Washington Reporter?"

"No, sir. Just checking the weather. Cloudy, continued cold. According to my mom. She's a weather nut. Besides, no one told me not to use the phone."

"Consider yourself told as of right now," York said.

Surely, this cop would understand that she couldn't be scooped by a small-town Podunkville reporter. York was just snarling at her for the benefit of his colleague. On second thought, perhaps he wouldn't understand.

The state cop looked tightly wound. The newcomer wore a short dark haircut and was dressed in a navy sports jacket, white shirt, conservative tie, and khaki slacks, neat and sharply pressed. Like his attitude. He carried a badge. His face was all hard angles, which seemed at odds with his soft, southern Virginia accent. He asked her who she was and what business she had there. He curled his lip at the mention of *The Eye Street Observer*. Lacey knew this was just pro forma for some cops whenever they met a member of the press. Or the contempt might be meant for Claudia. Lacey ignored it.

"And you are?" she asked politely.

"Special Agent Mordecai Caine, Virginia State Police Bureau of Criminal Investigations. Lead agent on this crime scene. Don't go anywhere. And no calls." He spun on his heel and marched off. Lacey thought he had something very stiff up his backside.

From her lonely perch, Lacey had a view of velvets spread out on long tables. She could see hundreds of rolls of the shimmering fabric, stacked high, ready for shipping, in a cavalcade of colors, blues, yellows, greens, pinks, and purples. Staring at the material, she had the urge to sink her fingers into it.

The cloth made her think of a blue velvet dress from the 1940s that her great-aunt Mimi had left her. She'd worn it at Christmastime. At times like these Lacey's first instinct was to run home to Aunt Mimi's trunk, her personal antidote to a stressful day. She might find a perfect pattern for another evening gown, something that would make her forget the dead man and the ruined spool of velvet.

Leafing through the patterns and pictures and vintage fabrics in the trunk always calmed her and made her think of women who had lived through worse troubles than she. Women who worked in factories converted for war production, who built weapons and airplanes while their men went to war. Back then, a velvet factory might have switched to producing wool and cotton for soldiers' uniforms.

Unfortunately, Mimi's trunk was in Lacey's apartment in Alexandria, Virginia, and not here.

Mimi would tell Lacey to slap on some war paint, put on some nice clothes, and show her best face to the world. *If you look strong, you'll be strong.* That was what Mimi would have advised. Lacey checked the mirror in her purse and freshened her own war paint.

She was ready for battle. At least, that was what she told herself.

Recession Depression Got You Down?
Dress Up in the Downturn!

So the economy is in a downward spiral. The wolf is howling at your door, your future uncertain. Is that any reason for a Depression-style fashion statement? When bad things happen, some women carry around their own personal gray cloud. Even worse, they dress *down*, anticipating the worst. Not exactly the style of a survivor, is it?

There is a woman out there, smart and attractive, but down in the dumps. You may know her. You may even *be* her. But wearing ugly clothes in response to bad news is simply punishing the wrong person—*you*.

Ask yourself: Are you spiraling down into the dismal colors, the grays, the beiges, the taupes that steal the blush from your cheeks? Passing up the makeup and forgetting to comb your hair? You might as well say, "I give up! Depress me! Wake me when it's over!"

No, no, no! Do not give up. Do not wear those baggy sweatshirts to the office, not even the unemployment office. Do not let the jerks win. Not while you've got breath in your body and cute clothes in your closet.

Even when you (and your pocketbook) feel empty, there's a simple reason to fight back with fashion. When you feel like a loser and dress like a loser, you tend to look like a loser. Who wants to hire a loser? Hang with a loser? *Date* a loser? No one.

My advice: In this iffy economy, your own attitude is the only thing you have any control over. So face the world with bravado. Punch it in the nose. Change your sad rags for glad rags. Dress like a winner. And for heaven's sake, don't give in to stretch pants with elastic waistbands. The economy may be sagging, but that doesn't mean *you* have to sag too.

It's hard to be brave when your livelihood is on the line. Sometimes bravery requires faith, hope, a bit of magical thinking, and oh, what the heck, maybe even sequins. Okay, sequins are optional. But your best and brightest clothes do you no good hiding in your closet, waiting for your ship to come in so they can help you strut your stuff on that happy day. Dress to welcome that luxury liner into port, and the *Good Ship Glamorous* just might cruise your way.

What to wear with those sleek dark-wash jeans? That velvet jacket you never wear, or the old reliable denim rag that looks like something out of a Depression-era photograph? Go with the velvet. It's stunning and striking, and as soft and comforting as a security blanket. Or those high heels and your best silk blouse in the perfect color that enhances your eyes and your outlook. Declare your own holiday party and celebrate being the stylish survivor you are.

So if you're down in the dumps, head for your closet. Dig out buried treasures you've been saving for, well, for right now. Fight that depression by getting rid of torturous togs. When in doubt, throw it out. Pretend those ugly clothes are all the demented employers who have ever tormented you. Dump them in a trash bag. They can't hurt you anymore. Now, don't you feel better?

This is the time to do something radical, to look your best and wear your best. Don't give in to the blues by wearing gray. Resolve to dress up in the downturn! And when your ship sails in, you'll be ready for it, wearing that great outfit.

The chicest woman on the dock.

chapter 4

"So you're Lacey Smithsonian," Special Agent Mordecai Caine said. "Reporter. What exactly do you do for that newspaper of yours?"

After everyone else had been questioned and released, Agent Caine came back to speak with Lacey. He gave the word *newspaper* a snide twist.

She wondered if he'd left her cooling her heels simply because he disliked the media. Or to keep her from interviewing the other witnesses for her news story. Or because he thought the other witnesses were more knowledgeable, and had a more personal connection to Gibbs and a motive for killing him, and therefore, should be questioned first. Or all of the above.

She didn't know and she really didn't care. She was itching to get out of the factory and into some fresh air that didn't have the stench of death and dyeing. By the time he got back to her, she didn't like him very much.

Through the office window, Lacey could see Vic leaning against the back wall, chatting with Officer Armstrong. Their body language told her it was a friendly conversation. *Great. Vic gets the good cop. I get the annoying cop.*

Caine's body language told her he was an adversary. She folded her arms in response. *Let him wait.* He cleared his throat.

"I'm a fashion reporter," she finally said.

"Fashion reporter? Why are you at Dominion Velvet?"

"To write a story about the factory closing and its effect on the workers. It's one of the backstories of fashion."

He invited her to sit down. She perched on the edge of the desk. He looked at her with hard eyes. "Is that a typical story for fashion writers?"

"I hope not. That's why I'm writing it. I try to write about more than just fashion. How it influences our lives, and how current events influence fashion. For instance, the blue and gray colors of the Virginia State Trooper uniform were chosen deliberately to reflect both sides in the Civil War. You probably knew that."

"Yes, ma'am, I knew that. A policy decision, not one involving fashion."

"Exactly. That's one way fashion, or even a uniform, evolves. Style is something else entirely."

Lacey wondered how this factory closing would impact other businesses, like the firms from which it had once bought yarns and dyes and other products that kept the machinery moving. And what of the industries that bought fabric from Dominion? Would they resort to lower-quality velvet from foreign manufacturers? Would they close their doors? Would Special Agent Caine care?

"Did you know Rodney Gibbs?" Caine asked.

"No. I spoke to him on the phone the other day to set up the tour and an interview," Lacey said. "He was my only contact."

"But you didn't meet him?"

"Not until they pulled him out of the dye. He was missing this morning, so Tom Nicholson agreed to give me the tour. Do you have a strong suspect?"

"No comment. Have you ever been to the town of Black Martin, Virginia, before today?"

"Nope." Lacey knew there was no reason for long answers.

"Yet you decided it was interesting enough for a story?" He jotted down a note in his notebook.

"Yes, and to be frank, it's more interesting now. Will the state police work in conjunction with the local police department or handle the investigation alone?"

"My job is to ask the questions, Ms. Smithsonian. Yours is to answer them."

That's hardly fair. "My job is also to ask questions," Lacey said. *Reporter here.*

Caine grunted and pressed his lips together in a straight line. "Then I suggest you contact the state police Office of Public Affairs."

In Lacey's experience, that might be the kiss of death as far as getting information goes. She smiled. "Yeah, sure."

"That Vic Donovan out there, is he your boyfriend?"

"Yes." *The term* boyfriend *seems so goofy when you hit thirty,* Lacey thought. But she decided saying Vic was her "main squeeze" would be a little flippant.

"Wouldn't that impact your reporter's objectivity on this story, seeing as how Mr. Donovan is going to handle security for the company?"

"I was writing a feature article on fashion and the impact of the factory closing, not a news story. Vic's work starts after they close. So I would say no."

"Then I suggest you stick to fashion, not murder, and stay out of my investigation. And out of my way," Caine said. "Rod Gibbs's death is not your story."

"Wow, did you know that is absolutely the worst thing you could possibly say to a reporter?" Lacey was so shocked she started laughing. "You might as well have called me *girly* and patted me on the head. Don't you tell me what my story is. I'm the reporter here." Lacey narrowed her eyes in the best manner of the nuns back in school. It was a look that could chill men to their core. *If I were a nun.*

If Caine felt a chill, he kept it to himself, but he cleared his throat again and changed the subject. It was a short interview. Caine knew enough not to ask to see her notes. And though she was sure someone had told him she took a couple of photographs, he didn't ask about those either.

By the time Lacey was dismissed, the light was gone and the air was February frosty. Crusted snow from a week-old storm reflected the glow from Black Martin's streetlamps in front of the factory. Dominion Velvet's building didn't look like a factory to Lacey. It looked more like a midcentury elementary school, squat and L-shaped, red brick with a roof with multiple angled vents, giving it a sawtooth profile. Scarred wooden picnic tables were scattered around the grounds for workers at lunch or on breaks, but they looked ghostly and untended in the dark. The trees and bushes were winter stark.

Their breath came out in puffs as Lacey and Vic walked around the corner of the building to the street. All the clouds had cleared from the sky and the stars began to light the black night. Vic hugged her tightly as they walked.

"How are you doing, sweetheart?"

"Agitated and bored, and not in a good way. Special Agent Caine is a real treat. I didn't get to follow the police around and listen to all their theories about what happened to Mr. Gibbs, like *someone* I know. On the plus side, I have no desire for Max Factor's newest foundation, Indigo Number Nine."

"There is that." Vic flashed a grin that made her feel better. "You're in the pink."

"But blue is all the rage. Blue is the new black."

"In this case blue is the new *dead*."

Though the air was far colder than when they arrived that morning and the wind chapped her cheeks, Lacey was glad to be outside and out of the velvet plant. They headed for Main Street, two blocks away.

"You called your boss, didn't you?" Vic asked. "Told him the story was getting bigger and messier? You've got that air of self-satisfaction."

"I do not," she protested.

"I recognize the look. A reporter getting one over on the cops. You did it to me often enough."

"I did? How sweet of you to say so. Seems like old times." She laughed at the expression on his face. "I had to, darling. It's my job. Besides, Mac has to know, so he can alert Claudia that the dogs of scandal may soon be barking at her door."

"The local law enforcement boys won't like reading about this."

"I'm just spreading the joy," Lacey said. "What's the local police role in this anyway?"

"VSP will take the lead," Vic said. "But Black Martin PD will assist with whatever they can provide."

"So Armstrong will work with Caine?"

"Theoretically."

"Great. Caine doesn't seem the type to share information with the press."

It was Vic's turn to laugh. "Not his job, darling."

"My whole story just exploded, and now I have to play catch-up and write something very different. You have to admit, this story took a twist nobody could have predicted."

"Unless they knew your track record with fashion fatalities," he pointed out. She ignored him.

"*The Eye* cannot find out about the colorful death of one of Claudia Darnell's business partners from somebody else's newspaper, particularly when I'm on the spot. That's a firing offense, especially in this economy."

"You made your point."

"What I don't get is why Gibbs told me the factory had a bright future when clearly it doesn't."

"Propaganda, Lacey. They say Napoleon sent reports to France of his glorious victories in Egypt, while he was really just getting his ass beat. They didn't know that back in Paris. They thought he was the conquering hero. Good for morale."

"You're saying Rod Gibbs wanted to put one over on me? So I'd write a story about how good things are coming if everyone would just be patient, when really, there's no way this place was going to ever reopen."

"That seems to sum it up."

"So he can look like a hero long enough to make a getaway? I hate people like that," Lacey said. "But then, he didn't get away, did he?"

"The big question for me is why today, sweetheart, when we're here? The day that Lacey Smithsonian has a meeting with the deceased."

"There can't be a link, Vic. That would make his death somehow our fault, as if he were killed so he couldn't talk to us, and that's crazy. We don't know these people. We've never been here before. No one but Gibbs even knew we were coming today."

"The last day of anyone's job is tense enough without a reporter on scene. Workplace violence happens, especially with an unstable employee or two and a whole factory shutting down," he said. "You never know how close to the edge some people are."

She thought about it. Tempers could get pretty peevish at the newspaper, but most reporters were nonviolent, or at least not fit enough to be violent. They'd chosen to believe the pen was mightier than the sword and that was how they dealt with their enemies. "Have you seen a lot of it—violence on the job?" Lacey asked.

He frowned. "I've seen the aftermath of people going berserk on the job. But it usually involves fists or guns. Never seen anyone dyed blue before. And what happened to the so-called night watchman? If they'd called me in a week ago, this wouldn't have happened. Not on-site anyway." He stopped and held Lacey's arm, turning her toward him. "I suppose it wouldn't make a difference if I asked you to stay away from dangerous stories."

"No. But I appreciate the concern." Lacey kissed him. "Besides, a story is never dangerous until it is. Unless it involves mocking Christmas sweaters, which I would never do. That's *really* dangerous."

Vic knew he wasn't getting anywhere. "Speaking of dangerous, are you hungry?"

"I'm starving to death. Could that be civilization up ahead?" She tugged at his sleeve and they headed toward the lights.

Black Martin's sleepy downtown was all of four blocks long and two blocks wide. But the early twentieth-century architecture along Main Street was rather grand for a city of its size, a collection of attractive buildings from a bygone era when the town was flush with money from textiles and agriculture and catered to soldiers looking for nightlife. Handsome pre–World War II facades sheltered too many empty storefronts, victims of the recession that had hit Black Martin harder than any other area of the state.

The county had the highest unemployment rate in Virginia. Since the Army had pulled out of the nearby base a few years back, Black Martin had become the kind of town where the sidewalks rolled up at six p.m. Only a couple of downtown restaurants were still open.

The first one was a café named Good Eats. The menu in the window featured Southern comfort food, like chicken-fried steak and vanilla tapioca pudding. It was brightly lit and half full of sedate senior citizens.

"What do you think?" Vic asked. "Is Good Eats good enough for us?"

"I feel my hair turning blue at the very suggestion. Not a good color choice under the circumstances."

chapter 5

La Puerta Roja, the Mexican cantina across the street, seemed to be the only happening place in Black Martin. Multicolored lights beckoned to Lacey and Vic, and when the front door opened, they heard the blare of mariachi music.

"Now this is more like it," Vic said. Inside, the place was warm and welcoming. The aroma of sizzling fajitas filled the air. Pitchers of margaritas were flowing. The décor was bright. Little pink and red cupids wearing mariachi hats hung from the ceiling. Signs invited them to the St. Valentine's Day fiesta.

Lacey and Vic headed for an open table near the bar. They recognized some of the Dominion Velvet factory workers. Apparently they'd come straight from the factory to spread the news of Rod Gibbs's blue death. *So much for the cops' warnings to keep it quiet,* Lacey thought.

"That's right. He was Midnight Blue! How's that for a send-off?" someone was saying.

"It'll always be midnight for Rod now," someone else replied.

Lacey craned her neck to see who was speaking, but she couldn't tell. The remark was swallowed up by laughter. Those who witnessed the body were already instant celebrities, and if they weren't toasting the dead man, they were certainly roasting him.

"I swear the devil himself came for Rod Gibbs," someone said. "He was stabbed with a pitchfork! I saw the marks myself." There was more laughter.

"No, really, he had a hole in his chest. I'm just saying," the voice insisted.

Lacey turned to Vic. "Eyewitness to a pitchfork murder," she said. "Satan sought for questioning. Details at eleven."

"This may be a reporter's dream, Lacey, but it could turn ugly fast."

"Don't worry, honey. If I smell sulfur instead of mesquite, I am out of here."

"Anyone ever tell you you're a smart-ass?"

"Yes, I believe there was a certain police chief, Victor Donovan, but that was a long time ago." Lacey flashed her most dazzling smile.

She felt someone at her elbow. It was Dirk Sykes, the velvet shearer, from the factory. "Come on, sit down with us, Ms. Smithsonian. Have a margarita. We're having a wake. Everyone's invited. You too, Mr. Donovan." Sykes started pushing tables together.

"A wake for Rod Gibbs?" Vic inquired.

"Hell no. A wake for us. For our jobs. The Blue Devil, he's the only upside of all this. His being dead and all." Sykes lifted a margarita and turned his face to the light, which highlighted the wicked scar down the side of his face. Lacey had noticed it that morning, but it was larger and deeper than she remembered. She tried not to stare. He saw her look and he ran a finger down the length of the healed gash. He grinned.

"It's okay, Ms. Smithsonian. No offense taken. Gives me character."

"Please call me Lacey. What happened?"

Despite the Hawaiian shirt, he looked a bit dangerous, like a retired pirate, with his scar and swarthy coloring and black ponytail.

"Had a little accident with a blade, shearing the velvet. Long time ago. You gotta respect the machinery. Damn near lost my head. Course, I nearly lost my job too when the plant got an OSHA citation for it." Sykes winked at her. "It's not so bad. Some of the ladies find it irresistible. Ain't that right, Inez?" He winked at Inez Garcia, who sat at the table, sipping her margarita.

"Oh, Dirk, how you talk." She giggled, and Lacey watched a romantic spark pass between the two.

"The ladies think my scar is romantic. Like Long John Silver." The only thing "Long John" Sykes lacked, Lacey thought, was a parrot on his shoulder and a pirate hat. "Why, I'm a damn romantic hero." He traced it again with his finger and winked at Lacey.

"Romantic hero, my ass." Hank Richards shook his long hair out of his eyes. Next to Sykes's pirate, Hank looked like a bearded blond Viking. "Shut up and give me a hand." Richards and Sykes joined the rest of the tables together and grabbed chairs for Lacey and Vic. "Have a margarita. We got another pitcher on the way," Hank said. "It's not often we get a big city newspaper visiting our little town. Seems we depress people. Hell, we depress ourselves."

Lacey and Vic shared a look. "Just one drink," Vic said, and held out a chair for Lacey. Inez and Blythe made room.

"Do you actually read *The Eye Street Observer*?" Lacey asked him.

"Never seen it," Hank said. "Heard of it. Claudia Darnell's paper, right? Sometimes I pick up the local rag. Don't take me long to read that."

Kira Evans arrived late, looking frazzled, and scooted into the last empty space next to Hank Richards. She ordered a white wine spritzer. "I had to drive my daughter to basketball practice, but I figured everyone would be here. I didn't want to be home alone." She leaned back and rubbed her eyes.

"What's the matter, Kira? You afraid of his ghost?" Inez asked.

"Maybe I am. I don't want to think about him at all," Kira said, hugging herself to get warm. "But I'm sure it's nothing a little wine won't cure."

"Look at it this way, Kira," said Hank. "The world is a little bit better place today. Whether we got jobs or not."

Lacey felt a little awkward about being a "mere" fashion reporter and about working for Claudia Darnell, whom these people seemed to know better than she did. She just hoped that no one knew about her history with fashion and murder investigations. It could be *awkward.*

"So Kira, why the turtleneck? Covering up a love bite? Who's the lucky guy?" Inez asked, proving she didn't miss much. Heads turned from Inez to Hank, who wisely said nothing.

Kira blushed and pulled her turtleneck up higher. "Just got a chill. Think I'm coming down with something."

"Yeah, a case of too much lovin'," Inez cracked.

Blythe was happy to pour Vic and Lacey margaritas from their pitchers while she stared appreciatively at Donovan.

"You've got quite a reputation, Ms. Smithsonian," Blythe said. Lacey looked at the woman in surprise. She wore elastic-band slacks and an oversized top in an unflattering mustard yellow.

"You read my fashion column?" Lacey asked.

"Fashion? Oh, heck, no," Blythe laughed. "We read all about you on that Web site, Conspiracy Clearinghouse. You know, DeadFed dot com?"

Oh no. Did Blythe really read Lacey's nemesis, Damon Newhouse's Web site? Lacey's cheeks did a slow burn and Vic had the nerve to laugh.

"Oh, Lacey knows all about DeadFed," Vic said.

"I never heard about it till today," Hank said. "But these guys are catching me up on it. Sykes here is the Internet wizard. Wouldn't know it to look at him though, him being a romantic hero and all."

"That Damon Newhouse is a real pistol, ain't he?" Inez said.

"He's a real *something*, all right," Lacey said.

"Oh, come on. Tell us all about him," Inez implored. She leaned toward Lacey. "I love that Web site of his. It's like that Drudge Report. But with aliens."

"Seems to me he really tells it like it is," Blythe added. "An honest man in a dishonest world."

Or a crazy space cadet from the Beatnik Galaxy, Lacey thought.

Damon Newhouse, creator of the Conspiracy Clearinghouse Web site, aka DeadFed, fancied himself a journalist of the people, a cyberhotshot who embraced every crackpot theory the mainstream media wouldn't touch. Still, he craved the legitimacy of a real news organization, one with words in print on real paper. Damon knew he would never break into *The Washington Post,* so he had set his sights on *The Eye Street Observer.* He dogged Lacey's tracks, following her stories and giving them his own cracked twist, finding a conspiracy behind every bush, around every corner, and underneath every bed. He drove her nuts.

"I understand the two of you are close," Blythe said. "You've broken some big stories together."

Lacey choked on her margarita and Vic slapped her on the back. *Together?* "Not exactly," Lacey said when she stopped choking. *That's how Damon wants it to look.*

"Most reporters are full of crap," Hank Richards said. "Couldn't tell their ass from their— Well, you know. But I kind of like that DeadFed thing. Kind of like the *National Enquirer,* but without all the celebrity diet crap."

Lacey did a mental eye roll, but tried not to show what she thought of Damon in front of these apparently rabid fans.

"If it wasn't for people like him and DeadFed, we wouldn't know half of what's happening in this country," Sykes said. "He's like a frigging light in the wilderness."

What about my light? My stories? "I must be in an alternate universe," Lacey said under her breath to Vic.

"Just like being back in Sagebrush, Lacey, where the natives are all friendlylike," Vic murmured. He turned around to hide his smile and wave over a waiter for an order of nachos and some fajitas. Lacey barely heard her cell phone through the noise and the music. She excused herself from the table to answer it.

"If that's Damon on the phone, y'all say hi for us," Sykes hollered after her.

"Will do." Lacey sneaked a peak at the number. It was from the paper, not Damon. She went into the restaurant's foyer and answered. "Hello?"

"What are we going to do with you, Lois Lane?" It was Tony Trujillo, *The Eye*'s police reporter.

"Hi, Tony. What's up?"

"You tell me. You leave town, find a body, and you don't

even tip me off? Where's the love?" He sounded a bit annoyed. Lacey was two and half hours away from D.C., so he couldn't readily horn in on her story. She allowed herself a small smile at Trujillo's expense.

"You talked to Mac. He remembered me. How nice."

"He says we ought to tag you with a GPS just to keep track of you. And maybe a hit counter for the bodies."

"You're hilarious, Tony."

"Is Clark Kent there? Sorry. I mean Superman."

"Vic is here." She looked over at Vic, who was helping himself to some tortilla chips. A waiter passed by with a tray of fajita platters. The aroma made her stomach growl.

"Mac says the dead guy was blue. Like really blue, dyed blue. That for real?"

"It's for real. The corpse was tied to a gigantic spool of velvet and stashed in a tub of dye."

"That's what Mac put out on the Web."

"The deceased was also the guy I was supposed to interview."

"Whoa, that's weird," Trujillo said. "Either way, he gave you a story. So, a crime of fashion?" She could hear the smirk in his voice. "Seems like maybe you need backup. Maybe we could send you Kavanaugh."

"You wouldn't dare!"

Tony laughed at Lacey's discomfort. Kelly Kavanaugh was Lacey's latest irritant, a freckle-faced overenthusiastic transfer to fashion from Tony's police beat, and Tony was glad to be rid of her. Kavanaugh was there ostensibly to free Lacey to seek out more complex stories. But Lacey suspected the young reporter was there to deliver payback from her editor, Douglas MacArthur Jones. Kavanaugh wouldn't know a ruffle from a bow, and just forget the subtleties of ruching. Kavanaugh's heart was set on dramatic crime stories, and from where she sat, Smithsonian's beat was on fire. Lacey didn't know what to do with her. She hadn't even told Kelly about the velvet factory story, or that she'd be out of town for a day.

"Is there anything else you want, Tony?"

"Do you need me, Lacey? I can be down in a couple of hours in Mustang Sally." Trujillo couldn't wait to get in his sleek black beauty with the white rag top and drive like a speed demon to Black Martin to steal her story.

"Thanks, but you can rest your horses. I'm sure you've got enough crime in D.C. to keep you busy. And I'm fine, really."

"When are you coming back to the office?"

"I'm going to try and scare up some interviews in the morning. I'll be back in town tomorrow. Late, maybe five or so. I'll file something from here or from home."

"Hey, you get any photos of this guy?"

"I took a few pictures before being glared down. They're not very good, but you can see that he's dead. And blue."

"What would your mother say, nice girl like you taking pictures of a dead guy?"

"She'd want to fly to D.C. and help me out, and she'd bring my little sister for some serious family bonding and crime fighting."

Tony snorted with laughter. Lacey hung up and headed back to the table as the nachos were being delivered. She took three steps when her phone rang again. "Good grief!" Lacey looked at the number: Brooke Barton. Normally she would like to talk with her BFF Brooke, but the timing was very suspicious. *What did Brooke know and when did she know it?*

Brooke Barton, Esquire, one of Lacey's two best friends, loved democracy and conspiracy theories in equal measure, and she had an eerie ability to know when something was up with Lacey. Brooke was always ready to lend her aid in a crisis, whether it required legal chops or sharpshooting skills. But she was also dating Damon Newhouse of Dead-Fed fame. And that could spell trouble.

"You rang, Ms. Barton?" Lacey said.

"Is it true?" Brooke sounded far too excited.

"Is what true?"

"Don't play with my nerves, Lacey. I have it on good authority that you stumbled onto another crime scene, interestingly tangled up in a fashion-related factory, and the corpse was purple."

"You talked to Damon, and he was not purple. Did Damon say he was *purple*?"

"No, the story is on *The Eye*'s Web site," Brooke said. "I threw in the purple to test you. Yes, he was blue, according to the story. But it was maddeningly vague as to the exact shade of blue. And why did you think Damon knew? Is there something more I should know?"

Bad move, Lacey. Now she's really *interested.*

Lacey looked over at the table of Dominion employees, madly scarfing up all the nachos. They'd heard the name *Damon*. They waved at her, mouthing words of greeting for their hero Newhouse.

"No reason. Other than the body is blue and Damon might think he's a dead Martian or something. And we know Damon just has a way of—*dogging* me." Lacey thought about her recent private investigator's class that Damon had also intruded on, once he found out she was there. Really, he was like a puppy, she thought, Brooke's overgrown puppy. *A puppy with a Web site. And fans.*

"Don't be silly. Damon adores you. He just wants to walk in your footsteps. So, what's the story on the dead guy?"

"You can read it when I write it. I'm not sure now what the angle is for my feature."

"How about the blue angle?"

"Yeah, there is always blue. The social meanings and symbolism of blue."

Brooke lowered her voice. "Do you need me to come down? I could be there in a couple of hours."

Along with Tony and Brooke and Damon's fan club, it would be a swell party.

"Chill, Brooke. We don't need our superpowers just yet." What Lacey needed was a good meal. She was beginning to feel lightheaded. Lack of food and that yummy margarita were sailing straight to her head.

"Oh. Okay." Brooke sounded let down. "You sure? I have a new Wonder Woman cape. A blue one."

"Ah, bad news. They've redesigned Wonder Woman's signature look. It's awful. She looks like a rocker chick in a metal band now. We should protest." Lacey took a breath. "They took the body away. You wouldn't even have a chance to see the blue guy. I kind of doubt there's going to be an open casket. It would be beyond tasteless."

"Damn. And cremation is all the rage too. What will future generations of archaeologists play with if we leave them no preserved remains?"

"Luckily, we are not here to worry about future generations right now."

"I guess you're right. But, Lacey, if you need me, all you have to do is call. You know that."

Lacey smiled to herself. "A friend in need and all that. I get it. I love you for that." She hung up and headed back to the table. The nachos were nearly gone. She scooped up the last bite. "Gee, thanks for sharing, guys."

A man approached the table. He was slightly built and wore a shirt and tie under his puffy purple parka, which was almost formal for Black Martin. His posture was overly erect, as if he were trying to be taller, and his serious glasses meant business. Lacey decided the young reporter looked like a congressional aide in training.

"So you're Lacey Smithsonian." He made it sound like an accusation.

"Not my fault. It's the family name," Lacey replied. "You must be Will Adler." Lacey put out her hand to shake. He ignored it. She had gotten only a glimpse of him before, but she recognized the posture and the attitude. She'd had a similar one when she was a reporter in Sagebrush, Colorado. No local reporter wanted a big city reporter to ride in and snatch some juicy story away.

"Did you come to town just to sneer at my newspaper and steal my story?"

"Hey, I'm from *The Eye Street Observer*. I only sneer at *The Washington Post*."

"I am Will Adler, reporter for the *Black Martin Daily Ledger*, and you are treading on my territory."

"No, I'm not. I'm writing a fashion-related story on the factory closing. Because of the velvet. That's not exactly your territory, is it, Will? Are you a fashion reporter?"

He looked like he was wondering if she was joking. "The factory closing is old news, and it's not about fashion. I wouldn't be covering a fashion—"

"See, we're working completely different angles." Lacey smiled. "Have a margarita."

"You're sure about that?" Adler suspected a big city reporter trap. "What about Rod Gibbs's blue body? Who tipped you off?"

"I was touring the plant when they found him."

"You were there? That doesn't sit well with me."

"Can't help you with that one." *Jealousy.* Lacey knew he was annoyed at missing all the action in his own town. She felt his pain. But Adler's antagonism was beginning to remind her of the cops. He pulled up a chair and sat down. The former factory workers regarded him warily.

"Even if you were there," Adler challenged her, "I've got good sources, and I'll get more from them than you will with your eyewitness account."

"Knock yourself out. Work your sources. That's the way it works in a small town, right, Vic?" Lacey turned to Vic to help her out.

He nodded. "That's the way it works."

"Your little paper, Adler, is nothing but lies and more lies." Hank turned on the local reporter. "I wouldn't train a puppy on it."

"Nice to see you too, Richards." Adler didn't look at Hank. He focused only on Lacey, his fellow reporter. *Rookie mistake*, Lacey thought to herself. *Follow the story, not the competition.* "So what do you think about Gibbs? Is this the work of a serial killer?" Adler asked.

"Gee, I haven't heard of any similar murders," Lacey said. "But if I hear anything else about victims being strung up and dyed all different colors, I'll let you know."

"It would be good not to mock me," Adler said.

Lacey had to laugh. "Are you really a reporter? 'Cause I get mocked all the time. Part of the job. All I know is that Rod Gibbs apparently had a lot of enemies."

"I understand this death had cultlike aspects," Adler said. "It was ritualistic. Who dyes their victims blue? A cult?"

Inez spilled her drink. "You don't mean like some kind of crazy witch thing? Like covens and black magic?"

"Yep, now we have a cult in Black Martin," Hank grumbled. "What are you drinking, Adler? Crazy blue Kool-

Aid?" Will Adler adjusted his glasses and tried to look knowing.

"Who have you been talking to?" Lacey said.

He puffed himself up. "I would never reveal my sources."

Great, Lacey thought. Cult murders would be exactly the kind of loose talk Damon Newhouse would gobble up with a spoon. She suspected that Adler was floating a trial balloon to see if anyone bit. Still, Rod Gibbs trussed up like a blue pig was unsettling. People wanted answers. They wanted to be reassured. They wanted to know that a crime like this didn't really happen to good people. The only comfort Lacey could find so far was that Gibbs was not considered a good person.

"Hey, Will." Sykes tapped on the reporter's shoulder and pointed. "Tom Nicholson just walked into the bar. No, don't look. I understand he's got some inside info on the Blue Devil's death. He might be a *source*, you know."

"They're calling Rod Gibbs the Blue Devil?" Adler's eyes opened wide.

"You heard it here first," Hank confided. "Old Tom knows all about it."

Adler abruptly stood up. "Thanks for the tip." Adler stalked off, a reporter in search of his story. And a clue. The rest of the crew at Lacey's table laughed at how easy it was to play with cub reporters. Sykes started chuckling. She raised an eyebrow at him.

"Was that nice?" Lacey asked, laughing too. She wondered how many times she had jumped when someone was leading her astray. Probably way too many.

"That boy's got no sense of humor," Blythe said. "We're just having some fun."

"Got him out of our hair for a while and into someone else's," Sykes added.

"Tell me, Blythe, everybody, why I am so lucky to have your attention?" Lacey asked, glancing from one to another.

"Because you're a friend of Damon's. Like us. And we're thinking about trusting you."

So Blythe Harrington thought she was a friend of Damon's? Blythe felt like she *knew* Damon because she read his Web site every day? Well, Lacey thought, it was time Damon Newhouse returned the favor and opened a few doors for her, instead of the other way around.

"I'm sure Damon would appreciate that," Lacey said. "You know, Damon's such an interesting character. I know him better than almost *anyone*. Why, the stories I could tell you . . ."

chapter 6

"Dyed blue and hung out to dry. Who do you all think disposed of Rod Gibbs in such a cruel and unusual manner?" Vic turned the conversation back to the victim. "I might as well ask. That's what everyone wants to know, isn't it?"

Faces turned toward Vic. He looked deceptively casual, but Lacey knew he felt bad that someone had died on his watch. *Almost* his watch.

Blythe's expression lit up, as if Vic had introduced a party game. "It's got to be someone who knows the factory. That's obvious."

"How many people are we talking about?"

"Just a handful now, we're the very last. But there have been hundreds over the years," Kira said. "It's a lot of suspects."

Lacey and Vic exchanged a look. "Gibbs couldn't have made everyone hate him," Lacey said. "That's not possible."

"You don't know Rod Gibbs like we know him," Sykes said. "The killer was some knight-errant, a stranger who rode into town last night on his stallion, or his Harley, and did us all a big favor. Like one of those comic book superheroes."

"A stranger on a stallion?" Lacey said.

"More than a stranger. An avenger! That's right, a Velvet Avenger who decided to right a wrong, and that wrong was Rod Gibbs. It's perfect that way." Sykes lifted his glass in a toast to their anonymous savior. "To the Velvet Avenger. Long may he *avenge*."

"Sounds good to me," Hank cracked. "To the Avenger." He clinked glasses with Sykes.

"I'm serious, Hank. Not about the horse or the bike," Sykes said. "But I'm thinking someone targeted Rod for death to do the world some good."

"Like one of those stories on DeadFed," Blythe said.

"That's right," Inez said. "I mean, Rod had such a reputation, it could have been anyone. Someone we don't even know."

"Maybe we should ask Damon Newhouse if he's heard about anything like this," Blythe said. "Post a question on his blog at DeadFed or something."

It's the margaritas talking, Lacey thought. At least, she thought it was the margaritas. *Margaritas calling Damon Newhouse, in the Galaxy of Grand Illusions!*

"Come on," Lacey said. "Let's get real here. Who could really do this?" But the workers didn't want real, they wanted a no-fault, mythical avenger to take the credit and the heat. That way no one would have to pay for Rod Gibbs's murder.

"See," Blythe lectured Lacey, "this is why Damon gets the good stories. He has the imagination to see how all these conspiracies work together. He'll get to the bottom of this case, I betcha." She sipped her margarita happily.

Vic tried to steer the conversation back to the dead man. "Tell me about Rod Gibbs then. Why would this altruistic avenger go after him?"

"A million reasons," Sykes said. "Gibbs just had a genius for gnawing on your last nerve. Like the day he cut our benefits, and the next day he showed up driving that new fancy-ass car of his."

"What kind of car?" Vic, Lacey knew, had theories about cars and their owners. Like Lacey had with clothes and their wearers.

"Blue Corvette."

Vic whistled. Lacey knew what he was thinking. The Corvette was what Vic called "an asshole car," but that didn't stop people like Rod Gibbs from loving it.

"It sure was a thing of beauty," Sykes said.

"Until someone keyed it in the parking lot. Damn

shame," Hank said, a hint of a smile on his face. "He didn't drive it to work much after that."

"Hell, any one of us might want to kill him," Sykes said. "Even our little sparrow, Kira, here." He lifted his margarita glass to her.

Kira hesitated before speaking. She seemed startled by being the center of attention. "I can't say I'm sorry Rod is dead. He was slime. Everyone knows how I feel." She started to play with a tortilla chip, breaking it into little pieces but not eating it.

"Rod was a pig," Inez said, "always saying dirty things, letting his hands brush against you." She waved her margarita for emphasis. "This one time, I had to knee him in the balls to get him to stop." She laughed loudly. "I swore it was an accident, but Rod tried to have me suspended."

"Were you suspended?" Vic asked.

"No, but he put a letter of complaint in my file, said he'd see me fired if it was the last thing he did. Guess he didn't have time. Damn shame." Inez howled with laughter.

Lacey turned toward Kira. "Why did you hate him?"

"All the same reasons. Like Inez, but I'm not that brave." Kira's large brown eyes started to moisten. "I filed a sexual harassment complaint against him last year."

"That's old news," said Hank. "Rod got a lot of those. Pass the chips, please."

"Did the complaint stop him?" Lacey asked Kira.

"Made him worse. Rod would come by and put his arms on my shoulders and his hands all over me. He only did it when no one else was around. He'd whisper things like how he owned me and that he could fire me in an instant. Or I could make it easier on myself, and I know exactly what he meant. He'd walk away and laugh and say someday I'd give in." Kira slumped back in her chair and lowered her eyes. "I was living in fear. Still am."

"It'll just take a while," Inez said. "But you're safe with us."

"We tried to make sure Kira was never alone much with Rod," Sykes said as he grabbed the pitcher and topped off their glasses.

"Why didn't you quit?" Lacey tried to put herself in

Kira's place. She knew it took a lot of courage to leave a bad situation.

"Jobs don't exactly grow on trees down here, if you hadn't noticed. I got a kid to support." Kira sipped her wine spritzer. She'd declined the margaritas. "And I figured Dominion was going to close soon. We'd been hearing that on the grapevine for some time." She shared a look with Hank. "Anyway, yes, I hated Rod, more than anybody I ever met. But I never would of thought of killing him. Dyeing him like a piece of velvet."

Inez glared at Lacey. "We can't all be reporters with a cushy job in Washington, D.C., at our Claudia Darnell's little paper."

It was Lacey's turn on the hot seat. The factory workers would be lining up at the unemployment office in the morning, Lacey thought. These days nobody's job was safe. *It might only be a matter of weeks before I join them.*

Vic gave her a smile and squeezed her hand under the table.

"It's not as cushy as you might think." Lacey looked around for the waitress. "I've got a job today, but it doesn't guarantee I'll have it this time next year. Or next month. Newspapers are in trouble. Major newspapers are folding. One of my hometown papers is gone. *The Rocky Mountain News* had been there for a hundred and fifty years. Ad revenues are way down, and even *The Washington Post* has been laying off people."

"What about *The Eye Street Observer*?" Inez demanded.

"There are rumblings about cutbacks. Layoffs." It was something Lacey didn't really want to think about.

"You mean Claudia Darnell is going to destroy her paper like she ruined the factory? She's killing more jobs?" Hank leaned forward into Lacey's face. Sykes too. Lacey felt a little cornered and she moved closer to Vic.

"I didn't say that. We have our own version of Rod Gibbs. If anyone's going to destroy *The Eye*, it's our Walt Pojack." Or as Lacey thought of him, Pojack the Destroyer. He'd spent some time as a PR flack for politicians, lobbyists, and developers before landing at *The Eye*. He had been an inadequate managing editor with no discernable skills for management, so he was shoved upstairs and somehow landed a spot on the newspaper's board of directors. His title was chief of operations.

"Who's that?" Blythe asked.

"Paper's resident snake. No one important." *I hope.* "Anyway, let me point out, Claudia Darnell didn't close the factory single-handedly. Did she?"

"No, she had partners in crime." Sykes knocked back the rest of his margarita. "The first one is dead."

Lacey and Vic's tablemates were several margaritas ahead of them, and tongues were loosening. What they said could be useful, or it could dissolve into useless barroom bluster. They might regret their words in the morning, and Lacey tried to remember that. But her ear was still cocked for a good quote.

"How many partners are there in the company? I thought it was owned by a family in New England."

"Massachusetts. That's where the factory started, the Connecticut River Valley in the late 1800s, where it was known as Symington Textiles," Kira said. "The Symington family moved operations here in the Eighties. Changed the name. They figured with cheaper labor costs and lower taxes they could save the velvet factory. It worked for a while."

"It was a union shop in Massachusetts, wasn't it?" Lacey asked.

"Until they moved the plant to Virginia. The union would have been better for all of us," Sykes said. "A union protects you."

But even the union couldn't keep the company from moving, Lacey reflected.

"The family still owns part of it, but they took on partners down here to help carry the load." Kira had access to all the records and she had absorbed the company history.

"How many partners are there, besides the family?" Lacey wondered how Claudia had become involved with the company.

"Three. Twenty percent interest apiece."

"So together, the outside partners have a controlling interest," Vic said. "If they vote as a bloc."

"That's right." Kira grabbed another tortilla chip from the basket and crumbled it with her thin fingers. "That way, when it came to the final vote to keep or close the factory, the absentee owners didn't have to look like the villains."

"Who is the third partner?" Lacey asked.

"That would be one Tazewell Flanders," Hank said.

Vic shared a look with Lacey and she straightened up. She told herself to be cautious, this could all just be bar chat. "Congressman Tazewell B. Flanders?" *And people think* my *name is funny.*

Congressman Tazewell Flanders had all the sincerity and telegenic looks of a television anchor: shiny white teeth, a spray-on tan, the Kennedy haircut, and that floridly Southern name. He also had a nice blond wife who raised two model children and stayed conveniently out of his way. But Lacey had heard that the Blue Dog Democrat from Virginia who talked moderation was heavy on cash but light on political bona fides. What on earth was he doing buying into a failing factory?

"Not too many people know that," Kira said. "I could be fired for discussing it, you know." She started to laugh. "Wouldn't want to risk my career after twenty-two years. 'Cept there's no one left to fire me. Someone tell me why I didn't leave this town long ago."

"Isn't Tazewell Flanders running for governor of Virginia?" Lacey asked.

"Not official yet," Vic nodded. "It's a pretty crowded field and the election is nine months away."

"Why he'd want to be governor, I don't know," Sykes said. "Seems like he's got a pretty comfortable life up there in Congress. And he's rich as sin. Everyone knows it."

"Why not run? Virginia has a lame-duck governor on a road to nowhere," Hank said.

Running for Virginia's weak one-term-limited governor's office indicated one thing to Lacey: Tazewell Flanders had no chance of winning his own district in the next election. He was banking on winning votes from people who didn't know him yet. Maybe he could fool the state at large, then take aim at another office with more permanency.

"Could be a long-term plan to be Senator Flanders," Vic said.

"I'm thinking the same thing," Lacey said. "But why is he involved in this factory? No, wait. Don't tell me he's from Black Martin too?"

It was Sykes's turn to be amused. "Just like Claudia Darnell and Rod Gibbs. Only he moved to a fancy house in Richmond on Monument Avenue. And now he hangs out on Capitol Hill," Sykes said. "Sitting on his butt is all I can tell he does for us. Maybe he and Claudia have nice long lunches together."

"What do people here think of the congressman?" Vic asked.

Sykes shrugged. "What do we think of any politician?" The rest of the table laughed.

"Save my job and I'll vote for you," Blythe said. "Do you know that fool offered to build a new gym for the high school if he's elected? Like that's more important than jobs."

Lacey made a silent note to contact Flanders's office for a statement on Rod Gibbs's death. His spokesman would, of course, have no comment. And dealing with any politician would make it look like Lacey was treading on the toes of *The Eye*'s congressional reporter, which was never pleasant. She was beginning to wish she had never heard of Black Martin, Virginia, or Dominion Velvet.

The ambient noise inside the restaurant was drowning out the canned mariachi music. It almost drowned out Lacey's thoughts. Vic finally got the waitress's attention. Lacey ordered fajitas and switched her drinks to iced tea.

The table quieted suddenly as a new woman walked through the door. Heads turned as she passed. They watched the showy blonde sway her way to the bar.

"Who's that?" Lacey watched with them.

Kira spoke up. "My guess is the happiest woman in Black Martin."

"Freed from Blue Devil Hell," said Inez. "The lucky widow."

"Her name's Honey," Blythe said, hefting her margarita glass. "She's celebrating, not grieving."

"Rod was a dog," Inez chimed in. "Now he's a dead dog."

Lacey looked at the newcomer with interest. She put the woman's age at midthirties, younger than Rod. In spite of the thick black eyeliner and the fried platinum curls with dark roots, Honey Gibbs still had an air of wholesome prettiness. With a clean face and a comb, she might be a knockout. Her bubblegum pink nails matched her lipstick. Her striped red top and black leggings, which were tucked into stiletto-heeled boots, looked almost painted on. Honey was proud of her body, perhaps a little too proud. She looked like she had something to prove. Maybe to her dead husband.

"She's a fine-looking woman." Sykes ogled her with a grin.

"If you like that type," Hank teased him.

"I like every type," Sykes allowed. Inez poked him in the ribs.

Vic was smart enough not to say anything, but he caught Lacey's eye and lifted one brow.

"It's 'cause she works as a trainer at the gym," Inez said. "She's gotta look good."

"Couldn't keep Rod from straying, now could she?" Blythe waved their empty chip basket at the busy waitress, who brought a refill.

At the bar, Honey downed a shot of tequila and sipped a margarita.

"Hey, Honey, you might want to slow down," the bartender said. "You got all night, you know."

"That's right. I got all day tomorrow too," Honey said. "Not only that, I got the rest of my life. I'm free!" She threw her head back and laughed. "And you know what, Pablo? I'll give a five-hundred-dollar Walmart gift card to the hero that put Rod out of his misery. And mine too."

"I don't know, Vic. What do you think of the grieving widow?" Lacey put her hand on his arm.

"It's grief talking," he said, his lips curving into a smile. "And laughing."

"Funny kind of grief. More like relief," Lacey said.

Blythe volunteered some history about Rod and Honey. It was common knowledge around town that the Gibbses were not a happy couple and unpleasant divorce proceedings were underway. There had been incidents of violence where the cops were called and found blood on the doorsteps. Honey Gibbs had filed the papers, but with Rod's death Honey would inherit whatever he had left. Rod would have hated that, everyone agreed.

"How do you know all this?"

"We have the same hairdresser," Blythe said. It explained everything.

Honey's voice soared. "Turning him blue was a judgment! You reap what you sow, Pablo, and Rod's going to hell dyed blue." The bartender asked her something quietly, to which Honey replied, "Open casket? Hell, yes! Let 'em all look at him! Take some pictures—take all you want. Put 'em on YouTube! I don't care."

Honey Gibbs ordered another drink: *a blue margarita.* The bartender just laughed.

chapter 7

"I'll be right back. I have to see a man about a job," Vic said. He squeezed Lacey's shoulder and nodded toward Tom Nicholson, who had settled at a back table and was trying to shake off intrepid cub reporter Will Adler.

"You're sure it's not a rescue mission?" Lacey asked and he just smiled. "Don't be too long. You don't want to miss your fajitas. They'll come as soon as you leave."

She watched him walk away, admiring the view as she often did. When she turned back, she found an envelope on the table in front of her with her name on it.

"What's this?" No one at the table seemed to know. They waited for her reaction.

"I think someone gave it to one of the waitresses and she set it down for you," Kira said.

Lacey looked around to see if someone would acknowledge giving her the envelope. No dice. She sensed some kind of gruesome practical joke, like an exploding snake, so she opened it delicately. She found a set of photographs and a flash drive. Lacey handled the photos by their edges and stifled a gasp. She wouldn't have to worry about her own poor photos of the corpse. The anonymous pictures were much better. Several close-ups showed Rod Gibbs's blue body hanging from the spool of velvet. One focused tightly on one of his hands, blue and swollen and tied with blue velvet strips. Another two photos were shot from farther away, showing the vat in context in the dye house. There was also a picture of Rod from his younger, nonazure days. For contrast. *A note would be helpful,* she thought, but there was none.

The pictures were macabre and compelling. One shot of Rod's Midnight Blue face was graphic and disturbing, not the kind of photo you'd want your children to see in the paper. But another from a distance, in profile, which showed more of the velvet spool, might be publishable. Another, better still, showed some of the shocked faces of the onlookers. Whoever took these pictures must have been in the crowd that day.

The Eye wouldn't print such photos, Lacey was pretty sure, but they might come in handy anyway. At any rate, whether to publish pictures of a dead man wouldn't be her call, but Mac's or some other editor's. Perhaps even Claudia's. Lacey didn't remember anyone else taking pictures when the body was discovered. But the body had riveted all her attention. For all she knew, the photos were leaked by someone at the Black Martin police department, hoping to embarrass the state police. That kind of friction could be helpful.

"Okay, somebody knows who gave me this envelope." Lacey stared at her companions one by one: Inez, Blythe, Hank, Sykes, Kira. One by one, they shook their heads.

"Looks like someone wants to help you out with your investigation," Inez suggested. "Wasn't me. If I'd taken them, I'd sell them to the *National Enquirer*." Blythe agreed. After all, they could use the money and it would be payback for some of Rod's more egregious sins.

"Maybe someone sent them to DeadFed too," Sykes added helpfully.

That would be just perfect. Exclusive pictures of a Martian Blue Devil! Alien autopsy at eleven.

"Maybe you and that nice Damon Newhouse can work together on this story," Blythe suggested.

"How'd you get interested in DeadFed anyway?" Lacey asked.

"All my fault," Sykes said with pride. "I turned everyone on to it."

The Hawaiian-shirted pirate. It fits. Lacey held her tongue.

"It's about time someone put Black Martin on the map," Sykes said. "These politicians need to slap a big fat tariff on foreign imports. Stop those bandits from China. Slave labor factories. Hell, they probably got lead in all their fabrics."

"How would they get lead in fabric?" Lacey wondered.

"Lead in the dyes. It could happen," Sykes said. "Who knows? Maybe they wash 'em in cadmium. DeadFed says it's worse than lead. And now they're putting cadmium in toys."

The discussion turned to politics and foreign countries trying to poison Americans, in addition to stealing their livelihoods. Lacey's attention was caught by a cool breeze from the cantina door opening. Officer Armstrong swaggered into the restaurant like he owned the place. Lacey tucked the envelope with the photos in her purse and smiled to herself.

Armstrong paid no heed to her table, but headed straight for Honey Gibbs. Lacey was surprised by the intimate embrace the two shared.

"Oh, Gavin, it has been one hell of a day," Honey said loudly.

Lacey strained forward. The room quieted to hear the cop say, "Don't worry, Honey. You're free of him now." Armstrong, aware of his audience, flashed a warning glare. Heads swiveled back.

"What's that all about?" Lacey asked the table.

"Comforting the widow in her hour of need, so to speak," Sykes leered. "We all need a little comfort sometimes. You know what they say about pretty widows."

"Shut up, Dirk." Kira rubbed her arms. "Honey's had her troubles with Rod. He roughed her up more than once. Until she walked out and threatened to deprive him of his precious man parts."

"She looks pretty friendly with the investigating cop," Lacey commented.

"That's between the two of them," Kira said.

"And no one wants to piss off the local law," Hank said.

Something private in this town? Lacey doubted that. It was a small town. People knew everyone else's business. It reminded her of another town she knew.

When Lacey had been working in Sagebrush, Colorado, the attraction between her and then–Chief of Police Vic

Donovan was palpable. However, Vic's divorce was not final and Lacey refused to go out with him. He was still technically married, besides being the chief of police. It would have been a major conflict of interest for her, and she had had her a boyfriend at the time. But gossip about her had been rife.

Vic showed up in her life again six years later, finally free. It was a great relief to Lacey to find out he'd been married to his ex, Montana McCandless Donovan, in some fly-by-night wedding mill in Las Vegas. Vic was free to marry in the church, if it ever came to that. A lucky technicality. He hadn't asked. She wasn't sure she would say yes. *Yet.*

Lacey studied Armstrong and Honey with some empathy. She decided for the moment that their private relationship was none of her professional business, unless it had something to do with fashion or murder. And judging from Honey's get-up, fashion was out. Lacey's friend Stella had already cornered the style market on spandex, and Lacey hadn't figured out a graceful way to write about it. Stella, on the other hand, might have appreciated Honey's outfit.

"Who can blame her?" Inez said. "That cop is hot. I wouldn't kick him out of my bed."

"Looks like someone might get lucky tonight." Sykes winked at Inez. She dissolved into giggles and fell onto his shoulder, her black braid tickling his chin. Maybe Sykes was talking about himself.

"You're right." Lacey smiled brightly. She didn't want the conversation to downshift into who might be hooking up with whom tonight. "Can you give me a little local history? Where did the name Black Martin come from?"

Hank Richards drew Lacey an invisible map on the table with his finger. "You come into town off the highway across that little creek? That's the Little Nottoway River. Town started there. Used to be two little settlements, Black's Ford and Martin's Crossing. They kind of grew together, way back when things were booming hereabouts. That's been a while."

"I guess it's been a while since you had a murder here too."

"We may not have many," Blythe said, "but what we got

are pretty spectacular. Why, we got the ghost taxi murders! And they've never been solved."

"The ghost taxi? Oooh! Tell me more."

Inez jumped in. "Back in the Fifties, a man and a woman were found in a burned-out taxi parked in the local graveyard. Nothing left but charred remains. They never even identified the bodies. No DNA or anything back then. Course legend has it they were the driver and his female passenger. But no one knows for sure."

"Ghost taxi." Lacey wondered how she could work that into the story. "Are there ghosts to go with it?"

"According to anybody who ever walked there at night," Inez said.

"Round Halloween, we can't keep the local kids out of the cemetery." Sykes had a raspy chuckle. "One year some high school punk boosted a big yellow taxi from out of town just to park it in the graveyard. The town nearly had a meltdown."

"That punk was you, Dirk," Blythe said.

"Can't prove that, Blythe." Sykes was laughing hard. "Now they say the lady and the cabbie drive around these parts at night, trying to find their killer. Sometimes they drive silently through town in a ghostly taxicab. If it vanishes before your very eyes, it's them. If you call a cab hereabouts and it never arrives, *it's them*." Everyone laughed.

"We got a community haunted house to raise funds for charity," Hank said. "And every year the legendary haunted taxicab bit gets bigger and more ridiculous. Actors jump out of the car now in these half-burned-up clothes, fake flames coming out of everywhere, screaming bloody murder."

"My kids nearly wet their pants at that," Blythe said.

Sykes just grinned. "I wonder what they'll make out of the Blue Devil this Halloween. Bet it'll be good. Maybe Dominion will donate that big steel spool for a prop. Or maybe we should just steal it."

"That is in really bad taste," Kira said. She lowered her eyes and reached for another chip to crumble.

"Don't be a poor sport, Kira," Sykes said. "Scary got nothing to do with good taste."

"Lay off her, Sykes. She's taking this thing hard," Hank cut in. "But you're right: A velvet spool might have to be liberated, in the cause of a good scare."

"My ears are ringing." Lacey shook her head to clear them outside La Puerta Roja. The air was getting even colder as they walked back to Vic's Jeep. "It was hard to escape that place."

"Something else hard to escape: Valentine's Day is coming up," Vic said.

Lacey moaned. Her friends were all in a lather over Valentine's Day. Stella and Brooke were rhapsodizing in harmony over how romantic it was. As for Lacey, it was something to avoid at all costs.

"I heard that moan," Vic said. "What does that mean? Is that what Valentine's Day does to you?"

"Valentine's Day? Let me see. It means—false hopes and endless disappointment." Lacey was half-serious, or more than half. "You might say I haven't had the best of luck with the day of hearts and flowers." In fact, her past Valentine's Days were a series of disasters that did not fade with the passing of time.

There was the boyfriend who sent her a dozen red roses on Valentine's Day—to break up with her. He included a note: *Like Mick Jagger says, these roses are living to be dying by your side. But we can still be friends.*

Another boyfriend never even showed up for their big Valentine's date—because it was too much pressure. He didn't send flowers. One Valentine's blind date set up by "helpful" friends showed up two hours late and drunk as a skunk. And another time— No, there was no sense in brooding over the past, now that she was with Vic. She squinted up at him. *Yep, still there. Still handsome.*

"Don't torture me," she said.

"Maybe they knew about you."

"Knew what about me?"

"That you used to flee at the first sign of commitment."

Lacey's mouth dropped open. There was perhaps a *tiny* grain of truth to this accusation. "So they had to choose Valentine's Day to humiliate me?"

"Darling, your luck has changed." He leaned in for a kiss, but she pulled away.

"Tell me more about my newfound luck in love."

"You've got me now. But I remember those days. You have an interesting past."

She stopped walking and looked at him. "You're never going to forget I left Sagebrush, are you?"

"Me and everyone else," he smirked. "No, Lacey darling, it's *how* you left. Cowboy asked you to marry him and you hightailed it out of town so quick his head spun clear around."

Sagebrush was the wild and woolly Western Colorado town where Lacey cut her teeth as a news reporter. Vic had been the chief of police there. It had been almost seven years since she'd left that small town behind. And since Vic had unexpectedly come back into her life, the cowboy who had asked Lacey to marry him seldom crossed her mind— except around Valentine's Day.

"Most people called him Tucker. And he was a rancher, not a cowboy."

"What's the difference?" Vic was teasing. He knew the difference very well.

"You were the cowboy cop. If you have to ask— Anyway, I hate small towns and big gossips."

"Isn't that why you're a reporter, Lacey? So you get to be the one spreading the gossip?"

"The *news,* darling, the *news*. There's a difference. Most of the time."

Vic laughed. "Most of the time." He opened the Jeep's door for her.

"It wasn't just Tucker I was fleeing. I was escaping Sagebrush." *And you.* At the time, Police Chief Vic Donovan seemed to occupy more of her thoughts than the man she was dating. Tucker had made it clear he would never leave Sagebrush; it was his home and Lacey would have to be the one to compromise. After all, she was the *girl*. It seemed like some silly, primitive man-woman thing. Sagebrush was Tucker's territory, his tribal homeland, and if she married him she'd be stuck there forever. It made her crazy. Did Tucker really like living in a place where the winter temperatures dipped to forty below zero? Did anyone?

"Besides," she went on, "Tucker married somebody else right after I left town—and on Valentine's Day!" Six short weeks after Lacey fled the icy winter of Sagebrush, Tucker wed a woman he had just met, adding injury to insult by choosing Cupid's little holiday to seal the deal. "It was the ultimate betrayal."

"People do have to go on living after you leave, honey," Vic said. "Hard as that may be."

"Six weeks, Vic! He married the first woman who crossed his path!"

Lacey remembered how her heart sank at the news. Tucker could have waited a decent interval. Just because she couldn't live in Sagebrush didn't mean she hadn't loved him. She had loved him too much to marry him and then hate him for making her live there, in the middle of freezing nowhere. But she didn't love Tucker the way she loved Vic. *Have I told Vic that? He knows. Doesn't he?*

"What do you expect? He knew he could never meet another Lacey Smithsonian, with her big eyes and long hair and quirky charm."

"Quirky?"

Vic leaned over for a kiss. "Marrying another woman was like throwing himself off a cliff. Couldn't marry you, so he didn't care *who* he married. Just get it over with."

"Ha. It seems he forgot about me pretty darn quick," she said.

"He couldn't possibly forget you, Lacey. Even if he was a dumb cowboy. And I never forgot about you." He brushed her hair off her face and tipped her chin up for another kiss, then pulled the Jeep onto the road.

"See how pretty you can talk when you put your mind to it?"

"Do you still love him?" Vic asked. "Even a little?"

"Come on, it was so long ago. He'll always be my first big heartbreak, but how can I think about him when I'm with you? Unless you bring up that miserable holiday again!"

"Right. I'll be careful. Not another word about it. So, what do you want to do about Valentine's Day?"

"You're impossible." She glanced sideways at him. "V-Day hasn't worked out well for me."

He laughed. "You were just betting on the wrong horse. Besides, we have to do something."

"Like what?" Now she was suspicious.

"Nadine is planning a Valentine's party."

"Your mother? She's planning a *what*?" Lacey blew out a breath of cold steam. "I suppose that's only fitting. She drives a bright pink Cadillac. It's practically the official vehicle of Valentine's Day."

"She'd die if she heard you say that. It's not *just* a pink Cadillac. It's a 1957 Eldorado Biarritz."

"So it's a pretty pink Cadillac. With fins. Nadine's probably had a lifetime of perfect Valentine's Days to let her tempt the fates like that."

"We're invited."

"No!" *Warning! Disaster ahead!*

"You should see your face right now."

"I don't even want to think about the ramifications," Lacey said. "Something horrible could happen, Vic."

"Don't be silly. But—" He hesitated. "She'd like you to make some kind of dessert. That's one danger with impressing my mother. You have to keep doing it."

"She wouldn't be impressed if she'd seen the cake batter on the ceiling."

"Come on, you know she likes you. And the chocolate almond torte you made for Christmas turned out great. So about this dessert—"

"I can't be thinking about that right now. I still have to write an article about the factory."

"You could always ask your food editor friend to whip something up and you could pay her for it. She'd love that."

"It'll be a cold day in Hell, Sean Victor Donovan, before I'd ask Felicity Pickles to do my cooking for me. She'd probably manage to write *Felicity was here* in icing or something. And she's not quite a friend."

"About Valentine's Day?"

"You'll have to ask me later."

They were headed to a local motel, a cheap one-story affair. Lacey didn't care. All she really needed was hot water, clean sheets, and a good wireless connection. Lacey hadn't been sure whether they'd be heading back to Northern Virginia after the day was over. But since taking her private investigation course, she prided herself on having her PI "go bag" ready in case of emergency. It was a necessity, her instructor Bud Hunt had said, if a stakeout ran into the next day, or a surveillance carried you far afield.

It made sense to stay in Black Martin overnight. Lacey had interviews to finish in the morning, and Vic had work to do, rewriting the Dominion Velvet contracts and reworking his plans for their ancient security system. The Jeep turned into the motel parking lot.

"You don't really want separate rooms, do you?"

"This is a small town, Vic." She got her bag out of the Jeep. "Our every move is no doubt being monitored." Her smile carried an invitation. "Maybe we could get two rooms with a connecting door."

"Nobody cares, you know. This is not Sagebrush, Colorado."

"It might as well be. Besides, I need to work on my story, write interview questions, sort out my notes, check out whatever Mac posted on the paper's Web site."

He sighed and walked her to the motel lobby. "I'll be out late, anyway."

She stopped short. "What are you up to?"

"A little security work. Call it reconnaissance."

"Around the factory?"

"Yep."

"So that's what you talked to Nicholson about."

"No comment." He shook his head. "You're not getting anything out of me, lady."

"I'll make you talk, Vic Donovan."

"Oh yeah? How are you going to do that?"

She stood on tiptoes, grabbed his lapels, and kissed him hard. "I have my ways."

Two rooms with a connecting door.

chapter 8

The moon was half full. Vic opened the front door to the darkened Dominion Velvet factory with a key Nicholson had given him. He turned off the alarm system, which Nicholson had said didn't work anymore anyway. They peered through the gloom. The police had cordoned off the dye house with crime scene tape, a ribbon of yellow leading them into the darkness.

Lacey had finally convinced Vic to take her with him. She pointed out that the experience might help her if she ever decided to be a private investigator. And she'd already done the class work.

"I just let you come to keep you out of trouble," he said. "You know how you are."

"I hope you don't think that passes for witty banter," Lacey replied.

"Ha. I have not yet begun to banter." Vic motioned her in ahead of him, and he followed.

Lacey had taken a PI class the previous month, for several reasons. She wanted to see if private investigating skills would help her snag a better reporting gig. And Lacey's beat had indeed changed, though she wasn't sure if it was for the better. She also took the course to get a better idea of what Vic did for a living now, after he'd stopped being a cop. He was in the security and investigation business with his dad, and the work was booming. Even though it seemed to include sneaking around empty factories late at night.

"There's no harm in getting my PI registration," she said.

"That's what they all say." Vic turned on his flashlight.

"You want to do this sort of thing? Surveil spooky old buildings in the middle of the night?"

"Maybe I'll learn something by watching you."

"Don't hold your breath, darling. I just want to see the place the way Rod Gibbs did last night, when he met with person or persons unknown."

Vic was a quiet walker, a skill he no doubt perfected on the job as a PI. Lacey followed, glad her boots had soft soles so she could gumshoe along with the best of them.

"You're not going to turn on the lights?" she asked.

"I don't think Gibbs did. He knew his way around. Besides, there's enough light here to see." Vic pointed with the flashlight to the skylights and the rows of large paned windows that lined the top of the walls, just under the ceiling. "The exit signs, the parking lot lights through the windows, the moonlight. Just don't fall in a dye vat."

"Very funny." Their eyes soon adjusted to the dark, and Lacey found he was right. "You're not afraid someone else could be skulking around here?"

His smile caught the light. "There is always that. But Rod Gibbs seemed to be the target, so his killer has no reason to be here tonight. Just us skulkers."

"Unless the killer wants to destroy evidence," Lacey suggested.

"Not much left after the state cops got through with it," he said.

"Why are we here again?"

"For the atmosphere," Vic said. "I know how you like strolling around abandoned factories after dark."

A sharp clap startled Lacey, and Vic froze. "What was that?" she whispered.

"Sounds like a baffle opening and closing, maybe in the HVAC system." He pointed his flashlight at the exposed heating and air-conditioning ducts.

They stood still for a moment, aware of a small symphony of sounds. The wind whistling through the roof was joined by hums and pops and the creaking of old wood and tired machinery. It was a concert with a haunted air about it. The cacophonous melody struck Lacey as the breath of a hundred ghostly workers surrounding them.

And their ghost taxi is waiting outside.

"This place is definitely creepy after dark." Lacey shivered.

"Still glad you came?"

Lacey grabbed hold of Vic's arm and held tight. "Am I ever. Love the atmosphere. Cue the ghosts."

"Good. You can hold the flashlight while I take some photos." Vic snapped digital flash pictures of machinery, doors, windows, security cameras. He moved toward the dye house, shooting from behind the yellow tape.

"You think you'll find something?" Lacey asked.

"You never know. The police already took crime scene photos. I'm just looking at the security that was, or was not, in place. Mostly not." He leaned down for a couple of shots. Lacey pointed the flashlight. "I have to make sure nothing like this happens again, whether this factory ever works again or not."

"What are the chances of that?"

"The killer isn't likely to come back here." Vic straightened up. "High school boys, on the other hand, after a sensational murder? An empty factory? I expect chances are pretty good. This town's already had that famous unsolved taxi murder."

"What about the high school *girls*?"

"Girls usually have better sense than boys."

"Can you put that in writing for me, Vic?"

He laughed. "No way. And don't quote me around guys. I'll deny saying it."

"Girls do have more sense," Lacey said. "Except where high school boys are concerned. Before you know it, the story will turn into a horror film. The killer will have a vicious hook instead of a hand."

"Or a pitchfork," Vic said.

Vic and Lacey paced off the factory's interior dimensions and stopped at the back of the room that once held the looms. It occupied an L-shaped arm of the building. At the junction there was a dented metal door next to freight bays that could be opened to move large shipments of fabric into trucks. The cavernous room was nearly empty but for a couple of beat-up wooden desks and chairs. On the larger desk a small circle of light spilled from a lamp. Next to it sat a video surveillance monitor, turned off. Between the desks were a space heater for winter nights and a couple of trash cans that had seen better days.

"Is this where the ace security team hangs out?" Lacey asked.

"Looks like it. Plush, huh?"

"Very. Could be the newsroom in Sagebrush. Nicholson said there was a guard?"

"That's the rumor. Needs new security cameras. Needs everything." Vic poked around in corners, took photos, looked in the trash. "Yeah, they had a guard. Or a thirsty ghost. Look in here." The garbage can was half full of empty beer bottles. The faint stench of hops still hovered above the can.

"Wouldn't the police be interested in that can?" Lacey asked.

"They probably took a sample. But the crime didn't happen in here."

A clattering sound and a grunt sent Lacey and Vic to safety in the shadows. Lacey peeked around Vic. "Security guard?"

"Or a drunken ghost."

The door to the back offices opened noisily and a sullen-looking, heavyset man shuffled in. Vic stepped out from the shadows.

"Good evening."

The man yelled, stumbled against the back wall, and fell onto a garbage can. Vic offered him a hand and pulled him up to his feet.

"God damn it, you scared me to death. Who the hell are you? I could of had a heart attack, you know." He glared at them.

"You must be Wade Dinwiddy," Vic said. "Tom Nicholson said I'd find you here."

"Yeah." Wade looked surly. "I'm Wade. What business is it of yours? Who are you?"

"I'm Vic Donovan. I'm taking over the security contract."

"Huh. Moving in a little early, ain't you?" Wade had

recovered from his scare and was standing up and dusting himself off. "And who is she? The Queen of freaking Sheba? Or are you going to tell me that little thing is my replacement?"

Vic lifted one eyebrow at Lacey. "My assistant. You're a little late tonight, aren't you, Wade?"

"Crap. I been talking with the cops all day, half the night."

"About Rod Gibbs?" Lacey asked.

Wade sighed and leaned against the wall. "It sure as hell weren't for my health. Course it was about Rod. I hear he's blue. That true?"

"You didn't see him?" Lacey asked.

"Why don't you tell us what you told the police?" Vic said.

"Why should I?" He and Vic stared at each other. Wade backed down and sat on the desk. "Aw, hell. What do you wanna know?"

"You worked here for the last few months, is that right?"

"Yeah, that's right. I just wanted to pick up a few extra bucks. When Rod told me about the gig, I grabbed it."

"Rod Gibbs hired you?" Lacey was surprised.

"Hey, little girl, I can do security work just fine," Wade snarled.

"That's why he got killed, because you were on the job?" she said.

"I didn't have nothing to do with that! You gotta understand. Me and Rod, we get along okay. Or did, I guess I should say." Wade rubbed his face. "I did the job he told me to."

"Tell me what your duties were." Vic loomed over him.

"I just make my rounds, make sure no one's breaking in, scrawling bad words on the walls and stuff. It's not too hard. Staying awake is the hard part."

"Did you see Gibbs last night?" Vic asked.

Wade shut his mouth, then finally nodded. He looked embarrassed. "I told the police all about it."

"Were you drinking?"

"Did that cop tell you that?" Wade shot back.

"He didn't have to." Lacey tapped the trash can with one toe. The empty bottles clinked merrily.

"Okay, I was drinking. With Rod. He always brought the booze. He knows what I like. Pabst Blue Ribbon. Good old PBR."

"Why would he bring beer to work?" Lacey asked.

Wade seemed puzzled. " 'Cause we're buddies? You know. Rod liked to shoot the breeze. Hell, I liked to drink. So we shared some brewskis. Wasn't the first time. Guess it was the last."

"Let me get this straight." Vic's face was hard. "Gibbs was drinking with you?"

Wade didn't seem to think there was anything wrong with lifting a few brews at work with the boss, especially seeing as how there were "not hardly no workers no more," as he put it. And Wade pointed out he wasn't handling the dangerous equipment. "I maybe had a bit more to drink than Rod."

"What happened?"

"Guess I fell asleep. Musta hit my head or something 'cause it's pretty sore today. I got one hellacious headache." Wade pointed to a spot on the back of his head. Lacey shined the light on it. "I was out cold."

"There's a scab." Lacey tried not to make a face. Did Rod actually get Wade drunk, then knock him out to make sure he wouldn't see anything? Or was it the killer?

"Did you see Rod leave?" Vic asked.

"That a trick question? 'Cause I know Rod is dead. And I didn't see him no more after I fell asleep. And I wouldn't have seen him leave, I guess, 'cause somebody killed him after that. Somebody could have killed me! Anybody think about that? So don't ask me to go shedding no tears for him, when I coulda died myself last night."

Now that Lacey looked closer at the man, she thought he might have already had a few drinks to get through this night. His hair was greasy and smoothed over a bald spot—and the scab. His shabby, unwashed clothes stank. His shoes were worn at the heels. He was drinking away what little money he had. It was hard to see what kind of relationship he'd had with Rod Gibbs. Old buddies from school?

"How long were you asleep?" Vic asked.

"Hell, I don't know." Wade tried to think. "Couple hours, maybe three, four. When I woke up it was getting toward light, so I left."

"Did you see anything?" Vic leaned down into Wade's face. "Hear anything?"

"I didn't see nothing. I didn't hear nothing. I just went home."

"Did you check the factory one last time, or complete your rounds?"

"Man, my head was killing me. I couldn't hardly see for the pain of it. I locked the door and got in my pickup and drove home." Wade looked confused. "You want me to go home now? I'm supposed to be paid through this week. You firing me?"

"You'll get your pay," Vic said. "But I'll have someone else here with you the rest of the time, starting tomorrow. You can show him or her the ropes. No sleeping. No drinking. Got it?"

It was better news than Wade had expected. "All right. It's too much for me anyway. I work afternoons at the junkyard."

"You should have your head checked out," Lacey said. "You might have a concussion."

"Oh no." He pulled himself to his feet. "Not me. I got a hard head. I'll be fine."

"Go see a doctor," Vic said. "The company will pay for it. If you got hurt on the job, it's covered under workers' compensation. I'll inform Kira Evans."

"Workers' comp, huh? Well, all right. As long as I don't have to pay for it." Wade sat down at the desk and took a can of Coke out of the pocket of his parka and pulled the tab. He gulped it greedily. He was still slumped over, holding his head, when they left.

They got in Vic's Jeep and headed back to the motel.

"What do you think, Vic?"

"The man is pathetic. Either he's lying about what he

saw and heard and drank, which is a possibility, or Rod Gibbs wanted him drunk and out of the way. Rod knew his weak spot. But why bother even hiring this fool?"

"Maybe to make sure no one more competent was in place," Lacey suggested. "To hide whatever Rod was doing?"

Vic just whistled. "Who knows, darling."

"Did our junkman Wade see something he didn't report?" Lacey said.

"If Wade was unconscious when Gibbs was killed, he wouldn't have seen the body, because it was at the bottom of the dye vat. The half-dyed spool of velvet on top of the body wouldn't concern someone like Wade. It wasn't his job. If, on the other hand, Wade killed Rod, it was a pretty ambitious method for such a sloppy drunk."

"Doesn't seem possible. And he's the first person we've met who halfway liked Rod Gibbs."

Vic nodded. "As long as Gibbs was buying him beer. If Wade saw the aftermath of the murder, it might explain why he goosed out of there so fast, without checking the facility again. But why not just call the cops?"

"You don't really figure him for the killer?"

Vic snorted. "I figure him for a drunk."

"And maybe a fall guy. And what to make of Gibbs? Pretty ironic to incapacitate his own guard and then get himself killed."

"Rod Gibbs had the worst luck of his life last night," Vic said. "Now *my* luck, on the other hand . . ."

chapter 9

"It was a calling, really. More than just a job," Blythe Harrington said mournfully. "I mixed the dyes. It's harder than you might think. You gotta have a grasp of the chemistry. Making every batch consistent. Mixing special batches of dye for unusual colors. I thought of myself as a dye artist."

Blythe, the artist of her kitchen, poured Lacey a cup of gourmet coffee and sliced a piece of cinnamon coffee cake. The sun poured in over the oak table in the cozy room.

Morning had really come too soon. Lacey hadn't written as much as she would have liked the night before, and she had more questions now about Rod Gibbs, the big blue elephant in the room. If she was still sleepy, at least she was comfortable in a deep purple sweater and dark jeans. Her vintage jacket added dash.

Blythe squinted at Lacey through puffy eyes. "I don't think I've ever drunk so much in my life. I guess that's how you feel when it's all gone, like another drink doesn't matter." She took some Advil and offered the bottle to her visitor. "I'm feeling it now."

"No, thanks." Lacey was glad she'd stopped after one margarita. After all they had to drink the night before, the velvet factory workers proved to be pretty slow-moving interview targets this morning. "How long did you work at Dominion Velvet, Blythe?"

"The last fifteen years, after my youngest started all-day school. Dominion was like a family. Maybe not the best family, you know, but I had a place there. That's where the ballet lessons and the piano lessons for my children came from. I could only afford them because of the job." Blythe's eyes got misty and she took off her glasses to rub her tears away. "I don't know what I'll do now. Got a little severance, but my husband's on reduced hours, not much savings in the bank."

"It must be very difficult."

"I'm sorry to see Dominion go." Blythe sniffed and put her glasses back on. "It was good, you know, not just pulling a paycheck, but making something beautiful. I could show you."

Blythe left the room for a minute and returned with a lovely red velvet skirt, with elaborate gores and a sweeping hem, proving that she was some sort of domestic goddess. "I dyed this fabric myself."

"That's gorgeous." Lacey reached out to touch it. "Did you make it yourself too?"

"Oh, sure. Sewing is my hobby. I got lots more."

Sewing, but not fashion? Interesting. Lacey wondered where Blythe would wear such an elegant skirt in Black Martin. Perhaps a Christmas party. Perhaps it didn't matter. For some women, simply having something beautiful hanging in the closet just in case you might get to wear it one day was enough. Lacey could identify with that.

"It's beautiful, Blythe. Thank you for showing me. But I wanted to ask a few questions about yesterday. And Rod Gibbs."

Blythe hung the skirt on the door. "What about him?"

"Why did everyone hate him?"

"So many reasons, so little time," Blythe laughed; then her face darkened. "We had to take two pay cuts because of him. Longer hours, less pay. Fewer benefits. He said if we worked harder and took the cuts, he could save the factory, make it up to us later. Didn't work, did it? And yet he would flaunt his fancy car and his fancy boat and his money in front of us. We all lost our jobs because of him and his partners. Dirk says Rod must have had some secret deal, some payoff for closing down the company. I don't know." She helped herself to a forkful of the coffee cake.

"It must be hard to sell expensive fabric right now,"

Lacey said. "Times are tough. A lot of businesses are in trouble." *Mine included.*

"I suppose the velvet business here couldn't go on forever, what with cheap velvet coming in from China and India and Mexico. God knows how they do it. Probably use little children, practically slave labor. Slicing off their fingers on that dangerous equipment? Makes me crazy to think of it. But closing us down was just done so cruelly, in bits and pieces. Like the song says, 'Take another little piece of my heart.' Rod Gibbs was a cruel man. Now he's dead and I'm thinking maybe there is some justice in the world. At least he won't be living high on the hog anymore."

"Do you have any idea who might have killed him?" Lacey took a bite of the coffee cake. It was delicious. Felicity, the food editor at *The Eye,* would kill for the recipe. And then she would use it as a *weapon.*

"No. I don't really care either." Blythe poured more coffee. "Some people think it was his wife, Honey. I wouldn't blame her if she had. Except for throwing him in my dye vat."

Lacey had to admit the widow had seemed uncommonly happy that her ex was dead, but if Honey Gibbs had killed Rod, wouldn't she have made some pretense at sorrow?

"But how would she manage it? Tying him to the spool and working the machinery?"

"She used to work at Dominion. Believe you me, Honey Gibbs is not exactly a frail little princess. She is a very strong girl. Solid muscle." Blythe regarded her own physique. She had strong arms, but she was still a little chubby. "And Honey has a temper."

"What do you mean?'

"Rod beat her. Common knowledge. But he came in more than once with a big black eye himself."

"Are you sure it was Honey who did it?"

Blythe smiled. "No, but I like to think she did. One thing I can't stand is women being beat on."

"What about Sykes and his so-called Velvet Avenger?"

"That's a nice idea, don't you think? Someone taking up the cause." Blythe smiled and reached for the pill bottle. She took two more Advil for her headache and closed the curtains against the winter sunlight. "I mean, someone going around avenging our lost jobs? It's right out of a comic book or something. But why would some mysterious avenger start with a velvet factory and not, say—the car industry? Nope, this was personal. And somebody wanted to humiliate Rod, or his poor, sorry corpse."

It certainly feels personal, Lacey thought. Rod may have been cruel, but his killer or killers had a good measure of cruelty as well, to truss Rod up on a spindle and soak him in blue dye.

"So the Avenger is just a fantasy?"

"I wouldn't take anything Dirk Sykes says very serious," Blythe said. "He's got kind of a Spider-Man comic-book mind-set. And he likes to mess with your head some."

Exactly, Lacey thought. "He's a fan of DeadFed, isn't he? And Damon posts some pretty bizarre theories." *He'll love the Velvet Avenger. Maybe I should leave that part out.*

"Stranger than fiction, I'd say. I still love DeadFed, Lacey. And that Damon, he's a pistol. I hope y'all get to work on this investigation together. But don't you catch that Avenger too soon. He's doing good work."

Lacey got Inez Garcia on the phone, but she said she couldn't talk long. Inez was headed to the unemployment office. "I have three months' severance first, but you gotta keep on top of these things." She explained that she woke up really late, and then she giggled. The giggle probably involved Dirk Sykes, Lacey thought.

"You guys are a couple, then?"

Inez giggled again. "We better be, after last night. And this morning."

"So he's a passionate guy? Like the Velvet Avenger?"

"Oh, Dirk likes to talk. He's really stuck on that silly thing, I can tell you. Like the Lone Ranger or something."

"So if it wasn't the Avenger, who could have killed Rod?"

"No one and anyone," Inez said.

"What does that mean?"

"I don't know anyone who didn't hate him, but no one I know is crazy enough. People round here would feel bad if someone had to go to jail just for getting rid of a cockroach like Rod. But old Rod, he brought it on himself. I bet it'll be one of those cases that never gets solved, like those taxi ghosts in the cemetery. Rod might become a legend in spite of himself."

At least two people liked the idea that Gibbs's death would be an unsolved murder. Lacey made another call.

Kira Evans still had bookkeeping chores for Dominion Velvet that would keep her busy for the next few weeks. After that, she would also be looking for work.

"My daughter is getting a partial scholarship to college, but I don't know how we'll pay for the rest of it," Kira said. "I might be flipping burgers. Her too."

"Are you going to attend the funeral?" Lacey asked.

"It's not like I'm a family friend, but the whole town is going to be there. And maybe it'll be some closure for us." Kira sighed. "Closure. Like the factory."

chapter 10

"I feel just like a prisoner who's been let out of jail," Honey Gibbs told Lacey. "And here I am, back in the big house! My own big house."

She opened the front door to the home she had shared with Rod and that she'd recently vacated in the divorce proceedings.

Lacey was surprised Honey had agreed to talk to her so readily, but the dry-eyed widow said she had nothing better to do. Apparently she hadn't consulted her lawyer either, who certainly would have advised her against talking to the media.

Even though her eyes were bloodshot, Honey looked softer and at least ten years younger than the night before. The harsh makeup was gone and her big hair was tied back in a loose ponytail. She wore black workout pants and a tight hot pink T-shirt that said BLACK MARTIN GYM RATS. Her toenails were painted the same girly shade of pink and matched her flip-flops. She might be mistaken for a perky Southern college girl.

Honey had already attended to the funeral details with some gusto. Lacey suspected Honey had planned the final scenario in her head repeatedly before actually having to complete the task.

"I heard you moved out of this house," Lacey said. "But now you're back?"

The Victorian home Honey occupied offered a dramatic contrast to Blythe's little shoebox of a house. A large oak stairway dominated the two-story entryway, and rooms fanned out on either side.

"It's far more mine than it ever was Rod's. I moved back in last night. Yeah, I know, he was barely cold. But my little apartment wasn't nearly as nice as this place. Didn't even have room for my shoes. You know, I painted every single room in this house, and Rod never helped a bit. This house was the one thing he let me have my way in. I kept my keys, and he was too lazy to change the locks. Typical. Since we weren't divorced yet, this place is *mine*. My name is on the title," Honey purred with contentment. She ran her hand over the wood banister. "It's good to be back home."

She led Lacey to the tastefully appointed living room, which was decorated in chocolate brown and buttery yellow with light blue accents. Lacey sat near the gas fireplace in an overstuffed wing chair upholstered in pale yellow mohair. Honey turned on the fireplace with a click of the remote, and soon the flames were warming the room. She sat on the sofa, kicking off her pink flip-flops and curling her bare feet beneath her. She stretched.

"That's better, now." Honey smiled at her guest. "This morning I had to pick out his coffin and clothes. That's the strangest thing in the world to do, you know that? You pick out a box to shove a man in for as long as his bones will last." Honey shivered.

"Someone has to do it, but it must be hard." Lacey felt chills too.

"Hard? Oh, not so much. Just weird. Anyway, since you're a fashion reporter, you might be interested to know Rod's gonna wear a blue suit. Blue shirt. Blue tie. Blue coffin. Some kind of silver-blue metal. I thought it was important that he be color-coordinated. In the interest of keeping up the theme Rod ended his life with."

Lacey looked for signs that Honey was being snide, but she seemed quite serious. "I see. Blue is forever?"

"This time anyway. Besides, he'd look god-awful in green or brown. I mean, Rod doesn't really go with much of anything but blue right now. He is so damn blue! It was a shock to see him. I thought I was ready, but how can you be ready for a sight like that? He looks like the very devil.

Appropriate, I guess. They're not releasing the body till tomorrow or the next day anyway. The funeral will be Friday at eleven. Rod wasn't much for churches. Calling himself the Blue Devil and all." Honey closed her eyes for a moment before she spoke again. "He might really have preferred to be cremated, but that would kind of rob people of the sight of him. You know what I'm saying?"

"Are you really going to have an open coffin?" Lacey was convinced Honey had been drunk when she said that. Surely she must have thought better of it.

"Oh yeah. Absolutely. People are going to want to be sure he's dead. Don't want to leave any doubt. Rod was such an awful person, I wouldn't want to disappoint them. As I am the grieving widow, it's my call. Ain't that a kick in the head?" She laughed at the irony. "If Rod wasn't already dead, that would kill him." She broke out of her reverie and focused on Lacey. "I hear you're writing about the factory."

Lacey nodded. "A feature story about the closing of Dominion Velvet and its effect on the people here."

"Well, you can see the effect it's had on Rod. Blue as blue can be. I can't say it's been very good on anyone, except me at the moment. I feel for everyone who's out of a job." She paused for a beat. "This town's been collapsing for years. For a long time, the velvet factory was our one ray of hope. Hey, what kind of hostess am I?" Honey hopped to her feet. "You want a beer?"

It was ten o'clock in the morning. Lacey felt her eyes open wide. "No, thanks. I had something at Blythe's."

"She's a sweetie. Regular little Martha Stewart, ain't she?" Honey headed to the kitchen. Lacey heard the refrigerator door open. A pause. Honey seemed momentarily stumped by her inability to offer something more ladylike than beer. "Unfortunately, Rod had all the savoir faire of a big old frat boy. We got beer. Chips, hot dogs, mustard. More beer. I gotta restock this fridge." Lacey heard the door slam shut.

"Please don't worry about me. You go ahead."

"Thanks." Honey returned with a Dominion Lager. "This whole business is making me thirsty."

Lacey wasn't a bit surprised. "Where were you when you heard about Rod?"

Honey concentrated, though Lacey thought it was the kind of moment that would be frozen in memory. Perhaps she was just savoring it.

"I was at the drugstore. Someone said a body was found at the factory and it'd been dyed blue. She didn't say it was Rod, but I just knew. Maybe a wife, even one on her way to being an ex-wife, knows those things. A little while later I got a call on my cell from Gavin—you know, Officer Armstrong."

Lacey wondered exactly when he fit that call in. Probably after he sequestered the witnesses. "Still, it must have been a shock."

"I nearly sank to the ground! Maybe it was the relief, or the disbelief. It was peculiar, that's for sure. I never wanted anyone dead so much as Rod, and then he actually *died*. That never really happens, does it? Because I'd been wishing that for quite a long time—I mean, I thought a lot about him dying, but being shoved in the dye vat—well, that's just extra. But it's not like I caused it, is it? Thoughts don't make things happen. I keep telling myself that. I did not make it happen." She frowned.

"No. Thoughts don't kill. Not without action. Honey, isn't there anyone who might be sorry Rod's dead?" It took an effort for her to sound neutral. *Surely, somebody must have cared for him*, Lacey thought. Everyone has multiple sides. Didn't he have some redeeming feature? Other than keeping a drunken security guard company? Didn't he even have a dog who loved him once?

Honey switched positions, putting one leg over the arm of the sofa. "Well, that's a tough one! His mama's gone to her reward. His daddy's in a nursing home. Alzheimer's. Doesn't even remember Rod. He might feel a bit bad about it, for a minute. I'm not gonna tell him. Not one person at the velvet factory, or in this whole town, is going to miss him. I guaran-ass-tee it."

"Seems like a shame." Lacey stared at her notebook. "Did he have pets?"

"Had a hound once. Cleo. He'd chase her in his car,

hanging out the door, screaming at her to come home. This one time, Rod drove into the neighbor's dining room chasing the dog. The neighbors hated him. Cleo ran away. Look, Lacey, I know what you're saying—I do. You think there's got to be some little shred of goodness in the man, and I would agree, with any human being on Earth, excepting maybe terrorists. But not Rod."

"Why did you marry him?" It was a question that often bothered Lacey. How in the world did people wind up with the people they wound up with, for good or ill?

"Oh, my. I ask myself that question every damn day."

Honey stood and pulled down a photo album from one of the tall oak bookcases. She opened it on the marble-topped coffee table to a picture of Rod and Honey, young and fresh and beautiful on their wedding day. Honey was dressed in a profusion of chiffon and lace. Rod was grinning in a tuxedo. A blue tuxedo. *Naturally*.

"I don't know why we didn't throw this thing out. It's like those are two different people. Back then, Rod had a lot of charm, personality, money—anything he ever wanted. Smooth as can be. Confident. Good-lookin'. He was fun." She flipped through a few more pages. "But he wasn't as smart as he thought he was."

"I know the type," Lacey said. Life was full of people who thought they were the smartest one in the room. It was no surprise Rod Gibbs thought he was all that.

"It went bad pretty fast. Rod failed at everything he tried. I could see it eat away at him. His own father fired him. Here he was, God's gift to the world, and he couldn't hold a job, unless he owned part of the place. Good thing he had a trust fund. And there wasn't as much money as everyone thought. Last couple of years, he was running through it as fast as he could."

"So, you kept your job at the gym." Honey was a lot smarter than she'd looked the night before.

"I own a piece of it too." Honey laughed out loud. "And this house. I guess that makes me the smart one. Course after being married to Rod for a while, I wasn't the dewy-eyed bride anymore. There are things I'm not proud of. But Rod destroyed people. He liked it. He fired people for no good reason, except he hated them, or he was jealous of them. And if it was a woman, it was because she wouldn't sleep with him, or 'cause she did and he got tired of her. All I can say is, he liked to take things away from people, the things they loved most—like that stupid boat."

"You mean the *Blue Devil*? That boat?"

"Oh yeah, *that* boat." Honey nodded and closed the album. "That pretty little fishing boat wasn't called the *Blue Devil* back then. It was something like the *Gypsy Princess*. It belonged to Dirk Sykes and Hank Richards. Those boys really loved that boat. They scraped all their money together—I don't know how long—to buy it, so they'd have something to do on weekends. I was still working at the factory when they brought it to the lake. It was a secondhand Cobalt."

"Cobalt?" Lacey knew nothing about boats.

"Yeah. Most fishing boats, they're kind of dumpy. Like minivans? Or maybe Jeeps? Well, a Cobalt is like a Corvette. The Corvette of fishing boats. Well, Rod one day tells me it's his. They used the boat to pay off a debt they owed him. Hell, I don't know what he had on them, but it was a shame."

"So they had a motive to kill him? Over a boat?"

"Maybe." Honey paused. "But Dirk and Hank, they're sweet old boys. They're all macho talk and no action. Just daydreamers. I don't know if they can catch a fish. Even if they had a boat."

Sykes seemed the more likely suspect to Lacey, salting his alibi with that anonymous Velvet Avenger theory. They weren't *just* good old boys. Lacey felt sure of that.

Honey shifted position on the sofa again. "I suppose you heard Rod was screwing me to the wall on this divorce, fighting me tooth and toenail?"

"Didn't he want the divorce?"

"Oh, sure! We hated each other something fierce, but it hurt his pride that I was the one who filed. Anyway, he cleaned out the bank accounts and hired a fancy attorney to help him hide his money. What he had left. I was just glad he wasn't going after *my* money. For all I know, he was planning to and just got distracted. Rod was like that."

"What else did he do?"

"Anything to break my spirit. The prick. Sometimes I think that's why he married me. To break me. Sick, huh? There were days and days he wouldn't come home. I'd worry all night. At first. He'd call early in the morning and leave horrible messages on the machine, how I was terrible in bed and a shrew. And out of shape! And that is ridiculous—I am totally in shape, on account of my profession at the gym." Honey flexed some impressive arm muscles. "Rod would tell me how hot he was, screwing other women, and he'd be calling me right from some bimbo's bed. Did it just the other day, and I haven't been warming *his* bed for over two years, now."

"What did you do?"

"Yawned and hung up on him."

"Sounds like he didn't want to let you go," Lacey said.

"You think? Oh, it was real amusing."

"Do you still have the messages?"

"No. But my attorney does. He found them very helpful, building a case for adultery. Like I didn't already know the dumb-ass was catting around on me. After so many black eyes and a couple of broken ribs, don't think I cared. Except for those poor women who got involved with him. Excuse me for a minute."

Honey killed the Dominion Lager and replaced it with another.

Lacey was feeling light-headed just watching the beer going down. "I'm surprised he could get another woman."

"That's another mystery of the universe." Honey took a long pull off her fresh bottle of beer. "I thought to myself a hundred times, the only way I'm ever going to get rid of this jerk is if he dies. When I got that call yesterday, it was like a get-out-of-jail-free card. It was like a miracle."

"I'm sure Rod didn't feel that way," Lacey said, with a smile.

"Believe me, I'm trying to find a little sorrow over the whole thing. Looks bad for the merry widow to be dancing a jig at the funeral. But I seem to have mislaid my tears."

"Aren't you afraid you're a suspect?" Honey was proving to be a good interview. Lacey marked asterisks on quotes she might use in her story.

"I'd be surprised if I wasn't. Had me a real long talk with those state policemen. That sharp little mean one?"

"Special Agent Mordecai Caine? Tightly wound, isn't he?"

"That's the one." Honey sat still and contemplated the neck of the beer bottle. The sunlight cast an amber light on her face.

"Did he accuse you of Rod's murder?"

"Not exactly, but I could see it in his eyes. He wanted to know an awful lot about the time I had Rod thrown in jail."

"You pressed charges in a domestic dispute?"

"Domestic dispute, my ass. That son of a bitch tried to kill me!" Honey pulled another long swallow of beer.

"But you went back to him?"

"Pretty stupid, huh? I've learned my lesson. The first few times he hit me, he was real sweet afterward. He promised to change." She made a *pffft* sound.

Lacey had heard that story before from other women. Rod had chipped away at Honey's confidence, little by little, day by day. He built his complaints into a continual rant. Like so many batterers. How many ways did he tell Honey she was worthless? But there was one spark of defiance in Honey. She never believed him. She believed in herself. Lacey tried to stop herself from believing that Rod Gibbs deserved his fate, but it was getting harder all the time.

"They got my pictures in those files, all black-and-blue. Not a pretty sight. That's when I decided to get strong, build myself up." She flexed her toned biceps. "He was never gonna do that to me again. Yeah, I sure as hell had a motive. I just didn't do it."

"Why was he so brutal?"

Honey arched her back, yawning. "You know, I don't know. Not like I spend much time pondering it. I don't care anymore." She picked up the wedding album and flipped through a few pages: Honey with her bridesmaids, walking down the aisle, dancing the first dance with Rod. "Who were those people, I wonder. Who the hell was I?"

She smiled at the woman in the picture and lines crinkled around her eyes. Yet Honey was more attractive now,

Lacey thought, than that untried and untested girl. Despite the pink sugarplum-coated wardrobe, Honey had gained strength and wisdom, not to mention those muscles. And she did it the hard way.

"What was his connection to Claudia Darnell?"

"Oh, Claudia! They were partners. But you knew that." Honey gave Lacey a long, slow smile. "He always liked Claudia. So she had a little mess-up with that politician way back when. Didn't stop her. Claudia Darnell, she's the lady from the wrong side of the tracks here who made good. Between you and me, I think he wanted her fairy dust or whatever it was she used to get herself to the top. And she never gave Rod the time of day, till the three of them got together to save the factory. "

"Why did he do that, buy into the factory?"

"Rod wanted to be a hero. But the lower the factory sank, the worse he got and the more he tried to suck up to Claudia."

The publisher of *The Eye Street Observer* made it to the top because she was smart, but also because she had a burning drive to survive her Washington scandal. Maybe it was revenge that motivated her. Lacey appreciated Claudia's toughness, but as far as reading the depth of the woman, Lacey was beginning to think she'd only read the Cliff's Notes, the carefully crafted public image.

"I guess a lot of people would like to know how she does it," Lacey said.

"He wanted to sleep with her, but I bet you anything he never even got close. She's way too classy for him. And too smart. Rod generally wanted to sleep with anything that moved, if it was female and of legal age. Or not. Hell, I don't even know exactly how old Claudia is—in her fifties, maybe—but damn, she looks good. As a fitness professional, I can tell you she's spent time in the gym. You don't get arms like that lifting potato chips."

Lacey was all too aware of Claudia's attractiveness and power over men. In fact, she thought, Claudia should really give lessons. "Who do you think killed Rod?"

"There we go. That's the big old mystery. I been wondering how long it took whoever did it to tie him up the way

they said he was. He weighed a lot. That's a lot of work.
And dyeing him blue—that took some thought. Some kind
of cosmic message."

"Do you have an alibi?" Lacey couldn't help smiling.
There it went, the last of my journalistic objectivity.

Honey smiled back. "Yes, ma'am. I had company all
night. Real nice company. And a real reliable witness."

Take a wild guess, Lacey. "Officer Armstrong?"

Her smile turned into a big grin. "You are *observant*,
girl." *As if,* Lacey thought. Any fool could see the connection between the two. "Most everyone round here knows.
We tried to keep it quiet for a while, but you know how
small towns are."

"I do. It seems everyone in town has an alibi, but everyone has a motive too." Honey said nothing, but she
frowned. "Do you have a favorite suspect?"

"Everybody." Honey laughed. "Get the Black Martin
phone book. That's your list."

chapter 11

The yellow and black of crime scene tape were the new spring colors at Dominion Velvet. From Tom Nicholson's glassed-in office, Lacey could see the police tape marking off the dye house. A couple of state police technicians were working behind the thin yellow strip. The place had an air of desolation and death, despite the busy people there.

"They took the spool of velvet out of here yesterday, and they drained the tank. Took samples of God knows what and then some," Nicholson said.

He was still taking care of business, until the last lights were turned off. He had agreed to spare a few minutes for Lacey's interview, the one she was supposed to have had with Rod Gibbs.

Dominion Velvet had been on site in Black Martin for only about twenty years, Nicholson told her, after relocating from Massachusetts. The company, previously known as Symington Textiles, had become too expensive to operate in the Connecticut River valley, where the original mill was built in the nineteenth century. Times had changed. Cheaper transportation costs, nonunion labor, and local tax incentives drew the Symingtons away from New England, down to Virginia. It was an attempt to keep the company alive. It worked—for a while.

"Did anyone relocate to Black Martin?"

"Very few. Most had deep family ties to the community. Only the management came to Virginia, and not all of them. I moved with the company," Nicholson said. "I started back in Massachusetts when I was eighteen years old. I've done maintenance, I've sheared the velvet, I've washed it, dyed it, and put it through the dryers. Then I had an opportunity to get into management. It helps knowing every job."

"More than one person has told me they felt the factory closing was like a death in the family." Lacey felt some of the weight of their pain. "Does it feel like that to you?"

"It sure as hell does. Make no mistake, the town of Black Martin is going to suffer when we go dark for good," he said. "It's already suffering."

"What will you do when that day comes?"

"The same thing everyone else is doing. Apply for unemployment. Look for a new job." Nicholson looked morose.

"Here in Black Martin?" The only businesses that seemed to be thriving were the Mexican cantina on Main Street and a gas station on the edge of town. "Or back in Massachusetts?"

"I don't know. It's hard to think about leaving. But velvet's all I know." Nicholson had been idly flipping through a big sample book of the company's velvets. He handed it to Lacey.

There were velvets made of rayon, cotton, silk. Every fiber took a different kind of dye. The core colors every year were black, green, blue, and red, but other hues came and went as seasons and fashions changed. She stopped at a sample of shimmering pink that looked silver in the light at certain angles, and when it was folded or draped both colors shimmered against each other. "That's beautiful." She could imagine that velvet in any number of uses. In décor, in couture, even a wedding gown.

"That one's called shot velvet, or shot through. We say the two colors are shot through the velvet, or, in other words, one color is shot through another. See how the color changes, depending on the angle of the light? This pink is called Posy and the other is what we call Star Shine. Pretty, isn't it? It's kind of an illusion. Like this job."

Lacey sighed and closed the book, but she couldn't put it down. "Do you have any job prospects?"

"I've been talking to a few people, but let's just say it doesn't look too good on the old résumé to be the manager of a sinking ship. And that isn't for publication."

At the clicking of boot heels on the concrete floor, they both looked up. Special Agent Mordecai Caine clipped past the office to confer with one of the crime scene technicians. For a moment, he stared through the windows and decided to ignore them. Lacey tried to keep her focus on interviewing Nicholson.

"There's still work to be done, cleanup work, paperwork, personnel files, tallying up the inventory, shipping the last of the velvet out to our few remaining customers," Nicholson was saying. "I'll be one of the last out the door. A month, maybe two."

"But what about the velvet?" Lacey said.

"People don't want to pay for high-quality velvet these days. Anyway, velvet has always been cyclical. There's always some call for it at Christmastime. It's been in and out of fashion, but less and less of a presence in high fashion in recent years."

"I thought you made velvet for other uses too." Lacey reluctantly laid the book of velvet samples back on Nicholson's desk. She couldn't resist opening it again, and the samples made a rainbow of fabrics. She wished she could run her fingers through the fabric for hours and let her thoughts wander, but that wouldn't get her story written.

"Sure, jewelry boxes and earring cards, velvet to line your coffin with. Velvet is usually the last thing your body touches. Funny how people want the finest possible quality when they lay their loved ones to rest. But we've lost a lot of other customers. At one time, nearly half our production was contracted to Kodak."

Lacey looked up, puzzled. "Half the production? That's a lot of velvet. Why Kodak?"

"Kodak film. Each little canister of film you buy—if you buy film anymore—has two small strips of black velvet."

"Ah. To prevent light leaks."

"These days with people going to digital cameras, hardly any film gets sold anymore, so that market's about gone." Nicholson kicked his feet up on his desk and stretched his arms behind his head. "Hope you don't mind. Not very businesslike around here these days."

"I've always loved velvet." Lacey ran through a mental inventory of all her velvet items, from her jackets and dresses to her dark blue velvet sofa inherited from her aunt Mimi. "This is very depressing."

"I suppose it couldn't last forever, though we had a really good run. We're almost the last velvet factory in America," Nicholson said. "There's one velvet mill left in North Carolina. They make upholstery-grade velvet. The heavy stuff, for sofas and armchairs. Don't know how long it can hang on." Nicholson handed Lacey three swatches of lavender velvet from the samples spilling across his desk. "Now, these are from our plant, right here. Feel how soft these pieces are. That's cotton, this is rayon, and that's silk." He layered more samples in her hand. "Feel the difference? Velvet is an old, old craft, lots of hand work involved. It's always been a very small part of the textile industry. No one's poured money into research and development to automate it or make it easier or cheaper to produce. So you need cheap labor to make it pay. We don't have that anymore. Not in this country."

"I've heard your people say making velvet was an art, not just a job." Lacey examined the lavender fabric, imagining velvet dresses. Jewelry boxes. Coffins.

Nicholson smiled. "You've been talking to Blythe Harrington. Some workers like their jobs, but with Blythe it was personal. She was one of the best employees we ever had here. She took real pleasure in the craft of velvet. You can't have too many Blythes. Even if she was prone to temper now and again."

"She threw her scissors at the body."

"She doesn't generally throw things." He smirked.

Lacey gazed again through his windows to the factory floor. The massive machines that washed and stretched and dried the fabric were quiet. The spools with their sharp teeth to grab the velvet were empty. "What will you do with the equipment?"

"Try to find a buyer for it. We have some feelers out. It's old but it's solid, one hundred percent American-made quality. But who needs it? Hate to see it go for scrap." He slapped his hand on his desk. "Damn shame. Another American business bites the dust. Every piece of velvet you see in America will soon be foreign made. From India, China, Mexico, Turkey. It won't be the same quality. It won't be the same."

"It must be hard to be the one left behind to clean it up and close it down."

Nicholson checked his watch, then leaned forward and peered out the glass to the empty factory floor, as if he expected to see someone.

"It's break time. Can you tell? I can't either. No one left to take their fifteen minutes. It's hard to leave and know that people are going to suffer. With so many layers of management gone, you know a little too much about your employees, you know? Who's got a mortgage to pay, whose truck won't make it another year. We've got folks with kids in school, elderly parents. They're squeezed on every side." Nicholson sipped some coffee from a ceramic mug. "Sometimes I hate knowing so much about all these people. They become your shirttail relatives."

He rubbed his head as if it hurt. Nicholson cared. It was a side of management some people never see. But perhaps he was among the minority, like Lacey's editor. Mac Jones, for all his bluster, occasionally revealed a softer side. *And then covered it right back up.*

"What did Rod plan to do when the plant closed?"

Nicholson snapped a pencil in half. "I didn't keep track of Rod. I know people think he had some kind of secret deal going on so he would make money somehow when the factory went under, but that doesn't make any sense. He just got a little crazy when he knew the end was coming. Trying to hold on to what he thought was his."

Nicholson was distracted by the sight of someone walking through the front doors. Lacey recognized Kira Evans, her shoulders weighed down with worry. She disappeared into her office in back without looking up. "Rod started bothering some of the women. More than usual," he said.

"You're talking about sexual harassment?"

"He never did learn his lesson. I guess you heard about that. It got worse when Honey left him and when the factory was closing. He could be one mean son of a bitch."

"What were his duties at the factory?"

"Oversight, I guess. He had an office here. Told me he was a 'direct report' to the Symingtons. Didn't seem to do any real work. Maybe he did and I didn't know about it."

"Are you sorry he's dead?" Lacey couldn't see how he would be, but it was pro forma.

"Personally? No. But I can't say I'm enjoying the police investigation, so I'd much rather Rod would have gotten himself killed somewhere else." Nicholson shifted in his seat. "This is off the record, but I suspected Rodney was stealing money from the company. A little here, a little there. Moving money all around. But I'm no accountant."

"Rod Gibbs was supposed to be rich. Why would he do that?" Everything Lacey learned about Gibbs seemed to bring more contradictions.

"I think he regretted putting money in the company, and maybe he was tapped out, so he was trying to take a little back out. Can't prove it. I'm just slandering a dead man. But I asked Kira to look at our expenses and try to track it. Not that I could do anything with that information. Not now. I just want to see if I was right."

"Did Rod know you suspected him of stealing?"

"I kept it quiet. He would have caused real trouble if he'd found out."

"Were you trying to get him out of the company?"

Nicholson laughed. "I don't have any such power. Besides, these are the last days of Dominion Velvet. Maybe he thought no one would care."

"Where were you when he was killed?" Lacey ticked off another required question.

"Me? Are you asking if I have an alibi?" He looked a little surprised. "Not here. Rod wasn't here when I left around six. I went home. My wife was cooking dinner. I had too many beers. Never left the house after that. Shouldn't have had to work on Sunday anyway. They should have just let me close down at the end of the week like I wanted."

"Do you think the police will find out who killed him?"

"Don't know." Nicholson shrugged weary shoulders. "Not much incentive for it."

"What do you mean?"

"The community thinks justice has already been done.

That's off the record, by the way." It was the third time he'd asked not to be quoted.

Lacey stopped writing for a moment. She had no wish to humiliate Nicholson or anyone else, if they didn't deserve it. She wasn't that kind of reporter. Now, if he'd been wearing something ridiculous, she might make fun of that. But he was casually dressed in slacks and a blue oxford cloth shirt, neatly tucked in. For the first time, Lacey noticed how strong and muscled his arms were. His hands also bore old scars from mishaps with the machinery. Were they strong enough to lift Rod Gibbs and tie his dead body to a spool?

"Do you think Honey Gibbs had anything to do with his death?"

"Honey? Other than wishing for it?" Nicholson smiled at her name, the way many men in town did at the mention of the comely widow, with her blond hair and fitness instructor's body. "Well, Honey is a little pepper pot. But I think she'd just as soon have plugged him with her nine millimeter."

"Honey has a gun?"

"Rod bought her one for Christmas some years ago, when they were getting along. But she sure was pissed. He thought it was funny. Honey wanted diamond earrings, not a gun."

"Nothing says love like a gun," Lacey cracked.

"He said it was to protect her."

"It seems to me Officer Armstrong might also have been interested in protecting her from Rod. He's a mighty big guy."

"You think he had something to do with it?" Nicholson laughed, then straightened up in his chair and watched the crime scene technicians carry boxes out of the factory. "I don't know. Gavin may be a special friend of Honey's, but he's a regular Dudley Do-Right. That's kind of his nickname here, in fact. He's a divorced dad, a scoutmaster, coaches the Little League. Besides, he's the one who called in the state police."

Wouldn't a Dudley Do-Right want to get rid of the villain in true comic-book-hero style? And then call in the state police so he couldn't be accused of hiding evidence or conducting a sloppy investigation. Or maybe he knew they wouldn't look too deep? As Nicholson had just said, there wasn't much incentive.

"What can you tell me about Wade Dinwiddy, the security guard?"

Nicholson made a face. "Did you meet him?"

She nodded. "He makes an impression." *A sour one.*

"After the graffiti incident, just some nasty things scrawled on the front wall about losing jobs, we had to do something. Rod said he'd handle it. We had some old cameras here and there, but no one ever monitored them much. My jaw about fell on the floor when he showed up with Wade Dinwiddy, who supposedly had some security work in his background. I told myself maybe at least he would scare the kids off."

"Why would Gibbs come here at night and drink with an alcoholic?"

"Maybe Wade was the only one who could stand his company anymore."

Kira knocked at Nicholson's open door and he gestured for her to enter. "Sorry, Tom. I have those reports you wanted to see."

He sighed deeply and took the pages. "Is there anything else I can do for you?" he asked Lacey.

She stood up. "You've been very helpful. Thank you. I'll call if I have any more questions." She tucked her notebook in her purse. "Mind if I take a last look around?"

"Sure, just mind the crime scene tape. Our police guests might get upset."

Lacey walked Kira back to her desk in another glassed-in office down the hall from Nicholson's.

"Did you get everything you need?" Kira asked. She looked almost ill in the glare of the fluorescent factory lightbulbs. Lacey thought she probably looked just as bad. Fluorescent lighting was no one's friend.

"Hard to say. I'm just going to take a last peek around."

"Sure." Kira seemed lost in thought, but she gave Lacey a small, sad smile. "It's a little hard to concentrate, what with the crime scene tape, everything that happened here, all the empty workstations. My friends are already gone. I don't know what's going to happen to me now."

Without the hum of the machinery, the plant felt empty and chilly. Kira rubbed her arms for warmth. The woman had pulled her hair back in a ponytail and was wearing an unflattering gray turtleneck sweater that matched the shadows under her eyes.

"Are you all right?" Lacey asked.

"All right as I can be under the circumstances," Kira said. "I didn't sleep much."

"Understandable." *Dead bodies have a way of sticking in your brain,* Lacey thought.

"I just kept seeing Rod hanging on that spool." She picked up some files and shuffled through pages. Lacey got the message and left Kira's office.

She wandered around the plant, from the room that once held looms and weavers to the perimeter of the dye house. She moved past the remaining large spools and past the low dryers and the tall shearing machine. She was standing lost in thought in front of a rainbow of velvet when her phone rang.

"Smithsonian, what the heck are these photos you sent me?" Mac sounded irritated, and it wasn't even noon.

"Hello to you too, Mac. You must be talking about the blue body." They were the only photos she had sent. Lacey knew they were more appropriate to the Smoking Gun Web site than her newspaper, but she was sure her editor would want to see them.

"I can see that. Did you take these pictures?"

"Nope, I was taking notes. I have a couple of lousy photos on my little digital. These were left for me by an unknown leaker. They're pretty vivid, though, aren't they?"

"Unknown leaker? Swell. Smithsonian, do you expect me to publish these?"

"Not my call, Mac. That's why you make the big bucks."

"They're appalling, to say the least." Mac snorted into the phone. "I'll have to figure out how many readers would cancel their subscriptions if I print these."

"I aim to please." The velvet was mesmerizing in all its

infinite hues. *What shade will the Grim Reaper choose next? Or should I say, the Velvet Avenger?* Lacey found it hard to concentrate on Mac's harangue. "I just wanted to share. I still have to write my story."

"Make it snappy."

"What's the rush, Mac? My story is going to be in Sunday's paper."

"I'm moving your deadline up. You got a dead blue guy, and our publisher is involved and very interested. And you know how uncomfortable it can get when Claudia rides a story."

Lacey knew. "But I'm writing a feature!"

"Now it's a news feature. You've got tonight. I want to run it in tomorrow's paper. Front page. Below the fold, so we don't upset too many subscribers."

Lacey could think of a million reasons why that was a bad idea. On the other hand, her byline on the front page of *The Eye*, thanks to the Claudia connection? Her byline was getting to be a regular feature there, but she wanted to keep her streak going. *Job security,* she thought, as if there were any such thing in the newspaper business anymore. And she thought of another reason to jump on this story as fast as they could.

"Hey, Mac, can you pull up Conspiracy Clearinghouse and see if there's a story on Rod Gibbs in it? And no, I wouldn't give Damon Newhouse the time of day when it comes to news, but . . ." She turned around to see if anyone was listening. "He's got some real hard-core fans down here. Maybe the anonymous friend who leaked the photos to me sent the same stuff to DeadFed?"

Damon might already have posted it. If he had, Lacey was curious about his cockeyed take on the subject. Something along the lines of VELVET AVENGER STRIKES BLUE BLOW FOR JUSTICE.

"This just gets better and better, doesn't it, Smithsonian?" Mac said. "You think he's got some off-the-wall conspiracy angle?"

"If Damon's breathing, yeah. Whether it's true or not." Lacey waited while Mac connected to DeadFed dot com. "Well?"

"Nothing. There is no story. Unless he buried it, and why would he do that?"

Lacey was puzzled. "He wouldn't. Maybe the locals were just yanking my chain. I have no idea. Right now I have to go read the neighborhood rag and see what it says."

"Don't forget you have a deadline tonight."

"As if I could forget. But there might be more to the story tomorrow."

"That's what follow-ups are for."

"I'll file this story from home, then." No sense in tramping all the way back to *The Eye* in the District when she could write the story in her jeans on the sofa. Lacey could also avoid a lot of uncomfortable newsroom questions as to what exact shade of blue the dead guy was, and why Smithsonian was the lucky reporter. Again. Inquiring minds would want to know, and newsrooms are full of inquiring minds.

"Suit yourself. I'll see you tomorrow."

"You're all heart, Mac." Lacey hung up and called Brooke to find out what had happened to Damon.

"Hey, Brooke, I was sure Damon would hoist his sails on the Cyber Sea and write something about the blue death in Black Martin."

"Poor baby, I told him about the blue body. Damon's interested, but he's feverish and green around the gills," Brooke said. "It's the flu."

He must be at death's door to pass up this story, Lacey thought. "Better green than blue. Fix him some chicken soup. It's good for anything. Tell him not to worry. This story is really no big deal." She could afford to be magnanimous. Her scoop was safe. For now.

Lacey took a last longing look at the rolls of velvet, hundreds of them, stacked in long tubes on massive steel shelving. Colors in every shade and hue, dozens of purples and violets and reds, blues, greens, yellows, pinks, browns, and blacks. All of it, thousands of yards of the very last American-made dress-grade velvet. She took several photos of the fabric and the empty rooms with her small camera. *Might as well give Mac a choice.* For context, she took shots of the crime scene tape and beyond.

Nicholson was still in his office conferring with Kira, going over papers in file folders. Perhaps Gibbs's financial shenanigans. The dye house was empty now. The last crime scene technician had walked out with the final bits of evidence. Lacey turned toward the front door, past Nicholson's office, past the row of remaining management photos that were still mounted on the red brick wall.

Soon all of Dominion Velvet would be silent.

chapter 12

A waitress in a pink uniform with NELL embroidered on the pocket smiled and told Lacey to seat herself anywhere in the Good Eats Café. Lacey chose a table near the counter with a view of the front door. The air was a blend of homey aromas—bacon and eggs, burgers and fries. She opened the paper to see how the local reporter covered Rod Gibbs's death.

She wasn't surprised to find that Will Adler's news story was brief and contained little more information than she had given to Mac. However, Adler's story had a colorful description of the corpse, with its "protruding eyes and grotesque death mask." He reported that Gibbs's widow was "too distraught to comment."

Maybe he meant she was too drunk *to comment,* Lacey thought. *Surely, this guy couldn't have missed Honey's freewheeling remarks last night.* But caution seemed to be Adler's watchword, and he didn't report everything Honey had said. Or maybe he did, Lacey thought, and it was edited out. Adler didn't draw any connections between the factory closing and the murder.

He spent more column inches on a sidebar about the most notorious unsolved murder case in Black Martin, the famous bodies in the taxicab in the graveyard, which Lacey learned took place in 1954. The story included a plea for any information on the cold case, even at this late date.

"Well, if it isn't Ms. Lacey Smithsonian of *The Eye Street Observer*," a voice greeted her. She turned to find Dirk Sykes behind her.

He wore a pair of sunglasses and carried a sloshing cup of coffee in his hand. Despite the cold weather, he wore another Hawaiian shirt, his sartorial signature. This one was black with shocking pink flamingos. "Mind if I join you? I was talking to Hank over there, but he's not nearly as interesting or attractive."

Lacey glanced in the general direction of Sykes's hand and spied Hank Richards, who was sitting at a table in the back. Hank took her gaze as an invitation and grabbed his coffee to join the party.

"Where's your friend Donovan, Mr. Security?" Hank asked.

"Right behind me," Lacey said, hoping it was true.

"Let me keep his seat warm till he comes." He pulled out a chair and sat down.

Nell bustled over, set down a cup of coffee for Lacey, and took her order for an egg-salad sandwich. Nell eyed the men and left the coffeepot on the table. "Looks like you'll be needing this," she said, and patted Sykes on the head.

"You're a doll, Nell," he answered, as she quickstepped back to the kitchen. "Nice thing about this place, they know me. And they serve me anyway."

"So, how do things appear in the clear light of day?" Lacey asked.

"A little fuzzy," Sykes said, and Hank laughed. "But a wake's a wake."

"Any more thoughts about who might have killed Rod Gibbs?" Lacey did not want to let go of her train of thought.

"You don't think it was the Velvet Avenger?" Sykes snorted, then moaned and put his hand to his head. "He's still my first choice."

"I thought this Avenger stuff was nuts on a stick." Hank lifted his cup in salute to his buddy. "But I gotta admit, Sykes, it's growing on me. Sykes here has made a sound case for it."

"Who do you think killed Gibbs?"

"Me? Take your pick. I pick the Avenger." Hank topped off his coffee and poured more for Sykes. The sleeves of his blue work shirt were rolled up and showed off sinew and muscle. Factory work might be backbreaking, but it was certainly good for upper-arm strength.

"Who knew you had waitressin' skills, Hank," Sykes cracked. "Boy, I'd say you got a future in the restaurant biz, unlike the rest of us. You'll be in back flipping burgers any day now."

"Smart-ass." Hank pantomimed pouring the contents of the pot in Sykes's lap.

"Hey, cut that out. Unless you want to mop it up yourselves," Nell said as she set two sizzling hamburger platters in front of the men. Lacey was assured her order would be up in a jiffy.

"Best cure for a hangover," Sykes said, taking the burger in two hands. "Fat neutralizes the booze in the blood. A well-known fact. Puts you right as rain in no time."

Hank was also two-handing his burger. "I just like a good burger, no matter what the medicinal qualities." He swallowed. "I read your story online. Wasn't much to it, was there?"

"That wasn't my story. My editor wrote a news brief," Lacey said. "My article on the factory will be in tomorrow's edition."

"You're writing about Blue Boy too, aren't you?"

"Don't worry. He's the centerpiece."

"That's funny," Sykes said between inhaling fries. "I've never thought of the old goat-sucking *chupacabra* as a centerpiece before."

"We're all looking forward to it," Hank added. "Brings some color to our day."

"Me too," Lacey said.

"Damon Newhouse's been a bit slow on the uptake," Hank said. "I already checked."

"DeadFed has an alien brain virus today. I have it on good authority," Lacey said. Hank grunted in response and took another bite.

"He couldn't feel worse than I did when I woke up," Sykes said.

"Better not tell Inez that," Lacey said.

He smiled a little shyly. "Inez made it all better—that's for sure. You gonna use those photos your secret admirer gave you?"

"Would you happen to know who that might be?" Lacey was convinced they both knew who slipped her the photos. It was probably a big joke between them.

"No, ma'am. But whoever it was," Sykes said, "I'd guess it was a *friend* trying to help you do your job. One friend to another."

Lacey leaned back in her chair and looked from Sykes to Richards. Neither one batted an eye. "I sent them to my editor. It's his call, not mine." Lacey shrugged eloquently. "Was it you, Dirk? Did you give them to me?"

"Hell, it wasn't me. Wished I thought of it. Honest to God, I was shocked spitless seeing the Blue Devil trussed up like that, like a demon blue scarecrow or something." He polished off another bite, and Lacey raised a brow in question at Hank.

"I don't have a camera," he said. "Can't hardly afford my damn car payments."

The door opened and all three turned at the sound. Lacey breathed a sigh of relief. Her ride out of town arrived. Vic eyed the other men and smiled.

"Looks like a party." Vic took the fourth seat across from Lacey.

"I understand Nell's hamburgers are the best cure for a hangover," she said.

"I don't have a hangover." Vic quickly scanned the menu. "But the burger sounds good. They're not just for hangovers anymore." Nell waltzed out with Lacey's egg salad on rye with a few potato chips. Puny compared to the guys' platters. "I'll have a cheeseburger, well-done, fries, and a Coke," Vic said.

"Just like you to join the boys' club," Lacey said.

"Founding member. And I need fuel, not rabbit food," Vic responded. He took a chip off her plate.

"We were just discussing who might have killed Rod Gibbs."

"Figure it all out yet?" Vic asked.

"We think it was the Avenger," Sykes said. "The Velvet

Avenger. He started with Rod. Who knows who's next. The field is wide-open. Today the Blue Devil. Tomorrow the bad bosses of the world."

"Unless it was just someone who hated Rod's guts and decided to do the world a favor," Hank said. "The world thanks you, Velvet Avenger."

"The blue goat sucker had more than his fair share of enemies," Sykes added. "Actually, no, I take it back. He had exactly his fair share. Earned every last one of them."

"Where were you when he died?" Lacey asked. Sykes and Richards looked at each other. Lacey let the question hang in the air.

Sykes answered first. "I reckon I was having a good-bye drink at the cantina. I've been grieving my losses all week. I may continue to grieve all month. I'm still in the grande margarita stage of grief. Sooner or later when it lets up, I might move on down to the Bud Light stage of grief."

Hank smacked his lips. "I guess it would depend on what time Rod died. I pulled the late shift that night, the last one. Sunday hours are overtime, so the money's good. But I was gone early, by ten Sunday night. Things were real quiet. He had to been killed sometime after that."

"Did you see Rod when you were there?" Vic asked.

"Nope. All quiet."

"What about Wade?"

Hank smirked. "You mean Wobblin' Wade, the Junkyard Drunk? He must have stumbled in sometime after I left. You should ask him. Course if he saw anything, it might have been pink baby elephants. Anyway, I went over all that with that state cop."

"Special Agent Mordecai Caine?" Vic asked.

"He's special all right. Why, Officer Dudley Do-Right Armstrong looks like a slacker next to Agent Mortified Caine. I didn't see anything out of place, like I told him. Damn little to see at that plant anymore. Locked up and left."

"I understand Gibbs's car was in the parking lot all night," Vic said.

Lacey hadn't even considered the car. It wasn't the

fancy blue Corvette. She would have remembered seeing that. "What kind of car?"

"Black Mercedes," Hank said. "His formal vehicle."

"Caine said the car was in the factory lot the afternoon he died. It wasn't moved." Vic had been gathering information.

"Rod parked it there all the time," Hank said. "Didn't mean he was at the factory. He could have gone off with one of his lady friends or walked over to the Cozy Corner for a drink. We all preferred it when he wasn't around, believe me."

"Did either of you see him that afternoon?"

"Not me," Sykes said.

Hank shook his head. "No telling where Rod was. We never actually caught him working, did we? Woulda been a shock. He wasn't even in the building all that much. Kind of surprised he died there."

"But he called himself the night manager," Lacey said. "Didn't he?"

Sykes howled with laughter. "Midnight rambler was more like it. The *chupacabra* liked people to think he worked day and night, like a lot of managers want you to think."

Like Walt Pojack. Lacey thought about the resident management pain in the butt at *The Eye Street Observer.* The man with the ax. And the golden parachute.

"That's right," Hank went on. "I met Sykes for a drink after I got off. You remember that, Sykes?"

Sykes concentrated. "I seem to remember you bought a round or two."

"Oh, yeah," Hank agreed. "I bought a round or three, and you still owe me one. We closed down the cantina. Went on home." Nell hovered and asked if they needed anything else. "Of course, I been trying to get somewhere with Nell here for years, but she's *particular*."

Nell pantomimed a big yawn. She had heard this comedy routine before. "Well, Hank, I'm game, but my husband just wouldn't understand. But if you vacuum my house, do my dishes, and rub my aching feet, we got something to talk about." They all laughed and she bustled back to the kitchen to check on Vic's platter.

"I heard the two of you owned some boat before Rod Gibbs," Lacey said.

"It wasn't just some boat," Hank said.

"It took a lot of years, but yeah, Hank and me bought a boat, so we could fish Lake Anna and have parties. And be pirates," Sykes said. "It was a damn shame."

"She was the *Gypsy Princess* when we had her. Rod changed her name. Ought not to have done that. I hear that can give you real bad luck, changing a boat's name." Hank gave Lacey a grim smile. "Couldn't happen to a nicer guy."

"She was a Cobalt. A boat that would make your heart tremble, all sleek and fast," Sykes said, lost in a reverie.

"A Cobalt." Vic whistled, impressed.

"Cobalt: the Corvette of fishing boats," Lacey put in casually. "Did you guys know that?" Vic looked away and chuckled. Hank and Sykes just nodded sagely at her, as if to say, *Dude, you said it!*

"Beautiful boat. She was a real coquette," Hank said. "And a money pit. Like your ex-wife, Sykes."

"Can it, Hank." Sykes bit into his burger and chewed with a purpose.

"Your ex-wife, Dirk?" *How many threads are there to this story?*

"My ex, the heartless bitch." He swallowed. "Rod couldn't resist her either. They had an 'affair.'" He made air quotes. "Sleazy drunken fling was more like it. She left me for him. All that money was hard for her to resist. Then he dumped her. Served her right." Sykes poured himself another cup of Nell's coffee. "Then he had to go and take my one last pleasure in life. The *Gypsy Princess*."

"How did he manage to take the boat away from you?" Lacey wondered whether Honey's remarks had been accurate.

Hank worked his jaw, but said nothing. Sykes looked pained. "He flimflammed us. Had some business proposition that never existed. Sucker bait. He wanted us to put up money and we'd be in. But we didn't have any money. We just had the *Gypsy Princess*."

"Shut up, Sykes," Hanks growled.

"Shut up, yourself. It don't matter. He got the boat. We

lost her." Sykes sighed deeply. "We may be dumb sons of bitches, but Rod Gibbs was a lying snake in the grass. He just wanted to get the *Gypsy Princess* away from us. We were playing poker and getting blitzed one night and Rod, he says, if he loses, he'd put up the money, and if we lose, we sign over the boat to him as promise money."

"So he won and you signed over the boat," Lacey said. "What about the business deal?" Nell arrived and set Vic's platter in front of him.

"Rod said the deal fell through," Hank said, "but he still owned the *Gypsy Princess* fair and square. Of course he didn't, not fair and square, but the flaming cockroach had the title and we couldn't fight him on it." Hank downed the last gulp of coffee. "I don't suppose I have to tell you he was a card cheat too."

Lacey rolled her eyes. She refrained from agreeing about how dumb men could be.

"I see that look, Ms. Smithsonian. And you're right. We were, let's say, a little gullible," Sykes said. "Rod could make things sound real good. A business deal that would make us all rich. Then he used our gullibility against us. Would we really want people to know how he crooked us? Made fools out of us? Nah, we didn't say anything."

"A little blackmail between friends," Hank added.

"Only we weren't friends," Sykes said. "I'm glad the goat sucker is dead."

chapter 13

"I think we should call it 'The Black Martin Blues.'" Vic put the Jeep in gear and pulled away from the curb at Good Eats. He headed toward the highway back to Northern Virginia.

"Call what 'The Black Martin Blues'?" Lacey slipped on her sunglasses against the winter glare.

"The country song we could write about Rod Gibbs's death."

"You're writing a country song?"

"Not me. Maybe you should. Just saying we could."

Lacey flipped through the music Vic had on hand and slipped a disc into the CD player. Tom Waits wasn't country, but he made music to muse by. And under the circumstances, *Blue Valentine* was irresistible.

"Why not?" Vic went on. "It's the tale of two men and their *Gypsy Princess*, and the Blue Devil who came between them. Or the tale of workers done wrong by their dirty rotten boss man. You got heartache, hard times, no-good men, cheatin' women. And a boat. It's a country song."

"You never revealed this side of you before, Vic. I look through Aunt Mimi's trunk for inspiration, and you make up country song lyrics?"

"Don't know what's gotten into me, sweetheart. Must be all this country around us."

"I understand to have a great country song, you have to have a truck, a train, a dog, and a broken heart." Lacey lowered the volume on Tom Waits. "And Momma getting out of prison. And rain. Did I miss anything?"

"As I understand it, there were many broken hearts, and I'd guess the deceased probably kicked a dog or two in his life."

"You got me there. He did kick dogs, and you couldn't count all the lying, cheating, stealing things he did."

"Whoa, Lacey. Where is your famous reporter's objectivity?"

"Gone with the velvet. Lucky I'm writing a feature. I'm allowed to actually use adjectives. But you're talking motive, right?"

"Motive isn't as strong as opportunity, but it can be pretty compelling. Especially to a jury. But motive can also lead you in the wrong direction."

"You're right." Lacey flashed back to a woman she'd read about, a murdered woman who had been a prominent fashion writer. There were numerous plausible suspects: lovers, former lovers, would-be lovers, jealous wives, her father's girlfriend, even her own father. They all seemed to have motives for her murder. But after all their lives were turned upside down by her death and the police investigation, the killer turned out to be the man who picked up the garbage. Who had no apparent motive at all. Just opportunity. Motive was a trickster. "It could be the trash man," she said.

"Exactly." He smiled, his eyes on the road. "But for the song, let us not forget the eternal triangle, a Honey of a woman, the cop who loved her, and the husband who did her wrong." He hummed to himself. Lacey closed her eyes.

"Is Gavin Armstrong a real suspect?"

"Yes and no. Motive, yes, but it would be pretty stupid of him. And a cop wouldn't go in for the blue-dye theatrics."

"You mean they have no imagination. What does Special Agent Caine think?"

"Caine keeps his cards very close to his chest. He doesn't want this investigation to get out of hand. He doesn't share."

"So he's not going to be your buddy?"

"I'm an outsider."

"What about Armstrong? Will he talk to you?"

"More willing than Mordecai Caine. And he's worried about Honey."

"Because she's a suspect?"

"She's a very chatty suspect. Could talk herself into trouble."

Lacey hadn't seen a car in twenty minutes. The desolate highway past the old Army base was eerily quiet. It was an easy drive, but the whole area had an abandoned feel.

"You're quiet," Vic said.

"I'm writing. In my head."

"Country song?"

"Later. I'm working on the lede for my story." Lacey retrieved her notebook and jotted down some thoughts, including bullet points she didn't want to forget, names, and questions still to ask. "I hope it doesn't come out like some kind of low-down, roadhouse blues lyric. Mac would love that. But you never know. Might give it more flavor." She smiled at the thought.

"I wouldn't worry about the flavor. This story's got plenty of color already," she growled.

"Why so industrious?" Vic asked.

"Mac moved my deadline up. It's due tonight."

"Tonight? So much for a romantic dinner. And I'll have to take a rain check myself. Got some work to attend to."

My annual Valentine's Day curse is starting early this year, Lacey thought, but said nothing. She tried to focus on the victim in the story—the dead one, not the ones who were left behind without jobs, who had to somehow pick up their lives and move on. Lacey had fully expected something to come to light, some aspect of Rod Gibbs that was redemptive. Perhaps he had saved one person in some way. Maybe he gave the Little League its uniforms. Maybe he once fed a homeless person. But so far there was nothing.

"One thing bothers me," she said.

"Only one?"

"At the moment. Don't you think killing Rod Gibbs was too much work for one person? Stringing him up on the velvet reel? Then handling the machinery and drowning him in the dye? If he *was* drowned."

Vic kept his eyes on the road. "It could be done by one

very driven person with a serious mission in mind. And maybe Rod was drugged. Won't know till the autopsy's in, and the toxicology. It would be easier with more than one, but then you got a problem, Lacey."

"Oh yeah?"

"You got a conspiracy."

"Bite your tongue, Vic Donovan. Let's call it a partnership of two." But could there be more than two people involved in Rod's death? Maybe even the entire town? "All I need is for Damon to get going on this and come up with the Velvet Avenger conspiracy, a subset of the all-encompassing global conspiracy of everyone against everyone else."

Vic laughed. "It would be fun to read, you have to admit that."

"No, sweetheart, I don't have to admit anything." She sighed and leaned back against the headrest. "What about the boat? Why so much melodrama about a fishing boat?"

"Lacey, it's a Cobalt. The Corvette of fishing boats—you know that. And a wise man once said, 'There is nothing—absolutely nothing—half so much worth doing as simply messing about in boats.' "

"Let me guess. *The Wind in the Willows?*"

"You take your wisdom wherever you find it."

"I don't have a boat to mess about in."

"No, but you do have me."

"You expecting bad guys to break in?" Lacey teased him, as he checked every lock and window in her apartment. "Spider-Man, a cat burglar, or perhaps the Velvet Avenger with a bottle of blue dye?"

Vic favored her with his special exasperated look. He escorted Lacey home and insisted on checking it out for her. Even though she lived on the seventh floor, he inspected the windows and the balcony too.

"No harm in making sure, darling. And it makes me feel good. So how about humoring me?" Vic tickled her chin and kissed her when she laughed.

"You're really cute when you're overprotective, you know."

"Yeah, all my women tell me that." He concluded her apartment was safe. "Be sure and double-lock and chain the door when I go." He headed toward the door.

"You're leaving?" She blocked his path.

"You have a story to write. And I've got to see if someone's available to spend a few days in Black Martin before I choose a more permanent solution. Another security specialist. A real one."

"Like who?"

"My regular guys are all committed this week, and I didn't think this job would require special talents. But I need someone scary and who doesn't scare easily. Thought I'd call on a friend of yours. Forrest Thunderbird."

"Turtledove?" She had crossed paths more than once with Forrest Thunderbird, code name Turtledove—neither one his real name, Lacey suspected. He was a freelance "security expert" and he also pulled some jobs as a bodyguard for high-profile celebrities. Six-four and all muscle, he was built like a pro wrestler, but he was a gentle mixed-race man who was extraordinarily easy on the eyes. If that wasn't enough, he occasionally played trumpet in a jazz band. Lacey had heard him play at a little club in Old Town Alexandria called Velvet's Blues. *One more blue velvet connection and I will scream,* she thought. On the downside, Turtledove believed that Damon Newhouse was *not* completely crazy. But everyone was entitled to a quirk or two, Lacey decided.

"Good choice, if you want to alert the entire population." No one could miss Turtledove. "Are you expecting trouble?"

Vic sat on the arm of the sofa and pulled her close. "Hard to say. We don't see a lot of murders in these plant-security contracts. Vandalism, theft, drugs, embezzling, and when you have a factory shutting down, you might have to look out for drug drops, squatters, local teenagers looking for a place to party. But when you get something as colorful as a blue corpse, people jump to all kinds of crazy conclusions and do crazy things."

"The Velvet Avenger?" Lacey drew him closer into a hug.

"Crazy enough. I want someone down there for a couple of days who looks intimidating but doesn't have to act tough. Turtledove fits the bill." He stood up, reluctant to disentangle himself from her arms. "So I need to go. And I don't want to wind up as an unnamed source in your story."

"You're just teasing me."

"It's so much fun. Now, don't forget to lock up. I'll call you later."

"Promise." Lacey kissed Vic and pushed him out the door.

It was late afternoon, and the clouds had gathered and dimmed her apartment. She changed into a soft hunter green sweater and dragged her cell phone, laptop, and notes to the sofa. Lacey made an obligatory call to both the Black Martin police station and the Virginia State Police, neither of which supplied any new information. The case was classified as a homicide, but complete forensics and toxicology test results would not be in for a couple of weeks. Cause of death? No comment. Suspects? No comment. Persons of interest? No comment. *That figures.*

In response to Lacey's call for a comment on Rod's death, Symington Textiles e-mailed her a statement typical of a business that vetted its every word through lawyers. Symington said it was cooperating with the authorities in every way in this unfortunate death, which had nothing to do with the plant's security processes and excellent record of worker safety. The company's sympathies, naturally, were with the family and widow.

Just like everybody in Black Martin.

The factory closing and Gibbs's death were clearly connected. But somehow she found it hard to get a handle on the victim. Rod Gibbs never killed anyone, though he whacked away at their souls. He stole their livelihoods, their wives, their money, their dignity, and their boats. If anyone was ever asking to be murdered, it was Rod Gibbs.

Lacey started to write.

CRIMES OF FASHION

♙

Violence in Velvet:
Of Death and Dying in a Dying Industry

By Lacey Smithsonian

BLACK MARTIN, VA—Employees at Dominion Velvet say they don't know how part owner and "night manager" Rodney Gibbs wound up dead, dyed blue, and tied to a large spool of velvet in the factory's dye house. They don't much care who murdered the man they blame for killing their jobs. They say justice has been served, whether or not anyone is ever charged with the murder.

These workers will need to find new jobs in a town with the highest unemployment rate in the state, a town without many jobs even before their factory is shuttered. The last of the velvet has been prepared for shipping. The machines have been shut down. All that's left is the final accounting. That final accounting already came for Rod Gibbs. And Gibbs's coworkers have no time—or incentive—to mourn for the deceased.

The workers held a wake for their jobs at La Puerta Roja Cantina in Black Martin, but no tears were shed for the dead man. Rather than offering a reward for information leading to an arrest, Rod Gibbs's widow, who had sued him for divorce, facetiously offered a Walmart gift card for the killer. . . .

Lacey filed her story with five minutes to spare before her extended deadline of nine o'clock. She stretched and yawned. Her phone rang. Again. She had been ignoring the familiar number on her cell phone. But it rang again and again. Stella Lake, hairstylist extraordinaire and the Voice of Dupont Circle, would not be denied.

"Lacey, where have you been? I got a crisis here!" Stella's New Jersey accent was thicker under stress. "Nigel's mother is coming. Here, in, like, America. This week."

"Hi, Stella. I'm fine. Thanks for asking. What have I been up to? Funny you should ask—"

"Do you hear me, Lacey? Nigel's mother! The woman is a Gorgon. And that's not me saying that—that's what Nigel calls her. A Gorgon. Do you know what that is? Snakes for hair. And I can do a lot of things with hair. Miracles, even. But I do *not* do snakes, Lacey. I am not going to be able to deal with Gorgonzilla."

Nigel, Stella's fiancé, had done nothing but cause problems since he entered the picture, in Lacey's opinion. Now his mother was coming? Lacey didn't know if she had the strength to live through another episode in Stella's romantic soap opera. She thought her feisty little punk goddess hairstylist (with a heart of gold, as Stella herself would say), was perhaps the least likely best friend she'd ever had. And Stella had a talent for involving her friends in her personal dramas. Resistance was futile.

"I'm sure Nigel's mother does not have snakes for hair, Stella." Lacey collapsed into one of Aunt Mimi's wing chairs and let her friend entertain her. "Although, I grant you, if she's Nigel's mother, she may have other, um, character traits."

"She's got metaphorical snakes, Lace. And they're worse. And where the heck have you been all day? I called and called. Finally got ahold of Brooke and she said you were in like West Elbow, Virginia."

"Close enough. South Kneecap. Just working on a story. A story that made my head spin."

"Better put it back on straight, because I need you, Lacey. This is my hour of need."

"What on earth can I do about Nigel's mother, Stella?"

"How about some moral freaking support?"

Lacey moved back to the sofa and stretched out flat, reaching for a pillow for her head. It was hard to keep her eyes open. "I just filed a story, Stel, and I'm wrung out. I can't move. You'd need a crane to get me out of here right now. When exactly does the Gorgon arrive?"

"Thursday. Day after tomorrow."

"What's her name, Stella? You might want to start practicing it. You don't want to call her Gorgonzilla, do you? The snakes might take offense."

"You're right, Lacey. She might turn me to stone. Her name is Gwendolyn, Gwendolyn Griffin. Lady Gwendolyn, I am not kidding. Lady freaking Gwendolyn. That's what Nigel calls her when he's not calling her a Gorgon."

"That's not nice. Does he hate his mother?" Lacey anticipated nothing but trouble from what Stella was saying.

"Nah, I think he likes her okay. For a Gorgon. But I am terrified."

"And does Nigel have a father who's coming to town too?" Lacey suddenly realized she was hungry, but the kitchen seemed too far away for her to do anything about it. And Stella was in the way.

"The ambassador? Oh yeah, he's coming. It's Sir Ian or something like that. Yeah, Ian. Sir Ian and Lady Gwendolyn, the Gorgon Twins."

"I'm falling asleep, Stella. And I'm starving. You will find my carcass on the couch come morning."

"You can't abandon me, Lacey," Stella implored. "You have to help me strategize for the British invasion."

"Nigel's mother hardly merits an invasion." Lacey felt her eyelids slipping down, too heavy to keep them open. *I'll just fall asleep,* she thought. *Stella won't even notice. She'll go right on talking without me. Until morning . . .*

"Hello! Lace, she is coming here from England. She is invading me. She is a one-woman army. Like the queen. The redcoats are coming! I want you to come over tomorrow night after work, okay? We need to make plans. Lacey, are you listening to me? Lacey?"

chapter 14

"How do you like that? Some noxious bastard winds up in a vat of toxic blue dye and our Smithsonian is there. Talk about a nose for news!"

Harlan Wiedemeyer greeted Lacey with a copy of *The Eye* as she dragged herself into the newsroom Wednesday morning. Wiedemeyer, who had earned his reputation as the paper's "death and dismemberment" reporter, was more interested in offbeat crime news than any other *Eye Street* reporter.

"Front page, Lacey. Way to go! But Mac saved Little Boy Blue's photo for the jump." He rattled the paper and presented it to her. "Color too. Is that cool or what?"

"Let me see." She flipped to the inside page. The photo from her unknown source showed a profile of Rod Gibbs, his body strapped to the spool of velvet in the dye house. "I can't believe Mac ran it."

"Oh, please. Who could resist?" Wiedemeyer said. "This is a classic. I understand there were far more gruesome ones. This one merely blurs the line of good taste."

Lacey stared at him. Wiedemeyer and good taste had never met. Harlan sang a few bars of the old classic tune "Am I Blue?"

"How do you *do* it, Smithsonian?"

"I don't do anything, Harlan." Lacey bristled. "I am merely a reporter who happened to be on the spot when the body was discovered. Dumb luck." Lacey hung up Aunt Mimi's warm mouton coat and put her bag down on the desk. She wore an old reliable outfit, reserved for days when she woke up late and had to pull it together in a hurry: a camel-hair suit with a black turtleneck. Not vintage, but classic. It showed off her hair to nice effect. She added a gold pendant of Mimi's and gold and pearl earrings. Lacey looked professional, but she felt fuzzy-headed. In contrast, Harlan looked like a happy little corduroy-coated teddy bear with doughnut crumbs on his tie. She noticed something was missing.

"Hey, where's my chair? And where did this disgusting thing come from?" She kicked the notorious Death Chair away from her desk. She had almost *touched* it. *Ewww*.

Mariah "the Pariah" Morgan, the fashion editor before Lacey was saddled with the beat, died on that old-fashioned wooden office chair. By the time editor Douglas MacArthur Jones remembered Mariah had a deadline, the woman was in full rigor mortis. The next reporter who walked into Mac's field of vision was Lacey Smithsonian, and his personnel problem was solved. Mariah was gone, but her chair remained. Now painted with a skull and crossbones by some unknown newshound, the chair sailed around the office like the Rolling Dutchman of Doom. It was still a sore point with Lacey, and she refused to sit in it. Few people were willing to sit in it for long.

"That thing better disappear before I get back with my coffee. And I want my chair returned or there will be bloodshed," Lacey announced at large to the newsroom. "Or possibly blue dye."

"Ah, but the seat of doom always returns when there's been a death around Smithsonian. It knows it is home, Lacey. It knows."

Harlan Wiedemeyer laughed like a maniac, a jolly little maniac. As usual, he was hovering around the desk of food editor Felicity Pickles, in the cubicle across from Lacey's. "And people think *I'm* a jinx." Harlan chuckled at his reputation. He grabbed the paper away from Lacey. "Was he truly that blue?"

"Yes, he was that blue. Exactly that blue." Lacey searched for her missing coffee cup. Her extra pens, new notebooks, and stapler were missing too.

You go away for two days! And what? They think you died, so they can plunder your desk?

"You have a gift, Lacey," Wiedemeyer insisted.

"It's a gift I would like to exchange, or regift to someone who deserves it more."

"The world's a dangerous place, Smithsonian, and it's good to be aware of it. You just happen to have a talent for putting together fashion and disaster." He paused and stared at the picture of Rod Gibbs. "Poor blue bastard."

Lacey smiled at Harlan's favorite term of endearment for nearly everyone. "I've heard enough blue humor now to last a lifetime. But this guy was a solid-gold bastard, according to all accounts."

"What's making you blue then, my moody Smithsonian? You should be happy. That's quite a scoop—a big, blue scoop. Front page!"

"Not one person in the world seems to care or utters a kind word for the deceased. Other malevolent souls have friends. Every lying, cheating, dog-kicking politician in Washington has friends. But not this guy. I found just one drinking buddy who maybe tolerated Gibbs. As long as he was buying. That's all. Don't you think that's weird?"

"No. Unfortunately, my naive style scribe, there are reprehensible bastards too many to count in this world. And it says something when the bastard turns up dead and blue and the widow swears she's going to have an open casket funeral. By gosh, I'd like to see that myself. Maybe I'll have the blue flu on Friday."

Lacey growled. She was still looking for her coffee mug.

Tony Trujillo strolled around the corner, stopping at Lacey's desk. He took a seat in the death chair and balanced his highly polished cowboy boots on top of her wastebasket.

"How do you do it, Lois Lane? Is death the new blue this season?"

"Jealous, Tony? Believe it or not, death happens, with or without my presence."

"Just not as often. I'm planning to read your opus in depth after I've had my breakfast. By the way, where's your protégée?"

"If you are referring to perky Kavanaugh, I have no idea. And in point of fact, she is not my protégée. I still have no idea what to do with her. I'm hoping Mac will give her back to *you*. She doesn't know anything about fashion or anything else." Lacey leaned in close and stage-whispered, "Maybe we could give her to Sports." She opened her desk drawers. "This is ridiculous. I can't find my coffee cup, and my chair has been stolen. Why me?"

"Lacey's a bit sensitive this morning, Trujillo," Wiedemeyer confided. "The mantle of truth-telling lies heavy, and it's taken its toll. Witness the seat of death you're sitting on." He indicated the chair of doom on which Tony sat. The police reporter jumped out of it like it was a hot skillet. Wiedemeyer took up the paper again and mused. "Sounds like this bastard got his just deserts."

"Speaking of just desserts," Tony said, "have you seen Felicity? She said she would save me a cupcake." Tony started snooping on Felicity's desk, but not a crumb was to be found. He was sniffing the air for clues to today's specialty when the chubby food editor herself appeared, with an empty tray and a satisfied smile. Felicity wore another in a long line of sacklike dresses purchased from catalogs. This one resembled a yellow floral chintz sofa.

Felicity's china blue eyes and straight auburn hair always made Lacey think of a malevolent baby doll. But Felicity was in the blissful throes of her betrothal to Harlan and more cheerful these days.

"I'm sorry, Tony. Maybe next time. My red velvet supreme cupcakes turned out to be a surprise hit. Who knew?"

As if, Lacey thought. Felicity had the newsroom trained like a pack of nut-starved squirrels. She appeared and they sat up and begged.

Felicity was ostensibly writing about romantic treats for a special Valentine's Day food supplement. But her every waking moment was consumed with her upcoming wedding plans and what to feed her sweetheart Harlan every day, until he was stuffed like a Thanksgiving turkey. Felicity and Harlan's relationship was founded on love, mutual admiration, and fattening food. Theirs would be a marriage made in confectionary sugar.

"I think our cake should be red velvet with cream cheese frosting," Felicity said. "It's such a lovely Southern confection. But there will be a surprise inside. Chocolate, perhaps, or caramel, or—a *praline*!" Her eyes lit up at the thought. "I'm still working on it." Felicity's expression was pure mad scientist.

"The wedding cake?" Lacey asked.

"Of course, the wedding cake!"

"I'm sure it will be delicious, whatever you make, my sweet Pickles," Harlan declared loyally.

Felicity had already been through a variety of cakes that she had sworn would be perfect for the wedding. There were cheesecake and carrot cake, spice cake and brown sugar cake, chocolate cake and German chocolate cake, lemon cake and marble cake, and she'd even bounced around the idea of caramel apple cake. But Lacey somehow knew that red velvet cake was going to be the winner in Felicity's wedding cake competition, simply because everywhere Lacey turned, *velvet* was closing in on her. Even Marie, her friendly neighborhood psychic, had left a message that morning warning Lacey that she seemed to be "suffocating in velvet."

"Velvet. It's the obvious choice," Lacey said.

"Not too obvious, I hope. That would be terrible." Felicity looked stricken. "Now then, I haven't decided whether to have cream cheese or buttercream frosting. And don't forget the surprise inside!"

"Like a box of Cracker Jacks." Lacey had an urgent need for coffee to clear her head. She tried to concentrate on locating her belongings and not on Felicity's sugary diversions. Lacey lifted newspapers and moved files. No coffee cup. It was amazing what could disappear after only two days away from the office.

Felicity continued to rattle on, much like Stella did when the subject of weddings came up. "For the bridesmaids, I'm thinking chocolate-colored dresses with mango velvet bows. Or maybe red velvet dresses with whipped-cream-colored bands . . ."

All Lacey could think was that unless the wedding was interrupted by some disaster, which was entirely possible considering this was Harlan Wiedemeyer and Felicity Pickles, it was still six long months away. Six months of listening to recipes and guest lists, six months of listening to what everyone would be wearing, six months of Felicity changing her mind. Lacey would have to prepare for a long siege in Wedding Planning Land.

"But the flower girls would look sweet in mango-colored dresses—don't you think?—with a chocolate velvet bow. Yes, I think that's more seasonal," Felicity continued, not paying the slightest attention to Lacey. "The flowers will be a variety of fall colors: butterscotch, peach, lemon, and cinnamon roses. . . ."

Everything Felicity discussed these days referenced some kind of food. It might have been completely natural for a food editor, but it drove Lacey bananas. Maybe Mac Jones would let her change desks with somebody else? Maybe old Chester Bardwick, the senior obituary writer, who was off in a corner all by himself. A very quiet corner. Oddly enough, Bardwick didn't have to deal with the death chair.

"Hey, Lacey, did you know Dilly Pickles and I are taking dancing lessons for the big event?" Harlan confided, and he demonstrated a quick two-step with a turn. He was surprisingly light on his feet. "I'm going to be the luckiest bastard on Earth that day. One lucky dancing bastard."

Unabashed, Harlan starting crooning "Blue Velvet," took Felicity by the hand and led her out between the cubicles. They assumed their dance position and lurched into a foxtrot. Lacey thought they looked like a couple of dancing teddy bears. Felicity giggled and blushed, but love gave her courage.

Every newsroom had its hermits and its butterflies, and Harlan was an uninhibited butterfly, with his off-the-wall opinions and the occasional song and dance. But what surprised Lacey the most was Harlan's singing voice. He was doing his best Bobby Vinton impression. And he wasn't bad.

"Harlan, you can sing!"

"Can I *sing*, Smithsonian? I'm a man under the influence of love." He twirled Felicity and dipped her. "And I had a retro swing band in college. Harlan and his High-Stepping Hipsters. You should have seen us in our zoot suits."

Wiedemeyer danced Felicity back to her cubicle, then quickstepped off to his own cubicle across the large newsroom, where news of the strange, the curious, and the downright demented awaited him.

"Smithsonian, you're wanted upstairs—sixth floor." Mac Jones could be heard down the hall and charging her way. He passed the dancing imp. "And Wiedemeyer, I hope you're working on a story about how dancing kills or maims some poor bastard. Or causes brain damage."

"Oh, dancing never kills, Mac. Never dancing." Wiedemeyer sailed on.

Mac reached Lacey's cubicle. He glanced forlornly at the empty tray on Felicity's desk. "You hear me, Lacey?"

"Now? I can't find my coffee cup." She straightened up. "I haven't had my coffee. And I'm dangerous."

His eyebrows did a little dance, but not a foxtrot. "Claudia calls. She's more dangerous than you. She said as soon as you got here. You're here."

"But, Mac—"

"Go."

Lacey had already dispensed with the chatter-with-coworkers portion of the day. But Mac didn't give her a chance to settle in and go through the rest of her morning routine—the coffee, the e-mail, the press releases. "And my chair has been kidnapped."

"Breaking my heart, Smithsonian."

"It had better be here when I get back." She sighed dramatically, locked her purse in her desk, and marched toward the elevators to the sixth floor.

chapter 15

Lacey had never seen the publisher of *The Eye Street Observer* look anything less than perfect. But today was the day she saw a chink in Claudia Darnell's sartorial armor.

Claudia had a ragged nail. A button was missing on her stark charcoal-colored suit. A few strands of white blond hair escaped from the knot at the nape of her neck. Others might not notice, but it was Lacey's job to notice the small details. And search them for hidden meaning.

The hidden meaning of a ragged nail escaped her for the moment. She wondered whether the events in Black Martin, and her story on them, had jangled her publisher enough to break a nail. Whatever the reason, Claudia was clearly under stress. For once Lacey dreaded talking with her. But this was a command performance.

The publisher's office was the most luxurious at the newspaper. From the deep red oriental carpet to the cream brocade wing chairs to the impressive cherry wood desk Claudia sat behind, it was designed to make a visitor relax and yet be awed by the statement of quiet power. Lacey was duly awed, but not at all relaxed.

So far, Claudia hadn't said anything. She was jotting notes while listening to a phone message. She gestured for Lacey to sit down. Finally she hung up and flashed Lacey a thin smile.

"Lacey, thank you for coming."

"My pleasure." *Do I have any choice when my publisher requests my presence?*

Claudia looked at her notes. She seemed to be having a

hard time starting this conversation. *I've never known her to be tongue-tied before,* Lacey thought. *Bad sign?*

Looking around, she noticed an odd addition to the exquisite décor. A large fanciful dream catcher was hanging incongruously in one of Claudia's windows overlooking Eye Street. Dream catchers, Lacey recalled, were said to filter your dreams, trapping nightmares in their spiderweb so that the sleeper would dream only good dreams. The bent willow hoop was filled with an intricate spiderweb of leather and multicolored beads. Long streamers of white feathers fell dramatically to the floor. Beads and bits of stained glass cast colored prisms in the cool February light.

"That's very pretty," Lacey said, to make conversation. "The dream catcher. Is it new?"

"No, I have a little collection of them at home. Most of them I bought in the Southwest, where I lived for a while. I just thought bringing a dream catcher in to the office might—I don't know—"

"Let only the sweet dreams in?"

"Something like that."

Claudia Darnell was certainly not superstitious. But Lacey believed everyone was entitled to a bit of whimsical, magical thinking now and then. With all the troubles in the newspaper business and at the velvet factory and around the world, who wouldn't want to trap their nightmares in a web?

Claudia took a breath and smoothed the errant strand of hair away from her face. Her turquoise eyes looked troubled. "It's been one of those weeks," she said. "First of all, I'm sorry you had to witness such an ugly crime scene down in Black Martin. I sometimes wonder what would happen if we put you on the crime beat instead of fashion."

"I'm sure the world would survive. Do you want to transfer me?" Lacey didn't really want to go to a straight police beat, like Tony's. Too much night work. And she was finally getting Mac comfortable with the idea that she could write any story she went after.

"Sorry to disappoint you." Claudia shook her head. "I think features and crimes of fashion are more your particular forte, though I'm not sure of your Kelly Kavanaugh's aptitude for—*anything*." She raised one eyebrow and they both smiled. "Back to the subject at hand. I think you're the right reporter for this unfortunate story."

"I had no idea you were involved with the factory."

"There was no reason for you to know, Lacey. But it wasn't a secret. Black Martin couldn't keep a secret in an armored truck. My involvement in Dominion Velvet certainly wasn't newsworthy while the factory was a going concern. And my role was strictly hands-off. But I'm into it up to my neck now, it seems. With the plant closing, I'm one of the villains. It wasn't supposed to go that way." Claudia briefly closed her eyes, then shook her head. "I assume you have some questions."

Lacey hadn't planned on an impromptu interview, but it wouldn't do to admit it. "The employees there implied you voted to close Dominion Velvet, along with Rod Gibbs and Congressman Tazewell Flanders. True?"

"I had to. There really was no other choice. The reason I was a silent partner is because, believe it or not, I just wanted to help my hometown. When I bought in to the velvet factory, I was looking for some way to save it, even if the plant would never see its glory days again. The economy was flush. The rest of my business interests were solid. But now . . ." Claudia took a sip of coffee before continuing. "The factory was up against foreign imports, cheap child labor, a rapidly dwindling market for luxury fabrics. There was no future for it. All we could do was try to stave off the inevitable for as long as possible." Lacey wasn't sure whether or not to take notes. She decided not to interrupt Claudia's train of thought. "This is confidential, Lacey, not for publication. I'm tapped out. I had to vote to close the factory in order to save *The Eye*."

A chill crawled up Lacey's spine. "So *The Eye* really is in trouble?" Lacey wanted to ask if her own job was safe, but that would be the act of a coward. That wasn't what this meeting was about.

"Every big city paper in this country is in trouble. There is still a chance to save the newspaper. It won't be easy, but I will never go down without a fight." Claudia paused for a beat and lifted her own cup of coffee, while Lacey looked on, acutely aware of her need for coffee. "Now, tell me what else you learned in Black Martin."

"You read my story?"

"Yes, but a good reporter always learns more than she can fit in a story." Claudia smiled.

What I learned? Mostly slanderous things about the late Rod Gibbs.

"There may have to be a follow-up," Lacey said. "The official cause of death, leads, suspects, police statements— that sort of thing."

"I will draft an official statement for your story, as one of the owners of the factory."

"Thank you." Lacey had to walk a thin line with her questions about Gibbs. "Some of the people said you were close to Rod Gibbs."

"That's what they always say, isn't it?" For the first time, Claudia seemed amused. "It's all right, Lacey. I've already played the Scarlet Woman in this town. Rod's family and mine knew each other, but I never had a relationship with Rod. His family had money. Mine didn't. My father worked on his father's car. He was ten years younger than me. He was married. And he always seemed like such a boy to me. And not a good boy. A very bad boy, from what I hear. But rumors are always rampant in a little town like Black Martin."

"Not one person spoke up for him, Claudia. Not his coworkers. Not his wife. Well, they were getting a divorce. Was he always so hated?"

Claudia stared out the window for a moment. "No. Believe it or not, at one time Rod could be very charming. He was the town's golden boy. He showed a lot of promise. He was very attractive once, though certainly not in recent years."

You should have seen him blue, Lacey thought.

"When he was young, Rod had a lot of money and a lot of friends. He was the one who was supposed to be the big success in life. It certainly wasn't me. Then—" She opened her empty hands and noticed her torn nail. "Something changed. He changed. He became angry and bitter.

He thought people used him for his money. And though he had a lot of it from his father, he had no talent for making more. It made him desperate. He really was too young to think life had passed him by."

"When did you become a partner?"

"About five years ago. When he came to us with the deal, he sounded like the old Rod. He was going to find a way to retool the factory, modernize production, cut costs, save jobs. I guess he was caught up in some fantasy, but it was contagious."

Outside Claudia's window, fluffy white snowflakes were falling. Lacey felt as if they were inside a snow globe, momentarily safe and protected. It was an illusion, and Claudia was waiting for Lacey to say something.

"Black Martin. It looks like it had an impressive past. Once."

Claudia nodded. "We wanted to bring back its glory days, or at least the memory of them. Maybe with technology companies. The state was interested in creating tax incentives. There were big plans. Then the economy tanked."

"What was the congressman's role?"

"Same story. Tazewell Flanders comes across as a bit of a lightweight. He needs to change that image if he's going to move up in politics. He wanted to help resurrect Black Martin, implement change, save some jobs. But now it looks like a huge blunder, and the entire company is tarnished by a murder." She picked at her imperfect nail. "Are there any suspects?"

"Everyone who ever met him, apparently. There's no one strong contender. But the state police are being pretty closemouthed. Did they contact you?"

"No. I suppose there was no reason." Claudia looked up at Lacey, propping her perfect chin in her left hand. "Rod certainly turned into a bastard, but murder?"

"Someone hated him enough to go to all that trouble." The swollen blue face flashed into Lacey's mind. "I'm glad you didn't have to see him when he was found."

"I'm sorry you did. I asked Mac for everything connected to the story. He forwarded the pictures to me. Horrible. I keep thinking Rod shouldn't have named his boat the *Blue Devil*. Tempting fate. It might have been a self-fulfilling prophecy."

"Did you ever see his boat?"

"I never had that dubious pleasure. I heard it was a Cobalt. Expensive toy. He didn't seem like a guy who liked to fish. Thank you for keeping me in the loop on this story, Lacey." It was an order more than a thank-you.

"Claudia, is there any chance this killer might be going after others—after you or Flanders?" Lacey asked.

Claudia shielded her eyes with her hand as if the light bothered her. "There is always the odd threat," she said. "When you are in the public eye, anything could happen. A violent death creates ripples in every corner of the lake."

Something about the way Claudia answered made Lacey pause. "Have you been threatened?"

"I'm not sure. Perhaps a warning." Claudia hesitated. She pulled an envelope from the top drawer of her desk. A length of blue velvet ribbon, about twelve inches, tumbled out onto her pristine white blotter. "This came in the mail this morning."

The ribbon was Midnight Blue, the color of the ruined velvet, the color of many parts of Rod Gibbs. Lacey didn't touch it. "Was there a note?"

"No, but the postmark is from Black Martin."

"Are you going to the police?"

"And say what? I received a ribbon in the mail?" Claudia inhaled deeply. "I think it's just a prank. Don't you?"

Lacey stared at the velvet ribbon. "I don't know. I'd like to tell Vic Donovan about it."

"He's your boyfriend, isn't he?"

"You know Vic?"

Claudia laughed. "He was at *The Eye*'s Christmas party, wasn't he? It's hard to miss a man like him."

Lacey nodded. "Vic is handling some security work for Dominion Velvet. I'd like to tell him about the ribbon, even if you don't tell the police. Vic used to be a cop out West." He was also beginning to trust Lacey's hunches, but she left that part out.

"Very well. He might be the right person to know. Not

the police, not now. Just so we don't overlook a possible link to Rod's death. I can trust Vic's discretion? And yours?"

"Yes, of course." The ribbon wasn't part of the story. *Not yet.*

Claudia put the ribbon back in the envelope and handed it to Lacey.

"Is that all?" Lacey stood up, envelope in hand.

"For now. Thank you. By the way, Lacey, there will be a staff meeting this afternoon, in the large meeting room. For the editorial staff."

"The entire editorial staff?" That was unusual.

"Yes." Claudia averted her eyes and picked up the phone. Lacey opened the door. She glanced one more time at the sumptuous décor and the incongruous dream catcher in the window. It was still snowing.

chapter 16

Lacey felt ill.

A meeting of the entire editorial staff of *The Eye* couldn't be good news. Rumors had been swirling around the newsroom for weeks that the paper might be moving, perhaps even somewhere outside Washington, D.C. If so, it would devastate the paper's reputation and the staff's morale. This meeting had to concern those rumors. What else could justify an all-editorial meeting?

The Eye might not have been a great newspaper, but it was audacious and it had a sense of purpose and life. It believed in the nobility of its First Amendment mission. Nobody at the paper wanted *The Eye* to slink across the river to Virginia and die. Or even worse, to Maryland. It had forged its identity on Eye Street. *What could the paper possibly become, away from Eye Street in the District?* she wondered. *The Off-Off–Eye Street Observer?* It made her queasy to think about it.

The moment Lacey returned to her desk, Kelly Kavanaugh rushed across the newsroom to Lacey's cubicle, clutching a copy of *The Eye* in her hands. The one saving grace to having Kavanaugh plastered to Lacey's beat was that Kelly still occupied a desk in the police beat division near Trujillo. Lacey didn't have to babysit her every second.

As usual, Kelly looked like a truant schoolgirl, with her lustrous Buster Brown haircut, a thousand freckles, and nails bitten to the quick. She wore her everyday uniform of a plain polo shirt, baggy gray pants, and sturdy black shoes. She hated shopping, she had told Lacey. There was no way she could be transformed into a fashion writer. Lacey sighed at the sight of Kelly, and she still hadn't had her coffee.

"I don't believe it! You grabbed another great crime story without me," Kelly said, shaking the newspaper at Lacey. "While I'm suffering on this awful beat."

"Good morning, Kelly." After her meeting with Claudia, Lacey was really in no mood to deal with the cub scribe. Kelly plopped down in the Death Chair, which was still in Lacey's cubicle. But somehow, magically, Lacey's desk chair had been returned. "Mac tells me you don't like this beat. It's too 'girly' for you. Just remember, you asked for the girly beat. Girly."

Lacey was hoping there might be a brief scene, a snit, even a tantrum, and Kavanaugh would paddle back to her little corner of *The Eye*. Perhaps she would even beg Mac to give her back her old job of bugging police reporter Trujillo. Then again, with Kavanaugh being so new, she might be the first one to go in a RIF.

"But the stories you want me to write are totally lame," Kelly complained.

"The stories you've written *are* lame." Lacey picked up the previous day's issue and opened it to a story the young reporter had written. "Just what is this?" She read the headline aloud.

CLOTHES. WEAR THEM. OR WHATEVER.

By Kelly Kavanaugh

Kavanaugh pouted. "Mac thought it was okay."

"Mac was on deadline. And Mac doesn't understand fashion," Lacey pointed out. "Or fashion writing. Mac is a fashion philistine. He thinks the fashion beat is just filler to wrap around the Macy's ads. All he saw is that you turned in column inches that filled space. You could have written it in Romulan and he wouldn't have noticed. But I noticed. This *thing* you wrote is not exactly the school spirit we like to see here. And it's not that hard, Kavanaugh. It's only fashion."

Lacey knew exactly how Kelly felt. *Only different.* Lacey suffered deeply conflicted feelings about the fashion beat. She hated it. She loved it. She wanted off of it. She wanted to write more in-depth pieces, features, hard news, analysis, social commentary. But there was a crucial difference between her and the cub reporter. Lacey loved clothes and personal style, and she couldn't help writing about the way fashion affected people and how people used fashion, how their clothing revealed clues about them: Their attitudes. Their backgrounds. Their economic status. Their characters. Their ambitions, hopes, and dreams. Who they were or wanted to be. Lacey couldn't get around it: *You are what you wear.*

"Where are the real crime of fashion stories you handle? Real crime? Like this cool dead blue dude down in Black Barton."

"Black Martin."

"Whatever."

There might be a crime here soon if she doesn't stop bugging me. Lacey sat down. Somebody had changed the settings on her ergonomic chair. It was too low. She stood up.

"Listen, Kelly. I don't write the 'exciting' stories all the time. They happen when they happen. In between, we have the meat and potatoes of the fashion beat. Dresses, shoes, what's in and what's out, who's wearing what, where, when, and why, and how can we ooh and ahh over it or else have a little fun with it. That's what we do. It's not brain surgery. Would you care to try a Fashion Bite?"

Fashion Bites were Lacey's bite-sized bits of fashion folderol and snarky advice that she dished out in between her Crimes of Fashion columns. The name was her own inside joke. She kept telling Mac that *Fashion Bites* was not just a noun and an adjective, it was a complete sentence with a subject and a verb. *What does fashion do? Fashion* BITES. *And who is it biting? Usually* ME.

Trujillo, trolling the area for crumbs from Felicity's tantalizing desserts, stopped to eavesdrop. What reporters live for: sugar and gossip.

"Those are especially stupid," Kavanaugh huffed. "I

didn't go to journalism school to write that lame crap. Um, no offense."

Offense taken anyway. Lacey smiled grimly. "In that case, Ms. Kavanaugh, your next assignment is a Fashion Bite: Top Trends for Spring. You know, something like, 'The pinks of last year are now jejune, and navy and white are poised to make a spirited return this Easter season.' That kind of thing." The kind of thing Lacey could write in her sleep, and often did.

" 'Jejune'?" Kavanaugh's eyes went very wide.

"Mac will want to see it today. By four."

"By *four*?" Kavanaugh looked stricken. "You hate me!"

"No, I don't. *Hate* is such a strong word." *A growing dislike is more like it.* "Whatever."

"How do you expect me to come up with stuff like that?"

"Think. Go to the mall or a store or out on the street. Find out what the teenagers are wearing. What the adults are wearing. Compare and contrast. Or go to the Hill. The interns occasionally wear something mildly radical, like ribbons for belts. Go shopping. Pay attention to the details. Try to decode them into fashion statements, with subjects and verbs."

"Will anybody *die*?" Kavanaugh was pretty rebellious for a freckle-faced kid.

"Only if you miss your deadline."

"It's not fair!" Kavanaugh crumpled up the newspaper. "You get a dead blue guy, and I have to go to stores and look at *clothes*."

Lacey had had quite enough of Kelly. "Do not forget, Ms. Kavanaugh, I am the senior fashion reporter. You must pay your dues to be a reporter. Look through my archives for writing style. Look through the press releases for an idea. Someone is bound to be flogging some new frock. Make fun of it or play it straight, but just do it."

Trujillo settled into Felicity's chair. He was having too much fun eavesdropping to leave.

Kavanaugh's face was fixed in an unattractive pout. "Anything else?"

"Yes. If you go to Capitol Hill, you must wear a jacket in the press galleries. Or they'll throw you out."

Kavanaugh slumped in utter despair. Lacey pointed to a couple of jackets that she always left hanging on the coat rack, dry cleaned and ready for the next wearing, in case of emergency. One was a classic blue-black blazer, appropriate for almost any D.C. occasion and a lifesaver in a pinch. She had lent it to other reporters who were surprised by an assignment more formal than they had dressed for.

The other jacket was a dark teal with a nipped-in waist and ruffled collar and cuffs. It could be described as *girly*, something Kavanaugh was guaranteed to hate.

"Here, try this one." Lacey offered her the girly teal jacket. "If you're not going to wear something fashion-forward, you have to appear professional. For a reporter. As we know, standards of professional dress are lower for the Fourth Estate."

Kavanaugh shrank from the pretty jacket as if it were kryptonite. She whined, "I'll check the press releases for something on fashion." She fled back to her desk.

"'Jejune'? That was a little mean, Lois Lane." Tony watched Kelly Kavanaugh streak back to her comfort zone. "I liked it."

Lacey smirked at Tony. "Yeah, it felt pretty good." She spun around. "Who else can I torture with my fashion beat? Step right up." She noticed something in his hand and leaned forward. It was a black extra-large coffee mug. In big red letters it said: FASHION *BITES!*

"What? What are you looking at?" Trujillo realized too late he was holding Lacey's purloined cup and tried to hide it behind his back.

"That's mine! My missing coffee mug! You dirty mugnapper!" Lacey snatched it out of his hands and headed for the kitchen.

Lacey Smithsonian's

Fashion Bites

Shopping as an Art Form:
Shop Early, Shop Often, Shop Well

When you're shopping for clothes, the point is not to skip down store aisles and throw caution to the wind. The point is not to fill your closets with endless tops and pants and skirts and dresses and coats and jackets and ruffles and wraps. The point is to have the appropriate garments on hand when you need them. For most of us, unless you make your own, or have them made for you (oh, if only), that means you must *go shopping*.

You do not want to leave that big event, whether a business dinner, a friend's wedding, or an appointment with the Supreme Court, till the last minute. Trust me. When you buy a last-minute dress because you're desperate and it *sort-of* fits and it makes you look only a *little* sallow and not *too* fat, you will experience buyer's regret and declare you hate shopping.

It becomes a vicious cycle.

Believe it or not, you don't always have to have an objective, such as scoring a black pencil skirt, which will perform the magic trick of tying everything in your wardrobe together, or a red cardigan that won't make you look like a stuffed sausage. Often having a specific target only makes your desperation worse. The perfect top or best trousers may present themselves when you're not looking for them. However, just as in life and love, you have to be open to the possibilities. A sharply tailored blouse in a great color that flatters your complexion may actually be worth full retail. When you see it, you should buy it.

But you don't have to buy anything to shop, to get

an idea of what's out there, what's new, what's hot, what's not. Maybe this spring all the colors will be muddy mustards and vile avocado greens. Feel free to pass them by.

Too many women hate shopping these days. They aren't in tune with the thrumming of their hunter-gatherer blood. Shopping without an objective sounds like torture to Ms. Type-A Attorney. But what happens when she prepares her oral argument for the Supreme Court? Is she just going to slap on that five-year-old, shapeless black suit with the boxy jacket and wear it with the dingy white blouse and boring pumps? Does she want to look like an underpaid and undermotivated government agency lawyer? I hope not.

Alas, the days of Supreme Court sartorial whimsy are gone. I long for the days when the late Chief Justice William Rehnquist, after seeing a sparkling production of a Gilbert & Sullivan operetta, had *four sassy gold stripes* sewn on the sleeves of his black robe. Rank has its privileges.

Now, the black suit is a staple of any Washington woman's wardrobe, but it shouldn't be generic. There are few things as attractive or professional as a perfectly fitted black suit, even pinstripes if you like. The skirt should skim the knee and provide enough room to run. It should not be a rumpled mess, with the sleeves hanging to the second knuckle. And how about pairing that perfect black suit with some snazzy red heels? Imagination! Initiative!

To shop well, keep some things in mind.

- If you hate shopping, plan to reward yourself for doing it. Buy a skim latte, or bring a friend with an eye for fashion. Someone who won't mind hearing you complain or whine.
- Don't shop when you're too hungry or too full. Hunger makes you cranky and you'll grab the first thing you see. If you just packed in a huge meal, you will feel too fat to try on clothes. I

recommend a light, protein-packed breakfast or lunch. You can always take a coffee break.

- Don't shop when you're exhausted. Unless you're energized by shopping after a grueling day at work, it's best to plan a day trip when you're refreshed and ready for those weekend crowds.

- Wear comfortable clothes and shoes that are easy to slip on and off. Nothing is as irritating as having to keep buttoning and zipping and taking layers on and off. And if your underwear is presentable, you'll feel better in front of those three-way mirrors and ghastly fluorescent lighting.

- Beware of bargains! Yes, we all love bargains. Scoring a $400 dress for $25 makes your heart glad, but only if it looks good and fits well and works with your lifestyle. Take a breath. Does that sale seem too good to be true? The price could be rock-bottom because: Too many were ordered, in which case everyone else will already be wearing it; too few were sold, in which case no one would be caught dead wearing it; it doesn't fit *anyone* the right way; the color would only flatter a sick wildebeest.

- Always try clothes on. Never, ever say, "It's a six, I'm a six, so charge it!" Sizes vary with the manufacturer and the phase of the moon, and the fit will fluctuate. So do you. So do I. Trying it on will save you irritation when you get home. Because while shopping can be exhilarating, returning your mistakes is demoralizing.

Shopping well for great clothes is an art form, like writing, painting, or dancing in high heels. You need practice, practice, practice! No one can do it well without doing a lot of it and getting the rookie mistakes out of the way. Not even Hemingway, Picasso, or Ginger Rogers. So do it! Go shopping! To shop well, shop early and shop *often*.

chapter 17

"Don't tease me! What do you know?" Lacey eyed Vic across the table. "Tell me!"

"What? You want me to feed you more than lunch? I have to feed you information too?" He grinned at her and hid behind the menu.

"You know something. Please, Vic."

"As long as you said *please*." He reached for the bread basket, broke his bread, and buttered it *slowly*, letting Lacey's anticipation mount. "Okay. Someone may have told me the preliminary autopsy results. It might have been determined that the recently departed Rod Gibbs had some kind of nasty head wound."

"Aha! The killer knocked him out? It makes sense," Lacey said. "Gibbs didn't volunteer to be tied to that big spool of velvet. Tell me more."

Vic's information was good, but not as satisfying to Lacey as their impromptu lunch date. Lunch with Vic was the perfect antidote to her awful morning. He called and suggested lunch at a posh restaurant on K Street, and she jumped at the chance to get out of the office. In his leather jacket and cowboy boots, he stood out like an unsore thumb among the wonky Washington masses of bespectacled bureaucrats in their gray suits. He was fit and confident; they looked pale and pudgy and tentative. Vic's dark green sweater deepened his jade-colored eyes, and when he smiled at Lacey and said, "Hey, beautiful," her heart clenched.

The waitress took their orders, the meatloaf special for him, a steak salad for her.

"Ah, but the head wound didn't kill him," Vic added.

"No? He drowned in the dye?"

Vic shook his head. "Nope. Funny thing is—and this is the best part—it looks like Rod Gibbs died of a gunshot wound. In the chest."

"Shot? You're kidding!" Lacey remembered someone said the devil poked a hole in Rod with a pitchfork. Maybe that was what they were referring to. Who was it who said that? She couldn't remember.

"I never kid about autopsies. By the way, you didn't hear it from me."

"You don't have to worry." She opened her napkin and spread it on her lap. "Who did you hear it from?"

"Someone close to the investigation."

"I'm guessing the Black Martin cop, Armstrong. Special Agent Mordecai Caine is too fond of bogarting information."

"My lips are sealed."

"Really?" She touched his lips lightly with her fingertips. "I'll just contact the medical examiner's office for a comment when I get back to the office."

"They probably won't comment. You want the scenario?" She nodded. "Looks like he was hit in the head. Then someone decided to string him up and make the Blue Devil really blue. And then he was shot, to boot."

"That works. But we didn't see any blood in the factory. Of course, there was dye everywhere, and by then, it was blue blood. Maybe he bled out in the tub of dye? So someone knocked him out, tied him to the spool, *then* shot him, and then dunked him in the dye? Wow. I don't know what to think. Why shoot him *and* dye him? And who did what first? And why? And how many were there? What do you make of it, Vic?'

"Lacey, darling, it's pretty darn strange. Someone wanted to make a point. Make a spectacle of him. Or else there's no reason for all the drama. You hate him, you shoot him, you leave."

"What kind of gun was it?"

"Looks like a nine millimeter. A slug was dug out of the velvet."

"The slug was in the velvet?" Lacey drew a breath. "Honey Gibbs has a nine millimeter, a Christmas gift from Rod. She was pissed about it. She wanted diamond earrings. Motive for murder right there. See, smarty-pants, I have sources too."

He smiled at her. "Lots of people own nine millimeters." Vic paused. "Doesn't narrow it down much, unless they can match the bullet to the weapon."

"Can anyone join this party, or are you two exclusive?" They turned to the inquiring voice. Tall, dark, and handsome, the man grinned at Lacey and smacked Vic on the back.

"Turtledove! It's been a while." Lacey leaned in for a hug.

Turtledove commanded as much attention as Vic did. Lacey could see the surreptitious stares from nearby tables, and she was glad to be at the center of attention. Who cared if there was some low-level congressman in the corner and a deputy secretary of some agency or other hogging the center of the room? The good-looking guys were all with her. Turtledove was not the kind of operative who would fade into the background. He wore a tight short-sleeved polo shirt that strained over his biceps, and a leather jacket slung over his shoulder. An exotic mix of ethnicities, including black and Cajun and who knew what else, Forrest Thunderbird was a rare combination of spectacular good looks and a restrained and elegant demeanor. He took a seat.

"Forrest, nice to see you," Vic said. "I made it over to Velvet's Blues after your set last night, but I missed you."

Turtledove smiled. "Sorry about that. I got a little busy after the gig."

"Getting busy with the singer, or someone new?" Lacey asked.

The big man cleared his throat. "Remind me never to try and fool a woman. Especially this woman."

"So it *was* the singer," she said with a smile. He laughed and turned toward Vic.

"Now, I understand we have a situation down in Black

Martin, Virginia," he said. "I can be down there this afternoon if you need me."

"That would suit me," Vic said.

"You don't expect any more trouble down there, do you?" Lacey wondered if they were leaving something out.

"With all that talk of a deadly Velvet Avenger, you never know," Vic said.

"Oh. You saw my story." Lacey had slipped in some quotes from the bar talk about the Avenger at the last minute. She never really expected anyone to read what she wrote. She was the exact opposite of reporters who think the world checks in with them every morning.

"You had to put in that crackpot theory?" Vic lifted an eyebrow.

"Hey, it was just to illustrate that people are frightened and want a solution, any solution, and they're willing to believe in anything. I pointed out that this 'crackpot theory' is a measure of their desperation and wishful thinking." At least, that was what she'd thought when she wrote the story. "Besides, if I didn't include that angle, I'd be accused by some crackpot of hiding the facts."

"I liked it," Turtledove said. When he smiled, he looked both predatory and sexy. *It's no wonder women swoon over him,* Lacey thought. "Why didn't I read about the Velvet Avenger on DeadFed?" he asked.

"Damon has the flu, according to Brooke. No doubt his fingers will be flying over the keyboard as soon as he stops puking." *Besides, he wasn't there to hear about the Avenger,* she thought. *The Velvet Avenger is all mine. For the moment.*

"We don't need to aggravate a situation that could end with the workers taking over the factory and refusing to leave," Vic said. "It happened in Chicago."

"That was a union shop," Lacey said. "They were organized."

"Those workers believed they were sold out," Turtledove said. "Not much different from your textile workers in Black Martin. They already have one blue corpse down there. Nobody wants another one."

"Tom Nicholson is down there with a skeleton crew,"

Vic said. "He's vulnerable. Things could get ugly quick. The invisible security is being installed, and Forrest will be the visible security."

"I can be scary when I have to be," Turtledove said modestly.

"This might be scary too." Lacey reached into her purse. She pulled out a plastic bag with Claudia's blue velvet ribbon and the envelope it came in. Lacey placed it on the table while the men watched. She waited a beat. She had their attention. "Claudia Darnell, my publisher, got this in the mail today. No note. Just the ribbon." Vic looked grim. Turtledove inspected it closely through the plastic bag. "It's the same color as the velvet and Rod Gibbs. Midnight Blue."

"Fashion clue?" Vic scratched his head. He looked sidelong at Lacey.

"It could be a warning. A prank. It was sent from Black Martin, just before my story appeared. You can see the postmark."

Vic held the baggie up to the light. "The ribbon won't have prints. The envelope will have too many. And this isn't the kind you lick, it's an adhesive strip. So no DNA. Lots of drama, not much data. But I bet it scared Claudia."

"Did the ribbon come from the factory?" Turtledove asked.

"I don't think so," Lacey said. "They don't make ribbon. Or didn't."

"So anybody could have sent it?" Vic asked.

Lacey spread her hands. "Everyone who worked at Dominion Velvet knows about Claudia's partnership in the company and about Rod Gibbs, and they know what their Midnight Blue dye looks like."

"If the killer sent it, he might plan on traveling," Turtledove said. "He might not be in Black Martin."

"He?" Lacey said. She thought the killer probably was a man, but she couldn't discount the possibility of a woman. The dye and the ribbon seemed to add a feminine touch.

"He or she," Vic added. "I don't like it, Lacey." He put his hand over hers. "You finished your Dominion Velvet story. You're not working on a follow-up, are you?"

"You're kidding, right?" She kissed him on the cheek. "Obviously there's a follow-up. The funeral is on Friday. You don't expect me to miss that."

Vic folded his arms and grimaced. "Heavens, no. Don't expect I could stop you if I wanted to."

Turtledove clapped him on the arm. "Don't try, man. Don't even try."

chapter 18

The Eye's news staff gathered after lunch in the paper's largest meeting room. It was barely adequate for the task. The room seemed to vibrate with voices and apprehension.

Full staff meetings were rare, as someone at the newspaper always had to tend to the business of news. Tables had been moved from the room and chairs were set up in rows. Many reporters generally liked to sit up front so they could catch every detail, but this meeting was different. Most seemed to be hanging to the rear for a quick exit. Lacey tried to snag a seat in the back, followed by Trujillo, but all the rear seats were taken.

Wiedemeyer had saved seats close to the front and he was waving so frantically they couldn't ignore him.

"Smithsonian, Trujillo. Over here!"

Lacey had to step over Mac to take a seat next to Wiedemeyer. Tony stepped over her. Claudia waited on the dais and shared a word with Walt Pojack. Lacey groaned. If Pojack was speaking, the news definitely wouldn't be good.

Most of the staff liked Claudia Darnell, or at least they liked the idea of a crusading publisher who was unafraid of the Washington establishment. Claudia's platinum blond hair caught the light and contrasted with her dark suit. Her turquoise eyes sparkled and drew people to her, especially men of all ages. The man to her left, however, had the opposite effect. No one even wanted to shake Walt Pojack's hand, for fear it would leave a slimy film behind, like a slug.

Claudia took the podium and the microphone.

"It's no secret that the news business all over this country is in trouble. *The Eye* is no exception. While newspapers everywhere are trying to create a new business model to transform our industry, we here are taking immediate steps to make sure *this* newspaper survives. *The Eye* offers the sane news alternative in this town. We have no ax to grind but the truth and the people's right to know. But we have to change some things about the way we do business. We have to be leaner and meaner. We'll all have to make some sacrifices for the good of the newspaper. I'll stop there—I have a pressing meeting—but Walter Pojack is going to fill you in on some possibilities under consideration. Please give him your undivided attention. And thank you for coming." She exited the stage and left the room.

There was a ripple of unease through the crowd and a low hum of disapproval. No applause, which struck Lacey as ominous. Claudia always got applause. But the eyes of *The Eye* were on Walt Pojack. And what they saw did not please them.

Pojack was in his late fifties, with a round face and dull, puffy eyes. He combed over his thinning gray hair, sported a manufactured tan, and attempted to cover up a paunch with expensive suits. He had multiple divorces behind him, but still fancied himself quite the babe magnet. When Pojack smiled, his lips thinned into a humorless slit across his face. He reminded Lacey of a salamander. She'd seen some ugly salamanders recently at the Washington Zoo, where they were trying to breed them. *Maybe they've succeeded.*

No one in the newsroom could explain how Pojack jumped from being a political reporter to managing editor to his position on the board of directors. Wiedemeyer's theory was simply that scum always rises to the top. Trujillo said Pojack must have blackmailed Claudia Darnell. Whatever the truth, he moved onward and upward, leaving a dozen bad decisions in his wake, and somehow managed to claw his way onto the board, where he was firmly entrenched. *The Eye* was stuck with Walt Pojack.

He took the microphone with a flourish. He laughed, he lurched, he made lame jokes. "There are plenty of hot seats up here, folks. Get them while they're fresh. Why, anyone would think you don't like me."

No one laughed. The first two rows remained empty, even as reporters and editors lined the back wall and sat down in the aisles. All were armed with phones and notebooks and pens, and many with laptops.

Pojack launched into his remarks on cutting costs and creating revenue for the company. Newsprint cost was up. Circulation was down. New media was hot, old media cold. The print edition would have to shrink; the Web edition would grow. The board was considering selling online subscriptions. The staff would be trimmed, hopefully from attrition, and a hiring freeze was in effect. There were no buyouts planned, but open positions would not be filled. If that didn't staunch the bleeding, certain positions would be cut, he said. Every position would be examined, he promised.

Lacey wondered whether she would be able to weather the storm.

"So this is what they came up with from those 'Quality Content' meetings?" Wiedemeyer piped up. "Gutless bastards. The staff is what makes this paper great. Not the suits." Heads swiveled to stare. Felicity tried to hush him up.

But that wasn't the worst. Pojack cleared his voice and tapped the microphone. "Now, I know many of you are pretty fond of *The Eye Street Observer*'s offices and our high-dollar location on Eye Street. But the board has been exploring our options. The District of Columbia is a very expensive place to do business. Fair warning: Get ready to move. Soon."

Dead silence. Pojack savored the moment, a self-satisfied smirk on his face. For once, he had their undivided attention. Lacey felt a stabbing feeling in her gut.

"*The Eye Street Observer* is moving—to Crystal City," Pojack said smugly. There was an audible gasp. Crystal City? That concrete maze in Arlington, Virginia, across the Potomac? An unfortunate blot on the landscape near Reagan National Airport. No one moved their offices from the District to Crystal City unless they were at the end of their rope. Even the federal government was moving out of Crystal City.

"It's worse than I thought," Lacey muttered. Trujillo jabbed her in the side.

"Is he kidding?" Trujillo said. She pushed him away. "That's across the river!"

Mac was stone-faced and grim, but management hung together. He said nothing.

Felicity put her hand on Wiedemeyer's arm. A liberal sprinkling of the word *bastard* poured forth under his breath. The staff broke out in hoots and jeers at Walt Pojack. Someone booed, then another one. It became a roar.

Pojack seemed only mildly ruffled. "Crystal City is convenient. It's right across the river. It's got a great view of the District. It's on the Metro, and with its numerous underground tunnels, you never have to go outside in bad weather," he said. *Like moles*, Lacey thought. *Moles who never leave their tunnels. Yech.* "Lots of convenient eateries," Pojack was saying, as if that was a selling point.

"Eateries? Like McDonald's? Is he out of his mind?" Felicity moaned. "*The Eye Street Observer* belongs on Eye Street."

There they had the District, Farragut Square, restaurants, shops, and sunshine (sometimes). K Street was a block away, the White House only two, and the Capitol and Congress were a short cab ride or a couple of Metro stops away. It might not be midtown Manhattan, but the newspaper's location on Eye Street plugged them directly into the pulsing beat of the Nation's Capital.

"Just remember, those who hate the idea of working in Crystal City do not have to continue their employment at this newspaper," Pojack added. "Remember what I said about attrition? Attrition is good, people."

Lacey wondered if that was his game, to make everyone so miserable they would quit. "Tony, what do you think of this fiasco?"

Trujillo said, "Let's put it this way. If Pojack dropped dead tomorrow, I'd have a cocktail party."

"Kickbacks. There has to be a kickback involved," Wiedemeyer proclaimed. "Pojack would sell his grandmother to the devil if he thought it would help feather his own damn nest. How much has he sold out *The Eye* for? That is the question, the slimy, gutless rat bastard."

"Why can't this guy show up on your beat, Wiedemeyer?" Trujillo poked Wiedemeyer's chest. "The death and dismemberment beat. What do you have on him?"

Wiedemeyer spoke in a low voice that forced Lacey, Tony, and Felicity to lean in close to hear.

"Pojack used to be a flack for a certain Crystal City commercial real estate developer with big political connections, right? That developer has kept his crappy, not to mention ugly, buildings filled with federal workers, suffering from mold and malaise. Until now. With federal agencies fleeing Crystal City like rats from the proverbial sinking ship, said developer is left with big empty ugly buildings to refill, just to keep the whole damned eyesore alive. So who does our developer cozy up to? Someone with the morals of a tree toad, and the brains of a sponge—Walter Pojack."

"Okay, I like it so far," Tony said. "There's more?"

"Trujillo, is the White House white? Does the District overtax us? There's always more." Wiedemeyer's eyes glittered with the light of the righteous as he polished his theory. "This deal's got to go through or Pojack's dead meat at *The Eye.* So how does he ensure his comfy retirement and do a favor for the developer, the one he used to work for with the shabby Mussolini Modern office ghettos with their sick-building syndromes?"

"He trades *The Eye* for something?" Trujillo guessed. "For a big cheap ugly building and a kickback?"

"Ten points for Tony," Wiedemeyer said. "For our crooked bastard of a developer, greasing some sleazy weasel like Pojack a cool million or so under the table in exchange for unloading a Crystal City white elephant? Chump change. And if you've observed, our Mr. Pojack is suddenly driving a brand-new silver Cadillac Escalade Hybrid SUV, at a cost of a cool ninety grand. It's in the parking garage right now. Do real newspapermen drive such gangster-bait vehicles, ladies and gentlemen of the press? They do not. The hybrid part is just to pretend the bastard is going earth-friendly green. And the Cadillac Escalade part is because—well, pardon me, ladies—but you gentlemen all know this: If you're a prick without a dick, you *buy* one. My sources tell me the bastard's also been taking banking trips to the Cayman Islands."

"You're talking payoffs," Trujillo said. "Pojack's not smart enough. Is he?"

"So say my sources." Harlan Wiedemeyer smiled. "I have no proof. Yet."

Pojack is venal enough. "But Crystal City is not a done deal," Lacey said. "It can't be. Claudia wouldn't sell out the paper and move us to—"

"Pojack doesn't care," Trujillo said. He was an instant believer. "Don't you see? He starts telling people the big ugly plan, and the dissidents start quitting. Attrition! Payroll costs go down, Crystal City sweetens the deal, and things start falling his way. He doesn't have to *be* smart. He just looks smart to the board. He embarrasses Claudia Darnell with this announcement *after* she leaves the room. She's got other troubles, so he seizes the moment to lay the groundwork to move what's left of *The Eye Street Observer* across the river. And pocket his payoff. Have you seen those buildings in Crystal City? They don't begin to compare to ours. And they're across the freaking river! In Virginia!"

Lacey was starting to buy Wiedemeyer's dark tale, and it gave her a headache. She found it perfectly believable that Walt Pojack could conspire against Claudia Darnell and everyone who worked at the paper just to grab a payoff and run. Was she becoming as cynical as Damon Newhouse, seeing a conspiracy behind every bush? Or could it all be true? Maybe. *Definitely maybe.*

The atmosphere turned sour. It was impossible for reporters who had made their careers and reputations in the District of Columbia to picture the newspaper moving across the Potomac River, to the ghastly Crystal City business ghetto. Reporters stood up and filed out while Walt Pojack was still talking. The noise of chairs and feet and unhappy voices began to drown him out.

"How could you possibly move *The Eye Street Observer* off Eye Street?" Wiedemeyer shouted over the din. "It would be a completely different animal. You'd have to re-name the whole newspaper."

"To what, Harlan?" Lacey yelled back, as loud as she could. "*The Crystal City Curmudgeon*?"

"*The Crystal City Cadaver*," he shouted. "It'll be dead on arrival!"

Chapter 19

Murder victims might turn blue, newspapers might fail, weasels might conspire with bastards, but Stella Lake was getting married. And that was a *real* world-class crisis.

Lacey headed to her friend's apartment directly after work, still in her suit. If she went home first she was afraid she would sit down and fall asleep and never get up again, and Stella would hate her.

Stella lived in a large midcentury brick building lost in a canyon of similar apartment buildings on Connecticut Avenue, above Dupont Circle. A cab dropped Lacey off at the circle drive in front. She pushed through the heavy wood doors and pine-cleaner-scented lobby. The familiar concierge waved her on upstairs.

She met Nigel Griffin coming out of Stella's apartment.

"Do calm her down, Smithsonian," Griffin said. "I've been having a bit of fun with Stella about Mum, you know, and now she—Stella—is, well, you know how she is."

"I know how *you* are."

"Be a pal," he pleaded, as if they were pals.

The Englishman was wearing his usual uniform of slacks and a navy blazer, no topcoat in sight. Nigel was good-looking in a sort of effete British way, if you went for that kind of thing. Tall, thin, longish medium-brown hair, English-movie-star features. Cute accent. Stella had gone for it in a big way. Any fool could look good in a navy blazer, Lacey thought, but she was of the opinion that if a man looked good in his jeans, he would look good in anything. Like Vic. So far, she had never seen Nigel in blue jeans.

Nigel's smug act drove Lacey crazy, but he'd taken a dive over a cliff for Stella, which counted for something. Quite a lot, actually. And he had popped for a very impressive platinum and diamond engagement ring. Lacey had to give him points for that. He was off crutches now, still walking a little stiffly from his twisted ankle. Where once Lacey suspected him of complete disregard for anyone but himself, she now saw him look at Stella with a kind of adoring awe. Griffin was a man in love, or at least deep infatuation. A reformed "man slut," Lacey sincerely hoped.

Nigel Griffin called himself a "stolen-jewel retriever." In reality, he was some kind of specialized insurance investigator. He'd spent his teen years forming a sticky-fingered attraction to jewels and gaining expertise at lifting them from unsuspecting victims. After a major run-in with the police, he parlayed those skills to his advantage, finding stolen goods for big-ticket insurers. Lacey didn't quite trust his reformation. She still thought of him as a jewel thief at heart, working whichever side of the fence paid better. But Stella loved him, and that counted for a lot with Lacey. Not everything, but a lot.

Lacey reflected that Stella might actually have a lovely Valentine's Day this year. *Well, good for Stella, with her hearts, flowers, and chocolates. And diamond ring. I should probably call in sick that day and refuse to answer the phone or the door.*

"Smithsonian, you there?" Griffin brought her back to the present.

"I hope you're not just playing with her feelings," Lacey said.

"You're really checking to see if my intentions are honorable? Again? Stella and I nearly bloody died for each other. Remember?"

"There is that," Lacey admitted. But if Nigel hadn't been the kind of man who broke unsuspecting women's hearts, he and Stella might not have been on that cliff. It was the plummy English accent, she thought. Women fell for it. *Literally.*

Lacey would never forget that snowy day in January when they all ended up on the cliff above the Potomac River at Great Falls. Lacey and Brooke had raced there to try to save Stella from a killer, but they weren't able to keep her from going over the cliff. To his credit, Nigel dove right in after her. Stella broke her leg, Nigel wrenched his knee and ankle. They had all done things that day they had probably never dreamed they were capable of. Lacey shook her head to clear her thoughts. They were all safe now—that was the important thing.

"Do you think I'd be asking my parents—my bloody *parents*—to come from bloody England to meet my Stella if I wasn't crazy for her? *Crazy* being the operative word here. And I bought her the ring. I didn't steal the bloody thing, you know. You saw it, Smithsonian. Is that a bloody great ring or what? And they'd kill me if I married her without telling them."

"Bloody well scared, aren't you?" Lacey allowed herself a smile at his expense.

"Terrified." He leaned against the wall and ran his hands through his hair. "Do you know she's the only woman I've ever asked Mum to meet? I've gone to great lengths to avoid them meeting all the others."

"I'm impressed." Lacey inched her way to Stella's door. She felt uncomfortable chatting with Nigel when he started to seem human. It was out of character for him.

"Mum is terribly excited. It's the never-introducing-her-to-a-girlfriend-before thing, I suppose. The prodigal-son-getting-married thing. And really, the Gorgon is not all that bad. This engagement is awfully big for them. The poor old things had given up hope, lost in despair. All that rot." He looked directly at Lacey and gave her his puppy dog eyes. "Perhaps I've been telling Stella a bit too much. Now she's terrified of my mum. Not that I'm not. A little. With good reason. Please help, Smithsonian."

Griffin patted his jacket for a pack of cigarettes, but Stella had convinced him to give up smoking. He settled for a stick of gum. "It was just a bit of teasing. The Gorgon is formidable, but not—*evil*. Not exactly."

"Why do you call your mother that?"

He looked blank. "What? The Gorgon? Dunno. Always have. Dad calls her that. Affectionately, you know."

"Do you call her that to her face?"

"God, no. Don't want to be thrown in the dungeon. It's damp down there."

"You're a card, Nigel."

Stella opened her apartment door. "Lacey, where you been?" She looked from Lacey to Nigel. "Oh, that's so cute. You two are getting along. Bonding. You are adorable, you two."

"Don't jump to any conclusions," Lacey said, scooting past him into Stella's doorway.

"A temporary truce." Nigel kissed Stella good-bye again. "Someday, Smithsonian, we'll actually be friends."

"When we're eighty," Lacey called out.

"Or ninety," he rejoined. "If we live so long."

"Both of you here, in my hour of need," Stella said. "Nigel, honey, you sure you can't stay?"

"Later, love. Must get the home front ready for the ambassador and Lady Gorgon. Cheers!" Another passionate peck on Stella's lips and he was gone.

Stella let out a sigh of contentment. "He's so adorable."

"Yeah. It's the accent."

"That too. And the sex." Stella, who had dyed her hair every possible color, including blond, black, red, and purple, now sported short tousled cupid curls in a warm chestnut brown. It suited her—not in the same way as her usual short spiky hair in a rainbow of radical colors—but the curls reflected the softer side of her personality.

But cute and cuddly her outfit was definitely *not*. Stella paired a shocking pink satin bustier, which raised the Girls to new heights, with a short, tight red cardigan and a short black leather skirt. One leg showed off a red patent-leather stiletto. The other leg sported a new walking cast, which finally freed her knee. Stella demonstrated bending it.

"Ow. That hurts."

"Wearing that shoe and that cast together is dangerous, Stella. You could fall. Remember falling off that cliff? That one heel is nearly as high."

"What are you talking about? I gotta look good for Nigel's mother. And I have to decorate this sucker." Stella kicked up her cast. "I just got it yesterday and it's too plain Jane for me, but now at least I can bend my leg. Everybody has to help me paste some jewels on it. Don't you totally love glue guns?"

"More rhinestones?"

"It'll be a work of art, Lace. I'd rather be a rhinestone chandelier than hide my light under a brown paper bag, or however that goes. Come on in. I'll fix your favorite. Hot chocolate and amaretto." It wasn't really Lacey's favorite, but it was a cold night and Stella loved it. "And surprise!"

Stella opened the door wide to reveal another friend, Marie Largesse, of Old Town Alexandria and formerly of New Orleans. Marie was a self-described professional psychic, though Lacey had her doubts about that. Marie was raking long, red nails through her hair. Her impressive tattoos, including an Eye of Horus on each shoulder, were covered up for the cold weather. Nevertheless, she didn't need them to draw the eye, with her cascade of curly black hair and her milky skin. The woman was luxuriously large, extravagantly curvy, and proud of her size in a way that made people think of her as bountiful and abundant, not fat. Tonight she was wrapped in swirls of royal blue and purple fabric, which ended in a flared skirt that danced around her violet suede boots. Lacey was delighted to see her.

"Marie, what a great surprise! I didn't know you'd be here." Lacey found herself being hugged hard.

"That, sugar, is why I am the psychic and y'all are the reporter. I see y'all are *not* staying out of trouble."

"Psychic vibrations?"

"No, I read your story in the paper." Marie chuckled, low and throaty. "But Lacey, I fear y'all are not through with blue velvet. It's positively raining blue velvet."

"Is this a message from the stars?" Lacey asked. *Or the weather report?* Marie was usually better with the weather than human events.

Marie nodded gravely. "I'm seeing ribbons of blue velvet. Ribbons and ribbons and ribbons. Careful, cher, that y'all don't get 'tangled up in blue,' as they say."

There was only one blue velvet ribbon that Lacey knew about, but Marie's vision was acute enough to give Lacey chills, and she'd had enough of those lately.

"Well, there is no blue velvet here," Lacey said. "But I'll take that hot chocolate." The coffee table was full of burning candles. Everything in the apartment that wasn't pink or red was jet-black. Stella loved her punk princess atmosphere. "Stella, the place looks, um— This is your new sofa?"

"Yeah, real leather. And so red!" Stella stroked it with her pink-tipped fingernails, at the same time showing off that impressively large but tasteful diamond. One point seven-five carats. "It's like my accent color. Nigel helped me pick it out. I figured since we're going to be married, maybe he'd like some say in the matter. He wanted black leather. I wanted red. You like the red?"

"Red as can be," Lacey agreed. "Poor Nigel. Now, what about Nigel's mother? Marie, what do you think? Are you getting any vibes on the Gorgon?"

Marie pressed her fingers to her forehead and grimaced. "Nothing. My radar must be down. The Eyes of Horus are half-closed."

"Well, you're not fainting, so it can't be that bad," Lacey said. Marie famously went limp whenever her visions involved blood or violence.

"It's not bad. It's totally wrong!" Stella hollered from the kitchen.

Marie glided down on the red sofa, creating a pop art collection of bright colors: blue, purple, red. "I don't know. I just have the feeling that Gwendolyn and Stella will turn out to be the best of friends. Far-fetched, I know. But the oracle is the oracle."

"Yeah, me and Eleanor freakin' Roosevelt. Can you see it?" Stella returned with a pot of hot chocolate, a bottle of amaretto, and mugs on a tray. There were also chocolate cookies and a heart-shaped box of truffles.

"It's going to be a chocolate kind of night?" Lacey took the tray from Stella. "Sit down, please. Your mismatched footwear is disturbing me. You already have one leg in a cast. Let's not make it two."

Stella plopped herself down beside Marie while Lacey placed the tray on the coffee table. "Yeah, my doctor swears this sucker will be off before the wedding. So I can wear some killer stilettos. You know, Nigel is so much taller than me, I gotta wear heels. I want to look him square in the eye when I say 'I do.' "

"You'll need a ladder." Lacey sipped her hot chocolate with only a half shot of the amaretto. It was a school night for her.

Stella munched a truffle. "Endorphins, Lacey. I need strength, and chocolate endorphins are the best kind of endorphins. True fact. Everyone knows it."

"Yay for chocolate-covered endorphins," Lacey said.

Stella was ripping open the chocolate-covered graham crackers when a knock came at the door. "I wondered when *she'd* get here," Stella muttered. "Always late."

"It's Brooke. Open up in the name of the law." Brooke made her entrance, breathless, as usual. It was part of her charm to treat life as one big dramatic conspiracy.

"I didn't know Stella called in the posse," Lacey said.

"Of course she called in the posse," Brooke said. "I understand we have a crisis. Hi, Marie. All present and accounted for. Now, are we ready to save Stella from the fire-breathing Gorgon?" She squeezed Lacey's arm and gave her a significant nod. "And to interrogate our fashion reporter? I understand dead men get the *blues*?"

Lacey raised one eyebrow. She double-locked the door behind Brooke. Stella hobbled on her one stiletto to give Brooke a hug. The two had finally bonded over gunpowder, margaritas, and that terrible day in the snowstorm. Lacey thought it was possibly the least likely pairing she had ever inadvertently helped bring about. *Well, except for Stella and Nigel.*

Brooke had perfected her version of the sleek young D.C. lawyer look. Her usual Burberry trench coat covered an Armani gray pinstripe skirt suit, with a blue shirt buttoned up to the neck, black tights, trim black leather heels. Her long blond hair was pulled away from her face in braids, which were wrapped around her head like a Swedish milkmaid. Stella put her hands on her hips and regarded Lacey and Brooke.

"God, the way you two are dressed, you'd think I was having some kind of Chamber of Commerce meeting."

Brooke pointed to her larkspur-colored blouse. "What? I'm breaking out in color. I'm practically a rainbow. See?"

Stella sighed dramatically. "Brooke, I bet you look like a lawyer even when you're in your underwear. I bet you sleep in gray flannel pinstripes. And that hair! I don't even know what to say about that."

"Please, Stel. At least they're dressed." Marie was always soothing ruffled feathers in this crowd. "You're here, Brooke—that's all that matters. And we're all here for Stella in her hour of need. Now, Miss Stella, would you care to explain?"

"Right. As you know, Nigel and I have decided on an April wedding. The clock is ticking. Like a freakin' time bomb. I need your help. All of you. Um, there's a big fat *please* in there too, in case you didn't hear it. Anybody need more chocolate? More amaretto? More *pleases*?"

chapter 20

"Stella, don't you think you're rushing the wedding a little?" Lacey said. "I mean, six weeks! Not much time to plan a wedding."

"It's like seven and a half weeks. The cast comes off in four. And hello? Cherry blossoms! I have always wanted to get married at cherry blossom time, Lace. And I know those blossoms are sneaky. They come early. They come late. They pop out, and then bang! They're gone. But this year, they're supposed to pop in about seven weeks. If I wait too long, another year could go by. I could be dead. Nigel could be dead. I am grabbing my man and my cherry blossoms and going for the gold. And if you want my advice, Lacey, you should go for it too."

"Vic and I are fine. Thank you very much." Lacey didn't want to get into a discussion of Vic and why it had taken them so long to get together. It was complicated.

"You must really love riding the stubby bus of love." Stella made a cross-eyed face at Lacey. Brooke and Marie laughed. "I don't know why I bother giving away good advice. Anyway, more chocolate, everybody. Then we can discuss the emergency while you all help me decorate my cast. Glue guns are locked and loaded. It'll be like a bridal bonding experience."

"Decorate your cast?" Brooke stared at the stark white encumbrance on Stella's leg, from which scarlet toenails peeked out.

"Rhinestones. We're helping with the rhinestones." Lacey pointed to the jars of rhinestones amidst the candles on the coffee table. They were pink and red and clear, all of them extra sparkly. Hot glue guns stood at the ready. "And, Stella, the theme is—?"

"Swirling hearts, 'cause it's almost Valentine's Day. And stars, for me, Stella. And maybe a few arrows, 'cause love is dangerous."

"We all know about the dangerous part," Marie said. She poured hot chocolate for Brooke and added amaretto. Lacey hefted a jar of pink rhinestones, shiny and mesmerizing.

"You never know when some wack job who wants your man is going to kidnap you and throw you over a cliff. It happened to me. It could happen to anyone." Stella pointed one long, pink nail at Brooke. "I want everyone to help. All my maids of honor."

"Stella? Glue guns? Oh no! I. Can't. Glue. *Anything.*" Brooke was frozen in her lawyerly shoes. "I flunked arts and crafts. Martha Stewart wouldn't trust me with a glue gun. A real gun, yes. Glue gun, no. There could be injuries."

Brooke was a perfectionist. She had received A's in everything that advanced her career in law. But she was a failure in the most basic of crafts. She couldn't draw or paint or make collages out of pictures from cut-up magazines, and she couldn't glue.

Stella led her to the sofa. "You can supervise, doll. Or sue the glue gun company for damages. Whatever. Just have fun. Now come on. We have to make this ugly cast pretty. Or at least memorable. Thank God it will be off for the nuptials. You cannot imagine how hard it is to maneuver a cast and a man in bed. Nigel nearly injured himself. And me!"

"Too much information, Stella," Lacey said.

"Prude." Stella gave Brooke a little push. "And you, Annie Oakley, sit down already. I got things to tell you." Stella steadied herself with a slug of amaretto-laced hot chocolate. "My nerves are *shot.*"

Marie waved her hands gently, like a conductor. "Just be very clear, Stella. This is about Nigel's mother and how you are going to get along with her. Now, cleansing breaths."

"Right." Stella closed her eyes and took a deep breath,

reopened her eyes, and blew it out. "I'm focusing my core. Okay, Nigel says his mother is pretty much hell on heels. He calls her the Gorgon. Affectionately, he says. And she has never, I repeat, *never*, liked any of his girlfriends. Or even met them. Lady Gwendolyn Griffin is flying in tomorrow, and she wants to meet me. She's staying with him all week! And she'll be back before the wedding."

"Maybe you can elope," Lacey suggested.

"It crossed my mind, believe me. But no way am I sacrificing my wedding day, my moment in the spotlight."

"Damn right you're not," Brooke proclaimed. "Your wedding is a civil right."

You have a right to a wedding spectacle, or disaster, of colossal proportions. Lacey smiled at the thought.

"Everything will turn out as it should," Marie said, quite as if she could foretell the future. "It will be fine. After some trials and tribulations."

"I hope you're right," Stella said sadly. "I am so worried about the children."

"The children! Whose children?" Lacey asked. "Does Nigel have children we don't know about?"

"Our *future* children," Stella clarified. "My clock is ticking. You know when they say someone is horsey-looking? Or horse-faced? I totally never knew what that meant before Nigel showed me pics of his mother."

"She can't be that bad. After all, Nigel is ..." Lacey hunted for the right word. "Nice-looking."

"He is a babe. But genetics are a bitch. What if there's a throwback to his mother's recessive horse-face genes? Honestly, Lacey, I don't want to name our kids Seabiscuit and National Velvet." *Please,* Lacey thought, *no more velvet.*

Brooke broke into the truffles and handed one to Lacey, who ate the whole thing in one bite. "Stella, what does the poor woman look like? Don't keep us in suspense."

"Like Eleanor Roosevelt. Crossed with a Clydesdale." Three women gasped.

Stella passed around a photograph. Lacey gazed at it for a long moment before passing it to Brooke. "Maybe she just doesn't photograph well."

"I'm sure that's it," Brooke chimed in. "Wow. Clydesdale or Lipizzaner?"

"It's just bad lighting," Marie suggested over Brooke's shoulder. "Really bad."

"What did I tell you?" Stella said. "My Nigel is half racehorse. On the other hand, that would explain his—"

"I like her eyes," Marie said. "They're very, um, *direct*. Under all those eyebrows."

"Oh, my God, I hadn't even noticed the eyebrows!" Stella grabbed the picture.

"Stella, calm down," Lacey said. "You're just psyching yourself out. Gwendolyn Griffin might be just as nervous about meeting you."

"Ha. She is as cool as a cucumber," Stella said. "We gotta get her mind off me."

"Perhaps we should get your mind off *her*," Marie suggested.

"Yes," Lacey said, thrusting a glue gun into Brooke's reluctant hands. "Let's talk about the wedding." She couldn't believe what she was saying. She was sick of wedding talk. "How are you wearing your hair for the wedding?"

"I haven't decided, but it's got to make a statement, you know?" Stella wouldn't dream of not making a statement with her coiffure. "Part of me wants to go, oh you know, blue with platinum highlights. Something crazy, like a punk angel with little blue wings on the side of my face, like a Farrah Fawcett do?"

"Okay, maybe we should pick another topic," Lacey said. *No more blue either.*

"Don't look at me," Brooke said. "I'd probably look like a lawyer. Stella, I think the *something blue* part of the rhyme should not be your *hair*. I'd go with Grace Kelly hair and pearls."

"Okay, part of me says don't mess with the curls," Stella said, fluffing her locks. " 'Cause they're cute as a baby duckling, and Nigel really likes running his fingers through them. Curls and pearls! That sounds good, doesn't it? Not to mention the Girls."

"Um, the thing about weddings, Stella, is that you'll have the photos forever," Lacey said. "Your wedding is a moment in time. The punk angel look may not last forever. You might be sick of it in a month. But you could go classic and timeless—"

"Or I could be an embarrassment forever. You're right, Lacey. It torments me, and that's just the hair! I wake up in the middle of the night and wonder if I'll be like those brides from the Fifties with their little knee-length, shirtwaist white dresses and poofy chin veils and cat-eye glasses. And forever after, people will snicker when Nigel and I bring the album out." Stella made cat-eye glasses over her eyes with her hands. Lacey reached for more amaretto. "But you know, that might be cool. Just for the irony of it? And then we could hire an Elvis impersonator."

Lacey and Brooke looked horrified. "Stella, you're not really having an Elvis impersonator at the wedding, are you?" Brooke said.

"No, not really. Elvis tends to pull the focus off the bride."

Lacey jumped in. "What about your dress?"

"It's got to be fabulous! White as snow, with like a *lot* of beads or sequins or pearls or something. I don't have a clear picture of it yet, but my wedding dress has got to fit like skin and look like sin, and show off the Girls to their very best advantage," the bride-to-be declared.

"Well, y'all have a lot of decisions to make," Marie said. "But I say nothing goes smooth as silk for a wedding gown."

Stella's eyes lit up. "Oh, you're thinking silk? I was thinking like maybe a tight white leather minidress—"

Marie shared a look with Lacey. "What about the attendants?" she asked.

Lacey felt a tickle of anxiety. Her taste and Stella's taste were continents apart. But she was a bridesmaid and she was fated to fail in this decision.

"Black," Brooke said.

"Black?! Brooke, it's my *wedding*, not my funeral. And it's not like we're vampires or something. Black is out. Red, maybe. Red would match my sofa. But I was thinking leather bustiers in some cheerful color. Pink, maybe? Something that goes with cherry blossoms for my attendants."

"How about gray?" Brooke suggested, as a lawyerly compromise.

Lacey felt her eyes go wide. Her views on gray were well-known in this crowd. "Not gray," she whispered.

"Blue-gray? Mauve-gray?"

"No, Brooke," Lacey said. "No gray. And no taupe, beige, or brown."

"Yeah, what she said," Stella said.

"Cherry blossoms are pink," Marie said. "The color of hope and new beginnings."

Stella nodded. "Pink is good, but pink with some passion to it. Like shocking pink or maybe neon purple. This wedding has to make a statement." Lacey and Brooke both reached for the chocolate grahams at the same time. "And oh my God, what am I supposed to do with Nigel's mom?"

"Do you have to do anything?" Brooke asked, lifting her glue gun nervously.

"There will be photographs, Brooke." Stella picked up the picture of Mrs. Griffin and shook it. "And photographs are forever. People put them on the Internet!"

"Cleansing breaths," Marie sang out.

"I'm thinking because of her resemblance to the very late First Lady," Stella said, "Nigel's mother should wear something like I saw in the Smithsonian. Not you, Lacey Smithsonian. The museum Smithsonian. Eleanor Roosevelt's inaugural gown, in lavender velvet. And that color would go with whatever else I choose. Covered up, long sleeves. More regal than racehorse."

Velvet? Why am I not surprised? "That dress is not on display anymore, Stella. The museum has drastically reduced the First Ladies exhibit," Lacey said. "But I know the one you mean. Simple, long sleeves. It crisscrosses over the bodice. That would work."

"But how do I know she'll go for it? I mean, maybe she'll want to wear a horse blanket, or tweed knickers or something. Oh, my God! Tweed!" Stella slapped her hands to her face. "And one of those hats that's as big as a garbage can lid. The English are funny about their hats, you know."

"But you are so good with mothers, Stella. You wrapped my mom around your little finger," Lacey pointed out.

"Your mom is a doll, Lacey. His mother is a Gorgonzilla."

"That's only fitting for the mother of a Griffin."

"You know, we've never met *your* mother, Stella," Brooke said.

"You're not missing anything," Stella replied.

"You are inviting her, aren't you?" Brooke asked.

"Yeah, but at the last minute, so she doesn't have time to plan anything. Like coming! And ruining my wedding! A drama queen, that one."

It is going to be a very long seven and a half weeks, Lacey thought.

"Maybe we should talk about something else," Marie suggested. She hefted her glue gun and started pasting more rhinestones on Stella's cast. "I think Stella's aura is a little overloaded."

"I think my aura is starving. We need real food," Lacey said.

"Pizza," Stella agreed. "We need pizza."

Pizza. Close enough to real food. Brooke dialed the pizza delivery number written in ink on the wall by the phone. On top of all that chocolate and amaretto, it was going to be a calorie-bomb kind of night. Stella leaned back onto the sofa and breathed deeply.

"I'm feeling a little better. Thanks, everybody."

"Brooke, how is that young man of yours? I heard he's been ill," Marie said. "That's why you've been thinking about gray and black. Little storm clouds have been following you around."

"You're right, Marie. I've been in a gray mood. And Damon's better, thanks. He's looking into why D.C. has more cryptosexuals than any other place in the country."

"Cryptosexuals?" Lacey felt her eyebrows rise. *Involuntary, I swear.*

"You've seen them. We all have. They're a gender-orientation enigma. They aren't gay. They aren't straight or bi. They aren't metrosexual or retrosexual, or even asexual or nonsexual." Brooke stood as if addressing a jury. "Maybe they're postsexual. No one knows. They might not know themselves. They don't give you any sexual signals at all, or else too many conflicting signals. They're *crypto-*

sexual. The District is full of them. It's a mystery on a whole other level. No one has anything against cryptosexuals. What we're asking is, Why are they *here*, in Washington? Does something about D.C. attract them? Or were they recruited here for some reason? Is there a national security issue? Is there a conspiracy? How do they reproduce? Damon's all over it."

"I can't wait to read that one," Stella said. "It's like science fiction. With sex. Or not."

"But don't worry. Damon's also on the Velvet Avenger story for tomorrow's edition of Conspiracy Clearinghouse." Brooke sighed with satisfaction.

"Please tell me he's not calling it that!" *I never should have used that quote from that good old boy Sykes.*

"How could he not? He's just following your lead, Lacey."

"I can't believe I missed that, Lace," Stella said. "What's a Velvet Avenger? Some kind of a new drink?"

"Don't worry, Stella, sugar. I got a feeling y'all're about to catch up," Marie said.

Brooke was dumbfounded. "You don't know? You didn't read *The Eye* today? Good God. Lacey discovered another body."

"No way!" Stella jumped up and knocked over a whole jar of rhinestones.

"Not exactly," Lacey said. "There were multiple witnesses. I was just a face in the crowd."

"The dead man was completely blue," Marie said. "Lacey's aura today is surrounded by blue velvet. It's a lovely but heavy burden. Velvet auras can be suffocating."

"Why didn't you tell me?" Stella was stunned. "You got a velvet aura *and* a Velvet Avenger?!"

"You were busy! I was busy! It was in the paper," Lacey said. "I've been a little preoccupied. You too."

"That's no excuse for not telling me," Stella pouted. "I always tell you when I find dead bodies. Jeez, I can't believe you did it again, Lace."

"It wasn't just another body," Brooke said. "This is big, very big."

"So, was he, like, *totally* blue?" Stella demanded. "Like,

what kind of blue? Baby blue? Turquoise? Larkspur?
Aqua?"

"No, dead blue. Deep blue," Lacey said. She knew Stella
would keep at it until she was satisfied. "Awful blue."

"If you need our help, invoke the Code." Stella was referring to the Pink Collar Code, which bonded them together like a secret cadre of Nancy Drew fans. "We will be
there."

"Yeah, you with your cast."

"It's a walking cast. Just watch me kick ass with this
baby."

"I know all about your Code," Marie said, tapping her
head. "And if I am needed, I will come. But if I faint, consider it a warning." She smiled, and they all laughed.

"Lacey, this could be the answer to my prayers!" All the
women turned to stare at Stella.

"What? The Code?"

"No, the Velvet Avenger."

"I thought we were talking about Nigel's mom and the
wedding. Wait—please don't tell me you want to get married in a blue velvet dress—"

"No, no, no, Lace. Nigel told me his mom is a total mystery hound. Maybe I could get her going on this thing and
take her mind off me. Nigel says she loves it all, dead bodies, corpses, cadavers, stiffs. It's a win-win, Lacey."

"No, Stella. Not for me. And you don't want to be involved with this story. Neither do I. I'm leaving this one
alone." *Right after the funeral.*

A loud knock at the door startled them all. "Pizza guy,"
Stella sang out. *And just in time,* Lacey thought. She beat
Stella to the door and opened it wide to take delivery of
their pizza. But it wasn't the pizza guy.

"Kepelov," Lacey said. *It just gets better and better.*
"You're the pizza guy? So where is our pizza coming from?
Moscow?"

chapter 21

Gregor Nikolai Kepelov was beefy and muscular. His bald head, handlebar mustache, and cool blue eyes added to his formidable appearance. He was once a KGB agent, or so he said, and his Russian accent seemed to be genuine, if a little unpredictable. He scowled at Lacey, but he smiled down at Marie, his zaftig Gypsy fortune-teller. Marie jumped up and squealed at the sight of him. She grabbed him for a big hug and a kiss.

Marie, who said she could see into his soul, clearly adored the man. Lacey thought it proved love was not only blind, but the product of a heaven with a peculiar sense of humor. Kepelov's expression of ardor was that of any man in love. While Lacey didn't trust the ex-spy, he was growing on her.

"Ah, Smithsonian, still you give me evil eye." His smile turned into a wide grin.

"I do not. It's more of a calculating reporter's eye."

His chuckle came from deep in his gut. "I forgive you, because you are Marie's good friend. And mine."

Kepelov and Stella hugged next. "Gregor, you guys want to stay for pizza? It's on the way."

"Another time," he said. "We have jambalaya in crock-pot at home. One of Marie's New Orleans specialties."

Kepelov and Brooke hugged each other as warily as two bears. Brooke said nothing, but she observed everything. Lacey knew her friend didn't know how much to trust the big Russian either. They had all been there in the storm the day Nigel and Stella were on the cliff,

Marie bringing them blankets in the snow, looking like something out of a Russian fairy tale, a spot of bright color in the white landscape. The experience had bonded the little group together in some way, yet Brooke always hesitated before offering her friendship. Lacey thought she was also probably hoping Kepelov would spill some dark, ancient, Soviet-era secret to her for Damon to report to the free world. Lacey was next in line for a Russian bear hug.

"Lacey Smithsonian, how long are you going to test me?"

He sounded like Griffin. Was it true? Was she such a tough grader? Did her friends' men have to jump through hoops to reassure her? Even her own man?

"Until I am sure you really love my friend Marie and aren't just using her psychic powers to find you Fabergé eggs. Or other lost treasures of the Romanovs. Or something."

Lacey was still half-afraid Kepelov might be trying to use Marie in some strange way for her dubious psychic powers. Marie was a dear and she seemed to have genuine flashes of ESP, but her abilities were sketchy. They came and went as the moon waxed and waned. Marie's psychic vibrations that famously tapped the Eyes of Horus on her shoulders, though often provocative, were not terribly useful. Except when it came to the weather. For predicting rain and storms, she was the cat's pajamas.

When Marie fainted because her visions were so frightening, her friends were alert to danger. But Lacey suspected Kepelov was still a jewel thief at heart, like his sometime partner Griffin—two would-be soldiers of fortune.

Kepelov found Lacey a little too amusing. "Can I not have both love and treasure? After all, Marie is my real treasure, I assure you. If she also leads me to the Czar's missing Fabergé eggs, why not?"

"Can you really have both, Kepelov, if you use one to get the other?"

"Smithsonian! You wound me."

"Don't squabble, you two," Marie said. She held on to Kepelov's arm and winked at Lacey. "My sweet Gregor knows my car is in the shop again and he just wants to see me home safely."

"You think a psychic would know an old Gremlin is a terrible car," Kepelov said. He helped her into her coat.

Marie laughed and placed her hand gently on the side of his face. She touched an old, faded scar from an ancient battle or a drunken brawl. "But I love my purple Gremlin, Gregor. It has all the right vibes."

"My darling Marie, those vibrations are telling you, 'Get new shock absorbers!' "

"I think he's right, Marie," Lacey said.

He suddenly turned to Lacey, and his smile was gone. "Smithsonian, I must tell you something. You must be on your toes, all ten. I read your paper. This new killer you have discovered? Very dangerous."

"Has Marie fainted?" Lacey asked, tongue in cheek.

"Not yet. The blue dye? It is showy, but obscure. A message, but what does it say? No one understands. So. This killer must send yet *another* message. There is the danger."

Lacey felt like a claw had grabbed her neck. "What kind of message?"

"How would I know that? KGB used subtler methods. Poison on tip of needle on umbrella. Simple shove over bridge railing. Car accident. Most effective is when victim disappears and no one ever knows. But this blue? In this factory? Looks like maybe political statement."

Brooke was on her feet. "Exactly what kind of political statement?" She blocked Kepelov's exit. The big Russian was smiling again.

"You always make me smile, Brooke Barton. You figure it out and tell me. Your friend Damon can break this exclusive story. It should be most entertaining." He turned to Lacey. "Be careful, my friend."

"Why, Kepelov, I didn't know you cared." *And how creepy is it that he understands the minds of other killers?*

"But of course I care. What would I do without you for amusement? And your fashion clues? Lead us to more diamonds. Who doesn't like diamonds?"

"Gee, I feel special," Lacey said. "And what about that

time you knocked me out in the basement?" She still held a bit of a grudge.

"Lacey, sugar, Gregor didn't know you then," Marie said. "And he tends to be a little leery of strangers, what with his spy history and all."

"That's a perfect reason to knock someone unconscious," Lacey said.

"As I have said before, I did not kill you, though I could have, and look at what good friends we have become. And there seems to be no brain damage."

Lacey wasn't sure about the "no brain damage." After all, what else could possibly explain why she was listening to Kepelov at all?

Kepelov was wrapping an intricate embroidered shawl over Marie's coat and tucking it around her with tender regard. The shawl's multicolored roses and leaves on a black background seemed to shimmer in the light. It caught Lacey's eye.

"Marie, that's beautiful." Lacey reached out to touch it.

"It is, isn't it? Gregor gave it to me. It's quite old. Full of stories."

"Really?" Lacey was intrigued. "What kind of stories?"

"I see your interest grows, Lacey Smithsonian. Romanov diamonds you care nothing about, but clothes and stories? Yes. Someday I will tell you about Marie's shawl." He winked. "It is a magic Russian shawl."

Right. "And someday we'll have barbecue at your mythical ranch in Texas."

"It is my American dream, Smithsonian. Have you applied for private investigator's registration yet? You would make a very unique private eye." Kepelov had taken over teaching a few of her PI classes from the regular instructor, Bud Hunt, after the events of last month.

"Um, I've got the paperwork. I'm thinking about it."

"Good. Be a PI. I think you will amuse me even more. You will be very dangerous as a PI." He put his arm around Marie and they left, laughing.

Lacey turned to Stella and Brooke. "I think that Bolshevik just insulted me."

*   *   *

Aunt Mimi's trunk beckoned Lacey when she got home, as it often did when she was exhausted and out of ideas. It was getting late, but she didn't care. She put a Cole Porter album on the CD player. Mimi had always loved Cole Porter, and so did Lacey.

The trunk also served as her coffee table. She cleared away the magazines, unbuckled the locks, and lifted the lid. She briefly leafed through a vintage *Vogue* magazine from 1939 before removing several layers of materials, looking for something she had glimpsed before.

She put her fingers on velvet that Mimi had cut into pattern pieces for a bolero jacket more than sixty years ago. And never finished. The dark moss green was woven through with gold threads, and it changed colors as it moved in the light. It was a prime example of shot through velvet. Lacey was glad she'd learned the term for this lovely fabric, though it gave her a pang of loss to realize she'd learned it just as the era of American-made velvet was ending. Mimi intended her bolero jacket to go with a high-waisted green velvet skirt. Lacey put the soft material next to her face and looked at its reflection in the mirror. It was beautiful, and as it changed colors it made her changeable eyes a deeper green.

"Oh, Mimi, it's beautiful. Thanks, old girl," Lacey said aloud to the empty room as she swayed with the pattern pieces to the smart and sassy strains of Cole Porter.

The velvet must have come from an American mill a long time ago, perhaps even Dominion Velvet's predecessor mill in Massachusetts. Lacey judged Mimi's pattern to be from the late 1930s or early 1940s, and the material was purchased before rationing was instituted during the war. Mimi must have had a vision of the final outfit, but she never got around to making the finished garment. Lacey liked to think that Mimi's habit of not finishing pieces and saving them forever meant they were destined to be hers. There were also many finished outfits that Mimi had left behind. Clothes were Mimi's passion, and the trunk was full of projects, finished and unfinished, to keep her thoughts and hands busy during the dark days of World War II.

Lacey decided the green-and-gold shot velvet outfit would be the next one she asked her favorite seamstress, Alma Lopez, to finish for her.

There was a familiar knock at her door: Vic's secret knock. She let him in, and he took a protective look around.

"Been communing with the spirits in Mimi's trunk, I see. Learn anything?"

"Only that I love velvet and I'm appalled that the textile business is dying in this country." She slipped the fabric and the patterns back in the trunk and closed the lid. Now that Vic was here, Mimi's spirit could go back to sleep.

"And how is the death of the American velvet industry related to the death of Rod Gibbs?"

"Haven't worked that out yet." Lacey closed her eyes for a moment. "Do you think it would be possible for us to forget about Rod Gibbs for one whole minute?"

"Works for me. We should both forget about him. At least for tonight." Vic leaned down and drew Lacey to him.

"Good idea. So all is quiet on the southern front?" she inquired.

"So far." Vic enveloped her in a big hug. "Turtledove is in Black Martin. We are here. No further developments. I'm done with paperwork for the night. You got a beer for me?"

"A beer? Vic Donovan, I've got more than that for you. Shut up and kiss me."

Lacey Smithsonian's

Fashion Bites

The Warning Signs of ADD:
Accessory Dysfunction Disorder!

Do you agonize when you accessorize?
Tear your hair and curse and swear?
Do scarves and shoes just make you mad?
Mix stripes with checks and dots with plaid?
Don't know the meaning of earring tree?
You might have a case of ADD!

Accessory Dysfunction Disorder is at large in the land. Some women fear accessories. Others pile them on like a starlet on a bling binge. Still others have a tortured rationale for hiding them away. Most cases of ADD fall into three categories, with endless variations. Do you have the warning signs of ADD?

- *My Life as a Rhinestone Chandelier.* These happy-go-lucky ADD victims believe that when it comes to accessories, the more the merrier. Three or four necklaces? Why not five? A rhinestone or two? Why not the whole rhinestone mine? Add some dangling earrings, an armful of bracelets, rings on her fingers, and bells on her toes. And her nose. You better believe she's got music wherever she goes. She wears them all with her swimsuits, too. She's been mistaken for a Gypsy fortune-teller, or a woman fleeing a burning house, wearing everything she owns. But don't be fooled. There're lots more where *that* came from.

- *Fear of Accessories!* These women don't believe in wearing anything extra. Accessory-phobes don't believe they *deserve* to wear anything extra.

They don't even wear belts unless their pants fall down. They believe that necklaces will turn your skin green and scarves will strangle you. They don't pierce their ears, so earrings are beside the point. Earring tree? What's an earring tree? They may have one strand of pearls they received for a birthday. But they don't wear them. Are they unworthy of the pearls—or are the pearls unworthy of them? Is it fear of the accessories themselves, or fear of calling attention to themselves? No one knows.

- *Don't Be Ridiculous. It's Too Good to Wear!* Perhaps the most puzzling category. These ADD victims own wonderful accessories and treasure them. They simply never wear them. This is the woman who inherits a vintage cameo ring from her grandmother but never wears it—because it's "too good." She won't wear that gorgeous silk shawl from her husband. She keeps it in a drawer—because it's too good. Her designer purses are wrapped in tissue and hidden on the top shelf of the closet. Why? You guessed it. We can only hope that someday this woman will believe she is good enough to wear her own lovely possessions.

What to make of these women and their Accessory Dysfunction Disorder? Personally, I'd much rather be a Rhinestone Chandelier personality who displays and exults in her treasures than an Accessory-phobe who lives her life in a plain brown wrapper. And to the woman who's afraid she's just not good enough for those pearls: Honey, unless you're hiding the Hope Diamond in your sock drawer, loosen up! You know you have beautiful things. Wear them. Live a little.

Release the butterfly from your cocoon.

chapter 22

Mac never lets me get away with this kind of headline.

Lacey stared at Damon Newhouse's story in Thursday morning's online Conspiracy Clearinghouse: DeadFed dot com. She couldn't wait to see what Damon had written in his flu-fevered dreams. Reading it at home before work made it easier for her to yell at the screen. Lacey read and sipped her cranberry juice. She frowned. The story seemed to be based on the same facts, but somehow it came out different, more lurid, more hallucinatory. More *wrong*.

WHO IS THE VELVET AVENGER?
CRAZED KILLER OR CONSPIRACY MASTERMIND?

By Damon Newhouse

Rodney Gibbs, a manager at Dominion Velvet, in Black Martin, Virginia: By all accounts, he was a monster, a playground bully on steroids who never grew up. He enjoyed torturing everyone he knew, from his wife, whom he beat, to the workers who filed harassment complaints against him. But this week, an avenger rose against Rod Gibbs, the so-called Velvet Avenger, who decided to forgo the courts and pass judgment on Rod Gibbs. A final judgment. But was it a personal judgment—or a political one?

Gibbs was strung up with his own velvet,

soaked in blue dye, and marked for death by
an unknown assailant or assailants, possibly a
secretive cult or shadowy conspiracy bent on
avenging lost jobs in America's industrial base.
Conspiracy Clearinghouse has learned that this
may be only the first Velvet Avenger murder of
many more to come, in retribution for the shat-
tered U.S. economy, which is the victim of vast
unseen forces conspiring to destroy American
industry and cripple . . .

Lacey had to stop reading before she turned as blue as
Rod Gibbs. Damon's story was accompanied by multiple
photographs of the dead man in all his deep-blue glory. *My
secret source sent Damon the same photos*. In contrast, *The
Eye*'s story seemed quite conservative, though certainly
more complete and accurate.

Lacey had read enough to know the story was vintage
Damon Newhouse. Damon's world was locked in an endless cosmic struggle of one shadowy conspiracy against another. She was grateful Brooke had warned her about the
story. Lacey closed her laptop and decided to think about
something more fun. Like what to wear.

Clothing, she decided as she dressed, could have magical properties. Protection. Passion. Transformation. But
that subtle magic depended on the wearer and her be-
lief in those transformative powers. Today Lacey needed
something fabulous. She pulled out a cropped black velvet jacket, with generous sleeves and frogs instead of
buttons. She paired it with a red wool skirt and a white
ruffled silk blouse, and she finished it with high-heeled
black leather boots. All that was missing from her look
was a whip.

Lacey would be ready for anything today.

She would need to be. Exquisitely bad timing found her
arriving at the front door of *The Eye* simultaneously with
Walt Pojack, the Newspaper Destroyer. She had taken a
moment to admire the paper's handsome location across
from Farragut Square. She picked up a colorful bouquet of
carnations, roses, and a few hothouse irises from the flower

seller on the corner outside the Metro. Then she ran into Pojack, and things began to go wrong.

He stepped into the first available elevator. Lacey couldn't avoid him gracefully or dash out rudely to avoid the sour vibes he emitted. After the Crystal City announcement, he knew he was unpopular, and yet he seemed to glory in it. Lacey sighed inwardly and walked in. She hit the button for her floor. She glanced at him and then stared straight ahead. She sniffed her flowers.

Pojack wore a boring brown suit, a tie with an Easter egg design, and a smirk on his face. He looked pretty jaunty for a man who wanted to gut *The Eye Street Observer*.

"Miss Smithsonian." He punched the sixth floor. "Our own little fashion reporter, isn't it?"

Is there a civil response to that? Lacey looked at him, in case he wanted to make a real comment. "Mr. Pojack." *Our own little Benedict Arnold.*

"Yes, I'm glad we met," he said. "You're on my list."

"Your list?" she said.

"When we reorganize the newspaper, there may not be room for the more superfluous departments. For instance, your little beat."

Little? His words hit her like a punch to the gut, and still he wore that supercilious smirk.

"My *little* beat? Why? I have a lot of readers." Lacey's head was suddenly swimming.

"That may be, and it will be taken under advisement, but consider this a friendly hint. You might want to brush up that résumé of yours, what there is of it," Pojack said. "It really is too bad there aren't any real journalism jobs out there anymore, isn't it?"

The slimy salamander had the nerve to smile. She loathed him.

The elevator opened. Lacey whirled to look Pojack in the eye.

"You can't cut my beat. This is Claudia Darnell's paper." And Claudia was depending on Lacey to stay on top of the murder at Dominion Velvet. She got off and glared at him. She held the door open for his answer.

"It's Claudia's paper for now, but remember, Ms. Smithsonian, nothing lasts forever," Pojack said. "Not newspapers. Not fashion. This is a newspaper, not a sideshow. Politics and government make this town tick. That's all people want to read about." The doors slid closed.

"Bet me! You—" But Pojack was gone. Lacey was talking to the closed elevator. "You bastard!" she whispered.

"Which bastard would you be talking about, Lacey?" Wiedemeyer overheard her as he scooted around the corner. "God knows there's a lot of bastards around these days." Wiedemeyer had a large cherry almond tart with a chocolate lace heart in his hand, today's love offering from Felicity. He licked some of the cherries, and Lacey fell in beside him as they trudged to the newsroom.

"Walt Pojack told me to polish my résumé. He's planning to kill my beat!"

"Your beat should kill his beat first. Except he doesn't have a beat. He's a filthy, dirt-eating rat bastard, the worst kind," Wiedemeyer declared, munching on his tart. "We can't let him kill your beat. Next he'll kill mine! He can't do this. He can't destroy *The Eye*. We won't let him."

"He said nobody's job is safe."

Wiedemeyer took another bite. "The Evil One has got to be stopped. That's all there is to it. How do we do it?" Lacey had just one small idea. It couldn't really make a difference, but *what the heck*. Wiedemeyer was still talking. "They can't take *The Eye* to Crystal City! The place is a black hole. A neurotoxin. A plague. A pox. A misery—"

"Harlan." Lacey interrupted his word association. "I hate to ask this, but do you think you might *possibly* cross Walt Pojack's path?" It was a vain hope that Harlan's celebrated jinx might somehow make Pojack suffer. But still, a hope.

"You're referring to my dubious reputation as a Jonah? Consider it done, Smithsonian." Wiedemeyer didn't take offense. He laughed out loud. "We'll wish a double whammy on him. He's on my list."

We all have a little list. Although no one really quite believed Harlan Wiedemeyer was a jinx, he seemed to have a curious effect on people. Lacey was nearly crushed to death by a Krispy Kreme Doughnuts sign after Wiedemeyer had insisted on driving her home in a rainstorm. After Wiede-meyer developed feelings for Felicity Pickles, her minivan was blown to pieces right outside *The Eye.* Immediately following a confrontation with Wiedemeyer, Capitol Hill reporter Peter Johnson's car was smashed by a D.C. Metro bus. *Coincidence?*

It was also widely accepted around *The Eye* that once you experienced the Wiedemeyer Whammy, you were in-oculated from further bad juju. *Reporters, not science majors.*

Logic and sense told Lacey there was no such thing as a jinx. Nobody could really believe Wiedemeyer was a bringer of bad luck or a boomerang of ill intent. Could they? Not even her editor, Douglas MacArthur Jones. Still, many people at the paper, including Mac, steered clear when they saw Wiedemeyer coming.

"It would be really nice, Harlan," Lacey said. "Very thoughtful of you. How about a triple whammy?"

He chuckled. "You know, I've never had the slightest interest in talking to that moron. But I'm going to hand that bastard today's paper. Personally. And I'll spit on it first. Maybe I'll even clap him on the back. All for a good cause, you know. Maybe his car will explode. Or the toad himself. Spontaneous human combustion. If he were human."

"All for a good cause." She was laughing again. Wiede-meyer always made her feel better. *Who doesn't appreciate a little death and dismemberment?*

Someone cast a large shadow that darkened Lacey's desk and hovered over her shoulder.

"Well, well, well. Lacey Smithsonian," a voice boomed. "My favorite reporter." Sarcasm was in the air. Like a fine shower of dust, it settled on her head.

Lacey glanced up at her visitor. A grin she recognized lit the face of the big African-American cop. "Fine day for a visit with my favorite reporter," he said.

"Detective Broadway Lamont. To what do I owe the pleasure?" *This can't be good,* she told herself. *He doesn't have a favorite reporter. He hates us all.* It was hard enough to concentrate after Pojack's bombshell, and now Broadway "the Bull" Lamont was dancing around her desk. What was up?

"I'm glad you consider me a pleasure. You must have a clear conscience," Lamont said. "Many people do not."

She raised her eyebrow at him. "Might have something to do with your being a homicide cop. And being so much larger than the average crook."

His laughter boomed across the cubicles, alarming Felicity. She popped up over the divider with a tray of cherry almond tarts and smiled at him. "Oh! I'd love to know what you think of one of my tarts, Detective Lamont."

He smiled broadly, like a shark. He ignored Lacey while he selected one of the tarts and took a bite, making a big show of it. "Mmmm. Mmmm." He gave a thumbs-up to Felicity, who beamed.

"We had red velvet cupcakes yesterday," Felicity said. "You missed them."

Lacey drummed her fingers on her desk. Wiedemeyer was away, laying the whammy on Pojack instead of where he belonged, making goo-goo eyes at Felicity. If he were there he would be retaliating at Lamont by telling some gruesome anecdote about radioactive German wild boars, or something equally appetizing.

"What brings you here, Broadway?" Lacey asked. "Tarts?"

"Ms. Pickles's tarts are a bonus. You got some coffee to wash this down with?"

"Follow me." Lacey grabbed her empty cup and led him to the small newsroom kitchen, where a fresh pot of the bilious brew awaited the unsuspecting. "Don't blame me if there are ill effects. Not everyone can handle fresh-brewed sludge."

Broadway helped himself to black coffee, without the help of cream or sugar. He took a sip and smacked his lips. "Just the way I like it. Police-quality coffee."

Lacey was dying to know what he wanted, but Broadway liked to draw out the suspense.

"I got to hand it to you, Smithsonian. No other reporter I know leads such an interesting life. But hey, we can't all be fashion reporters in the Nation's Capital, can we?"

"Lucky me. What's up?"

He drained his cup and poured another. "I got a call from the Virginia State Police. Agent name of Mordecai Caine wanted the lowdown on one Lacey Smithsonian. He Googled you. Seems my name popped up in some of your stories."

"Google strikes again," Lacey said. "Considering he didn't bother to spend much time questioning me, I'm flattered to be Googled."

"So, I asked what Lacey Smithsonian did to get on the radar of the Virginia troopers. I'm guessing it wasn't a parking ticket."

Lacey poured herself a cup of coffee and added plenty of cream and sugar. "What did he tell you?"

"Imagine my surprise! You, at the scene of a homicide. What are the odds? But this time, the stiff was blue." He shook his head. "That true?"

"You didn't read it in *The Eye*? Front page. My byline."

"Hell, Smithsonian, you know I try not to read the newspapers unless I'm in them. And especially not then. But I had to make an exception."

"What about Caine?"

"He must have read some of your stories. He thinks it's peculiar you've written about murder so often, seeing as how you're supposed to stick to hemlines and high heels. That sort of thing. Heck, even I think it's funny."

"Yeah, it's hilarious."

"Course, I think lots of strange things are funny. Caine asked me if you were trouble." Broadway paused for effect.

"I'm listening, Detective."

"I told him obviously you're trouble—you're a reporter—but for all that trouble, you were more interesting than most." He drained his second cup of coffee. "You got photographs? I saw the one in *The Eye*, but details get lost in newsprint. Photos can be manipulated."

"That photo was leaked to me by an unknown source. Really. Delivered anonymously and everything."

"An anonymous source? That all you got?" She was silent. "Don't play with me, Smithsonian. I'm not going to tell the troopers. I just want to view the hue of the dude. Between you and me, I got a bet running on this."

"Come on." She led him back to her desk and brought all the photos up on the screen. "I don't know who sent me the pictures. I turned them over to my editor."

Lamont leaned in for a closer view. "Whew. Smithsonian, that dude is really blue. You say he started out white? I've seen 'em a lot of colors here in D.C., black, white, brown, and every shade of café au lait. But I've never had a dark blue corpse. You mind printing that one out for me?"

"You going to win the bet?"

"Oh yeah, I'm gonna win that bet." He chuckled while Lacey made copies for him, several different shots of Rod Gibbs, full-length and up close. "These are real nice. You got a big envelope for these?"

Lacey rooted around and came up with an eight-by-ten envelope. "Stop by anytime," she said. "I'm a regular Fotomat."

"Stay safe, Smithsonian. And keep this crazy-ass murderer across the river and way down south."

"It's not me! Why does everybody think it's me?"

"You're just the chosen one. The messenger. If that Velvet Avenger makes it up to D.C., you let me know."

"What about the Virginia state cops?"

"What about 'em? Don't speed more than ten miles over the limit on I-95 and you'll be fine." He took a few steps, then added, "And you might try staying out of his investigation. I don't think Caine is as patient as I am. I am a saint. Did you hear?"

With that, Saint Broadway Lamont leaned over Felicity's desk, scooped up another cherry almond tart, and left the premises.

"You're a regular comedian, Broadway." Lacey contemplated her coffee and sipped. Police quality, Lamont called it? It was dreck. And now it was cold dreck. But at least she had custody of her FASHION *BITES!* mug.

chapter 23

It must be visiting day at the madhouse.

The guard at the front desk called Lacey: She had visitors. She wasn't expecting anyone. He hung up before giving her a name. She supposed she should be grateful for the warning. She'd had no warning about Broadway Lamont.

Stella was waiting for her in the lobby with Lady Gwendolyn Griffin, the Gorgon herself, who was not actually breathing fire or crowned with writhing serpents. *Maybe later.*

Gwendolyn Griffin looked perfectly normal, in a foreign-visitor way. She was standing next to Stella, who was showing off her now rhinestone-covered cast to the acclaim of all who saw it. The thing practically glowed. It was completely covered in valentine hearts, stars, swirls, and arrows. It must have weighed a ton. The cast almost competed with Stella's cleavage, which was displayed to advantage by a tight leopard-print sweater. Stella's Girls were entertaining the sports writers, a delivery man, and Tony Trujillo.

There was no competing with Stella, and Lacey didn't even try. Instead, she peered at Stella's future mother-in-law. Nigel's mother did indeed resemble a rather equine Eleanor Roosevelt, but not quite so much as her picture had suggested.

But why on earth were they there? Stella, no doubt, was planning some kind of diversion, and Lacey didn't have time for that.

"Lacey, this is Nigel's mom. Lady Gwendolyn." Stella

sent a pleading look to Lacey. "My best friend, Lacey Smithsonian."

"Lady Gwendolyn. It's so nice to meet you." Lacey shook the offered hand.

"Just Gwendolyn, please." She smiled with an alarming number of large, square teeth, and the woman hadn't heard of tooth whitener.

Gwendolyn Griffin was taller than Stella by a good five inches, and she had a couple of inches on Lacey. She was dressed in browns and beiges, pants with pleats and an elastic waistband, and sensible shoes. Lady G had pale blue eyes, a frizzy mop of mousy, gray-brown hair piled on top of her head, and not a stitch of makeup. Next to her, Stella looked like a bird of paradise. *Stella must be itching to get her fingers on that hair,* Lacey thought. But why come here instead of Stylettos?

"This is a surprise, Stella. I didn't expect you this morning."

"Lady Gwendolyn wanted to meet you," Stella said. "So I thought it would be a great idea to come here straight from the airport."

"Really? How special." *I'll never write a story today at this rate. Mac will not be happy.* "I'm pleased to—"

"You're *the* Lacey Smithsonian?" Gwendolyn spoke in plummy English tones, but she looked at Lacey with a discerning eye. It sounded like an accusation.

"Yes. Last I checked. But I thought Nigel would be showing you around, Mrs. Griffin. Or perhaps you would like to rest after such a long flight."

"Oh no, I slept on the plane, and my son and my husband abandoned me at the first possible moment. But that's quite all right. I wanted to see Stella's world all by myself."

"Isn't that nice," Lacey said. "Stella's world is right next door to my world." *Right next door, but around the bend.*

Gwendolyn pulled her lips back into that frightening smile. "Now, tell me, dear. Is it true? Are you the one who's been involved in all those murders?"

"I wouldn't say I was involved, exactly. I'm just a reporter. I just report."

"Lacey's so modest," Stella said. "But she's got lots of great stories. And she's tackled more than one killer. Literally. With all sorts of stuff. Like hairspray. And scissors."

"How lovely," Gwendolyn said. "Scissors can be so deadly."

"I had help. Even Stella has been involved in—"

"Oh yes, Stella saved all your news clippings for me."

"I'm sure she did." Lacey glared at Stella behind Gwendolyn's back.

"Turns out Lady G is a total mysteryholic, Lacey. Who knew?" Stella tried her *I'm so innocent* smile, but Lacey wasn't buying it.

"Thrillers, actually," Gwendolyn corrected. "I love the gritty realism of the hard-boiled, the noir, the seamy underbelly of society, if you like. The depths of human despair and depravity. That's my world."

"She likes those big fat books that are really bloody and gory," Stella added, as if it weren't completely clear.

"A really bloody thriller holds a mirror up to society, don't you think?" Gwendolyn pressed. "They show what depraved savages we really are." She had a frightening grin. People were starting to stare.

"Perhaps we should get some coffee. Or tea?" Lacey said, leading her visitors away from the lobby and the prying eyes of her coworkers. And especially coworkers like Harlan Wiedemeyer, the death and dismemberment specialist. Lady G would never let *him* get away. *And I will have jinxed Stella's future mother-in-law.* "I'll just collect my things." Lacey found them a bench. She whispered to Stella, "You so owe me one."

When Lacey returned, she found the women deep in conversation with Wiedemeyer. *Where did he come from?*

"Yes, indeed, Lady Gwendolyn," he was saying, "the world is full of scummy bastards! Why, I could tell you tales to make your ears bleed. Men turned into sausage, sliced to ribbons, drowned in chocolate. And just this week, a man stabbed to death with a rack of elk antlers! It's a wonder we walk out of our doors in the morning, and survive to go home at night."

Lady G was hooked. "And these ghastly accidents you've described, the sausage plant and the chocolate factory. Couldn't they all be *murder*?"

"Each and every one of them!" Wiedemeyer grinned.

Lacey gently wrested her away from *The Eye*'s documenter of doom. She dared not dwell on the havoc Lady G and Wiedemeyer could wreak if they teamed up.

"What a charming little man. I do hope we run into him again," Gwendolyn said.

Lacey escorted Gwendolyn and Stella across Farragut Square. Someone had built a snowman beneath the statue of Admiral David Farragut, mimicking his telescope-in-hand pose with a tree limb.

The women had barely settled in at the Firehook Bakery with their coffee and blueberry muffins when Lady Gwendolyn Griffin launched into her purpose: to pump Lacey for information on D.C.'s mean streets and slimy underbelly.

"The timing of our trip simply couldn't be better," Gwendolyn said. "I had heard something of your exploits from my Nigel. All the excitement last month, leg injuries all round, and the betrothal. And your sharpshooting. Well-done, my dear! However, I had no idea you'd be involved in yet another murder. And so soon. How nice."

"It's not like I plan these things."

"I understand the funeral is tomorrow. You'll be attending, I presume?" Gwendolyn had an unhealthy gleam in her eyes.

"Well, I do need to cover it for the paper...." Lacey tried to think of a way to head Gwendolyn off at the pass, but she was waving a copy of Lacey's own story in front of her. Stella shook her head as if to say, *What can I do?*

"I believe killers often attend their victims' funerals, do they not? Where is this Black Martin, Virginia? Is it far?" Gwendolyn inquired.

Lacey tried to catch her friend's eye, but Stella was deliberately avoiding eye contact. "Far. Far away. About two or three hours southwest from here."

Gwendolyn leaned forward, clutching the paper. "Your

story says the widow intends to have an open casket. Good lord! Do you mean to say she is going to put that freakish indigo man on display for all and sundry to gape at?"

"I don't believe that will happen. I'm sure she was just carried away by the moment. Surely she'll reconsider and do the right thing, especially after he's been through an autopsy. Don't you think?"

"How disappointing. I should so like to see that. It's a shame we have no time to attend, to see whether the widow does or does not. I've sometimes daydreamed about being a widow. Purely hypothetical, of course." Gwendolyn added sugar and cream to her tea. "I trust we can count on you to tell us all about it? In living color, as it were?"

"No problem." Lacey started to relax. "Color commentary, my specialty."

"What is your professional opinion, Ms. Smithsonian? How soon will this dreadful serial killer strike again? Soon, I suppose?" She took a bite of her muffin. "This is delicious."

"Lady G says this is just the first of many blue bodies to come," Stella said.

"It's obvious this is a fetish killer," Gwendolyn said. "They strike again and again, with savage brutality."

"A fetish killer?" Stella said. "I'm so glad you're having a good time, Lady G." Gwendolyn smiled her approval.

"This is an isolated case. So far as I know," Lacey said.

"This is what we know," Gwendolyn continued. "The Black Martin Avenger makes a trophy of his kill. He straps the victim to the heavy machinery, he binds him with velvet, a soft, sensual material, and then mocks the victim by dyeing him blue. The mockery is the tip-off. Don't you see? He's clearly sending a message. And he's keeping some souvenir in his lair. A deep, dark blue souvenir, I suspect, in a deep, dark blue lair."

"Perhaps you should write one of those gory thrillers yourself."

Gwendolyn giggled with delight. "I'm sure I could, if only I had the time to sit down and do it. Now, you two think about this killer. I'm going to find the loo."

Gwendolyn exited, leaving Lacey openmouthed. Stella

put her hand on Lacey's arm. "I know I totally owe you. But really, I think she's enjoying herself. Don't you?"

"She's a bloodthirsty old thing, isn't she?"

"Totally. And I'm completely terrified of her, but it's a little weird," Stella said. "I don't think she hates me. Not yet anyway. I never thought I could get along with someone like Lady Gwendolyn. And my guy's *mother*? Who woulda thought?"

"I suspect, Stella, you are her own priceless exotic souvenir."

"Good thing, huh? If it keeps her from sabotaging me and Nigel."

"What do you think about her hair?" Lacey was surprised Stella would be seen in public with her soon-to-be mother-in-law with that indescribable hair. After all, she was a stylist; she had a reputation to protect.

"Her hair! Oh my God! Can you believe that frizz? I just have to find the right moment to take her to the salon and introduce her to conditioner. Some product will work wonders. A good cut and color. That shade of dead mouse has got to go. Add some makeup, and who knows?" Stella counted tasks on her freshly rhinestoned nails. "If anyone on earth can make her look human, it's me. Right?"

"What about the brows?"

"Oh, God. The brows. Those thornbushes have to go."

Gwendolyn sailed back from the ladies' room, refreshed. "I'd so dearly love to go to that funeral. Don't you think there is *some* chance the blue man will be on display? This is, after all, a once-in-a-lifetime opportunity."

"Not really." Lacey looked to Stella. *Help me out here, Stella!*

"We have so much to do," Stella said. "With the wedding and all."

"And Stella is dying to show you where she works," Lacey said. "She might even be willing to demonstrate her makeover skills. She's the best, you know."

"I suppose you're right," Gwendolyn said. "I must say these two, my Nigel and Stella, really seem to be rushing things. Hence, I leaped to the obvious conclusion, but Stella assures me she's not in the family way. Not that that would be a bad thing. It would be wonderful, naturally. I love weddings and babies and so forth. Who doesn't? But a funeral! Oh, I do love a really good funeral."

A grandchild would always be welcome, but not quite as much fun as seeing a dead blue guy in a blue coffin. Lacey had to stop herself from laughing.

Stella has met her match.

chapter 24

"Smithsonian, what are you working on?" Mac was peering over her shoulder at her computer screen, his bushy eyebrows knit together in a frown.

"I have no earthly idea," Lacey replied. There were too many distractions in the newsroom today, what with unexpected visitors and all. It seemed destined to be the kind of day in which no actual work would get done. And she had an unexpected invitation in her e-mail. She was just reading it when Mac arrived.

"You better get an idea. That's what we do here."

It occurred to Lacey that another distraction might be good for her editor. And good for her.

"I have an idea, Mac. Felicity just made cherry tarts. Yum. Get 'em while they're hot." She grabbed her coat and purse and notebook, while Mac followed his nose to the tarts. Mac selected the most perfect tart and turned around.

"Cherry tarts! So, Smithsonian—" But she was gone.

An e-mail message from her publisher, Claudia, urged Lacey to meet her at the University Club. Lacey didn't know what to expect from the encounter, but at least she would get to see the inside of another grand old Washington building. One of the perks of her job, a job she might not have much longer if Walt Pojack had his way. *I'll be seeing the inside of the unemployment office.*

Lacey hailed a taxi on Eye Street. The University Club was only about five blocks from *The Eye*'s offices, just up Sixteenth Street between the *National Geographic* and

The Washington Post buildings, but with Claudia waiting for her, she wasn't about to take a leisurely stroll.

The University Club did not disappoint her, with its lush interior, the impressive center stairway, and the powder blue ladies' room. The entryway and lobby featured beautiful old paneling, plush red carpet, and three impressive crystal chandeliers. She briefly wondered how much the dues were. It didn't matter; they were obviously about two chandeliers above her pay grade. Her wardrobe might meet the club's dress code, but her salary never would.

As she walked in, the Taft Restaurant was to her left, and to her right, the club's library. Two women, deep in conversation, glided past Lacey and turned into the Taft. Lacey was riveted. The not-quite-middle-aged blonde wore a tight faux-leopard-print dress and sky-high matching heels. The other, a brunette of similar age, defied all Washington codes of dress in a hot pink suit and a pink-and-navy hat that looked like a gigantic piece of ribbon candy on her head. High-class working girls? Trophy wives? Divas on tour in a Broadway show? Delicious questions destined to go unanswered.

A hostess ushered Lacey into the red-walled library. Not every library could boast its own bar, but this one did, as well as cream-colored shelves full of books and portraits of club notables. The publisher of *The Eye* awaited her in a wing chair in the corner. Today Claudia was back in top form, wearing a navy pinstripe business suit nipped in at the waist. Every strand of her platinum pageboy was in place, and her ten perfect nails were all present and accounted for. She was wearing her game face.

"Lacey, I'm so glad you could make it." Claudia smiled broadly.

As usual, I wonder if I had some choice in the matter. Lacey smiled back. "What did you want to see me about?" She couldn't stand the suspense, particularly after Walt Pojack's nasty crack about the paper not needing a fashion reporter. She hoped this wasn't about her résumé.

"I wanted to discuss this Rod Gibbs mess outside of the office. It's a very curious affair."

Lacey relaxed slightly. "Everyone is curious about it.

But I'm a little surprised we published one of the photos of the body."

"We had to run it. Otherwise the world—and *The Washington Post*—would think we were hiding the truth. Either way it was dicey. Now we can be accused of mere sensationalistic journalism." She smiled. "Again. I'd rather go with sensationalism than cover-up any day. At least the public knows we're still here. We're still a newspaper."

Did that mean Lacey's job was safe? She tried to put it from her mind.

A waitress carrying a silver tray approached their table quietly. She set down cups and saucers on the small table in front of them. She poured coffee and left the pot and a plate of cookies. Lacey tried the coffee. *Mmmm, real coffee, not newsroom sludge.*

"Lacey, is Honey Gibbs really planning to have an open casket for Rod's funeral? After the autopsy? That can't be true, can it?" It seemed to be the question of the day. "She's not going to put him on display, is she? Like—like a prize blue marlin?"

"That's what Honey told me, so that's what I wrote. She seemed serious at the time, but she might change her mind. I was planning to go to the funeral for a follow-up." Lacey Smithsonian was not about to miss a blue guy in a casket, open or closed.

"You don't intend to unmask a killer while you're there, do you?" Claudia smiled.

Lacey wasn't sure whether Claudia was teasing. "Nope, not a chance. I have no idea who the killer is. I just want to follow up on my story."

"That's good. I've decided not to attend," Claudia said. "It will be a zoo, and I think it best not to add any more fuel to the fire. Keep your eyes and ears open. I expect you to report back to me."

"That's my job." Lacey paused for a minute. "Claudia, I have to ask one thing. I ran into Walt Pojack this morning."

"That man!" Claudia snorted. She played with a large cocktail ring on her right hand. "I imagine you have all kinds of questions. I've been getting them all morning. All I can tell you is that his announcement about moving to

Crystal City was very premature." She lowered her voice. "As I said, I don't want to add more fuel to the fire."

"Then the move is not a sure thing?" Lacey held her breath.

"Nothing is a sure thing at this point. Crystal City is just one train of thought. I want to stay right where we are, but I'm exploring every option."

"But why Crystal City?"

A look of annoyance crossed Claudia's face. "Walt's idea. He has a line on a building we can get very cheap. He has both the State of Virginia and Arlington County throwing tax incentives at us to move. He's working all the angles for us, and he's been lobbying for it for a while now. But I'm not at all convinced that move would be wise in the long run."

Lacey nodded. Some kind of power struggle was playing out on the sixth floor of *The Eye*. Was Pojack sneaking around behind Claudia's back, making deals, trying to force her hand? Wiedemeyer's theory was gaining credence.

"A lot of people are alarmed about his big announcement," Lacey said.

"Don't worry about him. I'll take care of Walt Pojack," Claudia said. Lacey just hoped Claudia would win this battle.

Claudia glanced up over Lacey's head. Lacey turned to see the third Dominion Velvet partner walk through the door. Claudia put out her hand and he clasped it.

"Tazewell, good of you to come. I want you to meet Lacey Smithsonian, our lead reporter on Rod Gibbs."

"Pleased to meet you," he said, and shook her hand, but Lacey guessed that *pleased* was the last thing Congressman Tazewell Flanders was. His smile merely twitched the corners of his mouth. Lacey wondered if he had been Botoxed. She was willing to bet on it. But at any rate, he wasn't going to waste a campaign smile on her.

Flanders dressed in a navy bespoke suit, crisp white shirt, and dark red tie. His politician-issue tan was buttery, his brown hair streaked with gold strands, and his teeth were whitened. He certainly was ready for his close-up, and his yet-to-be-announced, highly anticipated campaign for governor of Virginia.

"Congressman Flanders wanted to talk to you in person," Claudia said.

"So there is no confusion to my meaning," Flanders began. "This is the only time I plan to talk about the tragedy in Black Martin, at Dominion Velvet, or about Rod Gibbs—other than in my prepared statement, which will be issued by my staff later today." He handed her a single sheet of paper on his congressional letterhead. "Here's an advance copy for you, and I'll answer any questions you might have. You have a scoop, Ms. Smithsonian."

She quickly scanned the release. Politicians' news statements were routinely issued as late in the day as possible, after most of the print media's deadlines had passed, but miraculously just in time for the broadcast news. Lacey knew that game well. Broadcast anchors would simply regurgitate the congressman's press release, and no hard questions would be asked until the next print news cycle. It was another daily example of how politicians and their press secretaries used the media. But he owed Claudia a scoop, because they were partners, and presumably friends.

What more are they to each other? Lacey wondered how her publisher had gotten mixed up with such odious men—Rod Gibbs, Walt Pojack, and now Tazewell Flanders.

"What happened to Rod Gibbs is obviously a tragedy, Lacey," Flanders said. "It highlights issues of job creation I'll be talking about in my campaign for governor."

"So you really are running for governor of Virginia?"

"Yes." He smiled a smug little smile. "You heard it here first, Lacey. But it's not official yet."

Smart politicians always tried to remember the reporter's name and use it in every other sentence, to make the reporter feel they were sharing some special intimate connection. *Ick.*

"Rod Gibbs was a friend of yours?" she asked.

"No, Rod Gibbs was not a friend." Flanders said it a little too fast. "That is, we were associated through our business partnership in the factory. You might call that a case of—strange bedfellows. The truth is—" The congressman paused. "I'm from Black Martin myself and I have strong feelings for my hometown. We three tried to help keep the factory alive, keep those jobs alive. If not with velvet, then with some new high-tech industry at the plant. We were looking at every possible option. But the economy went south on us at the worst possible time."

"New industry?"

"If we'd found a compatible use, we hoped to update the factory to produce something more technologically advanced than velvet. It would have cost money, but there are state and federal grants for that sort of thing."

"But what about the velvet?" Lacey remembered the shimmering rolls of velvet and felt a pang of loss.

"Velvet is too expensive to manufacture here anymore, Lacey. Rod Gibbs was supposed to deliver a new business plan. Unfortunately, we sank a lot of money into it, and it didn't pan out. None of his plans ever did. Now Rod dead."

"What kind of business were you looking at?" Lacey asked.

"It's pointless to discuss that now."

"Did he produce a business plan?"

"Several of them. Unfortunately, not one of them was viable," Flanders said.

"How long have you been involved with the factory?'

"For about five years. That's when I bought my shares, along with Claudia."

"How did you get involved with Dominion Velvet?"

"I got a call from Gibbs, who informed me that some of the family's shares would be coming up for sale. It was a way to have a voice in the leading industry in the town where I grew up."

"And you trusted Rod?"

His jaw clenched. "I had no reason not to trust Rod Gibbs, not at that time. He was an old . . . associate. Our fathers were once, ah—friends. It sounded like a good business opportunity, a chance to give something back to the community."

Claudia set her cup down. "We knew that if we acted as a bloc we could direct factory policy and provide some oversight. The factory had only absentee ownership for so long. We, the three of us, believed it needed local control, to save local jobs."

"So that leaves us with the question, who wanted him dead?" Lacey asked.

Flanders looked to Claudia. His lips twitched again.

"Rod could be difficult to deal with, but I had no idea how much he seemed to enjoy bullying people," Claudia said.

"Rod Gibbs was a hard man to like," Flanders added. "But that does not excuse this barbarous murder. I'm sure the state police, in their investigation, will find the perpetrator. I won't be speaking about this ongoing investigation in my campaign. It's tragic, but it's in the past. I'll be talking about the future of Virginia, Lacey. It's time for all of us to move forward."

"But this thing might not be over. Some of the workers I talked to thought the killer might be some kind of avenger for their lost jobs. They say the killer isn't finished." *Why not yank his chain a little?* she thought. *See if he's up to speed.*

"That's preposterous. This was clearly some sort of personal grudge against Gibbs. It has to be."

"Do you think it will be damaging to your campaign for governor of Virginia to be involved in this?"

"I am *not* involved in this, Lacey. This unfortunate situation has nothing to do with me or my campaign for Virginia's future. But I do believe the Commonwealth of Virginia should establish a task force to explore how we can get our economy back on its feet and create more jobs, and as governor I will lead that effort. Our people, like our skilled workforce in Black Martin, are our state's most important resource," Tazewell Flanders said, sounding just like a sound bite for his campaign.

This meeting, it appeared, was not just the congressman's way of dealing with Rod Gibbs; it was a warm-up for a gubernatorial campaign speech. Was he just trying it out on her? *Do politicians never stop politicking?* Lacey sighed. She knew the answer.

"I'm curious, Congressman. Why didn't you speak to our political reporter, Peter Johnson?"

"The man's a dunderhead," he said bluntly. Claudia ducked her head and hid a smile. "Off the record." *His first unguarded comment,* Lacey thought. *And right on the money.* "I agreed to see you, Ms. Smithsonian," he continued, "because Claudia assured me you are an intelligent and balanced reporter. She said you have a unique, nonpolitical perspective." Flanders started to look over Lacey's head. He checked his watch.

"I want to make it clear that everything Tazewell says here is on the record," Claudia interjected.

He gave her a pained look, but he nodded. "Except that *dunderhead* remark."

"Will you be attending the funeral?" Lacey asked.

"I'm trying to clear my schedule, but I don't know if it will be possible." In politician-speak, that meant the congressman planned to be as far away from Black Martin and Rod Gibbs's funeral as he could possibly be. Another galaxy, if one were available.

"Do you know Honey Gibbs?"

He took a moment before answering. "I know the family. Not that well. I sent my condolences to the widow." Meaning the congressman's staff sent them.

"I understand you offered to build Black Martin a new high school gymnasium if you're elected governor. With your own money, if necessary."

Flanders had inherited his money. He'd never actually held a job, except in Congress, which many people, even in Washington, would say doesn't quite count. He shrugged. "Perhaps that was premature. But the town needs something to cheer them up."

"And it would cheer them up to have a new gym?" Lacey thought it was one of the sillier things she'd ever heard. *That week.* "Wouldn't more jobs cheer them up? If they had jobs, they could vote on a school-bond issue and build their own gym."

"Jobs are key, Lacey, but the gym is outdated. Small towns bond over high school sports. It builds community. We'll be looking into every possibility to keep Black Martin a viable community."

The gym idea probably also had something to do with

his own high school athletic career as a football jock. *Maybe they'll name the gym after him.* Flanders looked at his watch again.

Lacey knew he had said what he came to say, and perhaps a bit more: It was a shame about Rod Gibbs, but let the cops worry about it. He wasn't going to the funeral, and his campaign for governor was a hell of a lot more important than one dead blue guy. And a town full of lost jobs. *Let them drown their sorrows in high school sports.*

"Just one last question, Congressman Flanders," Lacey said. People usually relaxed when she indicated the interview was ending. "Where were you when Rod died?"

He looked startled. "That is impertinent, young lady. However, for the record, I was with my political advisers that night. A strategy meeting. Claudia can tell you. She was there." Lacey looked to Claudia, who nodded.

"And a follow-up question. Have you received a blue velvet ribbon in the mail?"

"What? Why would I get something like that? Is it a charity thing of some kind?" His puzzled look said he took this to be just one more sympathy ribbon, like pink ribbons for breast cancer, or yellow ribbons for loved ones in the military.

Claudia stepped in. "One came in my mail yesterday, Tazewell. Postmarked Black Martin. It could be a joke."

"Not very funny," Flanders said.

"Or it could be from Rod Gibbs's killer," Lacey said. That brought a moment of silence to the group.

"I'll check with my staff," Flanders said at last. "They sort all my mail. I only get what I need to see. I'm looking for a blue velvet ribbon, is that it? Is there a note of some kind?"

"I didn't receive a note with mine," Claudia said. "I wouldn't have thought much about it, but Lacey thinks it might be important." Flanders sighed again, exasperated.

"Rod Gibbs was tied onto the spool with strips of velvet," Lacey explained, "rather like velvet ribbon. The ribbon in Claudia's mail matched the Midnight Blue color that Gibbs was dyed. It might be a threat. Or just a prank."

"Very well. I see your point. I'll have someone check

and get back to you at *The Eye*. Just so you both know, I think this is ridiculous."

Claudia turned to Lacey. "Thank you for coming, Lacey. I'll see you at the office." *Dismissed again.* Lacey was used to it.

She looked back over her shoulder as she left the library. Claudia and Tazewell Flanders were putting their heads together in a tête-à-tête.

Lacey heard him say, "You can't be serious, Claudia. . . ."

chapter 25

The fading February sun cast a pale gold light through the windows of the newsroom. Lacey was filing her follow-up story, revealing that Gibbs was shot before he was dunked in the dye vat. The medical examiner confirmed that he did not drown. Rod Gibbs was already dead when he was dyed blue. Lacey added a sidebar with Congressman Flanders's comments

The sky was deepening, and a chilly night was settling on the fading day. Lacey leaned back in her chair and watched as lit windows in neighboring buildings created tableaux of workers getting ready to go home, comforting in their sameness, their everydayness. She became aware of heads around her swiveling at the sight of Vic striding into the newsroom. He wore the leather jacket that Lacey had bought him for Christmas.

Lacey caught her breath at the sight of him, a little click of the heart, and hoped he would always affect her that way. He noted her look and smiled back, lighting up his face.

"Vic, I didn't think I'd see you today."

"I was in the neighborhood. Figured I'd drop by before I head to Black Martin tonight."

"But—" It looked like Lacey would be driving down alone tomorrow.

"I need to talk to Turtledove and see how things are going, and I want to be on-site early, with the funeral first thing in the morning. Want to get some coffee? I might have some food for thought."

"Sounds appetizing. How about some real food? I haven't eaten yet."

"Your wish is my command."

"If only." Lacey laughed at the thought. She noticed Wiedemeyer listening in on their conversation. "Hello, Harlan."

"Ah, love is in the air. The pint-sized archer of *amour* unsheathes his arrows." Wiedemeyer drew an invisible bow and shot an invisible arrow at Vic. "Bull's-eye. Cupid strikes again, straight through the heart. You're doomed, Victor Donovan. I'm doomed. All men are doomed by their ladies' love. We're the lucky bastards, wouldn't you say? Doomed to love!"

"What's wrong with him?" Vic asked Lacey.

"Something in the coffee," Lacey answered. "Or the cookies." Felicity's second treat of the day. The food editor was cooking on all burners, and there seemed to be no slowing her down.

"Love, *amour, amore.*" Wiedemeyer trundled into Felicity's cubicle and drew heart shapes in the air. Felicity balanced a large tray of Valentine cookies and giggled as they kissed. This afternoon's delicacy was pink-iced, heart-shaped cookies with chocolate filigree on top. There were also arrow-shaped cookies with red frosting.

Lacey wondered how much time it took to produce the mountains of food that Felicity brought in every day. Sure, it was "research" for her column, but this was ridiculous. It was a full-scale sugar and carb attack. With the stress Lacey was under these days, it was getting harder and harder to resist.

"We're engaged." Felicity flashed her diamond solitaire for Vic's inspection. *Like he didn't know.*

"Seize the moment, Donovan. Valentine's Day is just around the corner. None of us is getting any younger. Someone could come after you with a rack of daggerlike elk antlers." Wiedemeyer helped himself to one of Felicity's cookies and gestured with it between bites. "Love is grand."

"Elk antlers?" Vic looked baffled.

Lacey grabbed her purse and coat and Vic. "Dinner, darling. I never did get lunch. Remember?"

"Another cookie for the road?" Felicity asked. "I'm writing about what to feed your significant other on Valentine's Day." As she offered the tray to Vic, newsroom feeders began to surface like a school of sharks, led by the most notorious sugar fiends of all, editor Mac Jones and police reporter Tony Trujillo. Felicity had trained them well. She beamed at them. They were her Pavlovian lapdogs, and she the mad food scientist.

Lacey held on tight to Vic and her warm, fluffy mouton coat to avoid taking a cookie. She and Felicity might be friendlier these days, but the food editor was still a one-woman diet-demolition team, skulking about with her sweets and treats. Lacey's stomach growled. Tony took a bite out of a cookie and made *yum* sounds.

"Felicidad, you are the queen of tarts."

"And the queen of hearts," Wiedemeyer added gallantly.

Mac grabbed a cookie too. "Are there more desserts for your feature, or is this it?"

"Oh, there's more, Mac." Felicity picked up one of her carefully crafted cookies and admired it. "I'm working on a special coffee cake with strawberries and chocolate for breakfast in bed. And what to bring to your office mates. I'm perfecting the red velvet cupcakes, with a twist. And this time the recipes will be simple enough for *anyone* to make." Felicity cast a glance in Lacey's direction, and everyone laughed. Except Lacey.

"I can cook perfectly well when I want to. I simply choose not to," Lacey said. "Not every day. I can shoot a gun too, when I want to. Keep that in mind."

Mac smiled and ignored her. A well-fed editor was a happy editor. "Keep me posted, Pickles. I want to ride shotgun on your story." He picked up another heart and an arrow cookie. "Pretty."

Vic began to reach for one, but Lacey grabbed his hand and led him away. "Don't want to ruin your appetite. For *amour*."

*   *   *

"You mentioned food for thought?" Lacey said. Vic took her to a Lebanese restaurant, where the waiters were setting down piping-hot pita bread.

"Yep, I did say that." Vic was enjoying making her wait.

"Hey, spill. Please! Spill!"

"You're so impatient," he laughed. "It's cute. Okay. I had a chat with Gavin Armstrong. You remember him."

"Dudley Do-Right. Who could forget?" Lacey sat up straighter. "So this is about our blue guy?"

"Sort of. Turns out the security cameras at Dominion Velvet were turned off that night."

"The night Rod Gibbs was dispatched to blue heaven, I take it?" She leaned forward. "So there are no pictures? No killer on film?"

"No pictures." Vic dipped a piece of bread from the basket in olive oil.

"What about fingerprints?" She broke off a piece of bread.

"That's the interesting part, Lacey. They had some of Wade Dinwiddy's prints. It seems when females worked late at the plant, he'd turn on the cameras and move them around so he could watch the women. He liked to spy on the ladies. He swears he didn't touch the cameras that night. The rest of the fingerprints belonged to . . . Rod Gibbs."

"You're kidding. You're telling me our dead guy turned off the very cameras that might have told us who killed him and dumped him in the tub?"

"Ironic, isn't it? Gibbs had no particular reason to mess with them, but apparently he did."

Lacey frowned. "So Gibbs arrived at the factory that night, he got the security guy drunk, and then he switched off his own cameras? But why?"

Vic perused the menu. "That's the million-dollar question."

"To hide something he was doing? Something illegal? Nicholson suspected Gibbs of stealing from the company. Maybe he went back to cover his tracks."

"Maybe. And something else. The state cops found a few things at the bottom of the vat."

"Stop playing with me, Sean Victor Donovan."

"Oooh, all three names. I must be in big trouble." He smiled at her reaction. "It seems they found Gibbs's wallet, some change, about a hundred dollars in greenbacks that are now bluebacks. And they found the gun that killed him. It belonged to . . . Rod Gibbs. No fingerprints."

"Gibbs's own gun?" She whistled. "And a hundred dollars? The killer may have been a worker facing unemployment, but didn't take the money? I wonder why."

"It would be interesting to find out. For the cops, for the state police, for the professionals. Not for you and me. They can figure out why Rod Gibbs was there and who killed him without our help. Right, Lacey?"

"I don't know what you're trying to say, Vic. I'm not getting any more involved in this mess than I have to. For my job. Besides, I already filed my story today."

Vic raised an eyebrow. "And by the way, you didn't hear any of this from me."

"Of course not, darling. But what about your country song?"

The story had hooked her and it would hook the reader. News was a funny business. Some stories caught the public's imagination. Others never would. There might be hundreds of murders a year in the District, and only a handful would receive any significant press. In a small town like Black Martin, Virginia, Rod Gibbs would be news for years. Gibbs was unimportant to the rest of the world, but throw a little blue dye in the mix, and he was sure to become notorious on tabloid newsstands across the region.

Vic ordered their drinks, and Lacey picked up Vic's copy of *The Washington Post*, which finally had a small story on Gibbs's death. It was hidden on the inside of the Metro section and given only three paragraphs, demonstrating how unimportant the story was to *The Post*.

"Typical of the Other Newspaper in town," Lacey said. "If they don't write it first, it doesn't exist." She read the headline aloud to Vic.

**BUSINESS ASSOCIATE OF EYE STREET PUBLISHER
FOUND DEAD: POLICE SUSPECT FOUL PLAY**

Lacey was aghast. Vic just laughed. "Oh, there's a classic headline for you to pass around the newsroom!" he said. "Gibbs was hit on the head, shot in the chest, strung up with velvet, and dyed blue—and they merely *suspect* foul play?"

"In the District," Lacey reflected, "the cops might have called that a suicide."

chapter 26

It's not every day a woman gets to bury a big blue devil.

Honey Gibbs made sure her husband's funeral would become a local—if not a national—legend, the kind of memory that Black Martin natives would savor and pass around till it was blown up into a tale of shock and awe.

"I saw him with my own eyes," they would say. "He was the color of a bowl of blueberries." Maybe they would add, "He really did look like a blue devil."

Rod Gibbs's body was on display, as Honey had promised, the center of attention, in front of the minister's podium. Rod was looking considerably more peaceful than the last time Lacey had seen him. His face didn't seem to be any the worse for the autopsy. But he was still many shades of blue. His cerulean eyes were now closed and his royal blue tongue was pushed back behind closed blue-black lips, with a trace of pink lipstick overlay. He rested in a light blue, eighteen-gauge steel casket with a white velvet interior, providing a nice contrast to all that indigo.

There wasn't much the funeral home could do about Rod's color. There had clearly been an attempt to mask the permanent dye with a little makeup, but his Midnight Blue tint bled right through. Rod was wearing the dark blue suit and shirt that Honey had selected. His hands were folded over his chest and a pale blue paisley tie (courtesy of Honey). Rod Gibbs looked like a prop in a surrealist play, not a real corpse. A play that Honey Gibbs was directing. A play that was assured of spectacular notices.

Lacey left Alexandria in her vintage green BMW before

six in the morning and arrived in Black Martin at eight-thirty. The funeral was scheduled for ten. But even at that early hour, the mortuary chapel was almost full of waiting spectators. Lacey felt they couldn't quite be called mourners. In anticipation of a maximum-capacity crowd today, folding doors on either side of the main room had been opened and chairs set out for the overflow.

Dressing for this particular funeral was tricky. Wearing black might communicate a grief Lacey didn't feel, and she might end up looking either mocking or morose. Wearing any shade of blue would be ridiculous under the circumstances. Red, which could signal hatred or passion, was always inappropriate at a funeral. Pink would be too perky. It was a fashion conundrum.

She finally settled on her dark green, vintage wool suit from the late Forties. She loved the green velvet chesterfield collar and cuffs and covered buttons. She appreciated the way it fit snugly at her waist. The suit made her feel strong and capable. A great pair of violet suede pumps finished the look. Lacey thought the outfit was both attractive and appropriate. And it featured a touch of velvet. Somehow this occasion called for a nod to velvet. And no more than a nod.

She told the mortuary assistant she was a member of the press, and Lacey was shown to a reserved seat on the side, near the front. She didn't know whether Honey Gibbs had loved or hated her articles in *The Eye*, but Lacey didn't question her good luck at snagging a ringside seat. The assistant even let Lacey bring her morning latte with her, as long as she disposed of it before the service began.

Lacey made herself comfortable. Soon she was joined by other reporters, including local newshound Will Adler, looking like a pallbearer in a dark suit, white shirt, and dark tie. A television reporter and cameraman from Richmond were informed they could not shoot footage during the funeral. They filmed Gibbs in his coffin, and contented themselves with setting up at the entrance and practicing news bites.

By far the most interesting character was a reporter from the *National Enquirer*. His press badge said he was

Glen Potts. The man was about fifty years old, pudgy, with thinning hair on a large round head. He wore a tan sports coat, white shirt, striped tie, and baggy khaki slacks. Lacey was willing to bet he wore a variation of that outfit every day of the week. *Inquiring minds want to know: Why do reporters dress this way?*

The *Enquirer*'s Glen Potts did not introduce himself to the other reporters. He walked right up to the casket and took up-the-nostril shots of the dead man with a small digital camera. He returned to his seat among the crowd and shunned the other press. Lacey didn't blame him. Even with its nomination for a Pulitzer, working for the *Enquirer* was its own punishment, and perhaps, its own reward.

"I didn't know they had actual reporters," Adler said. He seemed more pleasant today, being allowed to sit with the big city reporters.

"What did you think?" Lacey asked, amused. "Somebody has to make it all up."

"I thought the editors just sat around throwing darts at a big chart on the wall. Like they throw a dart and hit the fat-actress story block, so they write about how she only has two years to live because she's going to explode or something. Or they throw a dart and hit the Elvis block, so Elvis has to surface in a shack in Montana and he's going on tour, but his nose froze off and he's having plastic surgery first. That kind of thing."

"It would simplify the job, that's for sure. Maybe dead blue guy wasn't on the chart."

Adler smiled at her. "They'll have to add that now. And to think, Rod Gibbs is going to add a story block to the *National Enquirer.*"

"How does it feel to be part of tabloid history?"

"It's a proud moment for Black Martin. Those *Enquirer*s are going to sail off the grocery store racks here. Do you think they'll put him on the front page?"

"I'm just sorry the *Weekly World News* folded. We won't get to hear about Gibbs being a blue-skinned alien and Bat Boy appearing at the funeral."

"Ah, the golden days of journalism are over," Adler said. Lacey looked for Vic and didn't see him at first. Then out of the corner of her eye she spied him talking with the mortuary director. Tom Nicholson was with him. Lacey didn't try to distract him. It was enough to know he was in the room. She could tell by the slight turn of his head that he had spotted her. He smiled, looking seriously sexy in his suit and sunglasses. They were aware of each other.

Someone in front of the casket snickered. From where she sat, Lacey could just see Gibbs's blue nose peeking up above the velvet-lined casket. She walked over to take another look. Had she missed anything? No. Rod looked just as weird the second time.

Mac insisted he needed a photo to go with the funeral story. She scanned the crowd and was grateful when she saw *The Eye*'s head photographer arrive. Long, tall Hansen would spare her the indignity of taking out her own digital camera and shooting a photo of a blue corpse in his blue coffin. Lacey suspected Hansen was not just getting a photo for the paper, but documenting the event for Claudia. *Better Hansen than me.*

Hansen was formal today. With his usual blue jeans, he wore a blue tie and a rumpled navy blazer. *Blue. How appropriate.* Lacey waved at him and started back to her seat. Hansen took a position behind the casket and started snapping photos of the crowd.

"You reap what you sow," said a woman next to Lacey. "That's why he's blue. It's not natural. It's a judgment."

It was somebody's judgment, Lacey thought.

One mother took her young children to see the dead man. "That's what will happen to you if you do drugs," she said. "Now, are you ever going to do drugs?"

Their eyes were large and round. They shook their heads no. The boy stretched one fingertip toward Rod's nose.

"Don't touch him! Get away! You want to catch that?" his mother said. "You'd turn blue and everyone would know you touched a dead man's nose." She bustled her awestruck children to their seats.

Rod Gibbs was certainly popular at his last appearance aboveground. Everyone in town seemed to be there for the funeral of the Blue Devil of Black Martin. Killers might attend the funerals of their victims, Lacey mused, but they rarely wore a name tag to that effect. It would be hard to single out anyone among those who filed past the coffin. The parade of people wanting their own personal look seemed endless.

Lacey turned and nearly collided with her friend. She should have known Stella would show up after all. But the woman standing next to Stella made her do a double take. "Lady Gwendolyn?"

Gwendolyn fluffed her hair, pleased. The frizzy mop of hair was gone, replaced by newly colored auburn waves that grazed her shoulders. Her previously heavy eyebrows had become perfectly shaped wings over her eyes. And there was the slightest hint of makeup, mascara, foundation, lipstick, and blush. She looked much improved. Who knew? Maybe Stella could talk her into braces for her teeth. Lacey just stared at her.

"I meant merely to have a look around the shop yesterday after we left you," Gwendolyn said. "But before I knew it, Stella had my head in a shampoo bowl."

"Yes, Stella is very good at that."

"And then someone put color on my hair. It's rather racy, don't you think?"

"It's a great color, Gwennie, and it totally suits you," Stella said. *Gwennie?*

"The eyebrows." Gwendolyn pointed and smoothed them out. "Hurts, you know."

"Takes pains to be beautiful." Stella fluffed Lady Gwendolyn's curls, pleased with her handiwork.

"I thought my poor husband would have a coronary. Let him try to make another Medusa joke now." Gwendolyn scanned the crowd. Stella shot Lacey a *be careful* look. Lacey grabbed Stella's arm and pulled her aside.

"Stella, what are you doing here?" Lacey whispered. "And why did you bring Miss Marple with you?"

"You know why!" Stella whispered back. "We're, like, *bonding*, and she totally wanted to come. Like it would *ruin* her trip to America if I wouldn't take her. She's, like, a funeral groupie or something, Lace. And she's kind of fun in a *Twilight Zone* kind of way, though she might frighten the children someday."

"What did Nigel say about this?"

"Oh, Nigel doesn't know we're here." Stella grinned. "This is just us girls."

Lacey felt a tug at her arm. Lady Gwendolyn had a firm grip on her elbow. "Oh, don't blame darling Stella. I practically kidnapped the poor girl. Isn't she a dear to show me the sights?"

"That's right," Stella said. "She showed up with coffee to go at five-thirty a.m. And as I am totally a dear, we jumped in my Mini Cooper, and here we are."

Lacey could feel her mouth open, but she couldn't think of anything to say, so she closed it.

"I sneaked out of Nigel's flat and took a cab," Gwendolyn snickered. "Left a note, telling the two of them not to bother about me. I felt very wicked. But opportunities like this do not come every day. What a sight! Brilliant!"

What is it with women of a certain age? Lacey thought. *They suddenly get crazy and fearless?*

"Now, Lacey, I understand you have a *process*. Stella says you prefer to work alone at these things," Lady Gwendolyn was saying, "so we'll just quietly stay out of your way. Do let us know if you spot the killer. We'll be ever so discreet."

Lacey made an exasperated face at Stella. "It doesn't usually work quite that way," she said through clenched teeth. "Now please, Stella, for heaven's sake, keep a low profile. A little respect. It's a funeral, you know. It only *looks* like a circus."

Even as she said it, Lacey knew it would be impossible for Stella to keep a low profile. The outfit was somber for Stella, but not for a funeral: skintight black leggings with one leg cut out to accommodate the pink rhinestone-studded cast, the ever-popular black leather miniskirt, and a very tight black sweater with a lot of zippers, unzipped to reveal her lethal cleavage. She wore scarlet lips and big smoky eyes under her tousled cap of shiny chestnut-shaded curls.

Stella looks like a Kewpie doll in a motorcycle gang, Lacey thought.

Men went out of their way to offer Stella a seat toward the front so she could have a good view of the proceedings—and they could have a good view of her.

Stella's companion for the day was outfitted in tweeds and sensible shoes. Lady Gwendolyn might be mistaken for Stella's English nanny, rather than her soon-to-be mother-in-law. Stella clearly hadn't had a chance to take a whack at the woman's wardrobe. Yet.

"First, dear, we must have a good look at the guest of honor," Gwendolyn said, dragging Stella toward the coffin.

"Oh my God, look at him," Stella said in a loud whisper. "He really is blue."

"Of course he's blue," Gwendolyn said. "That's why we came. But he's a lovely, dark, dirty sort of a blue, isn't he?" She looked extraordinarily pleased. "We don't have anything like this in England. Not since the Celts and the Picts, with their blue woad and all that. Well, except for the bog people, those bodies in the peat bogs. Murdered centuries ago. They're usually brown. But blue? My, isn't he disgusting? It's simply marvelous!"

Nigel's mom could dine out on this story for years back home in England. *See the USA, the land of the red, white, and oh, so blue.*

"I didn't expect to see the two of you getting on quite so well, so soon."

"I come on a little strong, right, Lace?" Stella did a little Betty Boop hip wiggle. "Like a hurricane. But then I grow on ya."

"I was quite prepared to hate dear Stella, you know," Gwendolyn confided in chummy tones. "My Nigel marrying some awful American. Good heavens. But Stella's a dear and not at all boring, and I do like her, and I so adore a mystery, and if she and my darling Nigel manage to stay alive and not fall off any more cliffs, I may see grandchildren before I die. And free hairstyling for life? Things could certainly be worse."

"Like I said," Stella put in with a smile. "We're bonding."

"Where is the ambassador?" Lacey asked.

Gwendolyn looked nonplussed. "No idea. Out and about somewhere. Nigel will keep him busy. They'd both simply die if they knew we were here." Her smile was conspiratorial. "We're supposed to be doing something about the wedding. What was it, Stella dear?"

"Picking out the cake."

"Precisely, which Stella has well in hand. Don't you, dear?"

"I'm thinking cheesecake," Stella said. "Who doesn't like cheesecake?"

"Exactly," Gwendolyn said. "Can you imagine picking out a cake when you could see the not-so-dearly departed in shades of indigo? And a lovely unsolved murder? Now let us take our seats. I won't say a word."

Lacey returned to her own seat and took out her notebook in case good quotes came her way. She counted at least twenty exclamations of "Oh, my God, he really *is* blue," along with gasps and squeals and suppressed nervous giggles. She spied Brooke Barton and Damon Newhouse taking their place in line.

Brooke was wearing a charcoal gray pantsuit and a pink satin blouse. Pink on Brooke, Lacey knew, was to signal that she was in love with her companion, Damon, who looked rather ill. Normally Brooke disdained pink as weak and girly, but this shade had some life to it. And Brooke must have been feeling frisky, because she wore her long blond hair straight, rather than in its customary braid. Damon wore his own peculiar uniform of black shirt, black shoes, black trench coat and square black glasses. It could be the middle of July on Miami Beach and he'd be dressed the same. The attorney and the conspiracy blogger were a classic Washington couple. *Brooke is besotted, Damon is demented, and love is blind.*

Brooke broke away from Damon to say hello. Lacey met her in the aisle. She felt a headache tug at her temples.

"What are you doing here, Brooke? I thought you had briefs to prepare."

"Be serious, Lacey. The Blue Devil in a casket and the Velvet Avenger on the loose, and you expect me to stay in a stuffy D.C. law office?" Brooke smiled like the blond conqueror that she was. "Can you believe that color? I wouldn't have missed this."

"Do you want to sit with Stella?" Lacey indicated their stylist friend, who had also snagged front-row seats, playing her rhinestone cast for all it was worth.

"Stella's here?"

"With her mother-in-law-to-be."

Brooke craned her neck. "Oh, really? So that's the Gorgon? She looks like Mary freakin' Poppins. As Stella might say."

Damon sensed Brooke was no longer at his side. He scoped the room, spotted her with Lacey, and relaxed. He came over to say hello and was promptly swept away by the local online fans of Conspiracy Clearinghouse, led by Blythe Harrington and Dirk Sykes. In Damon's own wacky world of the Web, he was a celebrity.

Sykes cleaned up well in a sports jacket, slacks, and lavender tie, his ponytail smoothly pulled back. Inez, his funeral date, was signing the guest book and would be there in a minute, Sykes said.

"I knew you'd make it, Damon. We saved you a seat," Blythe said. "So sorry to hear you've been ill." She gave Lacey a thumbs-up. Blythe wore a stretchy purple top and skirt under a royal purple velvet jacket, and a pair of purple-framed glasses. She reminded Lacey of a bunch of grapes.

Inez Garcia rushed up the center aisle to speak with Lacey. She looked perky in a retro, full-skirted dress with black and white polka dots. Inez confided to Lacey that Rod's death seemed to give Sykes the push he needed to get romantic with her.

Sykes took Damon by the arm. "You got to see the Avenger's work."

Lacey cursed herself inwardly for publicizing "the Avenger." She regretted ever quoting Sykes's wayward fantasy.

"Smithsonian," Damon said. "Nice to see you. Thanks for the tip."

"You owe me. You have quite a fan club, don't you?" Lacey said.

He blushed. "Everybody knows I walk in your footsteps. Then I take a *turn*, you know?" He and Brooke were surrounded by a love fest of conspiracy theory fans, who escorted them to the body of Rod Gibbs. *As if Damon needed help finding a blue corpse.*

Brooke and Damon approached the casket and stood in

respectful silence for a moment. Then Damon whipped out his iPhone and photographed the last public appearance of Rod Gibbs.

Lacey felt a hand on her shoulder. Vic pulled her away from the crowd and whispered in her ear. "I see the whole musical comedy cast is here."

"Oh, please, darling. We're missing Broadway Lamont. Not his jurisdiction, but he was just as curious about this as everybody else when he showed up at my office. He made me print him some pictures."

"What on earth is Stella doing here with Nigel's mother?" Vic asked.

"You recognized the Gorgon with her makeover?"

"Hard to miss a woman who looks like Eleanor Roosevelt, even with a new haircut. I remember it was quite the joke in our prep school days. Even Nigel thought it was a little funny. So?"

"Seems Lady Gwendolyn the Gorgon is a fan of bloodthirsty thrillers, the gorier the better. She's loving every blue minute of this spectacle."

"She always was different from the other moms. Where's Nigel?"

"Don't know. She says he doesn't know they're here."

Vic smirked at that. "His mother and Stella are running around on Nigel? Couldn't happen to a nicer guy. I just want to know one thing. Can you ride shotgun on your friends?"

"I'm here for the story. I'm sure they can take care of themselves," Lacey said, and prayed it was true.

"As long as they don't get in my way." Even though there was an official police presence, Nicholson had asked Vic to keep an eye on things at the funeral in case there were any problems. "Tell them no jumping into the casket to see if all his parts are blue."

"Very funny." She spun around to make sure no one overheard.

"Hey, Lacey. I didn't expect to see you here." Hank Richards tapped Lacey on the shoulder.

"I wanted to see the conclusion. And write the ending," she said. "Or the epitaph."

"That's good." He inclined his head slightly. "You might have guessed I don't care much for reporters. Most of 'em anyway. But I wanted to let you know, I think you did a real nice job on the factory story, and you didn't hide Claudia Darnell's involvement." He gave her arm a quick squeeze. "We appreciate it down here."

"It's my job." Lacey noticed he was wearing a well-tailored suit and a tasteful tie. "By the way, Hank, you look very nice."

"My Rod Gibbs Is an Asshole T-shirt is in the wash." His smile softened his bearded face. "The suit is just to show a little respect for his wife. It's what you do. Honey's gone through a lot of pain with that idiot. Glad it's over for her."

The only member of the Dominion Velvet team who wasn't up front was Kira Evans. But as Lacey turned around, she saw her. Kira was dressed in a trim brown skirt and sweater, and she stayed in the back with her teenage daughter, even after Hank urged her to join the factory team up front. She shook her head no, and he shrugged. She seemed more comfortable out of the limelight, which Lacey thought was quite refreshing.

Hank took one long, last look at Gibbs. He stood next to Sykes and Nicholson. They all seemed different somehow out of their work clothes, less angry than the last time she saw them. They had needed someone on whom to focus their anger: That person was Gibbs. Lacey hoped some of that anger would be buried with him.

But Sykes wasn't quite through. He struck a fisherman's pose by the coffin and told Inez to take a picture of him with Gibbs. "Hey, babe, tilt the camera so you get both of us! Like he's a big dead blue trophy fish. Like a hammerhead shark."

Sykes's pirate grin looked sinister, especially with the scar on his face. Lacey decided he was still angry, but something like triumphant too. She didn't like this side of Sykes at all.

Inez complained she was too short, but Sykes grinned away happily and she angled for a trophy shot or two, before the frowning funeral director chased them away from the coffin.

"Man, that was seriously tacky," Hank said to Sykes.

Sykes laughed his raspy chuckle. "I never said I was Miss Manners, now, did I?"

The lighting in the room changed, cueing the crowd to take their seats. Finally they quieted in anticipation.

Honey Gibbs was the last to arrive. All eyes were on her. She was escorted to the front by the funeral director. The widow wore pink: an optimistically perky peachy-pink dress with matching jacket, which coordinated with her pink bag and pink shoes and pink nail polish. Her over-processed blond hair was tamed in a low ponytail, wrapped in a pink bow. Lacey thought Honey's pink veil was an especially interesting touch. She also sported pink earrings, necklace, bracelets, and ring, as if she had been hit with a pink magic wand by the Fairy Godmother of Accessories, swinging on a pink chandelier. The matchy-match thing didn't seem to bother Honey. All in all, Lacey approved. Pink was better than boring and bland. It was bold.

The widow approached the coffin and bent over the body of her husband, her nose wrinkled slightly in distaste. She sighed and shook her head. Lacey leaned forward to hear.

"Oh, Rod. You got your wish. You really are the Blue Devil now." Honey spun on her pink heels and marched to her seat in the front row, next to Tom Nicholson. He leaned over and patted her hand.

Officer Gavin Armstrong was in uniform, hovering near the door, but his worried gaze kept returning to Honey. As if she could feel his attention, Honey turned around and scanned the crowd. When she saw him, her face relaxed into a gentle smile and her shoulders dropped a bit. She drew a deep breath. Lacey followed Honey's gaze back to Gavin and felt as if she'd intruded on a personal moment.

Special Agent Mordecai Caine also watched this interaction between the lovers with interest. His lockjaw personality was still tightly buttoned up. He acknowledged

Lacey with a curt nod, then resumed his examination of the room, while a white-haired minister took the podium and asked for a moment of silent prayer. The moment was broken when a soloist with an ear-splitting vibrato attacked "Amazing Grace." The minister kept his head down.

Lacey wondered if he was praying for something to say about the deceased. Rod Gibbs was a hard case to eulogize. Indeed, the minister had some trouble coming up with the words for a proper send-off for Gibbs. He declared the evils of the world must have affected Rod, changed him and soured him. The dead man turned out to be a cautionary tale for these troubled times. The minister concluded by praying for mercy on the soul of the late Mr. Gibbs, and for the Almighty to spare others from the wrath of . . . the Velvet Avenger.

Lacey covered her eyes. *What have I done?*

The minister should have prayed for the soloist too, as she launched into a torturous rendition of "Poor Wayfaring Stranger." *Ouch.* Lacey realized the soloist must be her minister's secret weapon to encourage prayer in his flock. Every head in the funeral home was bowed in fervent prayer for this torment to end.

chapter 27

The minister is asking for trouble, Lacey thought. He invited anyone who wanted to share memories of the deceased to come up to the podium and speak. There was an audible intake of breath from the crowd and a few audible snickers. Apparently, no one's memory of Rod Gibbs was appropriate to the occasion. *If the Velvet Avenger is in attendance and looking for a platform for his or her message,* Lacey thought, *this is their big chance.*

Finally, Dominion Velvet's Tom Nicholson stood and said a few words for the widow. He thanked everyone for their kindness toward Honey Gibbs in her hour of need.

"It's been a trying time, as you can all imagine. Now I'd like to invite everyone for coffee and light refreshments, which will be served at the high school cafeteria." He noted that the school was available because it was a teachers' planning day. It was the only place in town large enough to accommodate the crowd. Or maybe the rates were reasonable. Dominion Velvet was picking up the tab. The burial, slated for later in the afternoon, was to be private. Presumably, Honey Gibbs did not want the carnival-like atmosphere to continue at the graveside.

Lacey watched the crowd file past the coffin, each nonmourner in turn silent or gasping or giggling or murmuring some irreverent comment that made their fellow nonmourners chuckle. Lacey looked at an older, noncolorized picture of Gibbs in the program, which listed his accomplishments. There was a lot of white space. On the back was a map to Black Martin High, home of the Badgers.

She waited for everyone to pay their last respects or disrespects to Rod Gibbs. She took her place at the end of the line. *No harm in filing past the coffin one more time*, she thought. But when she did, she was sorry. Nothing could wipe out the memory of that bloated blue face and the swollen hands that didn't even look human. And this time, Lacey noticed something new. Her stomach churned and chills tapped a tune on her backbone. Someone in this crowd had dropped a little memento into the coffin.

A blue velvet ribbon lay coiled through Gibbs's fingers like a snake.

She froze. She looked around. No one else seemed to have noticed. Lacey motioned urgently to Hansen. She said nothing, just pointed at Gibbs. After Hansen took one last series of frames, the harried funeral director gave the sign that the velvet cloth should be tucked in and the coffin lid closed.

"Lacey, you going to the coffee at the high school?" Stella was at her elbow. " 'Cause Lady G and me think it will like totally cap our day."

"Uh, sure." Lacey smiled as if nothing was wrong. "I'll be along in a while. I have to see a man about a quote first."

"I'll save you a seat." She swayed on her one stiletto and her cast and wobbled over to a happy Lady Gwendolyn Griffin.

Lacey watched the crowd. Everyone seemed to be heading for the high school. After all, who would want to miss a swanky, postfuneral coffee-and-cake reception at the home of the Badgers? She saw the funeral director deposit the dead man's watch and wedding ring in Honey's hands as they left the room. She spotted Vic and sprinted over to interrupt his conversation with one last flirtatious female mourner.

"Sorry," Lacey said, taking Vic's arm and pulling him into a corner. "Vic. Blue ribbon. Gibbs's right hand. Right now. It wasn't there before."

"Are you sure?"

"I'm pretty much the ribbons-and-bows go-to gal here. So yeah, Vic, I'm sure. They just closed the coffin."

He looked chagrined. "Our joker just put a velvet ribbon in the casket?"

"Joker? Or Avenger?"

Vic gave her a dirty look and folded his arms. "Please."

"I'm just saying it looked like a match to the ribbon that was sent to Claudia Darnell. So what are you going to do?"

He unfolded his arms and blew out his breath. "I'm gonna stop that casket." Vic moved swiftly to the pallbearers, who were getting ready to move Rod Gibbs to the limousine for the last ride to the graveyard. Lacey was right behind him.

Vic got some static from the pallbearers, who just wanted this job over and done with, but when Agent Mordecai Caine materialized, with whatever he had rammed up his backside, their protests faded. Caine called Officer Armstrong and requested his presence. The local cop went to Honey's side and sent her on to the reception ahead of him.

"Now, what's this all about?" Caine asked Vic, who then turned to Lacey.

Caine turned out to be more reasonable than Lacey had anticipated. He had the coffin opened up again. It was still a shock when the lid was raised and Rob Gibbs came into view. Still blue.

"Ms. Smithsonian, would you please explain what you say has been deposited in the casket, and why we should care about that. You may point, but please do not touch."

"The blue ribbon, right there. In his right hand. It wasn't there the first time I walked past the casket. It looks like a match to one that was sent anonymously to Claudia Darnell," Lacey said.

Caine turned to Vic. "You can confirm this?" Lacey bristled. It was apparent Caine didn't believe her. She glared at him.

"I can confirm it," Vic said. He put a warning hand on Lacey's shoulder. "I've seen Darnell's ribbon. It's in a safe at *The Eye*."

"And why is this important?" Caine asked. Mordecai Caine was not a reader of *The Eye Street Observer* or of DeadFed dot com.

Lacey took a deep breath and tried to control her temper. She didn't like being treated like an idiot. "It could be someone's idea of a joke, or it could be something else. Have you heard of the Velvet Avenger?"

"I heard." Caine set his jaw and looked bored. "But why don't you tell me?"

She filled him in. While he didn't seem convinced the killer was trailing blue velvet ribbons in his wake, he was willing to consider that the ribbon in the coffin could be something resembling a clue. Lacey refrained from calling it a "fashion clue" in a room with so much weaponized testosterone.

"Not a chance in hell we're going to get any forensics off that," Armstrong said. "And hundreds of people were here today, if not a thousand."

Caine nodded unhappily. "I'm also willing to bet nobody saw who planted the ribbon in the coffin." He then turned his beady eyes on Lacey. "And you're a reporter."

"Indeed I am," she said.

Vic said nothing, he just looked from Caine to Lacey with an eyebrow arched.

"Aren't you just supposed to be writing about ladies' dresses?"

Lacey smiled. "My beat is wide-ranging, which you know all about from my good friend Detective Broadway Lamont." She wasn't above being a little snotty. "And blue velvet ribbons definitely fit my beat."

Blue velvet ribbons—fashionable corpses will be wearing them this season.

"Get out of here, both of you," he instructed Vic and Lacey. "Stay available." Caine told Armstrong to close the partition between the rooms, leaving Vic and Lacey on the other side.

There was only time for one reassuring hug. "I'm going to check in with Forrest. Remember, the ribbon thing? Good catch, but it's Caine's problem now." Vic gave Lacey a quick kiss and was gone.

Lacey collected her things from her chair and put on her coat. The room was empty. An argument was brewing on the other side of the partition. It was amazing how easy it was to overhear. She quietly inched closer.

"Where were you?" Caine asked.

"Making sure Ms. Gibbs got away safely," Armstrong replied.

"Oh, really? Nicholson seemed to have everything in hand. You can cut the crap, Armstrong. Everyone knows about your personal relationship with the widow. It's what we'd call suspicious."

"Exactly what are you saying?"

"What do you think? You're a cop. You know the prime suspect is usually the one closest to the victim. Honey Gibbs had good reason to want her husband dead."

"He was an asshole. Everyone wanted him dead!"

"Including you, Armstrong?"

Lacey heard a chair overturn. She stepped back. It sounded like a shoving match.

"I had nothing to do with Gibbs's death," Armstrong said.

"Really?" Caine said. Lacey heard what sounded like the chair being righted. "The blue dye thing? And the ribbon? It's a little weird for a cop, the kind of thing that might throw someone off the trail. But a cop could do it. To help out his married girlfriend."

"I'm out of here." Armstrong stomped away, and Lacey heard a door slam.

"Give my regards to Mrs. Gibbs, won't you?" Caine called after him.

Lacey stepped quietly away from the partition. She crept to the door and peeked into the hall. It was empty. She sprinted out the door to her car.

chapter 28

"What's up, Lacey? You awake?" Stella asked. "Have a cookie."

Lacey was wondering why all school cafeterias had the same smell. There always seemed to be a hint of spaghetti sauce in the air. She sat down at one end of a long lunch table, with a cup of coffee and a plate of coffee cake and cookies that Stella had saved for her. But she felt as if the stuffing had been knocked out of her.

The good ship Dominion Velvet had sunk and the workers reached out to each other like survivors in a life raft. The factory group was sitting at the next table, laughing over multiple cups of free coffee, not knowing where their next paycheck was coming from.

Lacey didn't know where her next paycheck would come from either. She loved being a reporter. Sure, she would like a beat that didn't include the relevance of hemlines, but being a newshound thrummed in her veins. It made her blood pump. Most days. *Not today.*

"Lacey, it's like you're in a coma or something." Stella seemed utterly energized by the day's events.

"I might be losing my job," Lacey managed to say. "This could be my last big story. And I'm getting nowhere with it. People drop big fat blue clues right under my nose and I miss them. It's hopeless. I'm hopeless."

"WTF! No way. You are totally *The Eye* to me."

"Walter Pojack should hear you say that." Lacey laughed.

"What's a Walter Pojack?"

"The *Eye Street* exec who told me I should start polishing my résumé. Typical bully. Hits you when you least expect it."

Stella leaned in to commiserate. "Lace, I know the type. Self-important little prick. Weasel with a tiny dick, right?" Lady Gwendolyn looked alarmed. "They're the worst."

Brooke sailed over from the next table, where Damon was holding court. "About time you got here," she said to Lacey.

"Happy to oblige." Lacey yawned.

"What's wrong, Lace? Did your spring wind down?" Brooke asked. "We're taking bets on where the Avenger will strike next."

"Oh, Brooke. It's much worse than that," Stella said. "Some dinky-dick guy at her paper wants to get rid of Lacey."

"That's ridiculous," Brooke said. "Lacey is the heartbeat of that crummy excuse for a paper. Sorry, Lace. You know what I mean."

Gwendolyn put up one finger. "Pardon me. When you say *dinky-dick guy*, Stella dear, you mean *what*, exactly?"

Stella measured out an inch with two fingers. "Tiny. Dick. You know."

Enlightenment dawned on Nigel's mother. "Oh! You mean his Wee Willie Winkie! The dickless rotter! We shall have to do something about that straight away," Gwendolyn said, though she didn't offer any specifics.

"I'll represent you in a wrongful-dismissal suit," Brooke offered. "It'll be fun."

"I'm not gone yet," Lacey said. "Wrongful or not."

"Just in case," Brooke added. "How serious is this?"

"He told me to polish my résumé."

"He will rue the day." Brooke assumed a lawyerly pose, crossing her arms. "I promise you, Lacey. What's his name?" She got out her trusty BlackBerry to make notes.

Damon and the Dominion Velvet crew edged nearer to Lacey.

"It's good to have friends," Lacey said with a smile. "My job is just collateral damage. It gets worse. And everything I say, Damon Newhouse, is off the record."

Damon moved in closer. "There is no off the record, Smithsonian. You taught me that."

"How can it get worse than it is?" Stella asked.

"Pojack wants to gut the paper and send me and *The Eye Street Observer* to . . . Crystal City." Lacey put her head down on the table.

"Oh my God! Crystal City!" Brooke gasped. "That Stalinist gulag? Why, it's across the Potomac! What's this jerk's name?"

"Pojack. Walter Pojack." Lacey said, her head still down.

"The man apparently has a wee little dicky," Gwendolyn said. "Classic case of overcompensation."

"Ain't that a pisser?" said Inez. "It's always the guys with the little willies that want to put you down. Like Rod. I bet his was tiny. And blue."

Amid the general laughter, Lacey lifted her head. The crowd was growing larger and more boisterous and she didn't want strangers to get the wrong impression. She knew she shouldn't be complaining about her job. At least she still had one, and they didn't.

"Some swell funeral, huh? Any cookies left?"

Most of the crowd had dispersed. Lacey noticed an exhausted Honey, her head slumped forward, leaning against the wall. Armstrong stood next to her, glowering at all who approached. He reserved an especially sour look for Lacey.

"How are you holding up?" Lacey asked Honey.

"I'm managing." Honey squeezed Armstrong's hand.

"What do you want?" he asked Lacey.

Honey opened her eyes. "It's okay, Gavin. She's cool."

Relieved to hear it, Lacey said, "This day must have been hard to get through."

"Ask me tomorrow, after I read the papers," she said.

"My follow-up story won't be in till Sunday."

"It's weird reading the papers about Rod and seeing my name. I really shot my mouth off, huh?" Honey mused. "Well, I'm not taking it back. Can't wait to see the *National Enquirer*."

"I didn't put in everything you said," Lacey said.

"How tactful," Armstrong snarled.

"I did say I'd have an open-casket funeral," Honey said. "What was I thinking? I never expected this many people would show up. All taking pictures and videos." She giggled. "I hope I don't go to Hell for this. I sure don't want to see Rod again."

"Why did you go through with it?" Lacey could have sworn it would never happen.

Honey opened her hands wide. "Seemed like the right thing to do. Rod liked to humiliate people. Turnabout is fair play, right? And when someone becomes a legend, it seems kind of mean to deprive the world, or at least the whole town, of one last look."

"You're tired, Honey." Officer Armstrong tried to break up her reverie, but Honey was on a roll.

"God, he looked terrible. Rod was so vain, he'd like to die, if he wasn't dead already." She sighed loudly. "Besides, the body is just a shell. Isn't that what the preachers say? Rod isn't even in there anymore. And it's a good thing, because he'd kill me if he knew I did that to him. Put him on display like that. Blue as a blueberry muffin."

"About Rod—" Lacey started, but Armstrong stopped her.

"Leave her alone. I'll tell her about your little discovery, but it's too much right now." Gavin Armstrong was a whole lot bigger than Lacey, so she treated him to The Look. She could always call Honey later. "You want to go home, Honey? I'll take you home," he said. She looked around at the crowd. "You've done your duty by him. And more. The perfect hostess."

She smiled back at him. "I'd like that." Armstrong stood up. He pulled Honey to her feet and put his arm around her.

"Just one question." Lacey also stood. "Honey, do you want Rod's killer caught?"

"I don't really know." Honey looked puzzled. "I don't. I just—"

"This interview is over," Armstrong said.

"You have that lean and hungry look," Vic said. "You having steak?"

"Does the moon rise in the east? A lady needs her protein." Lacey ordered her steak medium rare. She leaned back and relaxed for what felt like the first time that day.

It was late afternoon before they got away from Black Martin, and her workday was not over. She had to drive back to Northern Virginia and file a story from home for the Sunday papers. Because they were in separate cars, Lacey met Vic for a very early dinner at Café Europa in Richmond's Shockoe Bottom district.

The restaurant was warm and cozy, and Lacey was in danger of falling asleep. Couples at other tables were leaning in to each other, starting an early Friday night.

"You have a dreamy look on your face," Vic said.

"It's date night for everyone but me and you. I have to go home and write a story. A story I don't have a finish for. One about blue ribbons." She brightened up. "But I am not feeling sorry for myself, honey. I am alive. I am with you. I am not any shade of blue."

"Rhyming again? You must be tired. Sweetheart, you want to go on a date tomorrow night? Your story will be over. My paperwork will be finished." Vic smiled. "A night on the town."

"Try and get out of it." She changed the subject. "How are things, securitywise, at the factory?"

"The building is secured. My guys have the new video surveillance and alarm system in place, all digital, all remote, can't be tampered with. And, most important, we actually turned it on. A couple of local guys are going to handle the night shift."

"Not Wade, I trust."

"Not Wade," Vic said. "Nicholson paid him his week and sent him packing. Forrest gets to go home and so do I. By the way, nice catch with the ribbon. What made you take another look?"

"The reporter in me, I guess. Oh, hell. A better reporter would have seen who left it. Caught the Avenger blue-handed. Velvet Avenger, one. Lacey Smithsonian, nothing. Why didn't I notice something, Vic?"

"You did. And you gave Mordecai Caine a big head-ache." He flashed his wolf grin.

"That's something. You just cheered me up, darling. I bet I'm on his list now. Right after Officer Armstrong."

"What do you know that I don't know?"

Lacey told him about the argument she overheard, the overturned chairs, the shoving match.

"No love lost there, that's for sure," he said.

"So are they still going to bury Rod?"

"Sure. The ribbon just delays things. The forensic guys will have to process the coffin. It'll have a thousand prints on it. Won't tell us a thing," he predicted.

The waitress came with their dinners. Lacey inhaled the aroma of her skirt steak and cheese potatoes. She took a bite and made *yum* sounds, which made Vic chuckle.

"Lacey, are you really worried about losing your job?"

"A little. I don't think Claudia would okay it, but Pojack seems to be doing an end run around her. And he doesn't like me."

"I don't know why. You're eminently likable."

She laughed. "I could always file my PI paperwork and switch careers. What do you think of me as a private investigator?"

"I don't think you've got the wardrobe for it. A PI's got to fade into the woodwork. Not be so darned cute."

"Cute." She sighed. Lacey hated being called cute. "You don't exactly fade into the woodwork, handsome." He snorted. She continued. "Maybe I could work with Bud Hunt, Hunt Country Investigations, where I took the class. You remember Bud Hunt. Old Grit, Guts, and Gumshoes?"

Vic took a bite of his dinner. "Sure. Good old Bud. All heart, no head."

"Or maybe Gregor Kepelov might have some crackpot jobs for me to work on. He likes me, when he's not trying to kill me."

"With Marie, his black-magic woman. The three of you

would make quite a team. Beauty and the Beast, and the Psychic Who Faints at the Thought of Danger."

"That's not a bad thing, Vic. Poor Marie, she's like the canary in the coal mine. I should have her around more often. I could have used her today."

"Fainting and falling into the coffin?" Vic said. "I don't think so."

chapter 29

Lacey was furious.

If that idiot Walt Pojack wants to fire me on my day off, I'll feed him through the printing press. Headfirst.

It was Saturday. Pojack had demanded by phone that Lacey come in to the office for an urgent meeting. It was ice cold outside. Beneath Lacey's seventh-floor windows, the Potomac River was ten shades of chilly blue, with a thick crust of ice hugging the bank. She just wanted to cozy up with a pot of coffee and a couple of magazines.

She dialed the one person who had promised to help. And wasn't completely crazy.

"It's Saturday, it's way too early, and this had better be a matter of national security," Brooke answered sleepily. "Who's calling?"

"It's Lacey. Pojack called me in to the office. I think he might try to get rid of me."

"Like hell. This is what you do if it happens, and it may not: Just say no. Don't let him get away with it. Claudia Darnell is the publisher. Insist she be the one to let you go. Pojack won't expect you to resist."

"You want me to stage a sit-in?"

"If that's what it takes." Brooke yawned into the phone. "Call me if anything happens. And bring a recorder. Get anything he says on tape. Or digital. Secretly, if you have to."

"Isn't that illegal in D.C.?" Lacey retrieved her pocket tape recorder from her desk.

"He probably doesn't know that. Don't tell him. And

you need it for ammunition. Better yet, insist on taping it. That might shut him up. Call me." Brooke hung up.

Lacey put fresh batteries in her tape recorder. She thought about getting dressed.

While she would normally throw on jeans and a turtleneck to go in to the office on a cold February weekend, there was no way she was going to look casual in front of Walter "Benedict Arnold" Pojack. She selected an early Fifties sweater that had been Aunt Mimi's, one of the few items Mimi left behind from that decade. The sweater was a soft red wool with three-quarter sleeves, and it featured a shawl collar with satin piping. It zipped up the side for a sleek fit. She teamed the sweater with a pair of charcoal gray slacks and a cream-colored jacket with patch pockets for the recorder. For presence, she pulled on her tallest black boots. For luck, Lacey also selected a vintage broach of enameled red cardinals. The birds, not the clergymen.

You don't scare me, Pojack. I'm going to scare you.

"Hey, Lacey, want a doughnut?" Wiedemeyer was waltzing through the office with a dozen fresh glazed doughnuts from Krispy Kreme. The intoxicating aroma of yeast and sugar filled the air.

"No, thanks, Harlan. My stomach is queasy. Hey, what are you doing here on a Saturday?"

"Just making up some hours. You seem glum, chum. What are you doing here?"

"Walt Pojack wants to see me. He called me at home and told me to come to the office."

"He what? Maladjusted bastard has no sense of priority. It's Saturday! You haven't actually updated your résumé, have you, Smithsonian?"

"Every week. But he blindsided me today. He can't do anything without Claudia. I won't let him."

"Gee, you just missed Claudia." He opened the box and grabbed one of the doughnuts. He took a bite.

"She was here?"

He nodded and swallowed. "I saw her driving out of the garage when I came back from Krispy Kreme."

That's weird. "She couldn't have told Pojack to call me,

could she? She wouldn't do that. Would she?" Lacey held on to a glimmer of a hope that she still had a job.

"I'm going with you," Wiedemeyer decided. He took another bite, sprinkling himself with crumbs. "He can't fire people on the QT. And on a Saturday. That miserable bastard."

Her stomach knotted and she grabbed her purse. Wiedemeyer marched beside her to the elevator. They headed to the sixth floor, where the high muckety-mucks had their offices.

"Why on a weekend? What can't he wait till Monday?" Lacey thought about Tom Nicholson at Dominion Velvet, being told it was gentler to fire people on a Monday. *Reason enough for Pojack to pick Saturday, I suppose.* She rehearsed Brooke's plan in her head and felt the recorder in her pocket.

"You can't trust a thieving weasel who'd send us all down the river to Crystal City," Wiedemeyer was grumbling away. "You can bet that's one rat bastard who's feathered his own golden parachute. He doesn't give a rat's ass for the rest of us."

Wiedemeyer had worked himself into a lather of mangled metaphors on her behalf. The pudgy little elf was pretty adorable, his loyalty touching, his courage encouraging. And maybe Wiedemeyer's jinx factor would work, if not in her favor, at least to the detriment of the evil Pojack.

The elevator doors opened onto the marble floor of the executive suite. Lacey straightened her shoulders and held her head high. Wiedemeyer pulled up his waistband and licked doughnut crumbs from his fingers. They marched down the hall to Pojack's office, where the door was slightly ajar. His accommodations were well-appointed, but not nearly as sumptuous as Claudia's.

Lacey adjusted the recorder's microphone, clipped beneath her lapel so it couldn't be seen. If Pojack had any sense, he would know that everything was always on the record. She turned on the recorder's voice actuation. The next voice it heard would start the tape rolling.

Pojack had his back to the door and did not turn around when she knocked, which made her mad.

"Rude bastard," Wiedemeyer said under his breath. Lacey heard the soft click of her recorder switching on.

She knocked again, harder. "It's Lacey Smithsonian. Here at your request," Lacey said. "What's so important that I had to come in on a Saturday?" She was thinking she should have simply refused to come.

Pojack didn't answer. They entered the room slowly. Pojack was too quiet. A familiar sense of dread descended on Lacey and she held her breath. Wiedemeyer followed so close he bumped into her when she stopped. Lacey spoke first.

"Oh, damn."

Pojack was slumped in the chair, his head thrown backward, his face turned to the ceiling, his eyes glassy and unseeing. His skin had taken on an ashy pallor. He was dead.

Lacey hoped for one desperate second that Pojack had died of natural causes. A clogged artery could have closed up and his cold heart failed, but the hole in his forehead said otherwise. Pojack's eyes were open and he looked terrified.

"Oh my God," Wiedemeyer said. "That is one cold, dead bastard."

This is what I get for coming to work on a Saturday, Lacey thought.

She inched closer to the corpse, careful not to touch anything. Wiedemeyer leaned over Pojack's face to get a good look at the bullet hole. His face drained of its normally rosy color.

"Holy smokes! This son of a bitch has been whacked."

"Don't touch him." Lacey was feeling queasy. She'd seen too much death lately.

"Nothing to fear, Smithsonian. I was just going to feel for some vitals." He felt Pojack's wrist. "No pulse. It's as flat as Kansas."

"That usually happens when you die."

"Oh, no. You think the jinx worked?" Wiedemeyer looked stricken.

"Don't be silly, Harlan. There's no such thing as a jinx."

"Yeah, but Smithsonian, I put the whammy on the bastard. Not the death whammy—more like the sperm-freezing whammy. I guess his swimmers are really frozen now."

Lacey circled the body and saw something clutched in Pojack's left hand, a trailing coil of dark blue. "Damn it."

"What is it, Lacey?"

"Blue velvet ribbon." Her words came out a bit strangled. Lacey hadn't divulged anything about the blue velvet ribbons in her stories. Not yet. She tried to remember everyone who knew about the ribbons. Vic. Claudia. Turtledove. The cops in Black Martin. Agent Caine. Congressman Flanders. And the killer. And there could be more.

Was the Black Martin killer here in the District? Was Claudia Darnell the next victim in his crosshairs? And possibly Congressman Tazewell Flanders? But why Pojack? Was he in the wrong place at the wrong time? Pojack had nothing to do with the velvet factory, but he had everything to do with threatening Lacey's job.

And yesterday too many people had heard his name, especially after Stella's take on his presumed penile size. News in a small town could go viral instantly, without the help of the Internet. Had someone decided to rid the world of another job-killing boss? Was Pojack's death her fault? Her stomach roiled.

First Harlan and his jinx, and now you? Stop it.

"I have to call Vic. Claudia too. She'll want to know."

But Claudia's words came back to her. She said she would "take care" of Pojack. It wouldn't be hard to find another blue velvet ribbon. And a gun. Was the Avenger a convenient excuse to cover up an unrelated murder? Using Lacey to discover the body? Too convenient. Too confusing.

This is crazy, Lacey. This wasn't the time for hypotheticals. This was the time to step away and let the police do their job.

"You're right." Wiedemeyer stood still for a moment, as if his legs were stuck to the gold-and-green oriental carpet on Pojack's floor. "Well, I suppose we should call the cops first."

"Right. I'll call the police. As soon as I call Vic," Lacey

said. "You call Tony. And get Hansen up here. He works Saturdays, right?"

"Good thinking, Smithsonian. We want our own crime scene photos for *The Eye*. Hey, you know what else this means?"

Lacey arched her eyebrow as delicately as she could. "No, what?"

"Trujillo's got to have a cocktail party now."

"Oh, Harlan, hush! Don't let anyone hear you say such a terrible thing."

Her warning didn't faze the death and dismemberment reporter. "He said if the bastard died, that's all. Nobody specified a cause of death. Ipso facto: cocktail party."

Lacey took out her phone and gestured that he should do the same. He reached for Pojack's desk phone. "No, no, use your cell phone."

"Right." The lightbulb in his head switched on. "Fingerprints."

Wiedemeyer made his calls to *The Eye*'s photographer and police reporter. Lacey called Vic, who said he was on his way. She took a deep breath and called the D.C. Metropolitan Police. She sent up a fervent silent prayer. *Please, send anyone except Broadway Lamont.*

Hansen arrived draped with cameras, film as well as digital. "Whoa, Lacey, what the hell! This is a little close to home."

"Way too close, Hansen."

He clicked on a new lens and started shooting photos. "The cops really hate it when I get there first." Lacey moved out of his field of view.

Wiedemeyer contemplated the corpse. "Pojack might go to Hell, Hansen, but at least the bastard doesn't have to go to the dark tunnels of Crystal City. He'll be underground, anyway."

"That's always the way with these bastards, Harlan." Hansen was usually good-natured with Wiedemeyer. Not everyone was. The photographer straightened up and put an arm on Lacey's shoulder. "You doing okay?"

"As long as you don't take my picture," Lacey said.

"That's asking a lot," he said. He pointed to himself. "Photographer here."

Police reporter Tony Trujillo trailed far behind Hansen, but he still made it with time to spare before the D.C. cops got there. He was Saturday casual, in jeans, a leather jacket, and a pair of black cowboy boots with silver tips.

"Tony, I didn't know you were in the building."

"I wasn't, but I was close. Luckily, Wiedemeyer thought to talk to me." He sniffed. "So why didn't you call me, Brenda Starr? I thought we were a team, Lacey."

"I told Harlan to call you, and you can have this story. I'll just go home and have a quiet little nervous breakdown, okay?"

"Brenda Starr would never have a nervous breakdown, and anyway it's not covered under our insurance."

"That figures," Lacey said.

It was pandemonium when the cops arrived. It took all their authority to prevent everyone else on the weekend shift of the paper from barging in and spoiling the crime scene. The sports writers were particularly difficult to fend off. Like a bunch of baboons, they treated the episode as if it were a sporting event. Detective Broadway Lamont arrived after the uniformed cops responded to the scene and he was not happy.

"I got a special call to come here, on my day off," Lamont said. "Somebody shot dead at *The Eye Street Observer*, and let me tell you, Smithsonian, damned if I knew whether to hope it was you getting shot or doing the shooting."

"I'm honored," Lacey said.

"I said to myself, *It can't have anything to do with one fashion reporter. That would defy the damned law of averages*." Lamont got in Lacey's face and she backed away. "And then the dispatcher told me it was called in by one Lacey Smithsonian. And since I got personal knowledge of one troublemaking fashion reporter named Smithsonian, I got to be the one to respond. Do you know it's Saturday?!"

She wasn't prepared for Broadway Lamont and his tough-cop routine, and she felt her eyes begin to sting. Things were going downhill very fast.

"You are not crying, Smithsonian." Broadway stepped back. He looked very much afraid that she might fall apart. "Reporters do not cry. Not even fashion reporters."

"I just have something in my eye." She blinked and rubbed her eyes. "I'd spit nails before I'd cry for you, Lamont."

"That's better." He looked much relieved. Broadway Lamont was a big, gruff bull of a man, but even though he looked irritated that his basketball game had been interrupted, she knew he wouldn't have missed this call. "Don't be crying on me."

"Gee, Broadway, sympathy? From you?"

"I take a personal interest in this newspaper, 'specially when someone's killed here. Kind of puts together two of your specialties, don't it, Smithsonian—the news business and murder? Just why in hell were you here? Ain't you covered enough blood this week?" Lamont snapped on his latex gloves and bent down to get a closer look at the bullet hole. "What's his name?"

"Walt Pojack, chief of operations."

"He married?"

"Divorced, three times," offered Wiedemeyer. "Three lucky ladies."

"Why were you here, Smithsonian? I'll get to your comrade in a minute. Well?"

The detective stared at Lacey and she fought to remain calm. She had observed Lamont in action. She understood that the intimidating cop act was his stock-in-trade. Bad guys might not have wept at his feet, but they quivered. She took a deep breath.

"He called me this morning and insisted that I come in."

Lamont folded his arms. "Why?"

"He didn't say."

"Smithsonian was called by the Terminator here," Wiedemeyer added. "Perhaps I should say the terminated? We suspected Pojack was going to lower the boom on our fashion reporter, put the kibosh on her job, send her to the long, cold unemployment line. It was RIF time. And I was probably next in line."

Lacey didn't need Harlan Wiedemeyer to go all purple

prose for the homicide detective. But Wiedemeyer lacked certain filters that most reporters had.

"That true, Smithsonian?" Lamont said.

"You just like saying my name, don't you?"

He favored her with the big Broadway grin. It was rather like that of a devouring lion. "Yep. It's museum quality. Now?"

"The paper's going through some changes. Earlier this week, Pojack told me I should polish my résumé."

"I'd say you've got yourself a motive."

"You think I'd kill that imbecile for the fashion beat?" Lacey leaned against the wall, not caring that it was a crime scene. "I have been trying to get off this damn fashion beat from the day it landed on me."

"That's true," Wiedemeyer said. "Our Smithsonian denies her gift, although she can read a seam like a clue, a neckline like a poem, an outfit like a novel."

Lamont grunted. "Anything else?"

"The word *imbecile* just slipped out," Lacey said.

"Don't matter. You can't hurt his feelings now. Or mine. Anything else?"

"Yes," Wiedemeyer broke in. "He's trying to move *The Eye* to Crystal City. The dumb bastard."

"Crystal City? Other side of the Potomac? Out of the District?" Lamont made a face. "So you got an even stronger motive."

"Are you through?" Lacey asked.

"Through? I haven't even begun to talk to you, Smithsonian. We're going to go into this nice conference room across the hall, and we're going to sit and talk."

"I should have stayed home in bed this morning."

"Amen." Lamont cast an evil eye toward the two of them as he directed them to the small management conference room. "After you."

"You know we didn't have anything to do with it," Lacey said.

"I don't know nothing. You getting gun happy, Smithsonian? After that incident last month?"

"That was self-defense. And I didn't kill anybody! And it was in Virginia."

"You draw nutcases like lightning bolts," Lamont said. "Maybe you or your little buddy here decided to take care of today's victim."

Wiedemeyer puffed himself up and thrust his hands into Lamont's face. "Maybe you'd like to run some gunshot residue tests on us?"

Lacey hoped Wiedemeyer wouldn't insist on it. Maybe he didn't know that he could refuse a test and the cops would only pursue it if a suspect was charged. Maybe he just liked playing tough guy for a change. Lacey's PI class had taught her that most GSR tests were not performed on the living but on the dead, especially in the case of suicides, to make sure the victim pulled the trigger. Everyone else knows to wash their hands. *Like Pontius Pilate. Or Lady Macbeth.*

Lamont glared. "I am not interested in wasting my time with goofballs."

"Careful, Detective. You'll hurt my feelings," Lacey said.

"Yeah, right. Follow me." Broadway Lamont turned to Wiedemeyer, trying to remember if he knew the man. Perhaps he remembered seeing Wiedemeyer hanging around Felicity's desk while Broadway was flirting with her. And her tarts. "What can you tell me, Mr.—?"

"Wiedemeyer. Harlan Wiedemeyer." The death and dismemberment reporter was wary of the big cop, mostly because of Felicity. She flirted using food the way other women batted their eyelashes or flashed a leg. And both big, burly Broadway Lamont and plump little Wiedemeyer were very fond of food. They sized each other up.

The three of them sat down in the large white leather chairs around the long mahogany table in the conference room. Meanwhile, back in Pojack's office, police technicians collected evidence and took photos of the deceased. Lacey could hear them working.

"What can you tell me, Smithsonian? Any *fashion* clues?" Lamont smirked at her.

"The dead man is clutching a blue velvet ribbon in his hand."

Broadway Lamont's mouth dropped open. "A what? A blue velvet ribbon? Blue, as in the same shade as Rodney

Gibbs?" He rubbed his eyes with both hands. "You saying this is connected to the velvet murder and you couldn't produce another blue dye job? I'm disappointed."

"I don't produce anything but the facts," Lacey snapped. She sat back in the chair and told Lamont about the velvet ribbon that Claudia had received, and the one that was dropped into Rod Gibbs's coffin. Lacey made a mental note to try to check on the congressman's recent mail.

Lamont scratched his head. "So, I might be getting another call from your trooper Mordecai Caine?"

"Possibly. And he's not my trooper."

"Anyone else up here, besides you two and the vic?"

"Claudia Darnell was here earlier," Wiedemeyer offered. "Publisher of *The Eye*."

"Darnell have any reason to rid the world of this Pojack fellow?"

"Sure she did," Wiedemeyer said. "Everyone did. He was a weasel. Selling out the company. He was a solid-gold bastard. Or scratch that. More like a rusted-out, diseased bastard. So Claudia had as much or more reason to kill him as anyone."

Lacey tried to give Wiedemeyer a look that said *Stop already!*

"What, Lacey?" Wiedemeyer said.

Lamont spun around on Lacey. "What do you know? You see Ms. Darnell today?"

"No, I didn't see her." Lacey suddenly remembered the voice-activated tape recorder in her jacket pocket and shut it off.

"What's that?" Lamont demanded.

"Um," she hedged. "Nothing."

"Don't try my patience, Smithsonian."

"It's a tape recorder." She pulled it out. The detective's eyes narrowed. "I brought it to my meeting with Pojack to record whatever he was going to say. Self-defense."

"You were going to tape him without his knowledge. Is that it? Something that is illegal in the District of Columbia?"

Lacey smiled. Pojack couldn't say anything now, pro or

con. "Heavens no, Detective. Journalists are always on the record. Everyone knows that."

"I suppose that machine will back up everything you and Weinermeyer here been telling me?"

"Oh, yeah, sure it will." She was beginning to feel on more solid ground. She popped the tape out of the recorder and handed it to him.

"Figures." Lamont eyed the tape glumly. "So, matter of curiosity. Why'd this Pojack want to get rid of you?"

"He didn't like me. He didn't like my fashion coverage. He thought my beat was frivolous."

"Ha. I'm surprised you didn't tell him it was life-or-death with you, Smithsonian." He sighed.

"Anything else?"

"Not now. Get out of here. Be sure you answer my calls. Day or night."

Vic was waiting at the door of the conference room. Lacey didn't know how he made it upstairs past the blue line of cops, but she didn't care. He was in jeans and a dark blue sweater under a sheepskin jacket. She thought he was the best thing she'd ever seen. He hugged her right off her feet.

"You'll keep her out of trouble?" Lamont asked, just to irritate Lacey.

"I can't promise that, Detective."

"Then just get her out of here, Donovan. For now, Smithsonian, day or night, I got a question, you answer it."

She gave him a weak smile. "Always a pleasure, Broadway."

"Smart-ass reporter. You too, Weinermeyer."

"*Wiedemeyer,*" the little reporter spat. "Spelling counts in my business, Detective."

Wiedemeyer glanced toward the door and his eyes lit up. Waiting in the wings was his Felicity, tearful but happy to see him, and dusted with flour. She'd broken out an eye-popping pink-sequined Valentine sweater, hearts and all, delivered straight from Cupid's love lair. The sweater was too much of a good thing, Lacey thought, especially with two or three layers of ruffles at the neckline. As Felicity flounced, her ruffles bounced—and revealed a dark smudge on her neck. Maybe chocolate?

No, Lacey decided, *that's no smudge. That's a love bite!* It was no wonder; they'd been getting romantic. Harlan had been dancing around Felicity like a love-crazed Cupid. Lacey smiled at the image.

"Why, Miss Felicity Pickles, is that a hickey on your neck I see, or a fingerprint?" asked Lamont. "You two think you're a couple of teenagers?"

"A what? Oh!" Felicity's hand flew up to her neck. She pulled frantically at the ruffles to conceal her mark of shame. Harlan's face turned a perilous shade of purple, and he looked a little stricken at being caught. And a little proud too. He and Felicity shared a quick guilty smile.

Lamont rumbled with laughter. He looked as if he were suddenly wondering whether Felicity might be as delicious as her desserts.

"Now then. You got anything for a starving man?"

Felicity's eyes glistened as she gazed up at Lamont. "Well, I just finished a new recipe and I was going to let Harlan test-drive it. With Valentine's Day coming up, our readers want the food of love. I think you need a little of that too, Detective Lamont. Don't you?"

Lamont beamed. Lacey wanted to gag, but she realized Felicity was cleverly offering Broadway Lamont a bribe that would leave no evidence.

A get-out-of-jail-free cake.

chapter 30

Detective Lamont shot a glance at a nervous Wiedemeyer, who was shifting his weight from foot to foot. At the moment, he didn't much care for Broadway Lamont, who was leering at his fiancée. But under the circumstances, Wiedemeyer was willing to share. He clapped his hands.

"Why not?" Wiedemeyer said. "Now, tell me, my delectable Dilly Pickles, what is your latest masterpiece?"

"A double-chocolate torte with pink raspberry-almond filling, spread over a layer of chocolate ganache," Felicity purred. "It does take some effort, but I think everyone will agree that it's worth it. For the one you love."

It certainly would be worth it, Lacey thought, *if it softens up Broadway Lamont.*

Indeed, Lamont looked a little happier. "Lead the way, Miss Pickles. Let's investigate that cake while I consider your boyfriend's story."

"My story? I'll always remember this as the day my death and dismemberment beat came to me," Wiedemeyer said philosophically. "But cake would sweeten the deal."

Lamont, Lacey, Vic, Harlan, and Felicity trooped down to the newsroom and Felicity's desk, where her latest calorie-filled creation was on display. It was a large many-layered thing with pink whipped cream frosting. Broadway's eyes lit up as Felicity carved out an extra-large piece of cake for him.

"Lacey, Vic, will you try some too?"

"No, thanks, Felicity. But it looks delicious," Lacey said.

"I'll give you the recipe. Before it's even published." Felicity pushed a copy into Lacey's hands.

Vic wrapped his arm around Lacey's shoulders and led her away from the others, behind a file cabinet. "Let them eat cake," she said.

"When you told me a body was found at *The Eye*, my heart stopped." He held her very tight.

"It was touch and go for mine."

"I don't like this, the killer being so close to you."

"I don't like it much either." Lacey's shoulders slumped against his chest.

"You want to talk about it?"

Lacey put her arms around him and held on tight for a moment. "Not really. Can we get out of here? This is Tony's story now."

She picked up her coat and bag from her desk, ducking the curious reporters milling around the newsroom. But Lacey and Vic were too fast for them. She crossed paths with Trujillo, who stopped her long enough for a quick statement. Mac wasn't around or answering his cell, but the weekend city editor wanted this story on the paper's Web site ASAP.

"You have to give me something to work with, Lacey." Tony stopped her escape. "I already had a *Post* reporter call me. We can't let the enemy get something we don't have, on a murder in our own building! Pojack wasn't really one of us, but then again, he was, in a way."

"I can't tell you anything. Broadway Lamont would have my head. However, why don't you ask Lamont if there is a blue velvet connection to the death in Black Martin, Virginia?" Lacey said. "Okay?"

Tony smiled. "Blue velvet connection. Got it." He sprinted toward the newsroom. Lacey and Vic made their escape in the opposite direction.

Lacey wouldn't feel secure until she was in her car, period. It was Saturday, and her vintage BMW was in front of *The Eye*, safe from the tenacious meter readers, the most efficient arm of the D.C. police department. But she'd never say that to Broadway Lamont. The twilight sky looked like sapphire silk and the air smelled like snow.

Lacey breathed it in as if she'd been underwater. She spotted a vehicle idling across the street. It was huge and pink and had majestic pink fins. It was a rare 1957 Cadillac Eldorado Biarritz.

The driver, Vic's mother, Nadine, was a no-nonsense cowgirl from Nevada who had married a Virginian and had mostly adapted to Washington ways. Now the image of an elegant East Coast matron, Nadine's wild side slipped out in subtle ways, like when she took the wheel of her Cadillac, her pink pride and joy. Wherever she went, men gathered to stare at her car. And her. She adored the attention.

"You didn't tell me you left your mother waiting outside," Lacey said. "In her pink Batmobile."

"You didn't ask."

Lacey jabbed him in the arm. "Very funny. What's she doing here?"

The woman in the car popped out and waved them over. Vic talked fast as they crossed the street. "She stopped at my place to ask about the party she's planning. She was there when I got your call. I had her drive me here so I can drive you home. And she wants to talk to you."

"Of course she does. It's that kind of day." Lacey liked Nadine, but now was not the time for a motherly chat.

They crossed the street, and Nadine gave Lacey a hug. "I won't pump you for information now, my dear—I know you've had a hard day. But eventually, I want all the details. Vic just gives me the glossy-magazine version of events."

"Thanks, Nadine. I can take it from here," Vic said.

"Just one thing, Lacey. Sean Victor won't give me a straight answer," Nadine complained. "Are you or are you not coming to my Valentine party?"

"I'm not really the Valentine-party type," Lacey said.

"It's a tradition in my neighborhood. Lots of fun. Vic will be there. And I know you don't want to disappoint me." Nadine wore a wicked smirk that said she knew when she had won. Lacey was trapped.

"Me? No, I wouldn't want to disappoint anyone. Except myself."

"I hate to exert pressure simply because I'm the mother of your boyfriend, but I will if necessary. With affection."

"I can't be held responsible if bad things happen," Lacey said. "I have bad luck with Valentine's Day."

"Don't worry about a thing." As mothers went, Nadine was pretty good, Lacey reflected, and not nearly so hard to handle as Lady Gwendolyn Griffin. "Then it's settled? All the ladies are wearing red or pink, but that's all spelled out on the invitation." She pulled one out of the pocket of her pink designer peacoat and handed it to Lacey. "And I would never insist, but if you wanted to make one of your spectacular desserts, I surely wouldn't complain."

Lacey told herself she should never have made that first dessert at Thanksgiving. "What did you have in mind?"

"You're the expert."

"Oh no. Not me. But I saw something today that Vic and I could make. Together," Lacey said.

Vic's eyebrows rose in alarm. Not Felicity's monstrous dessert? "Or we could always just pick up something at Bread and Chocolate."

"How does a double-chocolate torte with a raspberry-almond filling and layers of chocolate ganache sound?" The recipe was burning a hole in Lacey's pocket. And Felicity's words, *It takes a little effort,* terrified her. But Vic would help. He had helped her the last time.

"With pink icing?" Nadine inquired.

"What else?" Lacey linked her arm in Vic's. "I wouldn't dream of making it without Vic. He comes in handy when there's cake batter on the ceiling."

Nadine kissed Vic on the cheek. Mission accomplished. "I can't imagine what you two must be doing to get cake batter on the ceiling. Ah, young love."

They watched Nadine drive away in her big pink Caddie.

"You said you would never use Felicity's cooking," Vic protested.

"I said I would never let her cook for me. I didn't say a thing about not using her recipe," Lacey said. "Besides, she just gave it to me. It was like a sign. From above."

"Why did you go in today? You were supposed to be doing something restful, weren't you?" Vic was driving Lacey's BMW 2002. Her interrogation by Broadway Lamont hadn't been very restful. Now Vic was covering the same ground.

Lacey closed her eyes and leaned her head back against the seat. "Pojack called me and told me to get my ass down to *The Eye*."

"Pojack? The victim? On a Saturday? He's the one who wanted to let you go, right?"

"I guess I don't have to worry about that at the moment. You're right, it doesn't make sense that he'd fire me on a Saturday. But you never know. He was, as Wiedemeyer would say, a sneaky bastard." Lacey yawned. "Claudia told me he jumped the gun on the whole Crystal City announcement. I'd already spread that juicy news bite like a brush fire. So maybe he wanted to get rid of me in a hurry. But he doesn't seem like the type to want a face-to-face confrontation. He's a weasel. Was a weasel."

Vic drove the little Bimmer down the G.W. Parkway toward Old Town. The moon hung low in the sky, spilling silver light onto the Potomac River. A few boats were docked near Indigo Landing restaurant, some still wearing Christmas lights.

There was something else bothering Lacey. "This might sound crazy, but . . ."

"You're kidding? Something might sound crazy in a case where one man is shot to death and dyed blue and another is shot to death holding a blue velvet ribbon? And the one overwhelming connection between the two is Lacey Smithsonian? Darling, tell me what might possibly sound crazy."

"Is this that mockery thing I've heard tell of?"

"I learned it from the best."

"Pojack wouldn't call me on his own. I'm the last reporter on earth he'd want to talk with. And why fire me in person? Weasels have other weasels do their dirty work. But I was so freaked out, I didn't stop to think about it. What if someone *made* him call me?"

"Like with a gun to his head?" Vic considered it. "I like that. Our unknown suspect, the Velvet A, for lack of a better name, forces Pojack to have you come to *The Eye*, then kills the guy so that fashion reporter Lacey Smithsonian will be sure to find the body wrapped up with a blue ribbon."

"But why me?"

"Maybe it was a gift for you, Lacey. Pojack was going to RIF you, and now he's gone. Like Rod Gibbs."

"I don't like the way that sounds, Vic. But there is the ribbon."

"You're the only one outside of Tazewell Flanders and Claudia Darnell who would immediately understand the significance of the blue velvet ribbon." Vic pulled over into one of the little parks overlooking the Potomac. "Say it's all true. This killer wants publicity. He gets lucky, he gets you on the story. Now he wants you to write more about it. He's playing you, and he's moved onto your territory to do it."

"Am I safe or not?"

"He didn't stick around to harm you. This time. But he does want to use you."

"Like any source does." It was a common problem for reporters; they always had to ask what their news sources really wanted. This, however, was an extreme case.

"Darling, the killer is on the move and you're part of the game plan, because he likes what you've been writing. But what if Lacey Smithsonian starts writing something the Velvet A doesn't like? You're not safe."

The wind was whistling outside the car windows, sounding to Lacey like eerie laughter. The trees waved back and forth in the gusts. "One more thing bothers me. Claudia told me she'd take care of Pojack."

"You think she could have killed him?"

"Harlan saw her leave *The Eye* just before I got there. Her office is right across from Pojack's. And he was holding a blue velvet ribbon. She was the only person who knew about the ribbon and also had a strong motive. Besides *me*."

"Why kill him on her own territory? She's smarter than that."

"Smart people do stupid things."

"True." Vic looked tired and worried. The one curl he had so much trouble with fell over his forehead. "I hate this. It's all getting way too close to you."

Lacey played with his curl and kissed him. "I'll be careful."

"I really want you to come stay with me until this is all over," Vic said. He kissed her hand. "My place is more secure. I can keep you safe. Please, darling."

Lacey had a moment of panic. It felt like too much commitment too soon. Where would this lead? To sharing a toothbrush? And packing up her things seemed impossible at the moment. Her closet was a mess. Her shoes were all over the floor. She was still only half unpacked from their overnight in Black Martin. Her wardrobe needed serious remedial attention. She wished she had someone to do it for her. Someone like a Clothes Whisperer.

"Stay with me, Lacey."

She met his eyes. "Can I bring Aunt Mimi's trunk?"

"Darling, you can bring her whole elephant."

Whither the Clothes Whisperer?
Or: Taming the Wild Wardrobe!

Do you long for some mysterious stranger to ride into town and magically tame your clothes? Soothe your savage closet? Wrangle your wardrobe into apple-pie order? To stop your jackets and skirts from fighting with each other? Someone to persuade your pretty dresses not to jump off the hangers and hide in the dark behind their ugly sisters? Someone to make your unruly accessories work and play well together, so you can actually wear them with something?

Aha! You need a Clothes Whisperer, and so do I.

You have a closet full of clothes and nothing to wear. (Me too.) When you dig to the back of your deep dark closet, you discover clothes you've long since forgotten about. Your closet guards your clothes like a jealous troll, waiting to swallow up three Billy Goats Gruff, along with that perfect ruffled blouse you could swear you bought last year and haven't seen since.

Why do our clothes seem so much more attractive in our imaginations? Are they evil shape-shifters? Not only do they shift their shape, they shift *your* shape. You pull out a skirt you thought was oh, so flattering. But now you put it on and it makes your bottom resemble the hindquarters of a hippo.

Sure, there are personal shoppers and professional closet organizers. Are you brave enough and rich enough to hire a team of them? Do you have time to ride herd on them *and* your closet *and* your life? If so, lucky you.

The sad truth is that most of us have to face our

closets ourselves. All alone. Scary, isn't it? You and me, we have to be our own wardrobe wranglers. But how? Here are some suggestions.

- Clear a day to do battle with your closet. Accept that it will take all day. Put on some mood music and make yourself a pot of tea or coffee. Play something that will keep your spirits up and your energy high. (I like the Beach Boys.) If the very thought of closet wrangling exhausts you, remember all that lifting and tossing burns calories.
- Try on all your clothes, especially the ones you are iffy about and haven't worn since that last cheesecake. Yell and scream, jump up and down if you need to—there are no witnesses to put you on YouTube. I never said this would be easy, did I?
- A full-length mirror is essential. That's right. You have to see yourself top and bottom, up and down, left and right, front and back. Especially the rear view. This is usually where the yelling and screaming starts.
- Be ruthless! Ugly and rebellious clothes have to go. This includes the ones that never fit quite right, the blouses that have started to gap, the waistbands that won't quite close. The colors that looked good in the store but make you look like a corpse. Clothes that work for someone else but not for you have to go. Clothes that used to work for you but have turned on you, those especially have to go. Take no prisoners!
- Thin the herd. One pile for dry cleaning, one pile for mending and hemming, a third pile to ship to a toxic waste disposal site. Or Goodwill, or the charity of your choice. Caution: Do not try to give these discards to your friends and family. They'll just try to give them back to you someday.
- Round up the survivors. Corral all the clothes

that fit and flatter you, that work with your looks and your life. Arrange them by color and season. Separate the dresses, the skirts, the pants, the jackets, and the blouses. Save only the best, and the ones that bring back beautiful memories. Make notes on the survivors, pieces that work together and always make you look and feel good.

Haul out the losers and don't look back. Now it's time to reward yourself! Gaze at your lovely organized closet, full of promise and personality. You did it! You tamed the wild wardrobe, you Clothes Whisperer you.

chapter 31

"Why do we have to talk about murder and bake a cake at the same time?" Vic was pouring flour in a measuring cup. Lacey thought he looked adorable, a big boy playing house in her tiny kitchen. And he was complaining like one too.

"It's called multitasking, honey," Lacey said.

"And why did it cost eighty-seven dollars for the ingredients for just one cake?"

"Because it's for your mother." She measured out the white and brown sugars and stared at the recipe. There were too many steps. It was ludicrous. They needed a squadron of helpers. Or one Felicity Pickles.

"And why couldn't we have baked this at my place? My kitchen is bigger."

Just like a man, she thought. "Because you don't have the twenty-five cake pans and bowls and beaters and sifters and mixers and measuring spoons it requires. You don't have even one cake pan. Now, Vic darling, please measure out the baking chocolate. I'll get the sour cream." Lacey had taped the recipe to the cabinet next to the stove. She pointed to it. She was elbow deep in cake dough when the phone rang. Lacey cleaned off her hands and told Vic to keep working.

"Hello?"

"What happened?" Brooke never said hello. She thought it was a waste of time. "Did Pojack give you your walking papers?"

"No, someone gave him his walking papers. He's dead, Brooke."

"O.M.G. No one ever tells me anything. Is this on *The Eye*'s site?"

"Maybe, but there is nothing like reading real newsprint. You should buy a subscription." Lacey heard Brooke's laptop clicking in the background.

"Found it. Hang on." Brooke was silent for at least five seconds while she scanned Trujillo's story. "We're coming right over."

"*We* means with Damon?"

"That's right."

"No, Brooke, wait—" The phone went dead. "Uh oh."

"What?" Vic looked up from the batter.

"Brooke's on her way over with Captain Conspiracy." Lacey put the phone down and sank into a chair.

"The Conspiracy Cavalry to the rescue?"

"Apparently."

"Maybe they can help you pack your things."

Lacey stood up and returned to the kitchen. "First things first. We put the cake in the oven."

"Who else knows about the velvet ribbon in Gibbs's coffin?" Vic asked.

"Just us and the cops. And Claudia. I e-mailed her. She may have told Tazewell Flanders."

"All right. Our so-called Avenger was at the funeral," Vic said. "He or she may or may not have killed Gibbs. He or she may or may not know that the cops know about the ribbon and were all over the casket. The ribbon may be a warning of more deaths to come. Or a private joke. Or a deliberate misdirection. Or maybe the ribbon is his personal signature, for his private amusement. Or maybe it's his signal to you, because he knows how you like that kind of thing. Fashion clues."

"I don't like this game anymore," Lacey said. "The reporter is not supposed to be part of the story. Let's bake a cake."

Brooke and Damon arrived at Lacey's apartment door just as the cakes were coming out of the oven.

"You're telling me Lamont released you?" Brooke was asking her. Lacey got the impression this was taking some of the fun out of it for Ms. Barton, Esq.

"I was never detained. He added the stick-around-for-my-calls stuff, but that was it."

"You don't need an attorney, then?"

"Not at the moment. But knowing me, I'd like you to stay tuned for further developments. You don't think I killed Pojack, do you, Brooke?"

"Oh, come on. However, sometimes the system has a way of pointing the finger at the innocent. And that's a good thing. It lets lawyers get rich." Brooke slipped off her Burberry, and Damon set up his laptop on Lacey's dining room table. The lid was plastered with stickers advertising such things as *The X-Files* (THE TRUTH IS OUT THERE), *Battlestar Galactica,* and his own baby, DeadFed dot com. That sticker read: THE TRUTH IS IN HERE.

"Damon, what are you doing?" Lacey asked. Vic came out of the kitchen to see what was going on. Damon's fingers were flying over the keyboard.

"Sending out an SOS to our DeadFed friends list. Chatter's been low about our Velvet Avenger, but this will bump it up."

"Hold on, partner," Vic said. "Can you do that without writing about the murder today at *The Eye*?"

Damon stopped typing and considered Vic with some suspicion. "Why? Is there a connection? Trujillo's story suggested it, but he didn't quite come out and say it."

"Lacey?" Brooke asked. Neither Lacey nor Vic said anything.

"So there is a connection," Damon said. "Even better." He resumed his mad typing.

Lacey put her hand on his. "Don't jump to conclusions."

He leaned back and smiled. "There's got to be a connection. A murder at a factory where Claudia Darnell is a partner? A murder at *The Eye*, where she's the publisher? It couldn't be a coincidence."

"Sure it could," Vic said.

"But it's not. And you don't want me writing about it?"

Damon paused, fingers in the air above his keyboard, ready to attack. "Why?"

"If there is a connection, and I'm not saying there is," Vic said, "it would be jumping the gun, so to speak. Linking the two murders on DeadFed could make it much harder to find this killer. Or it might provoke him to escalate."

"You're saying that the Velvet Avenger reads Conspiracy Clearinghouse?" Brooke assumed her lawyer-in-court stance.

"If he didn't before yesterday, he probably does now. You were both at the funeral, weren't you?" Vic said.

"And you had a tableful of fans," Lacey added.

"And I got a great exclusive," Damon said.

"You weren't the only writer there," Lacey said.

"But I'm the only one working the conspiracy angle."

"We have to isolate what we know from what the killer knows," Vic said. "Pojack wanted to fire Lacey. She mentioned it to a lot of people yesterday after the funeral."

Lacey took a deep breath. "I'm going to tell you something strictly off the record, Damon, if you can handle that."

Brooke and Damon shared a look. "Okay. For now."

"Pojack had a blue velvet ribbon in his hand."

"Aha! And now he's dead." Brooke jumped ahead to the conclusion. "So they are connected! No question. But how?"

"One of my DeadFed readers could be the Avenger? Or an Avenger copycat?" Damon put his chin in his hands. For a moment, he looked both intrigued and repelled. Intrigued won by a landslide. "All right. We won't feed the beast. We'll just monitor all the online comments and ask for information," he finally said. "Let's see what's out there. Okay, partner?" he asked Lacey.

"We're not partners," she said.

"Sure we are." Damon smacked her in the arm.

Vic held Lacey back from slamming Damon's laptop on his fingertips.

The perfect chocolate cake rounds were cooling on the racks when Stella arrived, limping on one cast and one very high heel. She was followed by Nigel Griffin and his mother, Lady Gwendolyn.

"That's funny. I didn't schedule a party tonight," Lacey said at the door.

"Brooke called and invoked the Code," Stella explained as she handed her coat to Lacey. "The Pink Collar Code." Their sort-of-secret code that called out the Pink Collar Posse: the three of them.

Lacey spun on her heels and faced Brooke. "You didn't."

"I did. One for all, and all for you," Brooke said.

"Like you did for me," Stella said. "We are here for you in your hour of need. You got a murder. We got champagne. I gotta sit down." Stella hobbled to the sofa and collapsed. She pointed to the amazing Technicolor cast on her leg. "This thing is heavy."

"No wonder. We glued ten pounds of rhinestones on it," Lacey said.

Nigel plopped down on the sofa and looked at Vic. "Got a beer, mate?"

Vic dug a Dos Equis out of the refrigerator. "What are you doing here, Griffin?"

"Not quite sure, actually. My wounded dove, Stella, told me she was going to help Lacey figure out this murder business. There's another one, I take it? Because Smithsonian can't throw a stone without stumbling over some new cadaver." Griffin looked remorseful. "I expressly forbade Stella to get involved. And, well, here we are."

"Nigel *forbidding* me? It was hilarious, Lacey. Like something out of *Father Knows Best*. Lady G and I thought we'd bust a gut laughing. So cute." She combed his hair with her spiky fingernails and kissed his forehead.

Griffin put his feet up on Lacey's trunk. He was obviously loving the attention. "Next thing I knew, the three of us were in Stella's Mini on our way over here." His head swiveled from Stella to Gwendolyn and back again. "And I thought they'd hate each other. Shows what I know about women."

"But, Nigel," Lacey said, knocking his feet to the floor. "Aren't you glad they like each other?"

He sank even farther into the upholstery. "It's like putting two forces of nature together and creating a perfect storm." He put his hand against his forehead in a swoon, like Camille.

"Where's the ambassador tonight?" Vic asked. "So nice to see you again, by the way, Lady Gwendolyn."

"And you, dear Sean Victor. The ambassador is at Nigel's flat. Drinking your dreadful American beer and watching some sort of bizarre sporting event on the telly. Told us to have a wonderful time," Lady Gwendolyn said. "My, something smells delicious."

"Lacey, you're baking!" Stella said. "Whatcha making?"

"A cake for Vic's mom. A Valentine surprise."

"Let me help." Stella hobbled to the kitchen and studied the recipe. "Holy cow! You do need help. Lucky we came over. So now we make the filling? Where's your raspberry jam?"

"Really, Smithsonian," Nigel said. "You're at home on a Saturday night, domesticating? You're not out baiting a killer? I'm shocked."

"I've never smashed a cake on anyone's head before, Nigel, but there is always a first time," Lacey promised.

"Wait till I get my camera," Brooke said.

"I want a copy for my blog," Stella chimed in. "Stellarific dot com."

"Nigel, do behave," Gwendolyn said. "It's only men who can do just one thing at a time. Sometimes you have to do something restful with your hands, like cooking, while your mind works on an entirely different problem. Like murder. Now, do be quiet, and let the answers bubble up. We can discuss the murders while we bake. Victor, will you assist me with the bubbly?"

Vic popped the cork and Lacey poured hot cream over chocolate chips to make a ganache.

"Nigel, sweetheart, you can help me mix the raspberry filling?" Stella asked.

"Yeah, why don't you?" Vic said. "I like to see you working, Nigel. It reminds me that anything is possible." Nigel's mother snorted with laughter into her champagne.

After the troops went home, Lacey surveyed the crumbs of their culinary handiwork. There were just a few slices left. If they hadn't determined who the killer was, they had at least declared the dessert a success. She grumbled and rubbed her back, sore from stress and standing and stirring batter.

"What's the matter, Lacey?"

"I had hoped we could just make the thing and freeze it for your mom's party. And then the whole posse came over and we ate it. Every bite. Now we're going to have to do it all over again."

It was Vic's turn to grumble. "I forgot about that part. But next time we can do it without the posse. Right?"

"Only if they let us bake a cake at an Undisclosed Location."

chapter 32

"Smithsonian, what in the name of the sweet First Amendment is going on at *The Eye*?" It was after eleven p.m., very late by Washington standards. It had been a very long day.

"Hi, Mac. Yes, I'm fine. Thanks for asking." Lacey leaned back on Vic's sofa and closed her eyes. She heard the blender in Vic's clean and up-to-date and nearly empty kitchen, blissfully free of baking pans. Vic was whipping up piña coladas, another talent of his of which she had been unaware.

Vic had recently moved from his temporary digs near his folks' house into a newish town house in McLean, Virginia. Although it was an impressive place, with plenty of room and light, the oh, so desirable granite countertops, and a two-car garage, it felt very far from the action to Lacey, who loved her slightly funky and crowded Old Town Alexandria.

Aunt Mimi's trunk didn't exactly mesh with Vic's bachelor décor of leather and heavy wood, but its brass buckles glistened in the firelight and made Lacey feel more at home. She put her feet up on it.

"I just got some frantic garbled message from Claudia Darnell, and of course your name popped up in the middle of it," Mac complained. "Is it true? Was Walt Pojack shot dead right in front of you?"

"Um, yes and no, Mac." She reeled off the facts the way an obituary writer might put it. "Walter Pojack, chief operating officer of *The Eye Street Observer,* died today in his office, slain by an unknown assailant. The cause of death was not released by the Metropolitan Police, but sources said Pojack was shot once in the head. Foul play is suspected. He was *not* shot dead right in front of *Eye Street* fashion reporter Lacey Smithsonian. She just found the body, the way she always does." Lacey heard the blender shut off.

"I read all that, Smithsonian. Where were the security guards?"

"You got me, Mac. But you know there are ways to evade the guards. Like coming up through the garage and the back stairs. You might want to talk with Wiedemeyer for the more colorful commentary. He was with me when we found Pojack dead. I think the words *solid-gold bastard* might figure in pretty heavily."

"The jinx was there?" Mac tried to stay as far away from the death and dismemberment reporter as he could. "I don't want anything to do with Wiedemeyer. Not if I don't have to. And what on earth were you doing at *The Eye* on Saturday?" That looked like it was going to be the question of the day. "You filed your story. You were done. And why were you talking to Pojack? He's the last person on earth—"

"Hang on a minute." Lacey put the phone down. Vic came bearing drinks on a tray. She sat up and sipped the cool white concoction. She imagined Mac was likewise guzzling something soothing from his favorite blue bottle of Maalox. She picked up the phone again.

"I'm waiting, Smithsonian."

"Pojack called me at home. Said he had to see me. Told me to come to the office. Said it was important." *Ow! Ice headache!* Lacey closed her eyes and rubbed one temple.

"What on earth for? Don't keep me waiting, Smithsonian. I got the lede, now give me the jump."

"Okay, okay. I raced downtown because Pojack, the big jerk, made it sound like a matter of life and death." She paused. "Which I guess it was. But I really thought he was going to can me."

"Where the hell'd you get that idea?"

"From Walt Pojack! He told me the other day to update my résumé."

Mac paused a moment. "I don't know what kind of game he was playing, Smithsonian. Your beat's not in danger. Never was. And Claudia wants you on the Black Martin story. She's counting on you. I'm counting on you."

"Lucky me. Anyway, when I got to the office, I went to my desk. I hung up my coat and looked for coffee, because that's what I do. I ran into Harlan, and he volunteered to go with me and fight the dragon. That's what he does. We found Pojack shot dead. And that was that."

Lacey could hear Mac's wife, Kim, in the background, calling Mac to bed. Once upon a time, Mac would have been in the office six and a half days out of seven. Now he was a soon-to-be adoptive father of two young daughters and he was taking fatherhood seriously. That was the reason Mac hadn't been in the office today and was catching up with the Pojack story in the middle of the night, Washington time. These days he scheduled his weekends around bike rides and family time with little Jasmine and Lily Rose. Lacey heard him tell Kim he would be off the phone in a minute.

"Who's covering the story for the paper?" Mac asked.

"Trujillo. I thought he'd called you," Lacey said. "Check your messages, Mac. But I guess he could hand it off to Kelly Kavanaugh, if you like. She's dying for a real, meaty crime story."

"Bite your tongue, Smithsonian."

"Consider it bitten."

"And Lacey, are you all right?"

"Me? A little shaken up, but I'm fine."

"Good," he grunted. "Kim and the girls would have my head if anything happened to you. And, um, I'd be upset too."

"Thanks, Mac. Kiss the girls for me." Lacey hung up the phone.

Vic joined her on the sofa with his cocktail. Her cell phone rang again. Lacey handed it to him. "Whoever it is, tell them I'm dead. Wait, unless it's my mother."

Vic answered the phone and listened. He said a few words and handed it back to Lacey. "I think you're going to want to take this," he whispered. "Claudia Darnell."

She gave him the evil eye. Lacey sat up and swung her feet to the floor. "Yes, Claudia?" Her heart was beating fast.

"I can't believe Walt Pojack is dead. I've just spent the last hour answering questions from that Detective Lamont, but he didn't answer any of my questions," Claudia said in a rush. "He kept asking me if I'd been threatened. He said you were there! You discovered the body? That's dreadful. Are you all right?"

"Just another day at the office." The piña colada wasn't soothing her headache yet. "I heard you were at *The Eye* today too."

"That's right. The detective was all over me about that. I stopped by to pick up some things. I was going to do some paperwork. But Walt was there, doing God knows what," Claudia said. "I didn't feel like dealing with him, so I took my files and left. Apparently, I just missed the killer."

"You were lucky."

"Yes. It's just sinking in."

"What does Lamont think?" Lacey asked.

"He thought it would be very nice if I were the killer so he could wrap this up and go home. He dropped your name several times."

"Yeah, we're old— Um. Acquaintances. Unfortunately." Lacey took a cautious sip of her icy drink. "What did he say about the blue velvet ribbon?"

"He said anyone can pick up a ribbon at a craft store. And do I own a gun? At that point, I told him he could contact my lawyers. I was through with the interview."

"I'm sure he liked that."

"I don't particularly care what he likes. Lacey, tell me what you saw at *The Eye*."

"Walt was shot in the forehead. There was a blue velvet ribbon wound around his hand. It looked identical to the one you got. And the one I saw in Gibbs's coffin."

"But why Walt? He had nothing to do with Dominion Velvet."

"It doesn't make sense to me either. Unless—" Lacey hesitated.

"What? Go on. Nothing makes sense about this."

"Unless someone actually decided to be an avenger, not only in Black Martin, but at *The Eye* as well."

"I know Walt was kind of a wild card. He was spreading rumors to keep people on their toes, he told me. But he hadn't actually let anyone go. In fact, Walt was specifically instructed by me and the board not to fire anyone. If we have to lose positions, we will start through attrition."

He started today. "Walter Pojack told me personally my job was on the chopping block. And I was overheard telling a friend all about him while I was at the funeral yesterday. When he called and insisted that I come to work today, I was afraid he wanted to get rid of me."

"Walt called you? At home?" Claudia was aghast. "And you think that's why he was killed? To punish him for threatening your job?"

God, I hope not. "No, not for me specifically. And the killer might not have been looking for Walter Pojack." Lacey took a deep breath. "When he came to *The Eye*, I think he might have expected to find someone else, Claudia. Like you."

Claudia paused. "Yes, that crossed my mind." Claudia sounded cool, but Lacey couldn't believe she was as calm as she sounded.

"Instead, Walt got in the killer's, or the Avenger's way. It's a possibility. At any rate, he left his calling card. The ribbon. You could be in danger, Claudia," Lacey said, even though she still had nagging doubts in the back of her mind. But doubt was her business. "Did Congressman Flanders get a blue ribbon?"

"Yes. His staff said they found one in the mail. There was no note, so they thought nothing of it and tossed it, but they were able to retrieve it before the trash was picked up. That's where I went today right after *The Eye*. Tazewell wanted to know if it was the same as mine. It was."

"Then I'd say he's a target too."

"The worst possible time for his candidacy." Claudia sighed. "What are the police doing about catching this guy?"

"The usual, I suppose. The killer has crossed state lines. Virginia state cops and D.C. cops don't necessarily play nice together. And Black Martin is probably just pleased this killer has moved north."

"It could also be a copycat," Claudia said. "One of Tazewell's enemies."

"Maybe. Vic says if someone threatens a congressman, the FBI usually joins the party. But Claudia, you need some security of your own. At least until this is over."

"Tazewell has an important fund-raiser Monday night. I plan to be there. *The Eye* might very well be endorsing him for governor. And Lacey, your job was never in danger. Your beat is far too popular. You sell papers. The public likes you. I like you. And I rely on you. So stay safe."

Lacey felt a little dizzy. "Are you sorry Pojack is dead?"

There was a beat. "Let's say I'm sorry his death is going to cause us so many problems. That's for damn sure." She told Lacey again to be careful and clicked off. Vic took the phone from her. Lacey rubbed her temples again. This time it wasn't the piña colada. Trying to make these two murders fit together was making her head hurt.

Lacey moved their drinks off Aunt Mimi's trunk, clicked the buckles open, and lifted the lid. Mimi's bolero jacket pattern and the unfinished pieces of dark moss-green-and-gold shot velvet were still right on top. She handed Vic the largest piece of velvet.

"Isn't it beautiful? This is some of that shot velvet I was telling you about."

"I thought you said they called it shot through."

"Either one, I think. Shot velvet is called that because in the weaving process, one color is 'shot through' the other. See how it changes colors, depending on the way you look at it? The light catches each color from different angles," Lacey said. She turned the fabric this way and that, and they watched it change from gold to green and back again.

"Uh huh. Very pretty." He sipped his drink. Fabric was not his métier. "Shot through velvet. Kind of like Rod Gibbs. The bullet went through Rod and the velvet."

"Like these murders, Vic. Look at them one way and they seem to be all about revenge for lost jobs and a lost way of life. But look at the facts another way, and the motives for sending Gibbs to perdition are much more personal."

"Right. A political angle and a personal one too."

"The shot velvet uses two colors to make one fabric. What if the two motives are 'shot through' each other? The killer uses the so-called Velvet Avenger angle to cover his personal reasons for killing Rod Gibbs, and the personal motives to cover the political?"

"So was it basically personal or basically political?"

"Maybe both. Gibbs was a rotten guy," Lacey said. "And people are angry about losing their jobs. Everything in Black Martin is personal. And everything in Washington is political. Maybe both kinds of motives are at work here. But are there two killers? Or just one?"

"You have a wonderful mind for complications," Vic said.

"Claudia suggested a copycat killer." Lacey picked up her drink and held it to her throbbing forehead. "Maybe some political enemy of Tazewell Flanders, the congressman who's running for governor. And maybe the killer was looking for Claudia first. But they found Pojack instead, and so—"

"Slow down! You're heading into Conspiracy Clearinghouse territory. Maybe you should let Damon handle this one."

"That's not funny. I'm going to be the one to write this story."

"I have a great idea," Vic said. "Let's stop talking. Maybe the answers will come to us in a dream."

"Or a nightmare." Lacey wanted a deep, dreamless sleep. Vic started to massage Lacey's neck and shoulders.

"There is a time for everything, Lacey," he said in a voice soft as velvet, "and now is the time for you and me to stop talking about death. And start living." The knots in her shoulders were easing under his strong hands. She felt all her anxiety beginning to slide away from her. *Better than Aunt Mimi's trunk . . .*

"Don't stop. Sometimes you're really smart, Vic Donovan."

"You're just figuring that out?" His hands slipped away from the back of her neck and his lips took their place.

chapter 33

"Why do we have to stand at the back?" Vic asked Lacey.

"Because I'm a bad Catholic."

He grinned at her and she turned away to keep from laughing. "I'm not a very good Catholic myself, but I don't think God would prevent us from sitting until we can go to confession."

"Okay, but we have to sit in the back."

St. Luke's in McLean, near Vic's place, was more modern in architecture than Lacey's usual church in Old Town. It featured an impressive figure of the risen Christ instead of a crucifix, and it had an open layout where every pew had a good view. Unfortunately, that meant others could see them too.

"Good grief!" Lacey turned her head quickly.

"What is it?" Vic looked around.

"It's your parents."

As if she'd heard Lacey talking, Nadine Donovan turned her head and caught sight of them. She nudged her husband, who also turned and winked at the sinners in the back of the church. Vic's dad, Sean Donovan, had an expression of surprise and skepticism. Nadine waved for them to join her, but Lacey headed for the first open pew. She knelt and put her face in her hands to hide her embarrassment.

Vic knelt beside her and whispered, "We'll never live this one down—getting caught together in church? Instead of in bed? What a scandal. This will cost you some Our Fathers."

"Be quiet," she whispered back. "I'm praying."

"You can't pray your way out of this one," he said. "Oh the shame."

"I can try."

"You know we can't sneak out early now. We'll have to face the music. You temptress, dragging me into a church! What will we tell the children?"

Lacey ignored him and tried to concentrate on the sermon. It was a happy day for Nadine. She caught up with Lacey and Vic after the service and invited them to brunch.

"It would please your mother," Sean said to Vic.

"Unfortunately, Dad, we're about to take a short road trip." Vic pulled out his keys and rattled them.

"A rain check, Nadine," Lacey said. *What road trip?*

"Does this have anything to do with blue bodies?" Nadine asked. "Or the body at *The Eye*?"

"We read the papers, son. There's no use in fabricating," Sean said. "Your mother always finds out whatever she wants to find out. And the stories are all over the Web. You have a most colorful job, young lady." He winked at Lacey.

"We'll be careful," Vic said, as he whisked Lacey to the Jeep.

She waved good-bye. "Thank you." Lacey leaned over and kissed him.

"What for?"

"For not telling your mother I'm staying at your house. Near their house. And that's why we're in their church together. You know. I don't want her leaping to the wrong conclusion. Or possibly the right conclusion. Oh, you know what I mean."

"I won't have to. She'll find out. You heard my dad."

Lacey ignored him pointedly. "So what was all that about a road trip? I thought we were going to brunch." Lacey buckled her seat belt.

"We can get brunch in Black Martin." Vic put the Jeep in gear and waited for traffic before pulling out of the lot. "I'm not sure the local cops and the Virginia state troopers and D.C. homicide are going to pull this case together soon enough. There's too much bureaucracy. Too many motives. Not enough facts."

"Not to mention a lot of strutting around and territory marking. Guy stuff."

"That too. You want to go to Black Martin with me? Without traffic, we can probably make it in a couple of hours."

"Try and stop me, darling. I can't believe you want to get us more involved. But I'm game." Lacey thought of the many times he had tried to divert her from a dangerous story.

"That's actually the last thing I want, but we may be able to point them in the right direction before anyone else dies. You think the next targets on this nut job's list are Claudia and the congressman?"

"Yes. Blue velvet ribbons. The Velvet A was after Claudia yesterday, and Pojack just got in the way. I'm sure of it. About ninety percent sure. I'm hardly ever one hundred percent sure. So tell me, how are we going to help the police?"

"Delicately," Vic said.

Lacey laughed. "Maybe we can tie it up with a big velvet bow."

"The cops aren't stupid, sweetheart. They just look that way sometimes. They act that way too. But they have too much to do, and all of these jurisdictions—local, state, and the District, and heaven help us, possibly the Feds. None of them like each other much. They don't want to be told what to do, and they each have to think it's all their own idea."

"Just like you did when you were a cop?" He *grrrr*-ed at her. "So why do you want to help them?" she asked.

"Keeping you in one piece and in the pink and out of blue velvet is reason enough for me."

"Suits me fine." She smiled to herself. She felt like she had passed some invisible test, for Vic to include her willingly in an open murder investigation.

They picked up road-trip supplies and headed for I-95 South. She popped in a CD that Vic said he had compiled for her, titled *Songs in the Key of Blue*. It started off with "Blue" by LeAnn Rimes. It made Lacey laugh.

"When did you have time to do this?" she asked.

"Hey, men can be multitaskers too." Vic began a run-down of exactly what they knew. "Who heard you talk about Pojack at the funeral?"

"The usual suspects. Sykes and his band of DeadFed-heads."

"Jealous of Conspiracy Clearinghouse? Damon's fans are even wackier than yours."

"He can have them," she said. "You know. Dirk Sykes, Blythe Harrington, Hank Richards, Tom Nicholson, Kira Evans, and Inez Garcia. Same group we met at Dominion Velvet."

"What about Armstrong, the local cop?"

"I'm pretty sure he didn't hear me talking about Pojack. After his argument with Caine, he went straight to Honey Gibbs's side and stayed there, even while I was talking with her. He wouldn't leave her alone long enough to take a road trip to Washington to bump off Pojack." The next song was Chris Isaak's "Forever Blue." *Oh this is perfect!*

"What do you think of the merry widow Honey Gibbs as a suspect?"

"Why would she kill Pojack? She had no reason to kill anyone except Rod. And one woman alone probably couldn't drag Rod around and attach him to that spool," Lacey said. "But what if there are two killers?"

"One woman could have a partner. Honey Gibbs and Armstrong, for example. Could also be two women," Vic pointed out. "But we have another possible scenario. One person kills Rod with his own gun. For personal motives. Someone else likes the idea. Hears the Velvet Avenger theory. Kills Pojack with a different gun, for different motives. And uses the velvet ribbons to make a false connection. Blue ribbon equals red herring. We're looking for someone with a motive to kill Gibbs, but maybe Pojack's killer had no such motive. And might or might not be the same killer."

Lacey thought of Claudia. There was still that nagging doubt. "So Pojack's killer might have put the ribbon in Rod's casket, not Rod's killer? Why would a killer with a motive against Pojack be in Black Martin?"

"Unknown. It still brings us back to Black Martin." He

took a sip of his coffee. "Now let's come up with some idea of who to talk to by the time we arrive."

"There's time," Lacey said, checking the exit signs on the highway. "We haven't even hit Fredericksburg yet."

"What about Sykes? He came up with the Velvet Avenger theory."

They both knew Sykes's enthusiasm seemed to be fueled by reading Conspiracy Clearinghouse. For all the man's bluster, he struck Lacey and Vic as a guy with a big imagination and more enthusiasm than follow-through. When it came to action, Lacey thought, Sykes would just as soon go fishing. Or fish on the Internet. Vic offered another name.

"Blythe Harrington. She's hotheaded. She's really angry about losing her job. She threw a pair of scissors at the corpse." He lifted one dark eyebrow. "That's suggestive."

"Couldn't be her. She was really outraged about the ruined velvet. She might kill Rod Gibbs in a fight, but she would never have killed him in cold blood and then destroyed her own velvet. She loved that velvet."

"Inez Garcia. She strikes me as more of a follower than an instigator. So could she be the partner?"

"Inez hooked up with Sykes. Together they could have done it. Then Sykes comes up with his Velvet Avenger story. Misdirection?"

"Maybe." Vic sounded dubious.

"There were a lot of hookups the night we were there, after the body was discovered," Lacey said. "At least, it seems that way."

"Death does that. Death changes things. People realize life is short and brutal, and what are they waiting for? They go to bed with someone. They prove they're alive. It's romantic. It's all in Hemingway."

"Get out of here," Lacey snickered. "Anyway, as I was saying, Dirk Sykes hooked up with Inez Garcia. Honey Gibbs was with Gavin Armstrong, and I think Kira Evans might have hooked up with Hank Richards."

"What makes you say that?"

"I don't think they wanted anyone to notice. So I noticed. Hank Richards was pretty cool and collected that night. He didn't drink as much as the others, and he took particularly good care of Kira. Without making any fuss about it. I thought it was strange at the time that Kira was wearing long sleeves and a turtleneck when everyone else was in short sleeves and some were in shorts," Lacey said. "That's not the best protective gear, but it was hot in the factory and the dryers were on. Nicholson told me it could get to ninety degrees in there in the winter. Kira kept rubbing her arms. I guess the wool would have been pretty itchy in those temperatures. I was awfully warm myself. Inez teased her about having a love bite, which showed on her neck. Anyway, Hank diverted the conversation like a gentleman."

"All you're really saying is that Richards is a classier guy than Sykes. But yeah, they could have hooked up," Vic admitted. "So maybe Kira was covering up a hickey? And if that's the case, they might even have been hooking up right when Rod took his last stroll through the factory."

"I love these romantic chats, Vic. Hemingway, hickeys, and hookups." Lacey checked her watch. Ella Fitzgerald and Louis Armstrong were singing "Under a Blanket of Blue" on the CD player. "Why did Rod Gibbs derail the security cameras the night he died?"

"He disabled the cameras because he was up to no good," Vic laughed. "He was an up-to-no-good kind of guy. But what specifically was he after? If we narrow that down, we might narrow down his killer's motives."

"You said motive is misleading," Lacey said.

"Not always."

"In that case, Nicholson suspected Rod was skimming money from the company. But Rod couldn't have gone there to take money, because there wasn't any kept on-site. Maybe some petty cash. So why bother?"

"More likely he was after records," Vic said. "Files, documents, CDs, hard drives. Maybe he wanted to cover his tracks."

"Okay. But he was also a guy who was into immediate gratification. What if he went to the factory that night to pull more of his harassment-and-intimidation crap?" Lacey rubbed her face.

"What's bothering you, Lacey?"

"Something Nigel's mom said about having to find the quiet to find the answer. Or something like that."

"Has the answer boiled up, then?" Vic looked over at her, then back at the road.

"No, but I keep thinking about the one quiet person in all of this: Kira Evans. She was the bookkeeper. She worked late that night because Nicholson asked her to. She knew about Gibbs's embezzling. Maybe Rod went there to get what he'd been after for so long."

"She said she left before eleven," Vic pointed out. "Rod wasn't killed till later."

"Yeah, that's what she *said*. That's what everybody says. Her only alibi is her daughter. There are no security tapes to prove that one way or the other."

"Ironic, isn't it? Rod derailed the lousy security system that might have shown us his killer."

"What if it was Kira who killed him?" Lacey looked in the paper sack, hoping for some more muffin crumbs. The bag was empty.

"Her? Darling, you just took quite a leap."

"Kira Evans filed a sexual harassment claim against Rod. Remember, Honey Gibbs said Rod never forgot a slight. He always paid it back. Like the boat. He schemed until he got that boat, the *Gypsy Princess*, away from Hank Richards and Dirk Sykes. He slept with Sykes's wife. He tried to get Hank fired. He made Honey suffer." Lacey turned the music down a little. Madeleine Peyroux was singing "Blue Alert."

"Okay, Gibbs is a rotten guy. I get it."

"But Gibbs hadn't gotten his revenge on Kira Evans, not yet. He toed the line after her harassment complaint, but he was running out of time. He wouldn't have many more opportunities to even the score. To get her alone. What if he still wanted her sexually, and he wanted to punish her? Maybe it was the same thing."

"He planned to assault her that night? That's why he messed with the cameras, so there'd be no proof? But why, with all these likely candidates, are you settling on Kira?" Vic glanced sideways at her. "What's going on in that dangerous brain of yours?"

"Kira's love bite. And her reaction when Inez teased her," Lacey said. "Yesterday, Felicity had a hickey. She was all giggles and blushes when Broadway Lamont pointed it out. But she still smiled at Harlan. She really loves him, the poor schnook. She may not have enjoyed being busted, but she was proud of— Well, I don't need to go into that, do I, Vic? But there was nothing like that with Kira. No secret smile, no love. Just embarrassment and discomfort. So what if Kira's mark wasn't a hickey or a love bite, but something more serious? Something like . . . bruises?"

"From Gibbs? Gibbs left marks on her throat? If that's true, Lacey, then killing him was self-defense. Kira could say, 'He assaulted me, Officer, so I killed him.' Gibbs had a history. Everybody hated him. The cops down there would be happy to believe her. She walks. She's a local hero, in fact. So why the big cover-up? And why truss him up like some strange cult sacrifice to the Blue Velvet Gods?"

Lacey closed her eyes and went over what she remembered from her visit to Black Martin, the factory tour and the discovery of Gibbs's body, and that evening in the Mexican restaurant.

"Kira was quiet and edgy that night, when everyone else was rowdy," Lacey finally said. "She didn't drink margaritas with the rest of the laid-off workers. She had one wine spritzer."

"Well, aren't you the hall monitor." Vic grinned. "Doesn't make her a killer, sweetheart. She's mighty small."

"When will you macho men ever learn?" Lacey snorted. "Like Shakespeare says, 'Though she be but little, yet she is fierce.' You're right. She is small. But angry and backed into a corner, who knows what she'd be capable of? Rod was shot with his own gun."

"If she killed him, and I'm not convinced she did, she had to have help for the rest of it," Vic said. "Did she hit Wade the security doofus over the head? Did she dye Gibbs blue? And what about Walt Pojack? Did she do that too?"

"That might be where the Velvet Avenger comes in. Taking advantage of the first murder to lead everyone in the wrong direction." Lacey rubbed her head. "Or . . . I don't know."

"You don't know what?"

"I don't know how Kira could possibly dye the man blue! Or why! Except that it's sort of poetic justice. And I don't believe she killed Pojack."

"Okay, she's still the top of our list for the day."

"Think she'll talk?" Lacey liked his confidence.

"No harm in trying. And I'll have to give Mordecai Caine a heads-up." They pulled over at the next exit for a quick break to change drivers. Vic made a call to the state cop while Lacey bought sodas at a McDonald's.

"What did Caine say?" Lacey asked when she got in the Jeep's driver's seat and adjusted the seat and mirrors.

"What I expected. He thanked me for my interest and information. But to please remember that the state police have the investigation under control." Vic laughed. "It's like what I used to say to certain media busybodies."

"Yes, I seem to remember that." She poked him, then pulled the Jeep onto the highway. "But I was never a busybody. The word you're looking for is *reporter*."

"If you say so." He changed the subject. "We'll be having lunch with Forrest."

"Turtledove. My man."

"The man. He's checking on Kira's whereabouts, so we can talk to her later."

"We're not the police, Vic. So far, she's been a very quiet lady."

"I'm running the security contract for the factory she loves." Vic flashed his devastating smile. "And I can be real persuasive when I want information."

"What do you want to know, cowboy? I'll tell you everything I know." Lacey grinned at him. "Maybe."

chapter 34

"Swanky place," Lacey said. The Flaming Pit Bar-B-Q on the outskirts of Black Martin was crowned by a happy pig wearing a chef's hat, outlined in neon flames.

"Only the best for you, sweetheart." Vic opened the Pit's door for her. "It's supposed to have a great brunch."

Once inside the place, Lacey still had her doubts. It looked more like a burned-out Saturday night than a fresh Sunday afternoon. The walls were dark wood. The oak booths were scarred with graffiti, and the place had a smoky feel, even though Virginia's bars and restaurants had finally gone nonsmoking. The locals were watching a basketball game and paid no attention to the newcomers at the bar.

Turtledove was waiting for them. His grin was fierce, and Lacey was glad he was on their side.

"Armstrong," Vic nodded toward the window as someone pulled up in the lot. "I believe that's his pickup now."

"Why is he here?" Lacey asked.

"I invited him. Invited Caine too," Vic said. "Professional courtesy. Caine said no. Professional discourtesy."

The door opened. He wasn't in uniform, but Officer Gavin Armstrong still looked like a cop. With Vic and Turtledove, Armstrong made it look like a meeting of the Muscle Dudes Club. Everyone shook hands. A waitress showed them all to a booth, where they ordered brunch platters and drinks. It wasn't cutting the tension.

"I didn't think you were actively involved in the investigation," Lacey said to Armstrong, when their drinks arrived. He seemed a little less like a pit bull than the last time she'd exchanged words with him.

"Caine doesn't want me in on it. Says I have too many conflicts. I guess you know I have a personal interest." Armstrong looked tired and concerned. "But I am in on it. I want to see this killer caught. So what are y'all here for, Donovan? And you, ma'am? Another big story?"

"With my company taking over plant security, I just want to make sure everyone's safe," Vic said. "I'll offer any professional help I can provide. Maybe I can ask some questions no one else is asking. And if that means staying out of your way, and the state troopers' way, that's cool by me. I'd just like to get the lay of the land before I stick my foot in it."

"And yes, I want the story," Lacey said. "But I want to make sure it's accurate. I'm not the *National Enquirer*."

Armstrong chuckled. "Small blessing. That *Enquirer* reporter's been raising Caine's hackles to a perilous level."

"Heard you had words with Caine yourself," Vic said.

"I suppose Little Miss Peephole there heard everything?" Armstrong glared at Lacey.

"You were loud," Lacey said in her defense. "I could have heard you out in the parking lot."

He nodded. "Caine and me, we are not cut out to be bowling buddies, that's for sure. But we're working together on this case, when he remembers that. You heard what you heard fair and square. My apologies for flying off the handle. So, what can I tell you?"

"Who's first on Caine's list?" Vic asked.

"He finally gave up on me. Now he's trying to pin this killing on Honey Gibbs. But that won't wash. I know one hundred percent for sure that Honey had nothing to do with Rod's death. And he's got nothing on her! Nothing but motive. She had plenty of that, let me tell you."

So Armstrong knew Honey was innocent because he'd spent the night of the murder with her. Lacey had already heard that story from Honey, but the cop clearly didn't want to go on the record with it unless it became absolutely necessary. But it didn't really take them off the suspect list, Lacey knew. Their alibis were basically each other, so they could have killed Gibbs together and spent the night together too.

"Aside from Honey," Lacey said.

"All the usual suspects and the unusual suspects too. Everyone who ever worked at Dominion, even the ones who aren't around here anymore. Many folks who had reason to hate Rod left town to find new jobs. They're trying to narrow it down to just his enemies who stayed around town. That's still a hell of a lot of people to interview, lots of alibis to check. It's a big job. So mostly Caine's focusing on recently fired factory workers who had a serious grievance against Gibbs. Nobody looks good so far. Of course, there's poor old Wade Dinwiddy, the night security screwup."

"What do you make of Wade?" Vic asked.

"He's stupid," Armstrong said. "Not too stupid to kill someone. Too stupid not to leave a big, old forensic trail like a neon sign. But he could have gotten lucky. Be the first time ever for him."

Wade seemed to have a way of making people dislike him and pity him at the same time. "Still, he might know something," she said.

"If you can get it out of that booze-soaked brain of his," the cop agreed. "Seems he must have been there during the murder. Passed out drunk, it looks like. Banged his head."

"Who else besides Wade?"

"Well, it doesn't sit well with Caine that Blythe Harrington assaulted the corpse."

Their waitress arrived laden down with brunch plates. "What do you make of Harrington as a suspect?" Vic asked, when the waitress scurried away.

"Possible. Her alibi is just her kids asleep in bed. Husband works nights and wasn't home that night. But I don't really see it," Armstrong said. "If Blythe killed him, she woulda been more direct. Like those scissors she threw. She would have stabbed him and said to hell with it. Woulda called it self-defense."

"Blythe wouldn't have polluted the dye tub with Gibbs either," Lacey said, putting a fork to her steaming cheese omelet. "And then there's the velvet."

Armstrong looked puzzled. "The velvet?"

"She loved it. She wouldn't have ruined it," Lacey said. "She was all about the fabric. It was her art."

"You might have a point," he conceded. "Hadn't thought about that."

"Why is he focusing on the women?" Lacey asked.

"Caine doesn't see a guy throwing Rod in the dye vat. Simple as that. Says that's the kind of wacky thing a woman might do."

Lacey slapped her forehead. Vic chuckled into his eggs Benedict. "And men don't do wacky things? Give me a break! What about your wacky Dirk Sykes and his Ghost Taxi? And that little scene he put on at the funeral?"

"You got me there, ma'am. In fact, I think Sykes has got much more of a motive for the killing," Armstrong said. "He lost his wife and his boat to Gibbs. Men kill for that kind of thing all the time." Lacey stared at him. He caught her look. "I know what y'all're thinking. Yeah, I'd like to beat Rod to a pulp for what he did to Honey. Many's the time. But she always held me back. She always said blood begets blood." Armstrong focused on his brunch and bit into a sausage. "I'm not sorry he's dead, though I am a little pissed he's causing us all so damn much trouble. Just like Rod Gibbs to leave a big old mess in his wake. No pun intended."

"The forensics guys find anything?" Vic sipped his coffee. "Like blood evidence?"

Armstrong lifted his head and laughed. "Velvet factory lit up like a Christmas tree with blood evidence! You shoulda seen it. Looked like a bloodbath. It drove the forensic techs crazy. Turns out lots of folks have shed blood in that factory."

"Like Dirk Sykes." Lacey remembered the scar on his face, the one he said the ladies liked.

"Yeah, poor old Sykes was one of many. I don't know how many different blood traces they found. All over the damn building. You got twenty years of semi-cleaned-up industrial accidents to account for, bloody accidents. Plus lots of bleach and rust and chemicals of every description. Some of the dyes they used there for the velvet are organic, and you know there's dye splattered all over the place. False positives up the wazoo. Drove the crime scene guys nuts."

"And Rod Gibbs?" Vic asked. "Was his blood confined to the dye house?"

"Looks like," Armstrong said. "He bled some around the vat, a bit of spray on the wall, and he bled out in the tub. There may have been some blood spray on the killer's clothes and hands, but that's probably all gone now. It's not like on the TV shows. Forensics don't always figure it all out for you."

"What about the ribbon in the coffin?" Lacey said.

Armstrong shook his head. "That just gave us more questions. No answers. They didn't find a damn thing on the ribbon. Not like the perp spit on it or signed his name on it or anything helpful like that. And the coffin has every fingerprint in the whole damn county. No help there."

"You happen to focus on Kira Evans?" Vic said.

"Kira?" Armstrong's eyes narrowed. "That scared little rabbit? What do you think she knows?"

"Maybe she's got a reason to be scared," Lacey said. "She filed that sexual harassment complaint against Gibbs."

"Her and about two dozen other women, including Inez Garcia. Kira was just the latest. You think she got even with him?" Armstrong looked skeptical. "I interviewed her that day y'all found the body, and she had an alibi. Home with her daughter. Caine looked at her, sure, but she's not on the top of anybody's list."

Vic turned to Turtledove. "Any luck finding her, Forrest?"

"No, she's not home. It's a little unusual. Her normal pattern on Sundays, I'm told, is to go to the Methodist church in the morning and stay home in the afternoon with her kid. Unless there's some school-related thing going on. But the neighbors say she went away last night, told them she'd be gone for a few days. They're feeding her dog. Hercules."

Thank goodness for the dog, Lacey thought. At least they knew for sure Kira was gone.

"Do they know where she went?" Vic pulled out his iPhone and tapped something into it.

"Family," Turtledove said. "She's got a brother up in Arlington. I'm working on an address."

"What about her daughter?" Lacey asked.

"The kid went with her. Seems she likes to go to Tyson's Corner and shop." Turtledove smiled. "She's a teenager."

"If y'all really want to talk to Kira, let me ask Honey about Kira's brother," Armstrong said. "She might know."

"I didn't get the feeling they were friends," Lacey said.

"They weren't enemies. Honey knew what Rod was like. She supported Kira after she heard about the harassment complaint. That's when Honey moved out."

"Honey knew about that?"

"Small town." Armstrong grimaced. "You don't really think Kira had something to do with Rod's death? Now, Inez, she's a much more likely suspect. Kira'd faint at her own shadow."

"We just want to talk to her," Lacey said. "And her shadow."

chapter 35

"Kira gave this to me yesterday." Nicholson met them at the velvet factory. "It doesn't really help anything, now that he's dead, except to give me some peace of mind. I was right."

On his desk was a file detailing Rod Gibbs's illicit activities that Kira Evans had tracked for him. But Nicholson didn't know where she was today. He didn't know where Kira's brother lived. Vic told Nicholson they'd be in touch.

Blythe Harrington was busy at home, doing her laundry. She claimed she didn't know anything about the others' whereabouts. She added that she minded her own business. But she admitted Agent Caine had spoken to her on at least three occasions.

"I don't know what he thinks I know, but I put up with him," Blythe said, "because it's my civic duty. Nosiest man I ever saw." Blythe hadn't seen Kira, but said she hoped the woman was getting some rest, because she looked really beat down these days.

Honey Gibbs was at home, paintbrush in hand, touching up the front hall of her big house. "I don't know what the heck Rod was doing in this house. Playing football or something. Look at this: black streaks! That man!" Honey shook her head and covered up one streak with a swipe of the brush.

She told Lacey that at first she didn't care who killed Rod—she was just happy her nightmare was over. But now Honey would like it all to be cleared up so she could get

Agent Caine off her case and "off Gavin's ass." She was sorry, but she didn't know who actually killed Rod or who dropped a ribbon in his casket. She didn't know where Kira's brother lived. She asked Lacey and Vic what they thought about a pale peach color for her dining room. She was busily painting over every last trace of Rod Gibbs when they left.

Vic and Lacey found Sykes at Inez's place, watching basketball on TV. They seemed happy together and without a care in the world. Inez said she was going to think about being unemployed "tomorrow, like Scarlett O'Hara." Sykes didn't know anything about Kira's family or her whereabouts, but he said Hank Richards was out at Lake Anna, visiting the *Gypsy Princess*.

"Don't say I never take you to nice places," Vic cracked as they threaded their way down a narrow muddy trail between piles of greasy auto parts in the junkyard just down the road from Black Martin.

"It's homey. I like it," Lacey said as she stepped carefully to avoid slush-filled ruts, clusters of rusted fenders, and towering mounds of engines and transmissions. "At this rate, Vic, you are going to owe me a serious night on the town. I'm talking glitz, glamour, dressing up, and dancing. No dive bars and definitely no junkyards."

"Ah, if only women would tell us what they *really* want."

They found Wade Dinwiddy in the front room of the old mobile home that served as the junkyard's office, sound asleep and with his mouth open, on a tattered red plush backseat ripped out of an ancient Cadillac. His snores were making an awful *chuck-chuck* sound. Lacey thought he might be choking to death. Vic tapped the man's foot with his boot. Wade woke with a start, tried to clamber to his feet, slipped, and fell back on the makeshift sofa.

"What the hell?" The barely awake Wade shook his head and rubbed his face. He peered up at Lacey and Vic through squinted eyes. "Aw, hell. Now what do you want?"

"Why, just to say hello," Vic said.

"Nice place you got here." Lacey gazed at a mountain of grimy hubcaps piled behind the office's plywood counter.

The counter itself was glazed with grease. It held a greasy phone and computer monitor, a take-out container with a half-eaten submarine sandwich, and a couple of open Coke cans. Large metal shelves behind it were stuffed with auto parts: batteries, starters, alternators, old car stereos and speakers. Lacey wrinkled her nose at the aromas of oil, dirt, and gasoline.

Wade looked around and nodded. "Yeah, it's one of the best. Biggest junkyard in the county," he said with something like pride. "But I take it this ain't no social call."

"We just want to talk," Vic said. "We're not the cops."

"But we hear the state cops are looking at you for Rod's murder," Lacey said.

"Dumb-asses. Wasting their time, and so are you. All I know is I got my head cracked open that night."

"Did you see a doctor?" Lacey asked. "For your head?"

He scratched at a dirty bandage on the back of his head. "Yeah, workers' comp. Thanks for the tip on that, by the way. Got five stitches and the doc gave me some good pain pills for the headache."

"Did you remember anything? About that night, or anything else?" Vic asked.

"Nope." Now Wade scratched his nose. "I musta been out cold pretty much the whole time. I don't know why they're hasslin' me over Rod. I didn't kill him. I ain't saying we was blood brothers or nothing like that, but he never done nothing to me. I'd share a bottle with him anytime. I liked him okay, I guess."

He'd like anyone who bought him a drink, Lacey assumed. As if he could read her thoughts, he staggered up from the Caddy's backseat and grabbed one of the open cans of Coke. He took a long swallow and belched.

"The way I sees it," Wade went on, "whoever killed Rod wasn't someone dirty and low-class, like me. That's what the cops think. I know it. They think just 'cause I'm a dirty drunk I could maybe be a killer too. But they got it all wrong. It was someone who hated Rod and thought *he* was dirt. Someone high and mighty, like Rod always thought he was."

"Who might that high-and-mighty killer be?" Vic asked. Wade scrunched up his face, thinking. He took another slug of the Coke. "Don't rightly know. But I think it was someone real afraid of him. Like this dog—we had a dog here oncet. Little yellow thing. Cute. Not a real good junkyard dog, she was afraid of most everything. But you push that little yellow dog too far? Why, she'd go crazy on you, biting and snarling. Go after a big dog twice her size. Wouldn't let go. Scare a body to death, she would. Person who killed Rod was like that little dog. Just got pushed too far."

Wade turned his attention to the half-eaten submarine sandwich on the counter. He picked it up with grease-stained hands and took a big bite. Lacey watched the black sludge caked under every single one of his fingernails and permanently lost her appetite for submarine sandwiches. The phone on the counter rang, as black with grease as Wade's fingers, and he commenced telling the caller all about which starter motor fit which Ford pickup. Vic and Lacey exchanged a look and left the office.

"What do you think of the Little Yellow Dog Theory?" Lacey asked Vic as they picked their way back to the Jeep through the mud, snow, grease, and precarious piles of chromed bumpers.

"I think it's old Wade's crowning intellectual achievement. But you really think he's talking about Kira Evans? She's more like a frightened chipmunk. Could a chipmunk fit the Little Yellow Dog Theory?"

"Maybe. Maybe Wade's not quite as dumb as he looks."

An hour north of Richmond they detoured west off I-95 to Lake Anna, to find the place where Gibbs had kept the *Blue Devil*, née *Gypsy Princess*. It was a vast lake, with hundreds of hidden coves and inlets, and scores of marinas and private boat docks. Lacey was amazed at its size. She had imagined a tidy little round lake, but Lake Anna wandered through the Virginia woods for miles in every direction. One wrong turn sent them straight into Lake Anna State Park. They parked the Jeep at the closed visitors' center and stretched their legs on the boardwalk along the little sandy beach, partly hidden under snow, while Vic tried to make Sykes's directions match the GPS map on his iPhone.

They weren't far off course. It was a little off the beaten path, and Sykes had left out a few turns that were probably obvious to the locals. They finally found the small private dock, near the Lake Anna Marina on Sturgeon Creek, south of the state park. The gate was open and there was a pickup truck parked at the end of the gravel road. Lacey stepped out of the Jeep. She breathed in the cool pine-scented air on the breeze coming off the lake. It would be some time before the other trees leafed out, but at the moment it was a serene winter landscape, snow still on the ground, right down to the water. The sun was sinking toward the low hills west of the lake, lighting the smoke-colored clouds with brilliant oranges and pinks.

No wonder the factory guys in Black Martin wanted to own a piece of this place.

Vic caught sight of the boat first. The *Blue Devil* was sitting on her trailer beneath an open-sided shelter down by the water, where she was stored for the winter. A couple of other boats sat nearby. The big blue tarp was half off. Behind the wheel with a beer in his hand sat Hank Richards. With his shaggy blond hair and beard, he looked like a New Age hippie Viking in a puffy down parka.

He knocked back some beer and greeted them with a wave. "Y'all come on aboard."

"So this is the *Blue Devil*," Lacey said, shielding her eyes from the low winter sun. She'd heard so much about the boat, she thought it would be bigger. The *Blue Devil* looked sleek and streamlined, but she wasn't quite the luxury yacht Lacey was expecting. *This is the Corvette of fishing boats?* At least she was painted blue.

"Not for long," Hank said. "She'll be the *Gypsy Princess* again soon. Like she always was. New coat of paint soon too." He ran his hand over the wheel lovingly and hopped down from the boat.

"You're buying her back?" Vic asked.

Hank grinned. "For one whole dollar. Honey asked Dirk and me to take her off her hands. She didn't know what else to do with her. We just have to sign some papers. Pay some taxes. Course, I know she's just trying to put things right."

"She's trying to ease her guilty conscience?" Lacey asked.

"Honey's got no reason to feel guilty. She's just a decent lady." He sighed with satisfaction and nodded toward the boat. "We'll be fishing the spring bass soon. Mighty fine fishing here. So, what brings y'all out here? I don't imagine it's the direct route back home for you two."

"Just wondering if you've seen Kira Evans," Vic said casually.

"Kira?" Hank paused and thought about it. "We don't exactly keep company, you know, though I'd be happy to, if she showed an interest." He finished his beer and crumpled the can in his hand. "Haven't seen her since the funeral. Want a beer? Come on aboard. Lemme show you my boat. She's a beauty."

"We'd love to. Some other time." Vic pressed his lips together. "Got to get back to town."

"Why do you want to see Kira?" Hank asked, but he didn't seem overly interested.

"She was working on a project for Nicholson," Lacey said. "About Rod stealing from the company."

"Oh, that. Yeah, everyone knew about that. Only question was how much."

It was a typical small-town answer, Lacey thought. Everybody knows everything, except what might be important. And if everybody knew, did that mean Rod Gibbs knew they knew?

"Just wanted to touch base with her on it," Vic said. "See what she found out."

"It's the weekend. She's got family somewhere. Her daughter's a good kid. I'm sure nothing about Rod's so important it can't wait till tomorrow. He ain't gonna get any deader." Hank paused and looked away from them, out over the lake. "Be awful damn nice if people would just leave Kira the hell alone. She's had enough trouble in her life."

"You're right there," Vic agreed. "We just came out to see the lake on this beautiful Sunday afternoon. Thought she might be around, or maybe you might have seen her. Good to see you again, Richards."

As they turned back toward Vic's Jeep, Lacey called out, "I hope the fishing is good."

"Fishing's always good on Lake Anna," Richards said. "Rod only used this old girl a couple of times after he weaseled her away from us. He was a born fool." He climbed back into the boat and grabbed another cold one. He was still sitting behind the wheel, watching the sun drop low over the lake when they pulled away.

They drove in silence for a few minutes, lost in thought. Vic called Armstrong on his cell. He hadn't located Kira or her brother, and they'd already asked Honey. Vic called Turtledove. No answer. Just past the Lake Anna Marina, he turned the Jeep down a bumpy side road toward something the sign called THE ANNA CABANA.

It turned out to be a cute seafood restaurant on a little knoll right on the waterfront, with its own docks and boardwalk and a nice view of the lake. The deck was covered with snow, but there were boats docked and a few couples dining inside. Crab cakes seemed to be the Anna Cabana's specialty. Vic and Lacey ordered a crab-dip appetizer, but they didn't have much appetite. What they needed was to find Kira Evans.

Vic tried Turtledove's cell again. Still no answer. He left another voice mail. Their brief visit with Hank Richards and the *Gypsy Princess* hung over Lake Anna like a dark cloud.

"Richards didn't buy a word of that," Vic finally said, staring into the distance across the lake.

"He probably helped her with Gibbs," Lacey said, poking at the crab dip. She suddenly felt very sad. "I wonder which one killed him."

Vic was silent for a moment, and then he nodded. "Gut feeling or fashion clue?"

She sighed and put her knife down. "Hank's got a secret and he's very calm about it. He's made up his mind about something. And he's very protective of Kira."

"So we don't want to get him riled up, not before we talk to Kira," Vic said.

"You think he's on to us?"

"He's not stupid. He's got something to hide. Then again,

we're not sure what that is, or if he was the one who helped her. And how does he connect with Pojack and the blue ribbons? We're not sure about anything, are we, Lacey?"

"Not one hundred percent." She breathed in deeply and watched the setting sun light the lake aglow. It was a beautiful place. "More like ninety-seven percent. Yeah, he's on to us."

Vic's phone jingled. It was Turtledove calling back. He finally had something for them.

"You up for a late night?" Vic asked Lacey after he clicked off. He waved to the waiter for the check.

"Turtledove found Kira?"

"No. But he found her brother's address for us."

"You really want me there?" Lacey was flattered and a little nervous. They were walking fast toward the Jeep.

"She might find talking with a woman there a little easier. Less threatening."

"And you find me less threatening?"

"Good God, no," Vic said. "You terrify me, darling. But you can speak her language. That private language between women."

"That's better. I'd love to talk to her."

The sun set behind them on Lake Anna as Vic pointed the Jeep toward the highway.

chapter 36

It seemed a shame to shatter the Sunday-evening stillness of that quiet cottage home in Arlington, that family, and Kira's life. But other lives were in danger. Lacey gathered her strength and walked with Vic up the sidewalk to the door.

Vic rang the bell and Kira came to answer it. Her eyes looked frightened. She did not ask them in.

"We'd just like to speak with you about the night Rod Gibbs died," Vic said.

"I don't know." Kira looked behind her as if she was afraid of being overheard. "I'm not alone."

"Where's your daughter?" asked Lacey.

"Out shopping with her cousins." Kira looked around, almost ready to panic. "This is my brother's home, his family. My family. We can't talk here."

Vic suggested they get something to drink at Whitlow's on Wilson, just a few blocks away. It would be neutral territory. Kira reluctantly agreed. She picked up her coat and purse and told someone in another room she would be out for a while.

Whitlow's looked better when there were local bands playing and the lights were turned down low, Lacey decided. But even a marching band wouldn't raise her spirits tonight. They took a table in a side room where no one else was seated.

No one was in the mood for a meal, but Kira looked like she hadn't had a bite to eat since Lacey first met her.

They settled on the hot spinach-and-artichoke dip with pita chips, and sodas all around.

"I've answered all their questions," Kira said. "All those cops. I don't have to tell you anything."

Vic gave her a friendly smile. "No, you don't, Kira. But something is eating at you. Anyone can see that. I can see that."

"Did you know someone else has been killed?" Lacey asked. She left her notebook in her purse and folded her hands on the table. "It's in the paper today."

"I don't believe you." Kira looked miserable. The drinks came. She kept her head down, not meeting their gazes.

"Wait." Lacey left the table and walked outside to a news box on the corner. There was one last copy of *The Eye Street Observer*. She brought it back and handed it to Kira. "Someone at my newspaper was killed. Two more people are in danger. The killer sent them blue velvet ribbons in the mail. Blue velvet, like the ribbon left in Rod's hand in the coffin. Blue velvet, like he was tied up with when he died."

"Kira, we just want to prevent more murders." Vic reached out and touched her arm.

The waitress set down their order while Kira read the story on Walter Pojack's death.

"The papers all say this Avenger guy killed Rod," Kira said, spilling her Coke and wiping it up with napkins.

"The killer had to be someone from the factory, with knowledge of its machinery and layout," Vic said. "What they did with Rod wouldn't have come from an outsider."

"Tom Nicholson said you found Rod's paper trail, how he stole money from the company," Lacey said.

Kira nodded, unsure where this was headed. "It wasn't even that much, and he didn't need the money. He did it because he could, I think. Everything was a mean little game to Rod. He liked to put things over on people. God knows what he'd do if news of his skimming money came out. He might have blamed Tom. Or me. We had to be pretty careful."

"He knew you were on to him, didn't he?" Vic said.

"You were the bookkeeper. You could see discrepancies in the books. But time was running out. The factory was closing. Is that why he went there that night?"

"No. I'm not sure why he was there." Kira clutched her hands together. Her face was flushed. "I don't know."

"You saw Rod that night," Lacey said.

"No, I already told the police—"

"I'm just the security guy, Kira," Vic said in his most reassuring voice. It was low and warm. "What happened to Gibbs that night was not your fault, was it?"

Kira looked unsure of everything. She didn't know who to trust or what to think. She buried her face in her hands.

"There could be more deaths," Lacey said. "We think he's targeted two more people."

"But it's the Avenger, it's some crazy stranger, it's not—" Tears sprang to Kira's eyes. "Oh my God. What am I going to do?" She started to hyperventilate.

Lacey and Vic exchanged a look. He sat back, while Lacey leaned forward and took Kira's hands in hers. They were ice cold.

"It will be better if you tell us," Lacey said. "Everything can still turn out for the best, if you can help us. But it can't if you don't tell us what really happened."

"But I have a daughter."

"If it was self-defense, Kira—"

"Who's going to believe that? Rod being strung up and dyed blue that way," Kira cried. "It's awful. It's a horrible thing to do to anyone. Even Rod."

"You didn't do that by yourself, did you?" Vic said.

"No." Kira said it so softly it was hard to hear.

"Kira, the sooner you can explain what happened, the sooner this mess can be cleared up," Vic said. "Especially if there are extenuating circumstances."

Kira took a deep breath. Her words came out as if she were choking, but as she talked she calmed down. "The last crew had gone home. I just wanted to stay a little longer. It was easier to work on Tom's project that way. Nobody looking over my shoulder. I needed the overtime too."

"You proved Gibbs was stealing money from the company?" Lacey asked.

"Yes," she nodded. "It was pretty easy to see, if you went looking for it. No one was around after about ten. Wade eventually rattled around, like a big old friendly dog that didn't know what he was supposed to do. I don't think he even saw me. Wade wasn't much of a guard, and he's not the brightest bulb on the tree, but he's big, and I figured he'd scare off most anyone. Except Rod. Rod came back."

"What time was that?" Vic asked her.

"I'm not sure. It must have been after midnight. I got kind of engrossed in what I was finding."

"What about your daughter?" Lacey asked.

"Sara was home. She'd always call me when I worked late, and we checked on each other before she went to bed. Anyway, I didn't hear him come in. I looked up and there he was, right outside the glass wall of my office. Staring at me. I nearly jumped out of my skin. I tried to lock the files away, but he stormed in and grabbed them out of my hands. He didn't even look at them, just threw them on the floor."

"What about Wade? Where was he?"

"I don't know. I hollered for him. Rod said Wade was in no shape to help me. Everyone knows Wade's too fond of his liquor, but he never was that drunk on the job," Kira said. "At least not before that night."

That tallied with what Wade had said. Vic nodded slightly.

"Rod was there because of you," Lacey said. "He wanted to make sure his thefts wouldn't come to light. And I think he never got over the harassment complaint you filed."

"He never really stopped. I just wanted him to go away." Kira took a pita chip and dipped it into the artichoke dip, but she set it down on her plate uneaten. "I was so scared."

"We know Rod never let go—he kept hurting people till he crushed them. That's why he connived to get the boat away from Dirk Sykes and Hank Richards, why he was trying to take everything away from Honey in the divorce," Lacey said.

"You were the woman who said no to him. He never forgave you for that, did he?" Vic asked.

"He was determined to get what he was after for the last couple of years," Lacey said. "Did he assault you?"

Tears ran down Kira's face. "How do you know all this?" She put her head down and sobbed.

"You wore a turtleneck to work that day," Lacey said. "It was too hot in the factory to wear that. Inez teased you about having a hickey. But it wasn't a love bite you were hiding. It was bruises, wasn't it?"

"No." But Kira's hands went to her throat. Today she was wearing a brown boatneck top. Yellow shadows of the bruises remained.

"You didn't want anyone to see them because they might find out Rod slapped you around just before he died?"

"Rod told me I was going to have to pay." Kira gulped some air before going on. "He was drunk and he stank of booze. He kept breathing in my face and trying to kiss me. I tried to run out of there, but he grabbed me. He tore my blouse and backed me against the wall. Slobbering all over me. Slapping me. He kept saying I was gonna like it. Son of a bitch. He put his hands around my neck and started squeezing. 'How do you like that, you worthless piece of—' You get the idea. He'd let go of my throat for a second, then grab it again, two or three times, till I'd almost pass out. That's when I thought I was going to die."

"It's okay, Kira. Take a deep breath," Lacey said.

"I kneed him in the groin. Hard as I could. It didn't stop him. It just made him really mad. He slapped me and I didn't care anymore what happened to me. I didn't care if I died, if I could just hurt him. I wanted to kill him. I just went crazy. I felt for something to hit him with. There were some old softball trophies on the bookshelf. From back in the day. We used to have a team. I grabbed the first thing I touched. One of the trophies. It was heavier than I expected." Kira gasped for breath. "I hit him in the head. He went down like a ton of bricks. I killed him."

Lacey glanced at Vic, but said nothing. The autopsy showed the head wound was substantial, but it did not kill Rod Gibbs.

"What happened then?" Vic asked. Kira shook her head. "Someone helped you?"

"No," Kira was crying. "No, no, no."

"We know someone helped you," Lacey said. "Hank Richards?"

"I can't tell you anymore," she insisted. "It's all my fault. I killed Rod! Or near enough."

"You'll be safe," Vic said. "We won't let Richards find you."

"You don't understand! Hank went there to protect me! He knew what Rod was like. He saw what I did and he told me it was the right thing to do. 'This planet will not miss Rod Gibbs,' he said."

"Hank?" Lacey pressed.

"Hank. Poor Hank. But it's not his fault. I killed Rod."

"Why didn't you call the police?" Vic asked. "If it was self-defense, it would have stopped right there."

"I wanted to. I told him we had to." Kira wiped her tears with a napkin. Lacey handed her another one. "He wouldn't let me call the police. Hank said he would take care of things. And he said maybe Rod could do some good now that he was dead. He could be an example. I didn't know what to do. I had just done the worst thing anyone could do. I'd killed a man. I went to the ladies' room and threw up, and I wondered how fast the cops would come and arrest me. But Hank was calm. So calm. He told me to get myself together."

Lacey was afraid to say too much. She didn't want to lead the witness. But it was difficult to watch someone unburdening her soul and not try to help. She slid over next to Kira and hugged her shoulders. Vic squeezed Lacey's hand under the table.

"What happened to the trophy?" Vic asked. "Was there blood on it? Did Hank clean it up?"

"I don't know. It was gone when I came back from the ladies'. Hank had put things right in the office. I don't remember any blood. But Rod wasn't moving."

Kira was drained. She slumped back in her chair. "Hank told me not to worry. We could take care of things ourselves. That's when he decided to string Rod up. I about fainted when he told me what he wanted to do. But, oh God, I helped Hank tie him up. On that big damn spool of velvet."

She rubbed her hands together as if she were still cold.

"Why tie him up with those strips of velvet?" Lacey asked.

"They were there. That's all there was, no rope or anything." Her voice caught in her throat and she looked at Lacey, then Vic. "We dragged Rod to the spool and tied him to it. We wheeled the spool over to the vat to hook it on the chain." Kira closed her eyes and covered her face with her hands, but she couldn't get rid of the memory.

"You've gotten through almost all of it." Lacey squeezed Kira's icy hands.

"Rod woke up!" Kira blurted out, her eyes wild with the memory. "He wasn't dead! I'll never forget the look on his face when he realized where he was and how he was tied up. He saw the two of us. He started screaming."

Lacey took a deep breath. "You hadn't killed him after all, Kira."

"I said we should let Rod go, maybe now he'd learned his lesson. But Hank said no, people like Rod Gibbs never learned their lessons. Rod started screaming for Wade. But Wade didn't come. Hank said maybe we'd just leave him hanging there so everyone would see him when they came to work. But Rod made such a racket. Screaming and yelling and cursing. He wouldn't stop. So—so Hank shot him."

"Just like that?" Vic asked.

"Well, Hank talked to him some first. He said he wanted to make sure Rod knew he was going to die, and what a horrible moral degenerate he was, and how the Blue Devil was gonna go straight to Hell. And how he was going to wind up in the dye vat. And Rod started to cry. Cried like a little boy. But I didn't have any pity for him. I kept thinking about how scared I was when I thought he was going to rape me and kill me. Rod started cursing and yelling again. That's when Hank shot him."

"What did you do then?" Lacey asked.

Kira shook her head. "Nothing. My brain was wrapped in cotton. I just covered my ears and lay down on the floor."

"Where'd he get the gun?" Vic asked.

"Rod had it in his jacket pocket. I don't know why, unless he planned to use it on me. Hank found it when we were tying him up."

"What about Wade?"

"Never saw him. I guess he was out cold. Drunk." She looked as if she were thinking something over for the first time. "I guess if he hadn't been drunk, none of this would have happened."

Rod Gibbs set himself up for disaster, Lacey thought. He brought his own gun, he disabled the cameras, he got the security guard drunk, and he assaulted the wrong victim, with the wrong protector. He set up his own murder. *What a smart guy.* But why did he end up blue?

"Kira, why the blue dye?" Lacey had been wondering this from the beginning. "Because of the Blue Devil thing? To make a statement?"

"No, it was the only vat still full of dye. Midnight Blue. It was just meant to happen that way, I guess. Maybe it was fate."

"You have to understand something, Kira," Vic said. "If I have information about a crime, I'm under an obligation to report it to the police. But Kira, I want you to talk to the police yourself. You need to see Agent Caine with the Virginia State Police."

Her voice was very small. "I know." Kira looked straight at him for the first time, and she seemed relieved. She ate the pita chip. "I'm sorry."

"We know you are," Lacey said. "We are too. You just went back to work the next day, like normal?"

"Pretty much. It seemed like a nightmare. But it's funny what you can tell yourself." She picked up another chip. "I didn't think about him being under the velvet in the dye vat. I just put all that in a separate place in my mind. Like it was a bad dream."

"And Hank?"

"He told me to just play it cool. I wouldn't have to do a thing, he said. He'd protect me. He was so sweet, and I realized what a great guy he could be. Why didn't I ever see that before? I think I always kind of liked him, just not on the surface. He told me to remember I wasn't a murderer, because he's the one who killed Rod. And if anyone had to be punished for it, Hank said he'd be the one. But he said it was justified. And—" She stopped.

Vic prompted her. "And what, Kira?"

"He said there were other people who used people the same way Rod did. Because they were killing our jobs, they were killing us all, slowly. And maybe they needed killing too. I told him he was wrong and I couldn't listen to that kind of talk anymore. But he calls me every day since then, just to see if I'm okay. He's a good man. I can't believe he killed this other man too."

Kira had discovered her feelings for Hank, but he had gone too far now. *What a mess.* "Is that all Hank told you?" Lacey asked.

"He said something about killing two birds with one stone. I told him not to say anything else. I can't stand it when he talks that way."

Two birds. Both Claudia Darnell and Tazewell Flanders would be at the fund-raiser slated for Monday, Lacey realized. The very next night. So would Hank Richards. *One stone.*

Vic pulled out someone's business card from his wallet and started writing on it. "Don't talk to Caine without an attorney. Talk to the attorney first. Tomorrow morning. Very first thing. Stay at your brother's place tonight, and don't go home. Call tonight to set it up. I'm writing down that number, and I'll call them first myself. You won't have to face this alone."

"I can't afford a lawyer."

"Here's the name and number of a great attorney. She doesn't specialize in criminal defense, but she'll find you the right defender, someone who's a wizard at making deals. Ask about pro bono. And don't be afraid. You have a good story to work with. Just tell the truth. You'll be all right."

Kira took the card. Lacey recognized it. It was Brooke Barton's card.

"Thank you. I was wondering something," Kira said. "You think I could get a burger now? I'm starved."

chapter 37

Lacey had a 100-percent solid-gold scoop. But it was a little hard for her to appreciate this coup after midnight, long after *The Eye*'s usual deadline, with Mac Jones and the paper's attorney, Meg Wong, sitting over her shoulders, reading and second-guessing every word she typed. At least they liked her headline:

WITNESS NAMES SUSPECT IN BLACK MARTIN'S
BLUE MURDER;
MANHUNT IN VIRGINIA FOR "VELVET AVENGER"

"Fix that sentence fragment," Mac ordered, "and move that second paragraph."

Lacey sighed. *Why don't you move your—!* "Fine. Is that better?"

Lacey didn't reveal Kira's name, but everyone in Black Martin would know exactly who it was. There was an exchange of strong words and a protracted argument between Meg Wong and an irritated Special Agent Caine, who complained bitterly that Lacey and Vic should never have interviewed Kira Evans without him. Wong won. *The Eye*'s story triumphantly named Hank Richards as the prime suspect in the murder of Rod Gibbs and a person of interest in the death of Walter Pojack.

Caine grudgingly gave Lacey an official statement, confirming that Richards was a "person of interest" being sought for questioning in the murders by the Virginia State Police and the District.

Mac was grumpy, as usual these days when late-breaking news kept him away from Kim and the girls. But he had that familiar newsman's mad gleam in his eye, and he was hopped up on the idea of scooping the rest of the Washington media. And on late-night coffee and doughnuts.

"I think that does it," Meg said. "You've got one killer scoop, I've covered the paper's ass, and I'm going home." Meg was dressed in an oversized Redskins jersey, tight jeans, and a black leather jacket. She looked nothing like her daytime persona of buttoned-down Washington lawyer.

"Nice job, everyone," said Claudia. When their publisher showed up, coffee in hand, to oversee the final draft, the party was complete. And Lacey was completely frazzled.

By the time the last sentence was vetted, Lacey felt like she'd been pulled through a meat grinder, legally and editorially. She was also a little afraid that Hank Richards might materialize out of nowhere and pin a blue velvet ribbon on her. With a bullet. She was grateful when Mac waited with her until Vic returned to pick her up. It was after one in the morning. Vic had staked out Kira's brother's place himself until Turtledove took over for him.

"This is completely unnecessary, Mac. I'm totally safe."

"Yeah, that's what you always say." He smirked at her. Vic's Jeep pulled up in front of *The Eye* and Mac opened the passenger door for her.

"I'm not coming in till after noon," Lacey said.

"You always say that too."

By Monday evening, Kira Evans had an attorney, pro bono, personally recommended and approved by Brooke Barton: her brother Benjamin. He and Kira had an appointment to talk with the Virginia State Police. According to Brooke, Kira and her defender had a good chance at successfully playing Let's Make a Deal with the State of Virginia in exchange for her testimony. Kira and her daughter were under police protection in a hotel, at the proverbial "undisclosed location."

Congressman Tazewell Flanders was rehearsing his speech to announce his bid for governor of Virginia, and trying to ignore his temporary bodyguard, one Forrest

Thunderbird. Vic Donovan's new client, Claudia Darnell, also needed personal protection services. The Virginia State Police had an APB out for the arrest of Hank Richards, considered armed and dangerous, whereabouts unknown.

Fashion reporter Lacey Smithsonian had wrangled a pass to Congressman Flanders's political fund-raiser. She was on edge. Her gut was telling her to be on guard, but she also wished Hank Richards could go on fishing from the *Gypsy Princess* at Lake Anna.

Lacey had a lot of unfulfilled wishes. She wished she'd never seen the Blue Devil. She wished she'd witnessed Hank slipping a blue ribbon into Rod Gibbs's swollen blue hand at the funeral. She wished he could have been stopped there, before the Velvet Avenger killed again. But her wishes were not horses, and no one had seen Hank since Lacey and Vic left him sitting on his boat at Lake Anna. At least they knew his targets now, and she felt very relieved to be out of the bull's-eye.

The campaign kickoff was being held at the Torpedo Factory in Old Town Alexandria, Lacey's neighborhood. It could be a stroke of PR genius, or exquisitely bad timing.

"Tazewell Flanders is bound to be associated with factories for the foreseeable future," Lacey told Vic, when he showed up at *The Eye* to escort Claudia to the event as her bodyguard.

"Unfortunately for Flanders. Why on earth did he pick that place? It's a maze in there. Security will be a nightmare tonight. Glad I'm only handling Claudia," Vic said. "And you."

"She said Flanders picked the Torpedo Factory months ago, to fit his campaign theme of creative reuse of our industrial infrastructure as a foundation for Virginia's high-tech future." Vic gave her a look. "Yeah, I don't know what it means either. He's a politician."

Lacey walked him to the elevators and kissed him when no one was around to see.

With Hank Richards still at large, Vic made her promise not to return to her apartment without him, so Lacey had lugged her outfit for the evening to the office. She quickly changed into an emerald-green-and-black velvet dress with a flared skirt. That 1930s-era charmer also had a long-sleeve bolero jacket in black, with green cuffs that matched her green silk heels. *Very Claudette Colbert.* It was a sentimental favorite of hers. She didn't wear it often, but she loved the way it felt. She arranged her hair in a French twist. Not as expertly as Stella, but it would do. She freshened her makeup and called a cab.

While she waited, Mac administered a little fatherly lecture on her personal safety and steering clear of the suspect. And on rolling her eyes at her editor. *The Eye*'s security guard watched until she was safe inside the taxi and on her way to Old Town. She wouldn't have to worry about walking in those heels or about parking. Or about Hank Richards.

Since moving to Alexandria, Lacey had spent many hours wandering through the Torpedo Factory, perusing the art for sale, watching the artists at work, and admiring that large, lime green torpedo in the main hall, a sample of the weapons built there for the Navy. The factory dated to the World War I era, but it didn't reach full steam until World War II, when five thousand workers, many of them women, were slamming out torpedoes around the clock. It was the era of Rosie the Riveter. Her aunt Mimi had had friends who worked there.

The Torpedo Factory hadn't produced weapons for decades. It had transitioned in the 1970s into a community arts center for Alexandria, its cavernous interior partitioned into a maze of nearly a hundred small glassed-in artists' studios and cozy galleries. It found a new life.

Across America, factories of all kinds had closed down, many, like Dominion Velvet, because of foreign imports. Some had evolved into other uses, like condominiums and shopping malls and theatres. Congressman Tazewell Flanders would offer the Torpedo Factory as his shining example of what could be done to bring jobs back to an abandoned factory. But could the factory in Black Martin really be turned into something useful, like an arts center or condos, when the whole economy seemed to be in a shambles? Lacey had her doubts.

Flanders rented the two-story main hall for his kickoff

fund-raiser. With its massive ducts and exposed pipes and spiral staircase wrapped around an old industrial smokestack, it exuded both a gritty factory ambience and a politically correct, upscale art-scene vibe. In an economy when luxurious surroundings or a beautiful ballroom would be suspect, the Torpedo Factory, both industrial and funky, was perhaps the perfect venue for an up-and-coming politician's campaign kickoff. "Friends of Flanders" were invited to party with their candidate for one thousand dollars a ticket.

Lacey was neither a friend, nor did she have to pay a grand. She showed her press pass and was admitted to the hall. Small round tables and chairs filled the space, decorated for the event. Candles on every table cast a soft golden glow. Lacey strolled past studios offering hand-thrown pottery, jewelry, wearable art, glass, and sculpture. There were paintings and drawings, photography and fiber art.

She caught sight of her publisher in a studio on the main floor. Claudia was purchasing an extravagant piece from the artist to add to her collection, a very stylized dream catcher nearly three feet across. The thick copper hoop surrounded an intricately knotted spider's web, and it was decorated with a profusion of colorful feathers and beads in blues and greens. Claudia showed her the tag: more than a thousand dollars. *Pocket change for Ms. Darnell*, Lacey thought. *But why this sudden dream catcher obsession of hers? Are her dreams really in so much danger?*

Vic was a shadow in the background wherever Claudia went. He nodded to Lacey, but he was constantly scanning the area for Richards. Lacey knew Turtledove must be somewhere nearby as well, shadowing the congressman. That blue ribbon was persuasive.

"Here's hoping this is a crashingly boring evening," Claudia said.

"I'll second that. That's a lovely piece," Lacey said. "For the office?"

"Perhaps. It's bigger than I would like, but it seemed to call to me," Claudia said, tracing the web with her fingers. "But now I've got to carry it around all night." Vic couldn't carry it for her. It would only draw attention to her bodyguard. Claudia tucked it under her arm and turned to speak to a fellow Flanders supporter.

The airy heights of the central hall were filled with white lights and hundreds of giant floating paper snowflakes. "Friends of Flanders" and the media were milling about. Lacey climbed the stairs to the second floor to get a better view of the action below and to see what else was going on in the upper galleries. She wandered farther and farther back through the maze of hallways and studios, away from the crowd and the musicians setting up. She was peering through a window of the Alexandria Archaeology office on the third floor when she heard footsteps behind her.

"Stop right there, Ms. Smithsonian."

Lacey froze at the voice. "Hank? Hank Richards?" *Oh no. Did he read my story?*

"Pretty smart for a reporter. Don't turn around and don't scream. I have no cause to hurt you, but you know I could. Interesting story in the paper today."

Lacey felt something hard poking her in the back. Her mouth had gone dry. She gulped. Hank pushed her into one of the open studios, filled with fiber-art wall hangings and decorative clothing. She wondered why it wasn't locked. The studio lights were off, but it was well lit by the glass windows facing the hall.

"Where's Kira?" he asked.

"She's safe."

Lacey heard him sigh. "I don't want her blamed for any of this. Not her fault."

"How did you get in, Hank?"

"I have my ways. I've got a talent for locks. Spent a couple of years working as a locksmith, long time ago. Been hiding out in this maze all day. Big place."

She realized there was no one around to help her. Alexandria police were posted at the doors, on high alert for the suspect. Vic's job was to keep Claudia safe, and Thunderbird was looking after Flanders. Lacey was on her own.

She turned her head to look at her captor and her mouth fell open. She stared at him. Hank had shaved his long blond hair and beard and now sported a perfectly smooth, bald head. He wore a dark suit and turtleneck and could have passed for a slightly edgy lobbyist. Or a bodyguard. He was much more frightening this way than he'd been as an aging surfer dude and boat bum. She tried to catch her breath. "You've gone to a lot of trouble, Hank."

"You like the Velvet Avenger?" He smiled, but there wasn't much humor in his voice. "It was time for a make-over. A big change. You know how that goes. Sit down, Lacey. I'm afraid you're not gonna get to go to the party. But you ain't missing much. Flanders is a well-known bore." He indicated a chair and gently pushed her shoulder down. Lacey perched on it, ready to jump up. "We're pretty far back in a corner up here. I don't think anyone's gonna hear us. But I'm going to take some precautions. I don't want to have to shoot you. I really don't."

"Makes two of us." Her voice was a little too close to cracking.

Lacey memorized her surroundings, trying to keep from panicking. The artist's specialty seemed to be colorful faux flowers made of wire and fiber and felt. There were amorphous fiber wall hangings and some gaudy hats and vests. The artist had also helpfully provided a basket full of scraps, long felt strips in many colors for visitors' kids to play with. Hank eyed the basket while holding the gun on her. Lacey thought about kicking something to distract him, but he was much larger than she was and he was blocking the door. Unless someone walked right past the door, it was too soon to scream. And she couldn't forget that Hank had a gun. *Awkward. Way to go, Lacey.*

He pushed her behind a partition where the artist kept her desk and supplies. Lacey could see out of part of the window, but passersby would not be able to see them. Hank took her purse and set it down beyond her reach. Her cell phone was in there.

"You should know it wasn't your fault about that Pojack character at your paper. It just happened. Thought I'd find Claudia Darnell, but she wasn't there."

"If you were after Claudia, why did you kill him?"

"I didn't plan to. Darnell's one of the people who shut down my factory, killed all our jobs. But this guy was in there, in her office, poking around. He started giving me major attitude. Asshole. Reminded me of Rod. Told me his name like it was a big favor or something and I should be impressed. Walter Pojack. I remembered your friend talking about a Walt Pojack."

"Stella." Lacey wanted to kick herself, but she was tied up.

"He wanted to take your job away, right? We couldn't have that. I wanted you to write more stories. Until today. You kinda blew my cover today, didn't you? And I went to all that trouble to get you those great photos of Rod. But it doesn't matter now. I told that jerk I was the Velvet Avenger." Hank chuckled. "Your Mr. Pojack didn't know what the hell I was talking about. Idiot doesn't even read his own newspaper. I decided to do y'all a favor. I made him call you on the phone before I shot him, so you'd be sure to get the story. Ah, you shoulda seen that bastard sweat."

Hank related this story as casually as telling a joke in a bar. He was the ultimate in cool.

"Why the Velvet Avenger?"

He laughed again. "The more Sykes yakked about there maybe being a Velvet Avenger and that crazy-ass Web site got ahold of it, the more I liked the idea. Somebody needed to do something like this. Turns out it had to be me."

"You don't have to kill anyone else. You made your point."

"But I do. I have to make an example of someone. Let people know they're killing our factories, our work, our lives, our livelihoods. They're killing our jobs. Can't forgive that." He pulled a few long strips of felt from the artist's basket.

"This is insane, Hank."

"Yeah. Maybe. Probably. I gotta tell you, I stopped worrying about that." He put the gun down so he could tie her to the chair. She instantly jumped up and tried to run, but Hank was ready for her and grabbed both her arms. She got in one good kick in his shins. He yelped, then jammed her down in the chair, wrapping the felt around her and yanking her hands behind her.

"Be nice and I won't cut off your circulation," he said.

She felt him wrap the strips around her hands, pull them tight, and tie knots in them.

"You're hurting me!" Lacey shouted.

"Won't hurt you if you calm down." She stopped squirming, and he loosened them slightly. "See. I'm easy. I do *not* want to hurt you."

Keep him talking, Lacey told herself. *Keep him busy*. Besides, she wanted to know everything: the curse of curiosity. "Why did you go back to Dominion Velvet that night?"

"I was looking out for Kira. It was after I left Sykes at the Mexican restaurant. She was all alone after the crew left. Wade was useless. Rod went and got blasted that afternoon. I figured he'd be back sooner or later for his car. But if Kira was there all alone, he might try something, and sure enough he did. I waited for him."

"He didn't see you?"

"Nope. He was too busy fooling around with the security cameras. He was up to something. I gave him a few minutes. Then I followed. Wish I hadn't waited."

"What about Wade?"

"Poor old slobbering drunk. I just tapped him with my flashlight on the back of his head. He was down for the count."

"You heard the fight? You saw Kira knock Rod out?"

"Oh yeah." Hank sighed deeply. "Wish I'd been there in time to save her from that."

"You have feelings for Kira?" Lacey tried working her wrists to keep the blood flowing.

"I've loved that girl for so long," Hank said. "Every day she came to work, Kira was my sunlight."

"But you never said anything to her? You never told her? You never asked her out?"

"Kira's had a troubled life. Raised her kid all on her own. Worked hard. She couldn't love me."

"Oh, Hank. Why not?"

"Wouldn't work out. I'm not good enough for her. I'm not lovable."

Certainly not at the moment, she thought, wondering how to get out of this fix. She looked around the studio.

There were long strips of fabric everywhere. *Great. He can mummify me. Where the hell are the police?*

"Kira thought she killed him, right? But he woke up?"

"Shocked the living daylights out of both of us. It was one thing to think she killed him and he's already dead. But then he's not dead? We were in a real jam."

"You could have stopped then."

Hank shook his head. "When Rod woke up and saw me, he was damn scared. I thought he was going to have a heart attack or something. I enjoyed seeing him like that, at someone else's mercy. I told him I was going to dye him like a spool of velvet, 'cause he was no more good to anyone than that. Less, even. The look on his face? Priceless. He started screaming and yelling like a maniac. He couldn't be a man and just take what he had coming to him. He wouldn't shut up. So I shot him. With his own gun."

Richards leaned back against the artist's desk and evaluated his handiwork.

She reminded herself to keep him talking. "Did you plan to kill him?"

"Not right off the bat. Hell, I thought he was already dead. I just finished the job." He stretched his arms and cracked his knuckles. "I didn't know you were going to show up the next morning to see him pulled up out of the soup."

"Didn't Kira want to let him go?" Lacey asked.

Hank sat down on the desk and faced her. He gently pushed the hair out of her face.

"If it was anybody else in the world but Rod Gibbs, yeah, I'd have let him go. You know what his last words were? 'I'll see you in prison, Hank. I'll ruin you. I'll kill you.' "

"Famous last words," Lacey said.

Hank snorted. He rubbed her shoulders for a moment. "You all right? You know, I like you, Miss Smithsonian. I never had any use for reporters before, but you were different. You wanted to write about our factory and our people. Just a pretty girl reporter who likes pretty clothes and thinks they tell stories."

It wasn't the time to argue the point. "That's me. Listen, Hank, it's over. You don't want to do this anymore. You're going to get yourself killed. What will that prove?" The ties hurt her wrists, but the felt was soft. She thought she might be able to stretch them. A little.

"You think I care if I live or die? Everything's been taken away from me. Lost my job. No family. I can't have Kira. My boat? I'm leaving that to Sykes. Sometimes I think taking my own life would be a relief." His shoulders slumped. "I'm sorry for tying you up."

"Let me go and we'll forget all about it."

"Got things to do first. Velvet Avenger stuff. Gotta hand out a couple of blue ribbons." He took another strip of felt and carefully gagged her with it, pulling her hair out of her mouth. "Someone will find you up here. Eventually. Don't you worry, you'll be okay. You're safer up here anyway. I got work to do. Now be cool." He patted her head.

Hank picked up the gun and put it in his waistband. He took aviator sunglasses out of his pocket and put them on. With the shades and suit and his shaved head, he looked completely different from the shaggy blond Viking she'd seen sucking down beers at the lake the day before. Hank peered through the window and shut the door quietly behind him.

The Velvet Avenger was on the hunt.

chapter 38

Lacey told herself not to panic, but panic was winning.

Her cell phone started ringing and she couldn't reach it. It was probably Vic checking up on her. For a brief moment, she was glad he couldn't see her like this. She felt idiotic. Thank God there was no video of this to show up on YouTube. If only she could reach her phone. She tried scooting the chair over to it, but it wouldn't scoot; it was caught in some of the fabric.

Get a grip, Lacey! And figure out how to get out of this mess.

She could hear the music and the crowd gathering downstairs. Vic and Turtledove would be busy guarding Claudia and the congressman. The cops were guarding the entryways. No one else knew Hank Richards was already inside the building.

The felt could be stretched. Lacey strained her wrists against the fabric until she felt the fibers begin to pull away. She worked at it relentlessly until she could free her hands from the chair and tear the gag from her mouth. She stood up and rubbed her hands, sore from the effort. Her wrists were burning. She grabbed her bag and stuffed the felt ties into it, flipped open her cell phone, and headed for the door.

Lacey ran as fast as she could in her heels while trying to dial Vic. It wasn't working. Her fingers were too numb. She barreled into Turtledove herding the congressman up the stairs as she was tearing down them. She flattened herself against the big man and tried to catch her breath.

Flanders was annoyed. "Excuse me? I don't have time for this. I must get ready for my speech—" He tried to get around his large bodyguard, but Turtledove put out a restraining arm as solid as a brown tree trunk.

"Lacey, where have you been? Vic's looking for you. He gets really excitable when there's trouble brewing and he can't find you. You guys have a history."

"Tied up." She pulled one of the ties from her bag. Turtledove turned her wrists and looked at her bruises. "Literally."

"Vic is not going to like this," he said.

"Hank Richards is here. Inside the building. He got in early, before the cops. He has a gun. He's shaved his head. Bald, clean shaven, dark suit, dark sunglasses, dark turtleneck. He looks very different. We need to tell Vic."

She saw the color drain from Flanders's artificially tanned face as Turtledove pulled out his two-way radio.

"Code Blue Velvet. Lacey's fine—I'm with her." Turtledove was saying. "Yes, subject at large in the crowd. Location unknown. Armed. Altered appearance."

"Big-time," Lacey said. "He could pass for a cop or a bodyguard."

Turtledove relayed the details, listened for a moment, turned his gaze on Lacey, and clicked off. "Vic said to come with me. He's calling the cops. I'll lock down the congressman."

"Where's Vic?"

"Let's go. Vic's on the move." And so was Turtledove, dragging Flanders with him at top speed, back down the stairs toward the secure staging area for the speakers. He assumed Lacey was right behind him. But she wasn't.

She had no intention of getting locked down with Flanders when she could spot Richards and help Vic. She was the only one who had seen the new Hank Richards, the Velvet Avenger. She ran back up to the second floor and sprinted around the railing overlooking the ground floor's center hall to get a better view of the action. She could see the broadcast reporters below the podium, setting up cameras and mikes to catch Flanders announcing his candidacy for governor. Her cell phone rang.

"Lacey, what the hell—" Vic began.

"No time, Vic. Hank is here. He looks very different. I'm trying to spot him."

"Where are you? Aren't you with Turtledove?"

"No, I'm on the second floor by the circular staircase—you know, with all the sculpted faces on it." The decorated staircase wrapped around the old smokestack. Her view from there commanded the entire first floor. "Where are you?"

"Center hall, side stairway, first floor. Securing Claudia. Why didn't you go with—"

"Oh my God. He's there, Vic. Downstairs by the cellophane horses studio, walking past the pottery. Near the big torpedo. Walking fast."

"By the big—? Got him. I see him." Vic hung up. Lacey flew down the stairs right past *The Eye*'s head photographer. Hansen, as usual, was draped with cameras.

"Lacey," he said in greeting. "Wait. Where's—"

"No time, Hansen." She made it down the stairs and started pushing her way through the crowd, just in time to witness Vic tackle Hank Richards. The two men crashed to the floor and disappeared behind the throng. Partygoers were scattering in all directions, leaving a circle for the men to struggle in. Lacey caught a glimpse of them rolling on the floor, grappling and trading punches. TV cameras swung around wildly, trying to catch the action. People were screaming and running for the doors. Lacey was aware of Claudia Darnell running toward her, still holding her new dream catcher, and Hansen lifting a camera to his eye and squinting through the viewfinder. Claudia stopped next to Lacey, an expression of horror and fascination on her face.

Hank Richards was a strong, fit, and desperate man. He managed to scramble away from Vic and get back on his feet. Hank pulled his gun from his waistband, but Vic kicked it out of his hand. It went flying across the floor and skittered past Lacey's feet. Hank spun around, his eyes following the gun. He saw Lacey and Claudia. His face changed and his expression hardened. He pushed people out of his way left and right and headed straight for Claudia, who seemed glued to the spot.

Lacey shoved her publisher behind her and grabbed the only thing that came to hand, the way Kira had grabbed a softball trophy. Lacey barely had time to swing the big dream catcher by its heavy metal ring as Richards put his head down and charged. He was so intent on reaching his prey, he never saw the dream catcher coming.

Lacey slammed it down over Hank's shiny bald head and pulled the metal circle up as hard as she could, ensnaring his head and shoulders in the knotted leather web. She felt leather thongs start to pop and give way, but some of the knots held fast. Hank fell through the hoop, tangled and off balance. He dove forward, his hands outstretched to grab something, anything. Lacey couldn't tell whether Hank was trying to shove her out of the way or hold on to her, before she lost her own footing and landed on her butt, still holding on to the metal hoop. She was vaguely aware of her French twist coming loose. In a moment, she was aware that Vic was there beside her, diving onto Hank and driving him down to the concrete floor.

Lacey had managed to entangle Hank for the few seconds it took Vic to close the gap. Vic landed on Hank's back with both hands and ripped the tangled dream catcher from the Velvet Avenger's head and shoulders. He tossed the bent ring in the air, and Claudia caught it. Vic already had a firm grip on the killer's throat. He slammed Hank facedown against the floor and cuffed his hands behind his back in one smooth motion.

It was a madhouse. Lacey heard cameras clicking, uncomfortably aware that they were taking pictures of her on the floor as she got to her feet and dusted herself off. Uniformed Alexandria cops were pushing through the crowd, trying to bring order to this chaos. They took Hank from Vic and escorted him away. Vic caught Lacey's eye and smiled at her. He cocked his head. She nodded to say, *Yes, I'm okay.* Vic nodded back and went with the cops.

As they led Hank Richards away, Lacey heard him yelling, "You should have just killed me!"

Claudia stared after Hank until he disappeared from sight. She still dangled the crumpled piece of expensive art in her hands, its bent copper rim, its torn leather webbing, its tattered feathers and beads.

All Lacey could think of was the price tag on the thing she had taken from her publisher's hands and destroyed in a heartbeat.

"Sorry, Claudia. I just grabbed the first thing I could." Lacey swallowed and hoped her publisher wouldn't make her pay for this ruined, overpriced crafts project. "I'm sure they could make you another—"

Claudia turned around with a wry smile and quick hug. "No, Lacey. I like it this way. It may not have caught a dream, but it caught a killer. It makes a better story."

"Yeah," Lacey agreed. "A better story."

"Where's Hansen? Let's get a picture. Hansen!"

Lacey sighed with relief and leaned against the wall. It did make a better story. The picture might even make the front page of *The Eye*. An Alexandria policeman stepped up to Claudia. He cleared his throat.

"Ma'am? I'm going to have to take that for evidence."

Late that night, after it was all over, after all the police interviews, after all the media sound bites, after the cops and the crowd went home, in the nearly deserted Torpedo Factory, Vic held her tight for the longest time. He took her breath away with his embrace, and Lacey felt tears tickling her eyes as she closed them.

"So, how much did that fancy wall hanging cost?" he asked softly. "The one you and Hank ruined."

"A lot." She sighed. "But at least it's not coming out of my paycheck."

"So you still have a job?"

"The fashion beat will go on," Lacey said.

"I guess that's the way of the dragon slayer, isn't it? You slay one dragon and the beat goes on." Vic took her hand. "Let's go home, Lacey."

chapter 39

Everyone was mad.

Brooke was mad. Damon was mad. Stella was mad. Lady Gwendolyn Griffin was mad. Tony Trujillo was hopping mad. They were all mad at Lacey. All because they weren't there on Monday night to take part in the takedown of the Velvet Avenger.

But Lacey felt sure they would all get over it. *Eventually.* Most likely in time for Stella's nuptials with Nigel. Yes, definitely in time for Lacey to wear some perfectly atrocious bridesmaid's dress, playing second banana to the irrepressible and adorable Stella.

On the plus side, cub reporter Kelly Kavanaugh was so mad about missing another good story that she begged Mac to let her go back to the police beat. And Mac let her go. She had written her first, and last, Fashion Bite.

Lacey arrived at the newsroom Tuesday afternoon, looking as fresh as possible under the circumstances. She wore her favorite black vintage suit with the jeweled button covers, the one designed by Gloria Adams, a young designer in the 1940s who had died before her talent could be recognized. Lacey felt the suit gave her the extra bit of courage she needed. She refused to give anyone the impression she couldn't handle her own beat by herself. After all, it was just the fashion beat. And a little extra.

Mac Jones told Lacey to write her story of being abducted by the Velvet Avenger as an exclusive interview with the killer. Front page. Above the fold.

Mac thought this was a big plus, for Lacey and for *The*

Eye. But she balked at Mac's eyewitness-interview-with-the-killer angle. Her encounter with Hank Richards was seared into her brain. But it wasn't as if she had taken notes and flagged quotes. To her thinking, it wasn't quite a professional-quality interview.

Mac snorted. "From what I heard, Smithsonian, it couldn't be more exclusive." His dark eyebrows lifted, daring her to object. "It's a hell of an exclusive. It's practically front-line combat reporting. You're a professional. You had your eyes and ears open. And you're all in one piece, right? Who better to write this thing?"

"But I can't confirm my quotes, Mac. They won't let me talk to Richards yet. No notes, no tape. It's all from memory, too much excitement, and I might get something wrong. And it won't be very objective."

"That's what editor's notes are for." He wore his smuggest look. His eyebrows were happy. "I'll just put one at the top of your story: From the Editor. I'll vouch for your journalistic integrity."

"Yes, but if I say the reporter was tied up by the killer during the interview, it might be, um, awkward." *On beyond awkward!* "We don't want to give our crazy sources any fresh ideas, do we?"

"The facts are the facts, Smithsonian. We're fighting for circulation. And it's a great story. You want me to get Kavanaugh to write it?"

"God forbid, Mac. But my predicament during the interview is not important to the reader, or to Hank Richards's story. The facts should speak for themselves. I shouldn't be part of the story, Mac. You're always telling me that."

"Ha. You *are* this story, Smithsonian. And you're the wordsmith. Make it work."

Lacey's front page story, above the fold with its explanatory editor's note, would be teamed with a note from *The Eye*'s publisher, running below the fold. Claudia penned her own statement about the events at the Torpedo Factory and the tragic deaths at Dominion Velvet and *The Eye Street Observer*. And there would be a photograph, thanks to *The Eye*'s "Long Lens" Hansen. A big one. Lacey prayed it wouldn't be the one of Hank Richards snared in the web and her landing on her butt with her legs in the air. And yet that was the very one Mac selected.

"Best action shot of the bunch, Smithsonian," Mac said later with a malicious gleam in his eye. "It's visual. People like visuals."

It surprised no one that Claudia Darnell returned to work at *The Eye* that afternoon. That was the job of a publisher. She arrived looking fabulous in a winter-white skirt suit that showed off her brilliant aquamarine eyes and knockout figure. It was the right public relations move for the staff. Claudia Darnell sent the message that she was still a force to be reckoned with. *The* force at *The Eye*.

In an impromptu meeting with the entire staff, Claudia made all the appropriate statements about Walt Pojack: The newspaper regretted his death, and he had been an asset to the company. She reiterated that she and the paper's remaining board members were still looking at ways to cut costs and grow revenue. Nevertheless, she expressed her fervent hopes and her commitment to *The Eye*'s future, and she overturned Pojack's last and most unpopular announcement. *The Eye Street Observer* would not move to Crystal City after all. *The Eye* would stay on Eye Street in the District of Columbia.

None of these happy tidings was going to save Dominion Velvet in Black Martin, Virginia, or save the American velvet industry, or save Hank Richards from going to prison. But many people in Lacey's life found their wishes coming true that sunny Tuesday in February.

Mac had an exclusive interview with a killer on his front page, and a great visual of his fashion reporter in action, helping to stop the killer from reaching his next victim. Mac was a happy editor. Wiedemeyer and Pickles had a wedding to plan, likewise Stella and Nigel, and they had their friends and family to torment with endless blissful weeks of wedding planning. Damon and Brooke had a new conspiracy to savor, the cyberspace fans and followers of the Velvet Avenger. Lady Gwendolyn had her priceless memories of the Blue Devil's funeral, and her new best friend: Stella. The Blue Devil himself was now presumably enjoying the warm weather where blue devils go when they die, and it was no more than poetic justice. Kira Evans had a very smart attorney and high hopes for a prosecutorial deal that would let her go home to her daughter a free woman.

Lacey herself had multiple bruises and abrasions from her close encounter with the Velvet Avenger, but no bullet holes or broken bones. Or regrets. And on the plus side, she had a job, a fashion beat, a great suit, and Victor Donovan.

Tony Trujillo had a serious cocktail party to throw. The original party pretext, the celebrated passing of the late and unlamented Walter Pojack, had evaporated. It now looked like Tony's party would turn into a massive celebration for the capture of the Velvet Avenger and *The Eye Street Observer* staying right where it belonged, on Eye Street.

The Eye's publisher, Claudia Darnell, had a broken dream catcher, thanks to Lacey Smithsonian. But not a broken dream. It was a pretty good day in the newspaper business.

And tomorrow was Valentine's Day.

Lacey stood on tiptoes to kiss a small dollop of pink raspberry frosting off Vic's chin. She couldn't quite remember how it had gotten there. But no matter. The cake was finished. He had helped her make it, bake it, and crate it.

She had been on pins and needles all day, waiting for her usual Valentine's Day curse to strike without warning: the unexpected fight over nothing; the breakup she didn't see coming; the party where she drops the cake in her boyfriend's mother's lap. By the time Vic arrived to help cart the cake to his mother's bash, Lacey was a nervous wreck. Ominously, nothing bad had happened. *Yet.*

Instead, Vic surprised her with a bouquet of perfect pink and white roses. "I wanted to avoid that old red-roses-mean-I'm-breaking-up-with-you thing," he said. "Pink roses mean we're going steady. Don't they?"

"And the white roses?" Lacey prompted.

"Means I'm pure of heart. Knight in shining armor, at your service, ma'am."

"And smart too, Vic Donovan." She didn't say, *for a*

man. Lacey checked her watch. Just a few more hours to go and this Valentine's Day would be over. *So far, so good.*

"Still want to go to the party?" he asked. "Or shall we run away?"

"Oh sure, tease me now with lost chances. Do we have any choice?" What else could she do with this preposterous pink dessert she'd been intimidated into baking?

"Um. Not really."

"Yeah, I was afraid of that." Lacey frowned.

"You don't have to look like you're going to the guillotine, you know," Vic said. "It'll be fun. I promise."

Hesitating for just a moment to steal a kiss, Lacey and Vic stood outside his parents' home in the clean, crisp February air. They were all dressed up, per Nadine Donovan's Valentine's Day party precepts. (Pink and red for the women. Black tie for the men—pink or red optional.) Their fluffy, mile-high, carb bomb of a cake felt like it weighed a ton in Lacey's trembling hands. It was beautiful and it was dangerous, and it was very pink.

The heavy oak door opened wide and Nadine swooped down on them, a wicked grin on her face. She peeked into the cake box and her eyes lit up.

"Why, Lacey, you shouldn't have!" she said. "Even if I did practically make it a command performance." Nadine handed the frosted monstrosity to one of the caterers, with instructions to give the rosy pink torte a place of honor at her table.

"As long as you know that's all the holiday desserts I have in me," Lacey said. "No more tricks up my sleeves."

"Thank God," Vic added.

"Well, there's always our Fourth of July festivities," Nadine said.

Lacey turned to Vic, her eyes wide with apprehension. He shook his head sadly. "You don't want to know. Last year I had to carve a watermelon into a whale."

She swallowed hard and changed the subject. "That's a beautiful gown, Nadine."

Vic's mother was resplendent in a peony pink dress sparkling with rhinestones. It reminded Lacey of former

First Lady Mamie Eisenhower's famous "Mamie Pink" inaugural gown, once a favorite display at the Smithsonian Museum of American History. But the dress Nadine Donovan wore looked far better on her than on Mamie. Vic's mother was tall and trim and a very well-preserved sixty-something.

"This old thing? Just a little something I had whipped up," Nadine said. "The hostess must follow her own rules, you know. Now, let me see what our own fashion expert is wearing."

Lacey hated being held up as an example. Style was such a personal statement. Vic took her coat and handed it off to an attendant stationed in the foyer.

"Why, what a lovely dress, Lacey," Nadine said. "It is vintage, isn't it?"

"Yes." Lacey smiled. "It was my aunt Mimi's." She smoothed her hands over the deep red silk velvet. It was a classic, bias-cut cocktail dress from the late 1930s, dipping low in the back and hugging every curve. There was no embellishment on the dress—no lace, no beads, no crystals—but its rich velvet texture didn't need any adornment. Mimi had carefully stitched all the pattern pieces together, but she'd never worn it. She left it unhemmed—for Lacey to finish. The Valentine's party was its grand debut. *Thank you, Mimi.*

"Enjoy yourselves, darlings. I'm going to go taunt Vic's aunt with this divine dessert," Nadine said, disappearing into the pink-and-red throng.

A piano player was tinkling the ivories on a Steinway baby grand in the foyer as the guests arrived. Beyond the entryway, the great room spread out before them, sparkling with pink crystal chandeliers and pink shaded lamps and enough pink blossoms to make a florist green. Turtledove and his trumpet and his little jazz combo played Cole Porter tunes beneath a canopy of twinkling lights. Elegantly dressed men with roses in their lapels flirted with women in pink and red gowns. *This is the Valentine's Day party the Great Gatsby would have thrown,* Lacey thought.

After the dining and dancing and dallying, Vic pulled Lacey aside, into the library, away from the noisy crowd.

He slipped her a black velvet box that he'd kept hidden in one of those clever inside pockets men's suits always have.

"Happy Valentine's Day, Lacey."

Lacey was holding her breath. She relaxed a tiny bit when she realized the box was too large for a ring. Vic knew she wasn't ready for that particular step in their relationship. Had she mentioned how ridiculous she thought it was to get engaged on Valentine's Day? She was sure she had. Lacey cracked open the velvet box to find a chubby gold Cupid pendant on a gold chain. The happy little cherub had stubby wings of pavé diamonds and carried a ruby-tipped arrow in his golden bow.

A grin spread across her face. "Oh Vic! It's beautiful. Where on earth did you get it? It looks like an antique."

"It is an antique. It was my grandmother's," Vic said. He scowled. "But there's a terrible curse attached to this pendant, Lacey. It's a deep dark family secret. She got engaged on Valentine's Day and—" He sighed and shook his head in sorrow. "Lived happily ever after."

"Liar!" Lacey started to laugh.

"No, it's true. Ask Nadine."

Lacey put her arms around him and kissed him. "I think there's an awful strain of romantic sentiment in the men in your family."

"No! Couldn't be! We're all such heartless tough guys."

Lacey held the charm up to the light. She could almost swear the round little imp winked at her.

"Vic, this Cupid looks just like Harlan Wiedemeyer!"

He took a closer look. "Hmm. So it does. Maybe Wiedemeyer really is Cupid after all."

"You think so?" She raised her eyebrow at him. It was one of her talents.

"Sweetheart, I wouldn't be a bit surprised. And now that you have a Cupid of your very own, I'm going to break your Valentine curse once and for all."

Vic kissed her again. Lacey helped. A lot. The clock in the library chimed twelve. Valentine's Day was over, she'd survived, and she still had her boyfriend.

Lacey Smithsonian was out of the blue—and into the pink.

The Crime of Fashion Mysteries
by Ellen Byerrum

Killer Hair

An up-and-coming stylist, Angie Woods had a reputation for rescuing down-and-out looks—and careers—all with a pair of scissors. But when Angie is found with a drastic haircut and a razor in her hand, the police assume she committed suicide. Lacey knew the stylist and suspects something more sinister—that the story may lie with Angie's star client, a White House staffer with a salacious website. With the help of a hunky ex-cop, Lacey must root out the truth...

Hostile Makeover

As makeover madness sweeps the nation's capital, reporter Lacey Smithsonian interviews TV show makeover success story Amanda Manville. But with Amanda's beauty comes a beast in the form of a stalker with vicious intentions—and Lacey may be the only one who can stop him.

**Available wherever books are sold or at
penguin.com**

OM0016-110310

Designer Knockoff

A Crime of Fashion Mystery
by Ellen Byerrum

When fashion columnist Lacey Smithsonian learns that a new fashion museum will soon grace decidedly unfashionable D.C., it's more than a good story—it's a chance to show off her vintage Hugh Bentley suit. And when the designer himself notices her at the opening, Lacey gets the scoop on his past—which includes a long-unsolved mystery about a missing employee. When a Washington intern disappears, Lacey gets suspicious and sets out to unravel the murderous details in a fabric of lies, greed, and (gasp!) very bad taste.

Also in the Crime of Fashion series:
Killer Hair
Hostile Makeover
Raiders of the Lost Corset
Grave Apparel
Armed and Glamorous

Available wherever books are sold or at
penguin.com

OM0039

LOOK FOR THE BOOKS BY
ELAINE VIETS
in the Josie Marcus, Mystery Shopper series

Dying in Style

Mystery shopper Josie Marcus's report about Danessa Celedine's exclusive store is less than stellar, and it may cost the fashion diva fifty million dollars. But Danessa's financial future becomes moot when she's found murdered, strangled with one of her own thousand-dollar snakeskin belts-and Josie is accused of the crime.

Also available in the series
High Heels Are Murder
Accessory to Murder
Murder with All the Trimmings
The Fashion Hound Murders
An Uplifting Murder

Available wherever books are sold or at
penguin.com